A THIMBLE OF MEMORY

AUDRA DEHAN

Red Penguin

BOOKS

A Thimble of Memory

Copyright © 2021 by Audra Dehan

Illustrated by Ra Dahan

All rights reserved

Published by Red Penguin Books

Bellerose Village, New York

Library of Congress Control Number: 2021923864

ISBN

Print 978-1-63777-188-4 / 978-1-63777-189-1

Digital 978-1-63777-190-7

To papa – I miss you awful

ACKNOWLEDGMENTS

To Mom - wordsmith extraordinaire - thanks for teaching me the value of a poorly placed comma and an honestly won game of Scrabble.

To my Charly, who keeps my feet on the ground so my imagination can soar.

To Jonathan, Victoria and Ra - the universe has blessed us with a genetic rainbow of your kind and gentle souls.

Thimble of Memory

in this waning winter afternoon sun
    a finch
    alights from a branch
    that bounces slightly.

a fingertip memory
    scratches the gray matter of a brain,
    a ripple on the lake from
    the falling
    autumn acorn.

the thimble of memory
    pierces me, drawing blood from the needle tip.

the finch is lovely
    and dreadful.

the memory
    is true.
    it is a lie.

the ceramic thimble shatters on the frozen lake.
    the ice splinters,
    bursting in a violent rush of damned waters.

in the reflection
    the thimble of memory is revealed.

it is beautiful
    it is horrifying

the finch settles on the branch of a new tree.

THE WAREHOUSE EXAMINATION

My fingernails are blue with cold in the warehouse. Tap-tap-tap-tap- ta – ti-ti- tat- tat – tat, Tap-tap-tap-tap- ta – ti-ti- tat- tat – tat...clicks a pencil. Tick – tick – tick – tick-tick-tick tickity, tickity, tick-tick-tick, clangs my stopwatch. I'm working on one question for over two minutes now, well over the maximum allotted time of 1.8 minutes per question.

My palms start to sweat as my heart smashes against my ribcage. I close my eyes, put down my pencil, place my hands palms up, flat on my lap and take two cleansing breaths.

Tap-tap-tap-tap- ta – ti-ti- tat- tat – tat, Tap-tap-tap-tap- ta – ti-ti- tat- tat – tat - CRACK!, another pencil breaks. I want to toss the idiot next to me, chair and all, on his ass. I see myself, mad dog that I am, yellow foam bubbling like spoiled milk from the corners of her mouth, a mountain of hair teased into one gigantic knot atop her head, arms too long, dangling at her sides, swaying to and fro, posturing for the leap. Suddenly she lunges across the rickety table. Her nails, which had long since been whittled down to cuticle through endless hours of study, are suddenly freakishly long, resembling those on that Indian man in the Guinness Book of

World Records. Those nails are crusty with saffron bits of dirt and dried blood; they launch first at the schmuck's face across the table, scraping at his sweaty, fat cheeks and swollen bulbous eyes. *How the fuck could he be sweating!?* I thought to myself as I sat shivering and hunched over my area of the table on this damp and frigid February day.

Tap-tap-tap-tap- ta – ti-ti- tat- tat – tat, and I was snapped back into the work at hand, the gruesome image having startled me, to say the least. Holy shit—I was burnt out. But I stopped myself in mid-thought. No! No time to drift onto that wave to muse on what had happened...no time...time was the one precious commodity of which I had very little left at the moment.

I would not subject myself to this shit again, I knew, and therefore I must finish with a passing grade. There was no room here to fantasize at any excellence—passing was the prize—to make it, even if by the skin of my teeth. Success took on a whole new meaning in this alternate reality I had been operating in for eight long weeks, seven days a week, twelve to fourteen hours a day. "Pass, pass, pass," the mind whispered and teased. It was the second day of examination, and the mental fatigue was winning this battle.

No! In an instant, the mind retaliated against the failing psyche...rest and ramble would have to wait. We were almost there...so I put myself to sleep and let the mind do its work. Albert's breathing exercises took over. The panic was put to rest, and a resolute, mechanical retrieval of information took its place.

And the mind was able to do what was needed—and what brilliantly sharp work it could do. It was operating at its prime, a series of biological chips functioning at peak performance, unsettling in its excellence. The mind and me, we skipped the question that had side-tracked us, and the next answer came in a flare of simple reasoning. Snapshot flashes burst at us from each line.

The next questions, with four correct answers, were swallowed whole. Time stretched out and contracted, infinite and finite, warping in that lovely infinity symbol, weaving into and out of itself. The filament thread of legal reasoning stitched through each question was apparent to the mind, trained to discover the answer, the probe poking around my brain, blindingly cluttered only a few short hours ago, but now neatly compressed and compartmentalized, interrelated in a new understanding.

It was a time I shall never forget. Not only did I go back and answer that question, but I had time to spare to review, which I didn't dare do. I felt like Charlie (in *Flowers for Algernon*) at his peak, consumed with his ability, finally prepared to crash when he realized this was only a temporary awareness and soon all would be lost in the fog of his true reality.

I rode the train back from Manhattan to Long Island, my mind an empty page, scanning the gray February landscape, not feeling the numbness in the tips of my fingers nor the dampness that scalded my bones. The naked trees and ashen sky whipped past and then slowed as we made each stop along the Babylon line. Normally, I took the Huntington line; but as luck would have it (and the crappy Long Island Rail Road), the line was not running due to frozen switches in the February polar vortex. I enjoyed the timelessness of that ride —the season was perfectly suited to my passage home. Looking out the dirty window of the train, I thought "winter has color."

Winter has color—its palette calming the excited energy of summer. We ease into its quiet after the frantic pace of holidays. How it annoys me when people say winter has no color. Its complexion suits the climate and the temperament of its inhabitants in the northeast. We are creatures of changing seasons here. Much as we might bitch about the cold, who doesn't love the guiltless pleasure of hunkering down for a day or two, cooking, eating, marathoning television "because it's snowing and cold." We put on hot cider or soup and are relieved of our duties, like taking that one extra sick day off from life. Winter's hue is infinitely perfect and peaceful, expressionless. It cloaks us from the business and busyness of warmer months. It allows us our hibernation. As my mind wandered into these thoughts of winter's blush, I noticed I felt content. It was nice to think of something other than the exam which, of course, made me think of the exam.

I closed my eyes and saw the examination sector, a cold pier on the banks of the Hudson River in New York City, ceilings eighteen feet high, with scaffold-like supports throughout. The oversized Plexiglass enclosures were painted with many generations of soot, the resin of seaweed and murky steam rising from the polluted Hudson waters. We were in an enclosed docking area for ships, a container storage facility. I gave it the name 'The Warehouse'. As we filed in to find our designated seating, I felt the chill from the river rise to greet me, compounding my already frosty inner cold. A virtual sea of desks filled The Warehouse, hundreds of tables for two, with approximately three feet of separation, lined the territory. Everyone found his seat with little trouble, an organized mass of people each operating in his own sphere. My fingers were numb from the frosty zone, and in a flicker of cynical humor, I thought this must be another Rite of Passage, that the New York State Bar Examination Committee had discussed in a cigar-stenched, smoke-filled conference room, light dim and no face clearly visible...that the conversation went something like this:

"Gentlemen—Hear ye, hear ye, the committee is now in session. We have been called upon once again to perform our civic duty, our final task in sifting the wheat from the chaff. Let us be creative this year, gentlemen. Let us create lawyers in our image, after our likeness. Let us begin with the exam environment, physically harsh, emotionally strained, and, of course, mentally laborious. Our choice of venue is limited.

However, February provides a nice choice on the pier—let us quarter the captives on the docks with no heat and bring forth the paranoia lurking beneath the surface of each pupil. Let us demand the highest standards of the day and let us say 'Amen.'"

I managed to seat my frozen ass on the even colder metal chair and warm it up after a few minutes. Of course, at that very moment, I felt an uncontrollable need to urinate. That was one more measure of irritation for which I had the Almighty Committee to thank. The early morning silence that echoed throughout the cavernous Warehouse was suddenly disturbed as a voice boomed out. We sprang from our chairs in startled confusion. Rules were delineated, rules covering everything from my pee problem to expulsion.

The exams were distributed, proctors marching like soldiers—sentries down each aisle of tables, grave and somber people, and, I suddenly realized, old. It occurred to me that all the proctors were senior citizens. Maybe this was their silent revenge on a young generation of soon-to-be counselors at law. You know, those shysters and crooks always looking to bill for work never performed and results never guaranteed. You know, that guy who never got a dime from Aunt Millie's estate for you, even after you paid him $1,500! And that rascal who charged SIX HUNDRED FIFTY ($650) DOLLARS to fill out a few forms when you bought your house.

I saw the smoke coming from their ears. They were the enemy, as surely as the Examination Committee, each one of them. They were grim, without a trace of compassion or feeling for this young, arrogant, and disrespectful bunch of brats— "rascals" all of us, they thought, "scoundrels and rogues," and soon to be licensed to rob us all blind!

"THE EXAMINATION SHALL NOW COMMENCE", I heard. Incidentally, sometime later, great gigantic fans the size of helicopter propellers, hanging precariously from the ceiling, began to whir to life, the engines roaring in my ears. I could swear I saw the proctors simply giggle with glee as we all leaped in unison at the unexpected clang. I noticed at that time that the proctors were all suspiciously dressed for the occasion. Regardless, I was grateful for the small comforts, the temperature rose, making writing the essays bearable.

Two days later I found myself on the train back home, thinking about winter's color. I thought that stupid two-day exam was tough, never imagining that where I had been was simply the anteroom to hell.

A FIRST MEMORY

*G*rey trees continued to whip past me along the banks of the Long Island Railroad. The overcast February sky blanketed the view. An eerie silence accompanied me while I peeked out on the homes hunkered down for their long winter's nap. The ulcer I had developed in recent years began its inevitable and relentless upheaval of a volcanic eruption. It churned and exploded in rebellious fury at having been denied the pleasure of ravaging my intestinal walls for so long. Eight long weeks it had waited patiently, sleeping fitfully with the rest of myself, while the mind did its fantastic work.

I could finally crumple up in the seat like an old rag pile and let the swarming masses of rodent emotions wash over me. It felt awful to feel so much again, but at the same time, it felt wonderful to feel! I had denied myself the pleasure for too long. Pretty soon, I knew, the pain was going to become unbearable, but I was almost at my stop. Finally, the train pulled into Babylon and I began humming "By the Rivers of Babylon," looking forward to hearing Bob Marley and his soothing words. I threw my backpack over my shoulder and headed off to find a taxi, the last leg of this ride home.

The realization suddenly struck me, there on that train

platform, that if I had passed I would, in short order, be an attorney. I didn't know how I felt about that anymore. I had been so busy for the past three years surviving from one lecture to the next, one more final exam, one more paper, one more long night of torturous study, and lots of "Jolt" to think about joining the elite boys club. Well, I wasn't so sure that I wanted that membership card anymore. No, I wasn't sure, not one little bit, didn't know if I'd like it, sir, no, not one little bit. I began stomping my mental foot in time to *Sam I Am* and I did not like green eggs and ham. As I was meandering off the platform, preoccupied with this maelstrom of thought, I was abruptly cut off.

"You need taxi?" a little Indian man asked me. His voice was gentle, tinted with the melody of the King's English. I was surprised to see an Indian man in Babylon (wasn't Babylon in Iraq?) and I didn't answer him right away. He was a wiry little fellow with the gentlest of faces, smiling despite his lack of a winter coat and the wicked wind biting through my own.

"Sure—I'm going to Northport," I finally replied. I gave him directions as we flew along surprisingly abandoned roads. It was winter dark by that time, the kind of heavy lilac dark that descends so early in a February afternoon. It was the kind of dark that fades off around the edges of my peripheral vision. Pain gripped me and squeezed the air from my lungs. I was at an eight on the Richter scale of the ulcerous tempest in my gut. Despite the fiery furnace brewing in my belly, the exhaustion won out and I plummeted into blessed sleep.

I felt as if I had closed my eyes only a few seconds ago when I was startled awake by the lovely little Indian man suddenly shouting at me "Wake up! Wake up! You drunk? I don't take drunks! Out, out, out!" We faced off in the rearview mirror.

"What do you mean, get out? We're on the parkway. At least get off at the next exit. And no, I'm not drunk. I'm tired, you asshole!"

The car lurched to a sudden halt on the shoulder of the parkway as he continued screaming at me like a madman. "You fucking bitch—get out of my cab!"

I couldn't believe this. The gentle Indian man became a raving lunatic, and I couldn't get out of that back seat fast enough. There was not another car in sight then, nor for the remaining eleven long miles I had to walk to get home. As the cab shrieked into the inky night, I caught the little Indian man's face in his side-view mirror. The beady eyes in his petite face sparkled with a lightning bug's light. *Lightning bugs in winter...*I thought.

I began to walk home in earnest, trying to warm up by moving quicker. The calming hues I noticed from the train were not so soothing anymore as I did battle against the sharp cold on that abandoned parkway in the dark. Not a headlight or a taillight in sight. I couldn't help but think what a fool I had been, judging all those who bitched about winter. I was hating on winter, focused as I was on moving one foot after another. I was in terrible shape, having abandoned my usual exercise regimen and Albert's nagging advice to keep in shape. I was filled with regret now at not having heeded him. By the time I reached home, my hands were frostbitten. I stepped over the threshold and collapsed.

I woke up in Huntington Hospital and saw Albert sitting on the chair in the corner of the room. He always exuded an outward calm, no matter the circumstances in which he could be found. Albert, like our beloved Atticus Finch, could always be counted on saying "It's not time to worry yet," even when it was indeed time to worry. It was the first time I had known him to force a smile, intended to reassure me. It had the opposite effect as the smile dropped off his face when he delivered the news that I had lost the tips of two frostbitten fingers. My right hand was encased, a soft cast midway to my elbow.

"What a day," I snapped. "What a fucking day! I can't

fucking believe this!" I continued to shout until they sedated me again. I slept for another thirty-six hours as they pumped me full of antacid, antibiotics, and sugar water.

I was home in a few days, adjusting to two halves less of my digits. I took it well, my little fingers becoming even smaller, catching me by comic surprise. I was on my way to becoming the hobbit I had always dreamed of.

Albert didn't fuss and I welcomed his predictable reaction, which was no reaction. He took change in stride as if change were the natural state of things. I learned how to adapt to those shorter digits, buttoning a blouse, tying a shoe, chopping vegetables, over and over while Albert patiently waited. He didn't tolerate any dependence, as expected; and I understood I'd have to learn how to manage, which I did. It was really not so disruptive or disturbing in my life.

The pain those first weeks of the missing bits was mostly unbearable, but Albert discouraged the pain meds, and I had an intuition that he was right on that matter. He helped me breathe and meditate through the pain until the worst of it was over. The first days it was hourly, then every few hours...then once or twice a day after about three weeks.

The whole incident was soon a distant memory. Except once, I overheard Albert on the phone and I felt something alien in his comment about "the cab driver." I was shocked to overhear that he had been looking for the little man since my long walk home. Albert was a master of letting things go. This was a real departure from what I knew of him. It was also a real surprise to overhear him. I never heard anything he didn't intend me to hear. So I paid attention, wondering if I had missed an important warning when I got into that cab.

Albert was the mooring of my life, the rock that could anchor a container ship. We met when I was eight years old, the day I came to him in Northport, Long Island. He was my legal guardian, although I no longer needed a legal guardian. He was the closest person I had to family, having raised me since my arrival. Northport is a quaint New England town on the north shore of Long Island, about an hour's drive to New York City. It was in that three-bedroom cottage that I passed from childhood into adulthood with Albert.

My first memory of Albert was his greeting at the gate to what would become my new home. The house was just off Main Street in town, with a charmingly worn picket fence at the sidewalk. I remember stepping out of a car at the street as Albert swung the little gate open to greet me. It was twilight, with just enough light to make out the contours of the New England cottage, faded Wedgewood blue shingles with white trim, and front porch with a swinging seat. Norman Rockwell could have painted this scene— summer wildflowers in full bloom, hedges, and an American flag.

The first glimpse I had of Albert was his hands. He put out his hand as the driver took my bags to the house. I hesitated, then remembered my manners and reached out for his hand. As our palms touched, my attention was drawn to our hands. The warmth of his hand worked its way from my palm to my wrist, up my forearm, traveling through veins and capillaries, radiating throughout me until it tickled my belly. He knelt on the walkway while I continued to examine his hand holding mine, seeing it in amazing detail. The features of his long-fingered hand crept into my eye. I turned our hands to see the top of his, noticing spots of discolored skin, veins rising under the surface, gnarly knuckles of an older man. Reaching out with his other hand, he wrapped my little eight-year-old hand in his, the way a person would hold a butterfly. I added my left hand to the top of his, enfolding around mine like a blanket. The weaving of our hands was a lullaby to my troubled spirit.

I remember feeling completely at ease, soothed by that touch. I had been on a turbulent sea and had now docked in calm waters, the rhythmic sway of a moving sailboat rocking me in time to a daydream. I felt light and giggly at Albert's first touch.

I looked into Albert's pale blue eyes and he smiled. The smile moved and stretched from his lips to his eyes. Time seemed to stand still as Albert and I gazed long and deep into each other's eyes. And I let go of everything that came before. I don't recall any words spoken in those first minutes. It was easy, giving myself over to Albert who set my mind at ease without even a whisper.

I could feel Albert removing the backpack of memory from my mind. I felt lighter as I reached for the strap from my shoulder, somehow knowing he would keep that poisoned package as long as I needed. I held it out to Albert and he accepted the bag like a gift, his smile crinkling up to the corners of his eyes. I heard Albert's hypnotic, deep bass voice, say

"Hello, Sophia. That's it—just give it to me for a little while. We are going to have a peaceful time here together." He stood and let go of our hands. He touched my arm with the slightest pressure, guiding me up the slate walkway into my new home.

I don't recall much more of that first day except when he read me to sleep. Albert chose a Winnie the Pooh story, which I quickly grew to love. I would come to know and love the gentle cadence of Albert's sonorous voice. Later in life, I discovered that Winnie was actually teaching the path of the Tao, as was Albert. His pastel blue eyes were a constant source of reassurance for me from that moment forward. He always made direct and attentive eye contact, never distracted in the way that most people are when they communicate. He was the solace for my grieving child's damaged heart.

I grew to love the way his spidery hands would sweep through the air when he told a story, brushstrokes of artistry like wind painting a starry night in my eyes. Sometimes he would stand in our parlor on a cold wintry night, reading from a thorough collection of books lining the shelves, the shadows of his long arms and fingers dancing on the walls in the firelight throughout the room. At other times he would sit hunched over on a chair whispering a story from memory—stories that could continue for weeks on end. He was a master storyteller and there were important lessons in each story he told. When I asked to hear a particular story again, Albert would begin a series of questions. What did I like about the story? What parts were the most exciting, frightening, satisfying? I later learned that he would adapt our lessons based on my answers.

Although I went to school with the local town children, Albert had a curriculum that was all his own. The day after my arrival, I awoke to an unusually quiet household. It took a minute for me to remember where I was. I made my way to the kitchen where Albert had already put up a kettle.

"Ah, good morning, Sophia. Hungry?" he asked.

"Yes, thank you, Mr... Sir..." I wasn't sure what to call him.

"Albert will do just fine. What would you like to eat?"

I replied without thinking, "Pancakes."

"Okay—now what do we need for pancakes, Sophia?"

"Oh, I know, I know."

We prepared the pancakes together with a recipe from an old recipe book on a kitchen shelf. Afterward, Albert taught me how to do the dishes. It was a new activity for me in this new life. I enjoyed the responsibility and being treated like a bigger kid.

"Let's take a look around, shall we, Sophia?" prompted Albert when our chores were completed. I followed Albert to the backyard. There was a patio and a lawn scattered about with toys. A tire swing hung from an old maple tree. I jumped into it and Albert began pushing me.

"What kinds of games do you like, Sophia? I have..."

"Albert, I'm sorry to correct you, but you've been calling me by the wrong name. My name is…"

"Sophia—I know. Yes, it's going to be a little game. You were confused and now you are Sophia."

"Okay, I like playing pretend. Sophia is a pretty name. I'll be Sophia. But my old name..."

"Is also Sophia, don't you remember? We're going to play another game. I'll say a word and you repeat it after me, but first choose a toy. "

"I'd rather prefer the swing, Albert if that's okay."

"For today, let's start with a ball, if you don't much mind, Sophia."

He was so sweet and kind, I couldn't say no. But I resisted a bit and instead picked up a jump rope.

"Oh, that'll do just fine," said Albert.

I began to jump, one, two, three jumps.

"Repeat after me, Sophia—'garbage pail.'"

"What's a garbage pail?" Jump.

"You know it as a rubbish bin." Jump, jump, jump.

"What's that, Albert?" Jump.

"Garbage pail," he repeated.

"Oh, I think I'll just say rubbish bin," jump jump jump. The smack of the jump rope hitting the patio and my breath came in a steady rhythm.

"You're good at that jump rope, Sophia."

"Oh, my friend and I play jump rope all the time."

"Do you have a friend here, Sophia?"

"Well, she's not here. She's..." I stopped jumping. I couldn't remember her name. I picked up the jump rope again—jump, jump, jump.

"That's it, Sophia—garbage pail."

"You mean rubbish bin." Jump, jump, jump,

"I mean garbage pail," Albert replies casually but a little more sternly.

"If you want to get along in your new school and not have the other children tease you, you best say garbage pail."

"Oh, okay—garbage pail," I repeated after him.

"Excellent. Why have you stopped jumping?" he asks.

"I'm tired" Albert picks up a nearby ball and tosses it to me.

"Throw the ball, Sophia" he prods with a smile.

I did. He threw the ball on the first syllable of 'garbage' and I returned it on the second, he finished on 'pail'. We did this for the entire morning until he was satisfied with the way I repeated the words and phrases with his accent. I liked the pretend play. Albert was pleased with my quick work and we took a walk into the village. We went through our front gate, closed the latch, and took a walk down to Main Street of Northport village.

I was so excited to see my new town and loved that we were so close to Main Street. I thought maybe I could wander around on my own. I started to skip ahead and Albert caught up with me. We stopped for the best of American ice cream, and I was giddy with this new neighborhood and life. *Main Street looks like a movie set*, I thought to myself, with the barbershop and general store, diner, and ice cream parlor. It was charming and the people we met were friendly. This was how our lessons went. We could spend an entire day on two words that first summer, followed by a treat in town.

Activities—tossing a ball, jumping rope, regularly accompanied our lessons. It was a great partner to my high energy, and Albert taught me many new activities. We kayaked on the north shore of Long Island, repeating lessons to the slap of the paddles against the water. In winter, it was a brisk walk along the shore or a visit to our basement gym stocked with simple, effective equipment—like a military training room. Yoga, calisthenics, weights—there was a constant variety in our work together. Despite his age, Albert kept pace with my activity with little effort. Looking back, I could guess at his age, perhaps close to 40 at that time.

We trekked the cliffs and woods of the north shore while I repeated a story he told, putting on his accent in our ongoing game of pretend. Albert set the pace, always a rhythmic tempo, almost a march, but not quite. It was a very pleasant time for me. Albert was such a dramatic change from what I felt before, so kind, that I was eager to please him. Occasionally, he would ask a probing question when I started to sink into thoughts of my old life. It was as if he sensed my anxiety. I was afraid I'd be sent back or sent on to some new destination. And I wanted to be in Albert's company so badly that I learned quickly how to hide my brooding introspection.

One day I was resting in the hammock in the backyard, drifting into an afternoon nap, when I heard Albert ask me, "Sophia, can you hear me?"

"Of course," I replied as I sat up. But Albert was not outside. I left the hammock in search of him until I found him sitting in the parlor with his eyes closed. He heard the squeak of the old floorboards and opened his startled eyes. Albert quickly calmed his reaction into a bland face, but I had an uneasy feeling. I didn't ask how I had heard him. I intuitively knew not to ask. I turned and went to the kitchen for a drink instead.

At night, as a prelude to sleep, we meditated. Albert would hum a guided mantra of relaxation until I was deep under his spell. His calm voice was the last thing I heard every night for four years, until my twelfth birthday. I would wake in bed, never remembering how I arrived there, guessing Albert had carried me the night before from the parlor.

On my twelfth birthday, we took a trip to visit some friends at Orient Point on the north fork of Long Island. Orient Point had become somewhat of an artist's colony in those years. It was not our first time there. For the past three summers, I had spent many weeks at my friend, Sally's, summer house. Her parents were both artists and had a wonderful old studio in addition to the main house with many rooms for summer guests. It was more like a farmstead than a summer cottage. There was a two-acre organic garden, chickens for fresh eggs, goats for fresh goat milk. I loved summers there with Sally. She was fun and superficial, with little or no curiosity about where I came from, which made life very carefree for me during those weeks. We learned to sail on the sound with a camp of other summer kids, rode our bikes through town, and just lazed about, reading from the vast book collection, making fairy houses out of brick-a-brack about the house. And there was plenty of brick-a-brack. Her parents were enthusiastic suppliers for an active imagination and gave us free rein in their studio with very little limitation. There were supplies from buttons to canvas and every art medium one could wish for. Sally and I spent sunup to sundown in the meadows of our imaginations.

One time we were under the old weeping willow in the yard, hidden well beyond sight of the house. We were making fairy houses. A strong wind came up off the Sound, which was common. This was a cold wind, damp and bone-chilling. I turned to Sally to find her asleep on the grass. But she was just awake with me, talking about her fairy house. The wind swirled around me as I tried to shake Sally awake. She was lying on her side curled up in a ball. I rolled her over on her back, and her face was not her face. My friend's eyes were open, but they weren't her eyes. They were unfocused, drifting from side to side. It was upsetting to see Sally's eyes like that, like an old person who could not see. I put my hands over her eyes, closing her eyelids with my fingertips as you would do to a dead person. All the while my heart beat wildly in my chest; sweat broke out on my forehead and I was panting, my hands splayed out on the ground in front of me as I gasped for air. I began to talk to Sally like Albert would, calmly, trying to ease her out of this scary place she had gone to. She stirred, woke up, and looked at me a little groggily. The sky had opened up to a lovely blue again and the wind had died down.

"Oh, hi, Sophia, I guess we had a little nap", she yawned.

"Yes, Sally, a little nap," I replied, the lie falling gently from my twelve-year-old tongue. I felt someone nearby and looked up to see Sally's mom standing near the willow tree. She nodded at me and smiled, then turned toward the house.

After that trip, that evening, when we returned home to Northport, Albert suggested for the first time that I meditate on my own. He sat with me as I closed my eyes and easily recalled the words that he had repeated for the four years prior. Those first weeks he interrupted my meditation, guiding me to drop the words and concentrate on the breathing. In a few short months, I was able to slip into an uninterrupted ten minutes of silence in my mind.

I didn't ask Albert questions about who he was or how long I was staying. I don't remember even being curious about those things, as if Albert had already answered. We never spoke about my life before our time together. My fear of a return to that life overrode any curiosity. Strange episodes like Sally's "nap" would occur every so often and I accepted them, an inner intuition whispering in my mind that silence was best.

BEWITCHED IN THE SAHARA

*a*n eerie calm settled over the morning desert as Halima, the local healer, attended to Amalu. The sun was slowly ascending in the daybreak sky, gently splashing the horizon in sweeping fabrics of gold - serene and comforting. In the distance, three Bedouin men, dressed in their long white jalabias meandered along on their camels.

Four days earlier a sandstorm had swept up without any warning other than the animals' agitation. When Amalu began to bring in the goats, the sand momentarily blinded her. She fell and cut her fingers on some jagged rocks and the fingers became infected. It had been four long days of fever and infection that Amalu endured while Halima nursed the hand, attending to her with traditional Moroccan herbs. There was no chance to save the tips of two fingers, and they decided together that it was better to lose the fingertips rather than the whole hand. The infection had begun to spread—red and inflamed flesh tracking toward her palm. Both women glanced up as light followed Achmed into their clay home. "How is she?"

Achmed and Halima whispered while Amalu overheard all that was said. The fingertips...Halima prepared a sedative tea and Amalu was soon asleep at about the same time I was being wheeled out of Huntington Hospital. Amalu's hand, like my own, healed quickly, albeit not quite as neatly as my own. Her physical therapy was little more than the daily chores of a villager.

Achmed came to visit his lovely dark goddess one short week after the amputations. She was lying down midday to escape the sweltering sun. He sat quietly next to her on the blankets that served as their bed and eased back the gold and red embroidered cover to expose her in the heat of the day. She lay naked beneath the blankets. He was pleased by her comfort with her body, that she didn't feel the need to be covered. She was different from the village women and accepted now without judgment.

It often came as a surprise to him that Amalu chose him. He understood well that she didn't belong to him and would not be possessed. He loved the idea that she could not be possessed. He hated that she could not be possessed. It would depend on his mood of the day.

Achmed leaned over to caress Amalu's naked bottom, silky smooth and white as the day he met her. Her color was a mirage for strangers. She tanned herself in private, as she took the goats through the mountains and managed to sneak in an hour or so every day to keep up with the dark skin of Achmed's family. She stirred and smiled and tried to roll over without disturbing the bandaged hand. He was so proud of her strength and the light manner she accepted the loss of her fingers. He helped to turn her and was rewarded when she smiled at him, her white teeth in contrast to her mocha skin. My god, she was beautiful, exotic! Who could guess that little pixie frame would clothe such a large spirit? He took a moment to look at her, admire her fine and refined features, her pencil-thin lips, softly pointed tiny nose, deep round chestnut eyes. She was the tiny commander of his heart. He quickly undressed.

As Achmed lay with Amalu in his arms, he relived the day they met some two years earlier. He took pleasure in revisiting the minute details of their meeting, etched as they were into his heart.

He was returning with the rest of the men from the annual camel drive and marketplace, a journey of six hundred miles from their Atlas village home across the Sahara and back again. It was nearing twilight on the fourth day of the second week of the drive and Achmed was resting atop a dune facing the setting sun. Suddenly, he saw a woman walking toward him and thought at first it was a mirage or waking dream. He kept a keen eye on her and watched as she gently swayed and sank to the silken sand. The sun, a barrage of orange and red, reached out to capture her as she collapsed, the rays cradling her in the palm of a heavenly hand. Achmed cautiously made his way toward the figure, now convinced that this was no mirage or dream. As the last lights of day speckled the horizon, he walked toward her, certain she would be dead.

As Achmed neared the body, he saw the skeletal remains of a desert-ravaged woman. One arm was broken, twisted into an unnatural position, with dried blood smeared from shoulder to wrist, caked with sand. The desert sun had taken a toll on what must have once been milky white flesh. It was now open and weeping from severe burns, the worst being the soles of her naked feet. Her sky blue dress was violated with blood and sand. What an odd vision this delicate creature was out here in the desert, wrapped in French couture, pearls at her earlobes, wrists, and throat. The long dress was speckled with blood and torn at the sides from her armpits to her ankles, hanging only by the seams at the shoulders. Achmed knelt before the stranger and lifted her gown.

The dehydrated and scorched body did not surprise Achmed as he examined her with the cold detachment of a desert-dweller. This one was not meant for desert life. As

Achmed looked closely at her face, it sent him reeling in the moonlight. He expected the calm serenity of one who had known and expected to die in the harsh sun. But it was twisted into a mask of rage. This woman was not resting peacefully. Achmed laid his hands upon her heart, listening to his other voice. No, she was not resting at all. Instead, she was raging against the death that he was sure would arrive shortly.

Achmed closed his eyes and felt her breastbone beneath his hands. Her heart was racing toward death with the speed of hummingbird wings. She began to feel around in his mind. He was startled by her invasion but curious enough to let her in. She moved his hands with her will, her body an ouija board beneath him until his hands were resting over her heart, right between her breasts. His palms gently rested there as he felt a current run from her heart through his hands, up his arms, into his shoulders, then on to his heart, his life force.

Then she began to suckle through that current, drawing from the well of his life. She dipped her bucket of death into the deep well of his spirit, pulling with the powerful force of her will. Achmed knelt over her, silent, immobile, impotent against this theft. Leeching the life from him, slowly and steadily, a greedy babe nursing from his breast. It was the most alien sensation. Achmed felt the theft but it was liberating, almost erotic. He was lured by her even as his fear began to mount.

Her pulse began to slow as his quickened. The light of the Sahara moon concentrated itself on his hands as his heart rate climbed, racing toward the coming darkness. Achmed was slipping away, and he knew in a flash of chaotic understanding that she would take his life for her own.

He felt a calm fury in the slowing beat of her heart and began to resist in earnest; but the woman continued to draw on him, a vampire bat feeding on a goat. He tried to pull away, but she offered no release. Instead, he heard her determination to survive, her plan to punish those who had left her for dead. Achmed was catapulted from the sands beside her into the skies overhead before he could catch himself and before he could regain some control over her maniacal theft.

She is taking my life for her own, he thought to himself again. He rose above the dune, looking down on himself and the woman, the moon a white laser on his hands, her chest moving rhythmically. She was strong, and he knew that authority and intimidation would not move her. It could only be his other voice that she might hear.

Achmed's pulse began to slow, and he felt the ache to leave the desert. In a final effort of will, he continued to look down upon her although every fiber of his inner heart yearned to look behind him where the light of the other world would surely embrace him. He wanted desperately to turn around and rush at the light of what he had once known as a small boy—allow her this robbery and rest in peace.

Her eyes flashed open, blinding his other vision for a moment. At that moment, he awoke and called out to Hassan. There below, a figure jumped from a tent and sounded alarms, for he had heard Achmed's silent cry. The men sprang from their tents and rushed after Hassan. They arrived at the top of the dune to witness Achmed above and Achmed below. The men rolled down the dune like water bugs, their jalabias protecting them as they flew in the rising wind. They encircled Achmed and the woman, a flowing line swaying in the desert moonlight. As one, they began to hum . . .

. . . a poem of the lovers, Layla and Qays, a song learned at their mothers' breasts.

> *You kept me close until you put a spell on me*
> *and with words that bring the mountain-goats down to*
> *the plains.*
> *When I had no way out, you shunned me,*
> *But you left what you left within my breast.*

Achmed was bent over the woman, his chest heaving with the exertion of her theft. His tribe began another song, the haunting melody of Qays the bewitched, possessed by his beloved Layla . . .

I pass by these walls, the walls of Layla
And I kiss this wall and that wall
It's not the Love of the houses that has taken my heart
But of the One who dwells in those houses

Ahmed was swimming in the song; its rhythms echoing that of his own weakening heart. He felt it would be over soon and the music was a lullaby pushing him to sleep. Suddenly a clang and a scream and they bellowed to him:

Achmed! Achmed! You shall return!
To carry on you must learn
All she knows and all she sees
Come back, come back or we shall all be doomed!
Achmed! Achmed! sing with passion.
Whisper to the great one's pawn
Achmed! Achmed, time to conquer
All the fear and fury gone!

Achmed heard the clatter in the distance of a seaman's fog. The other voice spoke to him in its familiar accent.

"WAKE UP, SILLY BOY!" he heard.

"WAKE UP. OPEN YOUR EYES, MAN. IT IS TIME TO SEE THE UNIVERSE IN THE MOUTH OF A RIGHTEOUS ONE!"

Achmed opened his mouth and out came the song that he heard from below. The woman's rage subsided a fraction, but it was enough for him to break loose and hurl himself back from the grip of this creature. He was back on the ground again, the light gone, night closing swiftly around them.

He was sucked back into his body, now crumpled over the woman, both chests heaving in unison, desperate for another breath of the desert air. She gasped and he opened his eyes to look into her mouth. What he saw were a beautiful set of sparkling white teeth and a few gold fillings. He tried to concentrate and focus on the universe he was sure he would see in her mouth when her tongue darted out to lick her lips. He whispered to her,

"Open your mouth, righteous one, so that I may see the universe."

She did so again and all he saw was her beautiful teeth. Desperate with disappointment, he raised his eyes to her face. No longer twisted in fury, her features were as peaceful as those of a newborn suckling, drunk with her mother's first milk. A dim, foggy glow of moonlight still radiated from her. He touched her eyebrows, tracing their shape, then trailed his fingers around her eyes, to her nose, both thumbs gently massaging the thinned, parched muscles of her face, tracing each line to her lips, now wet with the water dripping from a skin above his head. The clan surrounded them as he moved to kiss her. She did not resist, but she also did not participate.

The men began to dance and chant around them and then holler and hoot with laughter.

"See the universe in her mouth?! What voice would tell you that!? All you will see in her mouth is your seed and the future of the clan."

They were jeering and lifting her, taking the woman to the tents to be cleaned and clothed and rehydrated. As Achmed tried to get to his feet, he fell to the ground, too weak to stand. Again, the men laughed aloud and carried him, too.

This had been Achmed's first camel drive, and the elders of the group knew it would be his last. As a boy, he was told Berber legends about the camel drive. Every year for as long as he could remember, the women of the village began a ritual in the early morning hours before their men were to depart and before the sun was scorching overhead. The eldest took the treasured tribe's satchel, covered with the tapestries of their legends and beaded with the precious stones of each elder wife who had come before for countless generations. It seemed such a strange contrast—that old woman, teeth gone, leathered face, handling that precious and beautiful treasure.

The ceremony began at the well where the satchel was lowered until soaked and then raised as the backs of the men were fading into the distance. The youngest wife of the village would then retrieve the satchel and pass it along the long row of married women until it reached the eldest at the village gate. She would begin a chant until the youngest male of the camel drive heard and raced back upon the finest Arabian mare. He galloped back to the village as the other men continued the slow trek into the Sahara, scoop up the satchel from the elder crone at the gate, and race around the outside of the village walls as all the village women raised their voices and joined the chant. "Safe travels to our riders and Inshallah, you shall bear witness to a wonder."

It was Achmed's honor at the start of this particular drive to retrieve the satchel. As he returned to the camp with the other men now, it was handed to him. Not knowing what to do, he opened the bag and found a simple white jalabia inside. It was decorated at the throat and wrists with blue sapphires. He understood and handed the robe to her. But the men laughed again.

"You must dress her yourself, boy—but don't you go playing any foolish games with her."

She was standing by that time and as Achmed started to gently put the robe over her, he heard another jeer.

"Remove her western rags first, you fool, and dress her in our colors as she should be—if we have to feed her, she'll wear what we say."

Poor Achmed was burning with embarrassment, his eyes darting every which way but to the task at hand—undressing a woman. He untied the knot at the back of her throat. She didn't move or moan or object to anything but stood gracefully before him, without shame. The gown fell to the ground, a halo of sky-blue silk puddled around her feet. She took one small and elegant step forward as one of the men scooped up the gown and dropped it into the satchel. He tied it closed and scurried away with the bag. The other men quietly and respectfully walked away, leaving only the old man, Hassan, to keep watch over Achmed and the stranger. Hassan brought a blanket for her to sit on, water, and clean cloths, and handed them to Achmed, who understood and began to clean her wounds and burns. Hassan opened the small silk bag at his waist, drew forth herbs, and began to mix them for a salve. It was a most exquisite moment, this nineteen-year-old boy, tending to a stranger with Hassan nearby, preparing a healing balm. Achmed began at her face, wiping it clean with the cotton cloth, then her neck and shoulders. When he reached her broken arm, he whispered, not knowing if she understood his language.

"Be still, this will hurt."

He cleaned the long gaping wound that ran the length of her arm, careful of adding pressure to the weeping cut. The arm hung at an awkward angle; her slim shoulder was red and swollen, having been dislocated, and the forearm was broken. Recognizing the smooth edges of a knife wound, he stopped for a moment, wondering who would have inflicted such an injury and why.

Achmed continued with his ministrations, on his knees before the stranger, patiently removing each grain of sand by the light of the moon and the fire crackling nearby. It felt like hours passed as Hassan waited for Achmed to clean the woman's injuries. All the while, this stranger sat quietly composed, watching his face.

The time came to deal with the arm, set the shoulder back into place, and tie the break. It was difficult for Achmed, even trained as all desert travelers were in first aid such as this. Hassan joined them, ready to help if he was needed. Achmed placed his right hand in the crook of her shoulder and the other at her elbow. He began to breathe slowly, in and out, demonstrating for her to do the same. He counted in Arabic, hoping she understood, as he told her, "Breathe slowly and evenly, counting your breaths."

Achmed twisted and pulled her arm until he could feel the ball of the joint pop back into her shoulder. He strapped a splint to the forearm and tied it with strips of cloth. Motioning, he had her raise the good arm so that the bad one could be held against her body, hand over heart. Hassan held the hand in place as Achmed started the wrap around her torso, then moved away again as the boy continued. She would be able to use her good arm while the broken one healed.

The stranger was humming a tune she had begun some minutes into the bandaging. It was strange but somehow familiar. She didn't so much as blink while he worked. When the job was done, he looked into her face and saw her eyes closed, her skin pale in the moonlight. The tune lingered between them, a hymn to the nighttime skies.

Achmed sat back, unable to continue, suddenly feeling as weak as he had when they found him with this stranger. Hassan took over, applying his salve to her arm, finishing the job of cleaning every nook and cranny of her body, searching for parasites, smaller wounds, and the redness of infection. He washed her breasts, lifting them to clean beneath, in that place where flesh meets flesh. She finally lay back on the blanket as Hassan moved over her belly, smooth and silky, then down to her pelvis, cleaning between her legs, front and back. There was no shame as Achmed observed his silent devotion to this one of earth's creations, wrapped in the skeletal remains of flesh and bone.

The young man watched the elder bathe her, worship her, worshipping all womanhood in the gentle caress of cloth and water. After finishing her legs, Hassan applied the salve to each wound and burn, gently massaging each mark as if it were the most important task of his life. He rose to his feet then and, though, in certain pain, she followed, looking up into his face. Achmed suddenly realized how petite she was and felt an urgent need for the warm smile she was giving Hassan.

Hassan continued in silence, reaching now for the long white jalabia, offering it up to her. The woman raised her good arm; he gently covered her, careful not to disturb the other arm, letting the jalabia's extra material drape her injured shoulder. He nodded to the younger man, turned away from the fire, and walked with the stranger to Achmed's tent. She leaned into him with the good arm snaking around his waist. Hassan had worshipped at the altar of her body and, as Achmed followed, he watched her thank the older man with a tender and enduring kiss. Hassan was not tall, but the woman stood on tiptoe to reach his cheek. Inside the tent, the woman laid down on the blankets. Settling onto her good side, she closed her eyes and, moments later, slipped into an exhausted sleep.

The tent flap was open and Achmed watched from outside as Hassan tended her badly burned feet—first washing, then massaging more ointment into them. Finally, after what seemed another eternity, Hassan left the tent and joined the quiet conversation at the campfire. Achmed remained where he was at the opening to his tent, awed by the music of the old man's devotion. He was imprinting the images of the day in his mind to recall later for his poems. The evening passed in the movement of the stars and the murmuring over the campfire.

Finally, weariness from the day's events overtook him. Achmed entered his tent, closed the flap, and stood over the woman. Her breathing was shallow but even. He moved into a corner and fell fast asleep, a comfortable distance from the stranger.

For three days they did not move from the campsite. The woman slept, awakening every few hours only for water from the nearby well, pita, nuts, and dried fruits. Achmed asked her name many times, first gesturing to himself and saying his name, then pointing at her and asking what her name was. She didn't reply but quietly looked past his shoulder in silence. There was understanding in her eyes as she searched for her name somewhere in the Sahara, a bit beyond Achmed's tent.

The men didn't speak about her much during those first days. Achmed was confused by this silence; how strange that they behaved as if she wasn't there. They only spoke about her when Achmed started a conversation. Finally, one evening Achmed was walking with Hassan and asked about this,

"Why, Hassan, does no one speak of her, or to her, except me? It's as if they pretend she isn't here."

"They respect you, Achmed. We were not called to the woman, you were. She is in your charge. To talk about her or to her without your consent would be an insult to you, poor manners for one of us."

"Why do you think I found her, Hassan?"

"You are your father's son, the little Sufi after all, although I think we need to replace the 'little'. There is not much about your spirit that is small. You must have called her to you, or perhaps her cries were only heard by you. All will be revealed in time. May I ask her name, Achmed?"

Achmed was stunned with the old man's deference toward him, the asking, and his tone so modest.

"She will not say, Hassan."

"Well then, let us leave her to her silence. She will have a name in her own time."

So she was referred to as "the woman" in conversation,

which worked fine. She was, after all, the only woman in camp. She was also understood to be this trek's "wonder."

On the morning of the fourth day, when the men woke they saw her sitting atop the one Arabian horse they took on each drive, the same one Achmed rode when they left the village. She was ready to go. The woman's transformation in those days was remarkable. Her injuries were still raw but healing, with no sign of infection. Her gray eyes were alert, shooting from her bronzed face with the intensity of arrows fired from a bow. Her strength had returned and, now rehydrated, her skeletal body looked flush in the desert wasteland. Camp was packed with military efficiency, and they were on the move within the hour. Achmed covered her head and face with a blue turban to protect her from the sun. She soundlessly rode beside the men, lost in her own thoughts.

Over the next three weeks, Achmed rode beside her, pleased that she knew to match the horse's pace with this camel's. He spoke now and again; she had yet to speak a word. It was a comfortable silence that accompanied the tribe through those weeks. The woman's tempo served as a finely tuned counterpart to the tribe, her rhythm in sync with theirs. Each night as the men sat around the fire drinking the last tea of the day, she would wander alone among the scarlet sands of the African desert. It was often many hours after Achmed had fallen asleep that she would return to his tent where they slept separately, divided by the meter of desert floor that stretched between them.

After two weeks, Achmed saw the woman approach Hassan one evening while he was sitting at the fire. She spoke to him, and they retreated to Hassan's tent. Achmed was surprised. She had kept close to him these two weeks, riding beside him and keeping pace, but never uttered a word. Did Hassan speak her language? A few minutes later, she emerged from the tent with both arms through the sleeves of her jalabia. She must have asked Hassan to help unwrap her bindings. Only the splint remained. For the next few weeks, Hassan greeted the woman each evening and massaged the stiffness out of the shoulder. She now rode comfortably with both hands on the reins.

Two days before they were to arrive back in the village, she came to Achmed's tent early, as he was beginning to fade off into sleep. She sat crossed-legged beside him and looked down into his face. And what a sweet face it was—with delicately drawn features and little round eyes, moving beneath his lids as he dreamed. His head was covered in wildly thick, healthy chestnut hair. Even in his sleep, this young Berber was an old soul, an ancient leader of his people. Achmed was thin but fit; and although his character was gentle, he could be fierce, being of the stronghold peoples, the mountain Berber clans. She gently lifted the blanket that covered him and moved aside the cloth of his robes to expose his chest. Achmed was instantly awakened and sat up, abruptly startled from his sleep. It was not like Achmed to be cruel or harsh. But he had her hands in a vice-grip before she could touch him, his eyes flashing open.

"I believe you have already stolen enough of my life, woman, some weeks ago. I will not allow you anymore." He studied the fingers in his grip. "Your greed may kill you before your time."

She flexed her hands against his, as the fingertips grew numb.

"Close your eyes, Achmed, and trust me," she whispered in his Berber dialect, although he did not notice and would not have cared. Her voice came to him in the silence of his heart, and it was music on the breath of his soul. She knew him from before. She opened her mouth—he did not see the universe or her gold fillings nor her beautiful ivory teeth. He saw her tongue dart out to moisten her lips, and she began to speak in a human voice.

"Six years ago, when you were thirteen, after your

circumcision, you were very ill. Do you remember? An infection developed and you were in bed for fourteen days. During the fever, you dreamed many dreams. I remember those dreams, Achmed. Do you not remember me? Please try to remember the dreams, Achmed. It would be such a relief for me to share this burden. Please try to remember and maybe we can help each other. We must have found each other in these impossible circumstances for a reason. It cannot be an accident that you of all people found me at death's door. You are the only one who could have saved me that day. Something has drawn us together, and I fear there is an urgent need for us to answer these questions."

Achmed did not hear anything she said, but he felt the plea for help in her words. All these weeks she had traveled beside him in silence. He thought she was quiet because she didn't speak the language. At times she looked like she understood everything the men said as they ate together. Then he thought she was a snob, too good to speak the language of the villagers. But now he heard her voice and could not hear a word she said. His kind nature overwhelmed him, and he felt a burning desire to protect and help her. Achmed loosened his grip as she spoke. He glanced at the imprints of his long fingers on her slender wrists and began to rub them, to warm the smooth flesh back to life. He was overwrought with worry —that he might have hurt her, but she didn't even seem to notice his gentle massage.

Achmed watched her mouth move and heard the murmur of her voice, as if in a dream. Her voice hummed and his muscles relaxed. He stopped rubbing her wrists and took one hand in his two, entwining their fingers. He lifted her hand to his face, moved his jaw against her touch. Opening her hand, she placed the palm flat on his cheek. Ah, that felt so very fine. Achmed dipped his face into her palm, all the while hearing the murmur of her voice, slipping into the pools of her grey eyes. Those eyes contained the entire cosmos in them, the pupils a center around which the universe burst into elegant song. He was not afraid as he saw her other hand slowly reaching toward his naked chest. He closed his eyes. She continued to speak calmly to him, her voice helping him to relax.

Her hand made contact with his heart and Achmed was swimming again in the hallucinations of those long days and nights. The movement started slowly, disjointed—like the beginning of a childhood memory—old words to a song. He was relaxed by the woman's hypnotic voice. The pace began to increase, dreams and memories twisting together, spilling over him, growing into a crescendo, crashing over him like a violent sandstorm against the village walls. His pulse increased with the percussion of the storm, swirling around him, the reds and oranges of the sands lifting him to the sky, pelting him, faster and faster. The sand cut him, nicking his entire body. The climax was coming—he was catapulted into the clouds drawn up by the strength of the sand and wind which had taken on the shape of a solid funnel—a tornado of spinning sand. Up and up it pushed him until he was above the desert sandstorm, then above the clouds, surrounded by stars and looking down into the funnel.

Achmed peered over the edge of the funnel, trying to see what was holding him in place. The sand twisted and moved until within the tunnel, the grains reformed, taking on the shape and features of faces—the woman's face, a childhood friend, the men who traveled with him. Each image moved in and out of the sand funnel. Then the sand took on the shape of a huge hand, and the hand began to move up the center of the cone. Achmed held onto the edge of the funnel, his grip tightening, as he peered over its edge. The enormous hand lifted, slowly closer, until he could see a body within the palm, curled on its side like a baby. It seemed to be struggling with some unseen foe, and Achmed wanted to jump in to offer help. He started to move further over the lip of the whirling funnel. All the while the walls of the funnel writhed and spun at great speed, shooting off millions of grains of sand. The body looked like it was being bitten, grains of sand digging into the flesh. Achmed was climbing, edging over the lip when the body turned onto its back. He could see the face now from a distance, but it was hard to make out features. Alive and naked, this was a grown man who sat up and began to rise to meet Achmed. The features of the face began to come into focus. As he came closer, he seemed to grow in size, his gray eyes shooting through to Achmed. The man reached out a hand, about to touch Achmed's face, but stopped, suddenly distracted by something beyond Achmed's shoulder. Achmed turned to follow his gaze and saw the woman, kneeling behind him.

The contact between this unknown man and the woman was electric and explosive—the air was charged with the smell of burnt copper and it was hard to breathe. Their instant connection left both gasping for air. Achmed was stunned and still, struggling to slow his racing heart. He watched the man turn back quickly toward the bottom of the funnel. Now Achmed could see a very small body again at the base where the man had been only an instant before. Achmed did not like the feel of this—this body was menacing and struggling with horrific violence. Scrambling to the base of the tunnel, the man waved Achmed off, a gesture commanding that both he and the woman behind him take their leave quickly. The woman had been touching his shoulder and she instantly broke contact.

Achmed's body regained its weight. He opened his eyes and found her in the same position as before the sand tornado, sitting near, but no longer touching his chest, which was heaving with exertion from the night travels. He recognized the quiet desert air—his Sahara home—and breathed long and deep.

"Who was that? Did you recognize him?" In his

excitement, Achmed rose, light-headed, and began to pace the tent. "I have seen him before many times over the years, but never in such detail, such detail!" His dark eyes locked on the woman's gray ones. "How did you do that? How were you able to come with me?"

Achmed was beyond excited at this turn of events. His head pounded, his heart raced—to have found a traveling companion—he had hoped since he was a boy that there was someone who could explain where he traveled, what he had seen. Finally, here was his answer, come to him in the most impossible circumstances. She had come to him to help him navigate his dreams, to enlighten him in the fearful and amazing sights he had seen. His visions and all that had come later—she could explain the separation of time and space—the shifting here and now of his days and nights. He could not count his questions, didn't even have the language to form them. He was within himself for these few moments until he turned to the woman who shared his tent and knew they were meant to be here together.

She was breathing heavily, in distress, leaning over on her hands and knees, trying to catch her breath. Achmed moved closer to her, not sure what to do. He ran from the tent and returned quickly with an overflowing skin. Still distressed, the woman was working to calm her breathing—sitting with her eyes closed, crossed-legged now, and breathing a bit easier. Her slim torso lifted, and Achmed could see the curve of her breasts as she inhaled. Her forehead was creased with deep lines, her hands tightly clenched. Achmed put the water skin aside and sank down across from her. He took hold of one of her hands, trying to uncurl it from its grip. He was looking down at the hand, massaging and kneading to open the fists when he heard her breathing had calmed considerably. When he finally looked up from her hand, he saw that she was observing him.

"Oh my," he heard the voice, pitched low and lilting, "you

have the most serene touch. How will I resist such innocent strength?" A whisper, "Achmed, you are so sweet, I'd like to curl up inside of you."

He wasn't sure if he was meant to hear, but her words were intoxicating and private. She let him continue to massage her palm, her fingers, the top of her hand. He moved to the other hand, the one that had hung useless at her side a short while ago. Achmed felt a heat rising in his throat and thought perhaps he should be finished now. He moved back a bit as if to lie down on his blankets. She moved with him, edging closer even as he leaned back. She reached out to touch his face, slowly moving forward, leaning on her good hand. She stopped as their lips were almost touching, waiting for him. The woman moistened her lips and watched Achmed carefully. He was frozen in place, anticipating, unsure. She brushed her lips against his and he felt that touch in the millions of little nerve endings, sparking like desert stars in his mouth. Her lips were soft like the outside of a fresh fig just plucked from a tree. She continued to move her head from side to side, brushing their lips, waiting for him.

Achmed was enjoying the pleasure of letting her do what she wanted with him. He swallowed, never taking his eyes from her. She moved her hand along his cheek and followed the contours of his face until she was touching his lips with her fingers, tracing their shape. Achmed's heart was sprinting, pounding in his chest. She was so petite, so gentle, but he felt the urgency of her touch begin to increase. She moved back and smiled.

She released him for the moment and he again was not sure what to do. She began to move back toward her blanket, holding his gaze. He didn't like this feeling of her slow retreat. No longer transfixed, Achmed moved with the woman as she edged away. He continued the sway of this new dance, its music warming. Now he was leaning toward her. The dance continued on a wave as she invited him with a warm smile, leaning back on her elbows. He came closer, his arms on either side of her hips, and finally found words, his voice, a dry whisper.

"What are you that comes to bewitch me in the desert night? The djin of Layla and Majnun?"

"Oh, Achmed, I am the one bewitched. You alone," she reached and touched the thick hair at his temple, "can help me find my way."

Achmed understood but something about her and her words cautioned him. He was inexperienced and she clearly was not. He was timid and she was bold. This ignited a flash of anger in him. Achmed sat up and she did the same. He saw that she was stricken, felt the sincerity of her words, and wondered at her truth. Achmed stood, walked quickly from his tent, nearly tearing the flap away in his fist. He paced along the desert dunes, struggling with the seduction and the woman's purpose here.

What if I have called this one here to help me? Is it possible for me to call someone? The man from my young dreams didn't exactly call me, but I was attracted to him. Maybe she can help me understand what I am supposed to do, who the man is. She has spoken to me, called my name, twice now in waking silence.

Achmed's musings began to calm his confusion. He found himself opening up to the possibility that this intriguing, seductive, little woman was a blessing. He would wait for all to be revealed. Yes, he was feeling more certain. Still, he understood nothing of this heated anger toward her, for usually, he was slow to burn. He resolved to be watchful, so unsure of these new feelings.

Am I afraid of her? Is it fear that makes me angry? Does she really think me the primitive village shepherd or is that my thought? Achmed had more questions than answers, typical for him, even when his mind was at peace. He was a deep thinker and this visitor would no doubt tickle his brain and pull at his heart for some time to come. He felt excited about exploring the meaning of her arrival, but it was tempered with a healthy dose of caution.

Achmed returned to his tent after some hours of walking and thinking about his visitor. Lifting the torn flap, he stepped inside to see the woman turned toward him. She lay curled up into a tiny ball, like a child. Her lips were parted slightly and from the safe distance of the tent opening, she looked comfortable. Interested in observing her while she slept, he came closer and sat nearby, gazing quietly, noticing the tiny details of her face. Sweat was beading up on her upper lip and her face was drawn and strained. This was no rest. He rubbed his face, touched the back of his neck, feeling the discomfort of her sleep creeping into his flesh.

Achmed lay down facing the woman, close enough to feel her breathing into his face. Her breath smelled sweet and a bit earthy, like mushrooms and onions. It was exciting, despite her uneasy rest. He reached out slowly, hesitating, holding his hand above her arm for a full minute before finally touching her wrist. He rested his fingers there and felt her pulse fluttering. Achmed closed his eyes and imagined himself beneath the leaves of his favorite Argan tree. He watched the branches bending in the breezes, swaying with the valley winds. He began to breathe, concentrating on the movement of the tree in his mind's eye. The woman's pulse began to settle, the crease in her forehead slowly relaxing. Achmed closed his eyes again and could hear her breathing in time with his own. He felt peaceful for the first time since she had stumbled out of the desert sun. He slept beside her through the night, his hand gently resting on the inside of her arm.

When Achmed woke in the morning, the woman was not there. He went out to join the men for breakfast and saw she was already sitting among them. They greeted each other with a smile and nod. He was relaxed but excited, so close to home. The tents were brought down and even the camels moved away quickly that morning, everyone anxious to return to the village.

That day while riding, Achmed began thinking about his nighttime dreams, those dreams that began a few months after the illness of his circumcision. He didn't remember the details of the long days and nights of illness except as a burning ache in body and mind. Sometimes the burning was simply fever. Other times, he felt a great chasm opening in his mind. He was falling into a giant gorge of mountains, pitched from a ledge by an invisible hand. The images were confusing and frightening—occasionally giant faces would emerge as snapshots, faces of strangers he had never met. At times he would see a mouth moving but hear no sound; at other times, there was a cacophony of strange and exotic languages. The hallucinations of those fevered days left a mark of disturbing and unsettling emotions. He often had a vague feeling that he was traveling to distant places in those fevered dreams, leaving an echo of memories behind.

Soon after he healed, Achmed discovered that he could indeed travel in his dreams. At first, it seemed random, as if an unseen road was choosing itself. Over time, he discovered that he could chart his own route. Leaving his body behind, the boy was freed to charge into unknown adventures.

ACHMED'S TRAVELS

*I*n the first months after his illness (which Achmed referred to as 'the change'), his nighttime travels were aimless wanderings. He was timid in the beginning, tethered to his corporeal body. It was frustrating in those early days, traveling just a bit farther than his daytime movements and limited to his local haunts. Each evening began the same. The boy was a sound sleeper, tumbling into a deep sleep within moments of putting his head to the pillow. He would lie down in bed, close his eyes, and in a matter of seconds be standing on the main street of his village, gazing toward his beloved Atlas mountain range. Almost immediately, Achmed was tugged on, as if by some invisible line from a ship, pulling him forward with concentrated effort, an eager determination to draw him on.

Turning his gaze west, a tunnel appeared, blurred on the edges—a mountain passageway, dusted with earth tones, striated lines of fantastic geological eons. It was unsettling, being suspended as he was, neither here in the village nor there in the tunnel. Achmed quickly learned that he could see through to the end of the tunnel. It fanned out like a great seashell. So, if he turned his gaze one way and stretched his neck a bit, he could see through to a different place altogether. It was a wormhole and Achmed could see the seashore. He stood in the road looking through the wormhole at the sea. The great expanse of the Atlantic Ocean overwhelmed his mind and senses, the distorted images too vast and confusing for his mind to grasp. The boy would quickly divert his eyes toward the east, facing his familiar Atlas Mountains. These majestic mountains were his village's backyard and held no fear for Achmed. He jumped in giant slow-motion leaps over his mountains until he was gliding above the Mediterranean Sea, touching down on land in Spain or Italy, France, or England. Achmed explored these places from the water, ground, or air—whatever appealed in the night. In time, he began to venture farther and farther, north to Denmark or Norway and east past Romania, Ukraine, and the great peaks of Russia's Ural Mountains.

After some weeks, Achmed became an expert at these evening travels. However, the journeys left him tired in the daytime, for he had not rested his mind. The weight of those nights began to grow on him. He tried to master his confusion and desire by repeating an evening ritual, chanting to himself throughout the day:

Remove the shoes
Remove the clothes
Close the eyes
Breathe — breathe — breathe
Calm the mind

But as soon as Achmed lay down, his will was defeated. A confident and persistent force lifted him, driving him forward against his best efforts to take charge. Achmed tried to retreat on occasion, but the flight was so light and intoxicating, his resistance was a few moments at best. The night flight was a drug that set him free above the world.

A contented sigh escaped his grinning lips once airborne, surrendering to the spidery web of silken threads drawing him out of himself. His first glance was always toward the Atlantic Ocean, the hum of rhythmic tides inviting his attention. The vastness of the waters weighed heavy upon his mind and heart. He could not fathom a way to cross the sea, although he sensed he must.

Night after night the Atlantic grew in his mind, a great Leviathan—until his thoughts became seized upon the idea. His obsession with the ocean started to seep into his days—a leaking roof dripping down the walls of his mind, the gray matter going soft with moisture—his brain wet like a drunk's. Achmed's mind began to soften like moss during the day. He craved the evenings to ponder the question of that great expanse before him. Each evening he found himself standing at the shore, peering into the horizon, minutes turning into hours. He was often jostled awake by his mother, resenting the need to leave his bed to tend the goats each morning.

His first thought as he was falling asleep was of the Atlantic, and it was his first thought upon each awakening. The ocean and its impossible size became an obsession, looming larger and larger in his mind until he knew that the only way to rid himself of this dead weight was to face it down or die trying.

The villagers started to notice a change in Achmed during this time. His patience was short; he was quiet and withdrawn, sometimes muttering to himself during the day. They tried to speak to him and whispered among themselves, saying a djin had possessed him. This happened sometimes, where the village mystic would lose his mind. There were many stories about a Sufi who became so immersed in spiritual wanderings that he would lose touch with his physical world. Achmed, of course, heard all of this but continued his nightly wanderings. He was an addict, enticed over and over to the cause of his own suffering.

Those nights stretched out into weeks, then months, years of him seeing the endless open breadth of that gigantic ocean, then flying with the jerky speed of unsettled fright back to the comfort of his mountain village. That ocean was the giant gaping maw of oblivion. Yet Achmed was lured back to the shoreline over and over, until it carved a groove in his mind, an obsessive addiction to that impossible journey. He stood at the shore, feeling the tide move over his naked feet, the sand retreating with each wave, his feet sinking deeper and deeper. He stood there hour after hour, the sand rising with each wave, awakening when he was buried up to his neck, and gasping for air to relieve the pressure on his lungs. Shivering in his own sweat, he would kick back familiar blankets. Achmed did not sleep, and the villagers whispered and worried.

At times, the boy tried to resist the ocean and traveled to small towns and villages, exploring the great cities of Europe. But he always felt the inevitable tugging in his torso and found himself returning there again and again. After years of waking in a state of frenzied fear, he decided to try to traverse the ocean. Achmed was seventeen now, and it was time. He went to sleep one night with the intent to cross the ocean or die trying. It was so strange, this other reality, that he lived in his dream. He reasoned these were only dreams and that he would probably not die; but the fear was so real, the touch and smell and sight of the shore so tangible, that he treated it as if it could indeed kill him.

That night as he went to sleep, his decision to cross the ocean brought a surprise visitor to meet him. Suddenly, a man stood facing him, his naked feet in the water, jeans rolled up below his knees. His face was olive, warm, and welcoming. This stranger smiled at Achmed and beckoned him forward with a wave of his hand. Achmed followed until his feet were also immersed in the familiar shallows; but as soon as his feet touched the water that night, he felt the heat, a scalding, as if the water were hot coals, not the cool soothing comfort of the ocean. He screamed and awoke in an instant.

The stranger beckoning to him continued for some weeks. Achmed dared not dip his toes into the water; he stayed just above the tide mark. The man's grey eyes seemed welcoming, but the boy felt that there was something sinister in his intent. Achmed was haunted once again, each time, by the lure of curiosity. He made his way to the seashore and there the man was, sometimes pacing, other times sitting in the sand before a crackling fire. New images began to appear, the stranger in an old rickety plastic chair before a shack. In Achmed's earliest memories of these dreams, he was an eavesdropper in the man's mind. He would sometimes hear him speaking to an old woman, talking of his daughter. When he was alone, his musings turned dark—to a woman he was making love to, but his thoughts were violent. This felt like a rape, but Achmed could see her face as if he were that man in the act, and she seemed drunk with her desire for him.

In the early years, these were the dreams that woke Achmed in the night, in a cold sweat, his sheets wet. He traveled no further than the shore. Then one day the stranger spoke to him. It was nighttime on the sand, a fire was flickering in the dark, warming the stranger. Achmed sat down across the fire, and the stranger looked through the flame directly at him.

"You are a people slow to act," he said. His voice was such a surprise that Achmed jumped. It was a different language; but strangely, Achmed understood and recognized it as English.

A SCRATCH ON THE
CHALKBOARD

*T*he alarm clock softly beeped at me at 4:45 a.m. Still dark outside, the street noises rose and seeped in through the open crack of my window. I could hear a garbage truck, a distant siren, a local merchant hosing down the sidewalk. While the water was running from ice cold to warm, I gathered the uniform for the day—stockings, pumps, navy blue skirt and blazer, white blouse, pearl necklace, and matching earrings. *Yeah, this is going to be one fun day*, I thought to myself sarcastically.

I had finally gotten a small place in Manhattan after a year of miserable commuting an hour and a half each way to Northport, compounded by twelve-hour workdays that often stretched to fourteen or more. Albert had stopped waiting up a long time ago. I was a second-year associate at a small "boutique firm," learning the ropes of New York trusts and estates law. Today, I had to deal with an avalanche of work, and I was already mentally reciting the priority of those files. It was not that there were a lot of different matters or scores of clients. The firm didn't need that many; a few select, high-net-worth clients were the cornerstones of the business model.

I stepped out of the shower wrapped in a fluffy towel as I

leaned toward the vanity mirror to apply the little makeup I wore. *It's not a bad face*, I thought, still plump with youthful collagen, shoulder-length, practical brown hair. The eyes, the eyes were the most striking feature of my small, round self, changing from honey brown to hazel, depending on the colors and moods I wore. I brushed on golden eyeshadow and extended the almond eyes with a little liner and some mascara. *No, not a bad face*, I thought every so often.

Aside from the grueling schedule, I was starting to like the work itself. The firm had a unique array of international estate clients, not that I ever saw them. I was relegated to the closet office for the grunt work, not yet seasoned enough to meet the clients. I did, however, know the scope and size of their loved ones' estates. They were impressive by any standard, even if I was easily impressed, and hung on every word that Richard uttered. Richard was one of the partners of the firm, with a sufficiently old European name to qualify him to service certain clients. I thought he was brilliant and intimidating, and I did almost everything in my power to please him, short of joining him for happy hour, no matter how many times a week he asked. I was not much of a drinker and didn't want to get to know my boss that personally. Truth be told, I was beginning to appreciate being in Manhattan, especially the little perks like the 4:00 p.m. bar cart rolling through the hallways during depositions or being able to order up anything, including a new pair of stockings if I ran one during the day.

It was a Tuesday when my life began to change. At 10:00 a.m. Richard called into my intercom to join him in the conference room with a client that he was meeting. It was a new client. His voice sounded more than a little strained,

"Sophia, please join me and Mr. Marlow in conference room 4."

"Yes, sir."

I got up from my desk and made my way down the

hallway, and in my very anxious state noticed the office as if for the first time—adrenaline pumping all the way—burgundy carpet, mahogany paneled walls hung with real and priceless works of art, and finally, the frosted glass surrounding the conference room. It was tasteful but very expensively designed and furnished. The exterior wall of glass looked out over the Manhattan skyline. Those of wealth knew and appreciated the care and expert appointments throughout the suites of Charles, Charles & Block, LLP. Block was dead and there was only one Charles remaining, that being Richard. There were other, unnamed and absent partners around the globe meeting with the clients who had interests in New York and elsewhere. Their names were on the letterhead, sure, but I would not have known them if I met them in their own New York offices. I didn't ask many questions; I was too busy trying not to look like a total dolt, scrambling around to simply learn how to get through a probate petition without having it rejected by the court.

I entered the conference room, frankly, for the very first time; and this would be the first time I met a client. I was surprised that Richard hadn't briefed me because I knew how he liked to be prepared for every meeting, down to the most minute detail.

Richard was standing at the head of a huge mahogany conference table. This was a table that could seat twenty comfortably. My boss was strikingly plain for a man who handled the estates of the rich and not famous, the intentionally unknown. He was really ordinary considering the breadth and depth of the clients he served. A little shy of six feet tall, he kept himself adequately fit, engaging in one hour per day of cardio exercise. He had a full head of mousy brown hair, rather pale blue eyes, and was clean-shaven. To complement his very ordinary physical gifts, he wore the most expensive clothing and accessories that money could buy. Like his offices, his person was elegant and understated in the most practiced way. Richard was absolutely rigid...no, rabid, about appearances. One of the five non-negotiable conditions to employment at his firm was a meeting with his personal assistant. Among her many jobs for Richard Charles, Katherine was charged with dressing and training the new employees in professional etiquette. It was an eight-week commitment and required two hours per night after work hours and full weekends. I admit that the new clothes were fun (especially for someone like me who didn't enjoy shopping). But the cost was outrageous. We were required to pay for the clothing, which would be reimbursed after five years (the probation period for all employees). As I entered the conference room, Richard turned and made the introductions.

"Mr. Marlow, meet Sophia Mason."

"How do you do?"

Mr. Marlow was a classical work of art, middle-aged and aging very well. He was olive-skinned, tall and regal like a Spaniard, kind in the face. His eyes were an opaque hazel, bordering on green. His chestnut hair was thick and shoulder-length, streaked with gray, beautiful, and healthy. He was dressed in a tweed sports jacket and jeans and was trim and handsome in an old European way. Jeans in our office were a rarity. In fact, I think it was the first time I ever saw someone in our office in blue jeans. They suited him. He was comfortable in his clothing and his skin. Everything about him exuded inner peace and good health.

He wore an intricately detailed necklace with some kind of family crest. It looked somehow familiar, and I glanced at it a little too long. He took my hand in both of his, his grip as strong as I expected but gentle, almost deferential. As I stared at his necklace, he stared at my bitty little fingers, including the clipped ones. When we caught each other staring, we burst into laughter. It was such a surprising couple of seconds that passed between us—blue jeans and belly laughing in the hallowed offices of Charles, Charles & Block!

We barely spoke above a church whisper in these offices. This was going to be an interesting day—if I didn't get fired. Richard was obviously uncomfortable with this personal exchange and showed us to the conference room table.

"Do you know each other?" Richard asked.

"No," I replied while Marlow remained silent and smiled his enigmatic smile that I would get to know over a lifetime of similar exchanges. Richard sat at the head of the table, indicating with a wave of his hand the chair he expected me to sit in, to his left, Mr. Marlow at his right. I moved toward the chair Richard indicated. Mr. Marlow proceeded to walk around the table toward my side at Richard's left. I stared at him curiously as he circled the room, clearly ignoring Richard's suggested seating, especially when he could have simply stepped behind Richard to come around. This, I realized, was a very calculated movement for my benefit. I understood that Richard's presence was an afterthought for Marlow as I also registered that I had mentally dropped the "Mr." salutation. Some instinctive knowledge crept into my brain that Marlow was his name, his whole name, and nothing more. This man in blue jeans was watching me the same as I was watching him. I saw his smile begin slowly at the edges of his eyes and work its way around his cheeks to an easy grin. Marlow pulled my chair out for me, sat next to me when I sat, while Richard's jaw practically dropped off, his mouth frozen into a cheerio "O." Once we were all seated, Marlow adjusted his chair so that it was angled toward me and finally answered, though I had forgotten the question by now.

"I do fine, Sophia, and you?" (Gigantic ear-to-ear smile— sparkling white teeth in his mocha face.) That smile could launch a thousand ships. I now understood the cliché and felt an overwhelming warmth and unexpected affection for Marlow, a favorite (and exceptionally handsome) older uncle that I had known all my life. Completely disarmed by him in a matter of moments, that impassive professional expression I had been wearing for so long now slipped off my face like an old, unwanted shawl. My smile emerged like the dawn, a Caribbean sunrise filling my chest with a lightness of being. The weight of the shawl hit the floor with a thud.

Richard began by telling me that Mr. Marlow had specifically asked me to join them at this meeting and that "our" new client had known me by name.

"I'm sorry, but have we met before?" I asked him.

Surprisingly, he answered yes, when I was ten years old. We had met in Orient Point during one of my summer visits there. I didn't recall ever meeting him.

"But how did you know I was here? "I asked.

"I didn't," he replied. "I noticed your name on the firm roster downstairs."

I tried to press him more, but he deftly avoided the inquiry. I knew there was no firm roster, as did Richard. There was no Internet listing of attorneys, no electronic or manual directory in the lobby of the building. The firm, like its clients, was not interested in making a name for itself. The members and associates cherished privacy. We were all registered with the Bar, but that was the extent of any public notice. As a matter of fact, I had never even applied for a position with Charles, Charles & Block. They hand-picked their attorneys and would not accept any solicitations from individuals or headhunters.

Shortly after I had recovered from my near-death experience of the return trip from taking the bar exam, I received an invitation from the firm. It was unusual, and I almost didn't attend. While struggling with my decision, I received a personal visit one day. A woman in her late twenties unexpectedly showed up at the gym where I worked out. She made her way toward me at the leg press as if she knew me. As she approached, I noticed her brown bob, pin-straight hair, brown eyes, cute little glasses, and her perfectly conservative skirt suit, pumps, and simple gold jewelry. She exuded an efficient, clean, sharp aura. She waited for me to finish my set then stuck out her hand brusquely to shake mine. She spoke shortly, not wasting any words except what was absolutely required.

"Hello, my name is Katherine and I work at Charles, Charles & Block. I've been sent to personally deliver this invitation to you. I have also been instructed to tell you that it is rude not to RSVP to an invitation unless, of course, you didn't receive it. In any event, Mr. Charles would be pleased if you could meet him for a luncheon at the firm. It is a social event but business, as well; and he is interested in meeting you."

Well, that was an unexpected invitation.

"Pleased to meet you, Katherine; but I didn't reply because I wasn't able to find out anything about the firm or whether it's a place I'd like to work. But this second attempt to reach me has now gotten my curiosity peaked. So consider this an RSVP and tell Mr. Charles that I look forward to meeting him."

"A car will pick you up at 12:30," Katherine replied and began to leave.

"Wait a minute," I responded. "Can you tell me what the firm does, why they are interested in me, anything?"

Katherine looked at me a little more closely, lifting her cute little glasses and peering under them at me. Her eyes locked on mine and I could feel her trying to get a reading of me. It was a small electrical charge that started at my scalp and grazed my back, like the nails of my old tenth-grade bio teacher on the blackboard. I knew there was something very wrong with him, and I felt it here, too. Her nails were scraping the chalkboard of my inner alarm system. She smiled tightly and said goodbye.

Back in the present, I felt those nails creeping around under the table; but Marlow's presence was such a lovely diversion, his charm and good looks so soothing, that I didn't mind the alarms nipping at my heels. The conversation turned to Marlow's business needs. I was mostly ignored during the remainder of the meeting while I took detailed notes. Occasionally, I would look up to see one or the other of the men observing me—Richard, with outrageous curiosity as to what I was doing there, and Marlow, studying me with focused interest. Richard took a short break at one point.

Alone in the conference room with Marlow, he suggested we break soon for some lunch.

"I'm sure Richard will take you someplace nearby," I replied.

"Couldn't you join us?" he asked. Knowing Richard would not care for that idea, I politely declined.

"I can sway Richard," Marlow said as if he understood my hesitation; but the nails were still scraping, and he sensed it. He gave me a way out gracefully, "Unless, of course, you have another appointment."

I took hold of that and ran with it. I was on overload as it was and needed some time to reflect on this meeting.

It was odd the way he held onto my hand as we said goodbye, a few seconds longer than propriety would dictate. I felt a little dizzy and then realized it was because I had stopped breathing, while he seemed to be searching my eyes for some information. Eventually, though, he won out and we did have lunch a couple of years later. It began innocently enough, with Richard, Marlow, and me having lunch together. Then I began handling his matters on my own, and we met for lunch when Richard was in London. It was at lunch some three years later when he told me the truth about why he had chosen our firm from the beginning. It had nothing to do with the firm and everything to do with me. He had a special assignment, and part of it included getting to know me, observing me, and determining whether I was up to the very difficult matter that was now in front of us both. It all sounded very mysterious, and I bit at the forbidden apple eagerly enough. I would soon be on my way to London.

A YANKEE IN LONDON

*A*fter four years at Charles, Charles & Block, LLC taking care of Marlow's business, we sat at lunch that day and he told me there was an important matter that required my travel to Europe as soon as possible. He was secretive and explained that he didn't want anyone but me handling the file. It was personal, an estate matter relating to a close friend, and extremely confidential. The file would remain in London and that is where it was expected I would do my work. No, he couldn't guess how long I might be needed—that would, of course, depend on me.

The following month, in the early days of July in the year of our Lord 2003, I was picked up by the company car and flown on a first-class flight to London. Arriving at Heathrow in the wee hours of the morning, I was met by a chauffeur holding a card with my name who shepherded me through the airport to a town car.

"You will be staying at The Honourable Society of Gray's Inn." I had already been so told but enjoyed the driver's baritone. "Of course, there is a long and storied history associated with the British Inns a' Court. Similar to your Bar association, I'm told, all barristers must belong to one of the four Inns, an' the earliest records a' Grays date back to 1370. That's right...1370."

I met his eyes in the rear-view.

"Course, you'll be wanting to see the offices a' Williams, Shepperd, and Brown in the morning. City Center, they are. We'll get ya' to a comfy bed first at Grays."

Williams. Shepperd. And Brown. The name was so vanilla and so similar to Charles, Charles & Block, they could be recited as a laundry list of white shoe names, names that I often referred to as "American cheese on white bread" or, in this case, "shepherd's pie." White potatoes, white bread—same thing. I glanced at my watch.

It was 3:35 in the morning, London time, so only 10:35 Sunday night in New York. The flats at The Honourable Society of Gray's Inn were let for attorneys only, or barristers and solicitors as they were called in the UK. Barrister made me think of a coffee barista, snobbish in the extreme. Solicitors made me think of elderly pasty-faced white gentlemen who solicitously hold open doors. Those two tiers of lawyers, of course, reflected the United Kingdom, built on two classes of people for millennia—the nobility and everyone else.

I looked around the flat, a small, functional London space, suitable for one. The door opened into a short hallway with a table and a mirror. The hallway flowed into the living area of the one-bedroom apartment. It was a small seating area with a short couch for two, one chair, and a side table with an antique lamp. There was a television on top of an old low buffet in front of the couch. The firm had let this apartment and furnished it for me. Someone must have known my taste. Everything was first class but simple and cozy, exactly how I like it. I could dress the part of the high finance lawyer, but in my private life, I liked jeans and comfy tee-shirts best. There was a small balcony to the right of the seating area with a door. On the stationary side of the door was a desk facing to the outside where I could work from home or surf the net. To the left of the entry hall was a small galley kitchen with a table for two pushed up against the wall. The hallway continued past the living room to the bathroom and bedroom.

The driver asked what time I'd like him to fetch me in the morning. I told him 8:00 would be fine. After saying goodnight and turning the two brass deadbolts, I got to the business of unpacking. I hung most of my clothes on wooden hangers in the bedroom closet and noticed the pleasant aroma of rose sachets when I opened the drawers of the dresser for jeans, tee-shirts, and the rest. Some of these had cushioned the personal knick-knacks I had thought to bring—pieces of Murano glass that I collected over the years. Marlow had said I might be here a while, so I brought five of my paperweights with me, scattering them randomly about the flat. My black-faced angel went on the little entry hall table. It was a gift from my childhood, but I didn't remember where it came from. I took it everywhere with me, like a favorite teddy bear. There, I felt like I had personalized my space. I went to see what I needed to purchase in the way of food; to my delighted surprise, the pantry had been stocked with all the things I liked. They were thorough, left no room for me to have to fuss so that I could get directly to work. I took a shower and got into bed and was quickly asleep after the long flight.

A different driver, crisp and clean, knocked on my door at 8:00 a.m. sharp. He gave a nod to my chocolate brown suit, and I smiled, feeling like I passed a test. The left lane drive into London took us along the Thames, past Westminster. I recognized the statue in Trafalgar Square. We turned a short time later and stopped in front of a lovely old historic home. The firm owned the building, my driver shared, and had painstakingly converted the Palladian structure into offices. There were upgrades like underground parking, a rare and precious perk in the crowded city of London. We pulled into the little alley driveway and made a turn into the underground parking lot. The driver got out with me. I took in the details of him, a huge black fellow with arms the size of tree trunks.

"Good morning, my name is Oliver. I am a member of the security team here. I will be showing you the security procedures in our London offices."

"Good morning, Oliver, nice to meet you," I replied.

When we shook hands, it was like putting my hand into a baseball mitt. Everything about Oliver was huge—his height, his arms, but most of all, his grin. I liked him immediately, and the English accent on this huge fellow was such a delightful surprise. That British accent, you either loved it or hated it, depending on who was wearing it. On Oliver, it was charming in the extreme. I wanted to squeeze him like a giant cabbage patch doll.

I followed Oliver to the door. He entered a security code and then we walked two flights up to the security office. It was small and bare, a perfectly neat desk with a file cabinet behind it and one chair for visitors where I sat. Oliver sat as well and leaned forward, his huge arms on the desk, all traces of his brilliant smile gone. Suddenly, he didn't seem so squishy and charming. He looked dangerous.

"Sophia, listen carefully. Open that remarkable brain file of yours and put all of the information I am about to share with you into it. You must be able to recall every detail in the most extreme circumstances."

He knew my name and spoke to me as if we had talked long and often. I was on hyper-alert and began to notice all the details of the room that hadn't registered before Oliver spoke. My eyes were darting around and I had jumped to my feet with the door to my left, not at my back where it was when I was sitting. There was a tiny square out of place in the ceiling, and I suspected it concealed a hidden camera. The garbage pail had several scraps of paper that should probably have been shredded. On top of the file cabinet, there was an ashtray with an old Dunhill butt in it but no smell of smoke in the room, or on Oliver for that matter. Oliver was holding it to dispose of elsewhere. The door was heavy and steel, with no windows in the room. It was a safe room. This happened occasionally where I would suddenly be tuned in to everything around me. I knew that someone must have taught me these things, but I couldn't recall who or when. I also knew that it was a good thing I couldn't remember.

"Good, I see I've got your attention," Oliver said. "Sophia, there is no room for error here. You must follow every procedure I am about to tell you, every time. Do not relax your vigilance, ever. You will be briefed in person on codes each morning. The codes will change every day, and you must recall them perfectly. You must never jot down the codes anywhere. You must never share them with anyone. Remember, Sophia, no room for error."

He handed me a key card, a skeleton key, a four-sided key (which I knew was a cruciform key), and one whose shape I didn't recognize, a sort of rectangle on top. Oliver explained before I even asked that it was an Abloy key, popular in Finland and almost impossible to pick. Three were for the office and one for my flat—the key card for the basement entrance from the parking garage, the skeleton key for my office, the cruciform key for the cellar, and the Abloy for my flat. In addition to the keys, each door had a security panel, therefore, the different codes.

"I'll show you around the office and go through the keys with you—remember, key first, code second. Sophia, key first, code second." Every time he uttered my name, I jumped into hyper-alert and filed the information in a safe place that no one could reach. Oliver stood, opened the door, and began my guided tour of the office.

It was a magnificent old building, not New York old. There was no old or antique in New York. This was Europe old, built by master craftsmen, meant to last many lifetimes. The building was a four-floor historic estate home, nestled among some of the more modern buildings in the business district. The ground floor was the basement where we had come in, the first floor held the grand foyer, with reception, library, and conference rooms, all displaying beautifully appointed furnishings. Lots of wood and stone, I noticed. The remaining floors were offices carved from the former home's bedrooms, a bit cumbersome because of the historic preservation requirements. I was shown to my office on the third floor where I deposited my purse under Oliver's critical stare. I raised my eyebrows and he explained that the entire building and each office were under constant video surveillance and therefore no need to hide the purse. The office was beautifully decorated, as was the rest of the traditional and very European décor, a lovely combination of modern technology elegantly situated among old-world antique furniture and collections. I glanced around to appreciate the paneled mahogany walls, button-tucked leather chairs, and beautiful and original works of art. One of the partner solicitors was apparently a serious collector. There was a kitchen on the ground floor with a back entrance for the staff, I assumed. Oliver took me through there to a landing with an emergency exit sign. Opposite the exit was another door. It looked like a supply closet. Beneath a false light switch next to the door was an electronic keypad. Oliver turned his back to me, his huge wall of a back, as he entered the key code. He turned to me when the door opened.

"You may access the cellar by calling me on this phone. It is programmed to work with fingerprint and retinal scanning." *Holy shit*, I thought, *this is like James Bond security.* "If you want to see the files, ring me up and I'll be here as soon as possible. If it's during business hours, I'll usually be here within a few minutes. However, if it is the weekend or holiday, it may take me longer." How interesting that the head of security at this firm would be at my beck and call. We stepped onto a landing and down to the cellar, one simple set of wooden stairs.

"Oliver, are you available to all the employees on such short notice?" I asked.

He didn't reply, instead, warned me, "Be careful, Mademoiselle, this is a historic home and the original stairs are maintained here, but they are worn smooth and a little slippery." He was right; I did almost slip on the smooth stairs. I also noticed the musty smell of the basement, but it wasn't bad. It smelled like a mushroom house I had once visited.

"Oliver, please call me Sophia. Do you have a French background?" I asked. I was met with the great wall of Oliver's silence in answer to my question.

When we reached the bottom, I glanced around the room and was confused for a moment as I didn't see any files. It looked like the basement of an old house. There was a boiler, some pipes running, and a door to what could have been a crawlspace. It was not well lit, a single fixture hanging in the center of the room. The entire cellar was maybe 20 x 20 feet; there was one wall with metal shelving and boxes marked with office supplies, mostly cleaning supplies. Despite feeling a little confused, I was not in the least bit uneasy or afraid. Oliver had the kind of demeanor that could stop a subway with a pinky finger. He had a reassuring aura about him.

Reaching behind one of the metal shelving units, Oliver pushed an unseen button. The entire unit was attached to a door that opened silently, like a bank vault. We stepped inside to a small room, a cell really. He closed the outer door with the push of another button and then turned and stepped maybe two paces to the far side of this very small room. He inserted his key and mine and then entered a five-digit code. I heard tumblers moving and the smooth swish of the second heavy door. We stepped through, and before me was another staircase heading further down, well below ground. The staircase was lit with yellow sconces, reminding me of an underground mining operation, and with it the thought of being trapped. At the bottom, we reached a hallway, lit every few meters by the same yellow sconces. We walked through the underground tunnel, walls of earth and rough-hewn stone, for several more minutes. We must have arrived at a place below another building altogether because the building owned by Williams, Shepperd, and Brown was not this big.

Oliver kept up a running dialogue the entire time.

"Some of the items brought from the Moreaux family estate are stored here. They were considered too valuable to leave behind after Madame's passing, just a year ago. Nothing has been touched since for various reasons, but many of the trunks are antiques and the contents haven't been inventoried yet. Due to the antique nature of many of the files, we have kept them in this art storage facility. The temperature and humidity are closely monitored to prevent decay. Mademoiselle, you are the first to see these files since they arrived. Before beginning the legal work, you will have to catalog and inventory all the documents, make copies, take photographs, etc. so that you won't be handling the documents directly after the initial inventory. Everything you need is here—a copy machine, paper, and cotton gloves for handling the originals. You will have an assistant upon request, but the client would prefer that you do all that you can by yourself for privacy reasons."

A team of file clerks could have had this all prepared for me already, and I was irritated that I'd be spending weeks in the basement of this lovely building, holed up like a mole. But I was excited to know that no one else, really no one else, had been permitted access to the documents.

The walls and floor transitioned to smooth concrete. On either side of the hallway were two walls of glass storage rooms. I was facing the one I would be working in. It was enormous, with a desk in the middle, a computer, a printer, and a copier to the side. There were shelves lined with boxes, trunks piled on the floor, some works of pottery, art, antiques, etc. I didn't know the first thing about valuing art or antiques, but that wasn't my part of the work in any event. The interior was well lit and seemed a little less claustrophobic now that I could sit facing the glass instead of another coffin wall. I couldn't see the end of the hallway on either side.

"This will be where I will bring you when you are ready to begin work down here." Oliver and I began the long walk back. When we reached the cellar off the kitchen, he reminded me, "Sophia, remember, no room for error. Whatever you do or see in storage is for no one but you." I remained silent, my heart tapping out a calm but alert beat, while he reminded me of the absolute need for secrecy. We then climbed the smooth polished steps back to my third-floor office.

During the day, several people stopped in to introduce themselves, including my assistant who was shared with two other attorneys. Katherine from New York was the assistant and had been relocated here two years prior. It was nice to see a familiar face, but she was her usual clipped self. She was on the same floor down the hallway, and I'd be sharing her services with Gabriel Hayes and another fellow named Harry. I had been reviewing the files that were in my office and was taking a break, my back to the door as I stared out the window while I stretched my arms up high, hiking my blouse out of my skirt.

"I am sure you were told that these offices are under video surveillance." I wheeled around with my hand on a paperweight in a flash. What a surprise to find a Murano paperweight here in my office, exactly where I expected to find it. There was a little note under it that I would look at later. At that moment, though, I looked up to see, leaning up against the door jamb of my office, Gabriel Hayes.

I lifted my hand off the paperweight and extended it to him as he approached. "How do you do? I'm Sophia Mason. Thanks for the warning. I suppose it's not so bad as long as I'm not picking my nose."

He cringed, not appreciating my crass Yankee humor. "My office is two doors down. I manage the corporate and business matters here and wanted to extend a welcome. You're the first American we've had here since I joined the firm a few years ago." It sounded like an insult the way he said 'American.' Ha, I was right on the money! His distaste couldn't be clearer. Yankees didn't belong here, but he would be polite as a proper Englishman should be.

This tidy snob put me off in a flash, standing in front of me, giving me the chance to see him in his nice three-piece pinstripe gray suit, lavender tie, shirt pressed to perfection, shaved to a baby smoothness. He was a tall man, about six foot two I guessed, about my age, late twenties. A little soft under that suit I also bet, brown hair and brown eyes—the boarding school British type. His unruly hair was the only renegade quality about him. It seemed he couldn't tame it, which brought me a small degree of satisfaction. He was pleasant enough, but there was something sharp about him, cold on the edges.

He would never be caught reading a trashy romance. No, Gabriel Hayes would be pontificating on the merits of classical art or music. No vampire works in his summer reading, but Virginia Woolf, Dostoevsky.

"Good day, Sophia, pleasure meeting you," he said as he exited. I picked up the envelope under the paperweight and opened it with a nearby letter opener.

Sophia,

I hope you enjoy your stay in London. Here's a little something to keep you company

~ Marlow

How thoughtful of him. He knew I liked the Murano, in particular, the paperweights. I turned this one in my hand to get a feel for it. It was medium-heavy, pink oleander in clear glass.

I met a few other solicitors, James and Philip, Martin and Mary. The names were perfect for the office, white shoe all the way...more protestant, less earthy. Most of my time was spent settling in, but I did notice a shocking absence of older attorneys. I started to get the feeling that they were watching remotely from video surveillance but not participating in the day-to-day grind. We were like rats in a maze, all we young'ns, chasing bits of promised cheese. Toward the end of my first month, I was introduced to some of the London partners at their monthly meeting one evening. It was a cursory hello and goodbye.

We were the workhorses and didn't see much of the older solicitors and barristers. But we all had our work to do, and no one discussed the obvious missing piece, the elephant in the room. We also did not discuss our files other than in the most generic, academic terms if a particularly troublesome issue came up. I might ask a general question about the heirship proceeding in the UK but never discussed any particular matter I was working on. As a matter of fact, my second week was spent learning the procedure for the UK heirship proceeding.

I began reviewing the part of the file that was in my office. There were about a dozen storage boxes all marked "Estate of Adele Moreaux." They were pretty well organized and what I would expect in an estate file—wills, trusts, inventories of assets, real estate holdings, business documents, and partnership agreements. It took me the better part of my first week to read everything, make my own notes and memos to have quick access to the documents. For the most part, I did not disturb the order of the files or their contents.

I had to prepare the documents necessary to petition the

court to probate the Last Will & Testament of Ms. Moreaux. The files lacked the most obvious document to complete that task, a family tree. My first few weeks at the firm were spent looking for any notes on the family tree. I felt like Alice slipping down the rabbit hole. The intake sheet on all estate planning clients almost always includes a family tree. I shrugged my shoulders and continued poring over files. In the evenings, I returned to my flat for dinner followed by a nice walk through a nearby park. I spent the first few weekends as a regular tourist exploring London and saw the Poet's Corner at St. Paul's, the chapel at Westminster Abbey, Big Ben, and the changing of the guard at Buckingham Palace.

Then one day a few weeks after my arrival in London, Harry broke the ice and invited me to join him and a few other associates at a local pub, The Seven Stars, which it turned out was walking distance from my flat. I eagerly accepted, having gotten more than a little bored. Harry and Philip were good company, much more relaxed outside the office. They seemed more Irish than English, and it turned out I was right. They had Irish roots but were clever enough to garner the attention of the firm which, upon hiring each of them, gave them a thorough lesson in the King's English so there was little left of a brogue in them. I asked how their families felt about it, and they both replied that they had no family, had been orphaned, and were now living together as partners for four years. It confirmed my guess that they were gay. We became fast friends and spent after-hours together regularly. We never discussed office files, but we did talk about politics, philosophy, the current state of affairs in the world, movies, fashion, music—everything but work. Harry and Philip took me to all the lovely gardens of the city parks and showed me the beautiful parts of London far from a tourist's camera. They loved to cook, as did I, and we began exchanging recipes. Although Gabriel, Martin, and Mary often joined us for a pint, they were not interested in pool or darts. Seemed they couldn't let their hair down at all. Where Harry and Philip roared over my humor, they kept their distance. They were snobs, through and through. Harry and Philip knew what it was like to be an outsider and made a conscious effort to include me.

At one of our nights out together I noticed a young woman talking to Gabriel. They were having a good time chatting, and I suddenly noticed that he was handsome. It hadn't occurred to me until then. He was sort of unremarkable in appearance, not a face or a body that would draw much attention. He could be lost on the streets of London, go by unnoticed for a lifetime. But talking to that woman at the bar, his face was more animated, he laughed a bit, head tipped back while he drank a whiskey. She was flirting with him, and he was enjoying the play. I was enjoying it, as well, seeing him have fun that way. He must have felt someone watching and glanced my way, mid-sentence with his companion. Our eyes met, and we both smiled. I never thought of him as a social companion before. But then again, I never saw him out of a suit or drinking whiskey, for that matter. I felt awkward and out of place suddenly and soon found a way to take leave of my Irish lads. On the pavement outside, Gabriel caught up with me and offered to call a cab, but I told him I'd prefer to walk.

At work the next day, I called Oliver to go to the basement so that I could start on the files down there to see what I could find in the way of family documents. When Oliver arrived, he suggested that I bring a change of clothes next time. The boxes and crates brought from the estate were old and dusty. Of course, there was a full bathroom in the storage facility with plenty of room to shower and a comfortable dressing room. When we got to the door, he inserted his key and asked for me to do the same, then entered the digital code.

In the climate-controlled, secure cellar, I began the painstaking work. The room where the bulk of the Moreaux estate property was kept was enormous, easily double the size of my glassed-in space. I estimated 40 x 40 feet. Pallet after pallet, marked with a name that until six weeks ago meant no more to me than Jones or Smith. Moreaux...Moreaux...Moreaux. Missing was any home furnishings of comfort —a couch, chairs, a lamp—nothing from Adele's daily life. After questioning Oliver, I discovered these personal items had remained at the country house, along with the elderly executor who resided there with a diminished staff and perhaps diminished capacity. After Adele's death, valuables deemed unessential but vulnerable to theft or loss had been packed and moved here to the underground vault beneath the firm's offices in London. Touched, packed, and crated but for some reason, no one took the time to conduct an inventory at that most convenient time. I often lost track of time down there, and while muttering to myself under my breath one evening, Oliver startled me by answering the question I had spoken out loud.

"No one took an inventory because these files were selected by the executor and sent here at various times by different people. Another late night, Sophia?" Rhetorical question. "Right then, just ring me up when you are ready to go."

The Moreaux family tree was a complete mystery. Under Adele's will, a 'friend' had been appointed as executor. He was long since retired and resting comfortably at her country estate in Devonshire. Under the terms of the will, he was also given the right to remain there for his lifetime, along with an ample allowance to support him and his limited staff. I would do all the legal work, and he would simply sign the documents.

I couldn't understand how the solicitor who had done so much planning never included a simple family tree. When I asked about phoning him, I was told that it wasn't possible, he had suffered a stroke in recent years. The little bit I could glean from his notes indicated that Adele never had children, nor siblings—no nieces or long-lost nephews. Her parents were gone, and their siblings were also deceased or had long since lost touch. Her will specifically stated she had no heirs and was leaving all to charities. Given that her estate had a value of approximately fifty million euro, distant heirs were expected to appear from the mist and rear their heads, but no such claims had yet occurred.

In any event, I was required to do my due diligence—to search for the next of kin who had to be given notice of the proceeding—or prove to the court's satisfaction that there were no remaining next of kin, not even a distant cousin residing in New Guinea. Her family had some relations in France at least at the end of the First World War. Adele's was an old European family, one that was likely studied by the cultured UK boarding school brats like Gabriel. And that was probably one of the reasons the office brought me in.

As confidences go, attorneys are notorious water cooler chatterers among themselves. So, no one in the London office was to know about the family I was servicing. I was, however, getting desperate for help. I caught up with Gabriel in the hallway one day and asked him if he could drop into my office if he had some free time during the day. Gabriel handled the business and corporate work in the office, and that sometimes included portions of estate matters. A bit after 8:00 p.m. Gabriel poked his head into my office.

"Hi, Sophia, I was about to head on but remembered that you asked me to stop in."

I looked up from my desk to see him leaning against the door jamb, obviously his favorite pose. He looked as tidy as the first thing this morning, as if he hadn't spent a fourteen-hour day at the top of his game and hard at work. I was completely caught off guard, immersed in my work, and had forgotten that I asked him to come by. I couldn't ask him for help in the office, not with the surveillance. But I was equally uncomfortable asking him to step outside. He would misinterpret it, I was sure. A few uncomfortable seconds passed before he cleared his throat and moved to the chair in front of my desk. He sat down, looking at me curiously.

"Gabriel, would you like to get a bite to eat this evening?" I asked and saw his head tilt, eyes inquiring.

"Sophia, are you ill? You're looking a little peaked," he replied.

Well, that was an odd reply, I guessed his way of saying no thanks. No real surprises there. He may have thought I was asking him out and didn't want to answer. I could understand. We were from quite different worlds, and I would never imagine him having an interest in me. It really was not hurtful in any way. So I replied to allow us both an easy out.

"As a matter of fact, I am a little under the weather and will be heading out myself in a short while. Have a nice night, Gabriel."

About a half-hour later I packed up for the evening and headed home, not giving any further thought to my little dilemma. I would put in the extra time to learn the family history as best I could, without any resentment toward my elitist colleague. Declining the company car, I began to walk home in London's steamy night air. A short time into my stroll, I really did begin to feel ill, a little lightheaded and weak. I sat on a bench in St. James Park and tried a few deep breaths that did not help the nausea. I rummaged around my little purse for a cracker or mint, something to help settle my stomach. I remembered then that I hadn't eaten since breakfast, which happened often, busy at work, not conscious of an empty stomach until I was on my way home and feeling the effects of it. This happened to me back in New York on the subway ride home pretty regularly. I found a little pack of oyster crackers and a mint and began nibbling. It didn't help. There was something else here, nipping at my gut, more than low blood sugar. I glanced up from my purse to see a man staring at me from across the path on another bench. Gathering myself, I stood and began a brisk walk across the park. I was mentally changing my destination when I heard footsteps behind me at the same pace as my own.

I turned on my heel and stepped back for leverage. The move was so unexpected that he passed me by and dropped a piece of paper as he continued walking. The paper read:

Head to the west exit. Cross into Hyde Park to Piccadilly to Park Land. Watch for Gabriel.

I wasn't afraid at all. In fact, I was now feeling better and curiously excited. Our conversation forgotten, I followed the instructions, paused for a second to get my bearings, and headed toward an unfamiliar park exit. This was Mayfair, an area I had not yet explored and foreign to me.

The walk twisted and turned around the bottom end of the lake, past the Victoria Memorial, across Constitution Hill, left and right, following the signs toward Piccadilly. I caught sight of Gabriel walking ahead of me—already about to cross the broad thoroughfare, but he slowed on the far side until I crossed, then walked south. It was getting dark as he took a sharp right. At the corner of Old Park, I lost sight of him but then picked him up just outside a pub with its own Victorian street lamps and heavy leaded windows. The Rose and Crown was busy with after-work professionals. He had passed through the crowd and taken a booth at the back, where I found him sitting. He didn't say a word, and I followed that silent lead as he got up and went through a back door and down a small hallway. Restrooms were on one side. The pass-thru went on and ended at the bottom of a roped-off stairwell. Lifting a heavy brass clip, Gabriel stepped back with the velvet rope, and I moved past him, down the stone stairs.

Gabriel didn't speak when we reached the bottom but held out his hand for my purse. He removed the RB&W office keys and left them in an old wooden decorative box sitting on a small table at the bottom of the stairs. The box snapped closed with the slight pressure of his thumb, I thought maybe his thumbprint. I followed him now into a beautiful wine cellar and watched as he closed the old wooden door behind me. All the while, I was calmly observing our surroundings, making mental notes—the name of the pub, the street, faces at the bar, counting the number of steps to the wine cellar, noting that the way in seemed, at first glance, the only way out.

The cellar had that great musky smell of earth and aging wood, mixed up with yeast and wine. A small wooden table and two chairs were set beneath a golden mellow light; on a sideboard, glasses were arranged for tastings. Gabriel held out a chair for me and I sat. He produced a wand that looked like the metal detectors at airports and scanned my body with it. He sighed and sat, poured a glass of wine for both of us, and reached into a small refrigerator for a plate of cheese and crackers.

"Eat, Sophia, before you faint. You have an awful habit of ignoring your body's needs."

I nibbled on the cheese and crackers, searching Gabriel's face for some message.

"Well, that was interesting," I offered. "Good cheese. If I were stuck on a desert island, I think the only food I would really miss is cheese." He practically rolled his eyes at my little diversion.

"Sophia, you have so little sense about your own safety, it's astounding. You wander the city without an escort. You walk through a park in the dark and follow a stranger's instructions without question. You ask to meet me after hours for a meal. Seriously, what are you thinking?"

He had a sharp tongue, a British sharp tongue that could cut like a knife, but it didn't really faze me. I'd been in boardrooms with far worse than this over the years, had adversaries who thought they were bullies, who couldn't even get a raised eyebrow from me.

With Albert's excellent help, I had mastered the art of never taking anything personally. He taught me by example that every person has his own story and baggage. Mostly, it had nothing to do with me and everything to do with ego. This art of understanding was a muscle that needed to be exercised regularly, and Gabriel was providing me with an excellent opportunity to do so.

I spread a delicious soft brie on a wheat cracker. Interesting that he thought I didn't have a care for my own safety. I really had no fear walking through a dark parking lot, wooded park, or alley. It wasn't so much that I was unaware of the danger. I was quite aware of my surroundings, but I was confident I could take care of myself. From a practical standpoint, that confidence didn't make much sense, given how petite I was. Nevertheless, I never found myself in a dangerous situation, so I had no fears.

"So, Sophia, what did you want to talk to me about that couldn't be discussed in the office?"

I hesitated, now not sure of the risk I was taking. It was quite possible that the cloak and dagger were a ruse to lure me into feeling I could confide in him. I searched his face and found a blank slate. There was not a hint of uncertainty, none of the telltale signs of deception, no flicker of the eyes up and to the right, no nervous tics, no twitching in his seat. He was perfectly comfortable with himself. Not sure how to proceed, I erred on the side of caution.

"Gabriel, I think you may have misunderstood me. There

isn't anything in particular that I wanted to discuss. I was interested in having some company for the evening."

"Sophia, I think you know quite well that as social companions, we are not well suited to each other. So what's really going on here? The little I know of you indicate that this is out of character. Incidentally, this is a perfectly secure location." He nodded toward the barroom over our heads. "They'll be shouting down the Arsenal game replay by no…"

This little bout of bossiness put me off—I didn't much care for being told what to do. I wanted to believe him but was relying too much on outward observation to be confident he was what he seemed to be. I thought I'd try something else.

"Gabriel, put your hands on the table if you don't mind, palms up."

"Why? Are you going to read my palms now?" He was acerbic in the most irritatingly polite way that only the British could perfect.

I raised my eyebrows in a challenge, implying he might be afraid. He bit and said, "All right, I'll play," as if it would all be a joke to him.

He placed his hands on the table but was staring intently at my face.

"Close your eyes, Gabriel. It's distracting." He smiled an arrogant little smile that piqued my irritation level another notch for a quick millisecond. But then he closed his eyes. Contrary to his expectation, I did not read his palms or even look at them. I stood quietly, so quietly he didn't hear. I walked around behind his chair and held my hands at my sides. I could feel his impatience, and I knew he was about to open his eyes when I whispered,

"Don't. Move." He was startled to hear my voice so close and behind him, and I saw the tiniest twitch of a hand. He hadn't heard me move. I closed my eyes and felt for him—not his thoughts or his feelings but his other self, the one that hovers around but outside of ourselves. That true self, that part of us that was not ego, was somewhere behind and above the head. I hadn't attempted this for several years (since the last time I had practiced with Albert), and it was a challenge to flex this muscle after so much time. Gabriel was hard to 'read,' so guarded I couldn't see more than the top of his head. I couldn't feel anything but resistance, free weights in the gym that wouldn't budge.

"Breathe, Gabriel. You're holding your breath. In through your nose and out through your mouth." I began to breathe rhythmically, and he soon joined the rhythm. He did as I asked and the sweetness of his breath washed through the room, mingling with the dampness of the earth and the wine and yeast. In and out, timed to a slowing heartbeat, we breathed together. First ten breaths, then twenty, then I lost count. Guarded was the only feeling that came to me. He had mastered the ability to keep people out. How very strange.

Deciding to come back around, I sat again, facing Gabriel. He was a puzzle that I was becoming more interested in working out. Maybe my unexpected proximity had gotten his guard up fast and strong. By the time I had returned to my seat, his eyes were wide open and his fingers wrapped around the glass of wine he had poured for himself. He was smiling that annoying little smirk, leaning back now in his chair.

Then his face was serious, his earth-brown eyes concentrating on my own. He spoke quietly, barely above a whisper, his voice hypnotic. "Sophia, what are you trying to do?" he asked. "Sophia, wouldn't you like to tell me what you are really about, trying to poke around in my head?"

He continued to speak, his voice soothing and rhythmic, his words touching me in a lazy kind of way. My name was so sensual on his lips. It was as if he knew how to say the three syllables quietly, before each sentence, so pleasant and sexy. It was amazing how he modulated his voice from that cold, clipped elitist to the warm sing-song rhythm, whispering, his voice hoarse...on and on his voice droned, "I would like...to get to know you...better, Sophia." I heard him say, but I kept missing pieces of his poetic monologue, watching instead the way his lips moved. I felt so strange as he repeated my name, leaning closer and closer to me over the table, the room starting to tip at an angle.

I closed my eyes and instantly heard, "Sophia, snap out of it!" My inner alarm, this time like nails scraping the back of my neck. I jumped to my feet, back to myself, hyper-alert and in high gear.

"Gabriel, I think I made a mistake. Yeah...I'll...I'll see you at the office tomorrow." I muttered.

As I headed to the door, he answered, "As you wish. Tomorrow then." Behind me, I heard wine being poured.

I felt off-balance the entire way home. I didn't understand what had happened. It was as if Gabriel knew something about me that I myself didn't know. There was a nagging anxiety that followed me all the way home that evening. I dreamed of Albert that night, holding my little-girl hands, keeping them warm. We were together at the Sound, walking along the familiar shore.

I was still sluggish the next morning as I woke before work and cold, too, as if I were coming down with the flu. I went through my morning routine, yoga, weights, my run through the park, but I couldn't find a calm moment. In the shower, I felt faint.

I arrived at the office, as usual, the next day, and the next and the next. No one would have noticed anything different about me. I continued my work over the next several weeks. I was where I was supposed to be—in the basement vault— when I was supposed to be, which was most of the long hours of my workdays. I continued the Moreaux inventory and my research over the next several weeks, but the sense of heaviness grew by the hour. The anxiety was mounting, growing into an unnamed dread. I didn't sleep well, nightmares that I couldn't recall leaving me weak and drained in the mornings. Dark circles took up residence under my eyes. I found it hard to concentrate, and it took me longer than normal to retain the information I was finally learning, Moreaux history—French, British, Spanish family lineages, wars fought and lost, and where my Adele fit in. I was feeling an affection and an eagerness to shape her lost history.

One afternoon several weeks later, Gabriel was on his way out with the usual gang of three when Philip and Harry asked me to join them. I accepted half-heartedly, hoping a night out with the Irish lads could help shake this dreary doom. The four of us sat in a booth with lamb sliders and beer. It was fun —there was a live band playing slow and easy blues. Philip and Harry went to shoot some pool while Gabriel remained with me. I was sipping on my second beer, something I didn't usually do, and feeling more relaxed than I had in weeks.

Aside from the heavy sense of dread, I was beginning to really like London—the work was progressing, and my colleagues were funny and, in the main, supportive. Stretching my neck, I rested my head back against the booth's leather cushion. The band and beer were just what the doctor ordered. I sighed and closed my eyes. An image of sand dunes began to swell and roll beneath my eyelids. I was carried along over the sand, rocking as if on a boat. I could smell the dry sand on the wind and felt minute grains slipping through my fingers as I reached out to touch them. I squeezed my eyes tight before opening them, suddenly alert and sitting ramrod straight, looking at Gabriel across from me. His brow was wrinkled and he was studying me.

I asked him without weighing the question, "Gabriel, what the hell are you doing?"

"Trying to know who you are and what you and that afflicted New York voice is doing here. You are too young and unpolished to be in this game. You don't know when you're being observed, and I repeat myself here, you have no sense of self-preservation," he finished.

Holy shit, I thought to myself, *that's the most I've heard this man say in three months*. The intensity on his face was comical. He was trying to get into my head and he and all his boarding school polish couldn't so he was trying to disarm me with that cutting tongue for a second time.

Quietly, and with a smile on my face, I replied, "Poor fellow is frustrated...well, that sucks for you...good evening, Gabriel." I got up to leave. Philip and Harry had finished their game and were returning from the pool tables. They tried to insist on seeing me home, but I declined. Watching Gabriel finish off his last pint, I wanted some time alone to walk and think. I was relieved to hear his voice again but not that nasty one. The early September chill helped to snap me out of my slumber as I began a motivated walk home.

The next day at work, Gabriel was nowhere to be found. His office door was closed, lights off. Same thing the next day and the next—for two weeks he was out. Finally, one day while in the storage cellar with Oliver, I asked where he was and Oliver answered, "Mr. Hayes is temporarily on assignment in another office."

Meantime, I continued to work on the estate, learning the British common law of descent and distribution, mapping out the family tree, and appearing in court to have the executor appointed.

Then one day he was there in his office, head bowed over work at his desk. I was glad of it, pleased to see his face; yet he was gloomy and withdrawn, politically polite, with no sense of camaraderie. *What a pity*, I thought. I was still working out the puzzle that was Gabriel, the challenge of getting past his very guarded self. I would miss that nasty banter of ours because it was familiar. Later on that afternoon, I decided to walk home; the weather had cleared for the first time in days. After the dog days of summer, September had no dawn, buried as it was from earth to sky in an unrelenting rain. The downpour had let up, and I enjoyed a stroll through St. James. It was easy to see that others had the same idea.

Partway through the park, I noticed a man sitting on a bench; something about him was familiar. Yes, it was the man who led me to the pub with the wine cellar to Gabriel...definitely the same man. I glanced at my watch and opted for the adventure. I took the western path, reaching old Park Lane, past the four street lamps, and heard the doorbells announce my entry into the pub. Remembering to deposit my office keys in the wooden box, I started down the stone steps and found it interesting how no one in the Rose and Thorn took notice of me. On the other hand, I took in the room in precise detail, counted heads and drinks with a glance, noticed who was dining and who was standing, made a mental note of the exit, and filed all this information neatly in its place, arming myself for instant recall.

No surprise, Gabriel was there—in the same chair—but he was obviously not expecting me. He got to his feet in a flash as his eyes darted around frantically, looking for something...panicked, I thought, surprisingly panicked.

"Sophia, how did you get in?" he asked in a fast whisper.

"I walked, Gabriel, you know, on my feet," I replied with a smile.

"Don't be an ass," he spit at me. "No one just walks in here without an invitation."

"Well then I suppose someone invited the Yankee in without your knowledge," I spit back at him; but his alarm was contagious and electric as it jumped in the air between us. The smell of an electrical fire and burnt copper filled my lungs. Gabriel moved quickly toward me and grabbed my wrist as if he was about to drag me back upstairs and out to the street. But he stumbled as I jerked my hand back, literally stumbled on his feet with the electric shock that passed from his hand into my wrist, like a Taser...or was the current running from me to him? I couldn't tell, only knew that screaming from the pain wouldn't help. I bit my lip until I could taste blood on my tongue, thinking that this hurt more than a Taser. How would I know that? I'd never been shocked with a Taser. Yes, I had, I realized as I tried to grab hold of some memory that was right around the corner. My instinctive reaction was to pull away with all my might, but it didn't help. I was swimming in those sand dunes again, about to black out, losing my footing. My knees buckled as I began to collapse to the floor. Gabriel tried to get me to my feet, but I was thrashing and fighting against him. All the while, I was withdrawing, silent as a church mouse, biting down and slipping deeper and deeper into a calming void. Gabriel grabbed my other upper arm and the current was excruciating, shooting through nerve endings from my arms up my clavicle, into my neck and head, and down my torso to my feet. On my knees now, my muscles in spasm, I tried again to pull away as I was falling into unconsciousness. He wrapped an arm around my torso as I fell over to the side.

I was silent in my intent concentration on the void. My eyes rolled back and the pearls I was wearing caught on a cufflink and broke apart. My head lolled across his forearm as I watched the pearls spill off their string and onto the floor. They began to bounce and shatter into tens, hundreds, thousands of smaller pearls, spreading all over the floor, splintering over and over like a hi-speed cell splitting many millions of times, a beautiful sand dune of grain-sized pearls filling the wine cellar, brilliant and bright, creamy colored pearls. I wanted to reach out and run my hand through them. I was sure the texture would be smooth and chilled, in perfect contrast to the fiery current flashing through my nervous system.

A voice whispered into my failing consciousness. "A life is filled in the most unexpected moments with beautiful images. Breathe and take note."

"Oh, how beautiful," I murmured, now on the floor in

Gabriel's lap. He didn't understand that he needed to let go, or he couldn't let go, I thought briefly as I felt his hands spasm over and over around my rib cage where one hand held me. The other was on my forearm, his grip almost choking off the blood supply to my fingers. The pearls kept coming and it looked as if we would be buried, both of us suffocated under a dune of pearls. A wind was rippling along the dune now from side to side on the floor of the cellar, the quiet waves far out on a calm ocean. It was so warm and comfortable, like being before a crackling fire in the dead of winter.

Hmmm, Gabriel smells good, I noticed for the first time, like fresh water at a mountain lakeside. I wanted to ask what cologne he was wearing, distracted for a moment from the slicing pain firing through my nerve endings.

Sleep. Sleep now. I wanted to sleep, sleep, sleep, and rest, rest, rest my weary bones. I let go of his shirt, let go of the silky fabric and the faint realization I was holding on in a death grip. All the tension was slipping from my muscles as I let the dunes of soft, soft creamy pearls rock me to the waves' rhythm. My head hung limp on his forearm as I continued to watch the pearl dunes move from half-open eyes dipping back into my skull. I wanted to sleep a sleep I had never had—one from which there would be no awakening. That thought soothed me, an unfamiliar swaddling embrace I had never felt. I could simply will myself into the big sleep, it occurred to me. I welcomed the freedom and relief I knew it would provide.

Then I felt cold water on my face and jerked away from it. I was moving in the air now and recognized Oliver's baritone voice, "Sophia, wake up, Mon Petite. Not time to sleep yet, love." I opened my eyes and Oliver was carrying me as if I weighed ten pounds. I could hear the crunch of pearls beneath his feet—no, gravel. We were out in a gravel driveway and it was dark—out in the countryside somewhere. I smelled cow dung and remembered a farm. I was so comfortable in his arms, I didn't try to get to my feet. I didn't care about being carried like a child, or dignity, or anything else. I wanted to recapture that lovely peaceful warmth of the pearl dunes. It was so inviting and I was mad at Oliver for spoiling that respite.

"Put me down, Oliver. I can walk now." Ouch, my throat hurt like hell—as if I had been in a desert for days on the brink of dehydration.

Upright. Dizzy. Pissed off.

A car came alongside and Oliver held the back door for me. The driver had been waiting for us. "What the hell did you do, Oliver? How did you know where I was? Where is Gabriel?" Searing pain in my larynx and desiccated mouth. I raised my hands to my throat, dropped them quickly, and pulled a compact out of the purse that Oliver had handed to me. My lips were swollen nearly twice normal size, blistered, cracked, and bleeding. They were so dry that my tongue touched slivers of skin, the skin of my face pulled taut over bones, thinner than usual.

"Water," I croaked as Oliver was opening and handing me a bottle. I finished the first bottle and asked for another. Damn, it hurt to speak.

"Found you, searched for you for three days, recovering from sedation."

"What—three days!? What the hell are you talking about?" I whispered, trying to save myself the pain of speaking.

"Sophia, you've been missing for three days. I found Gabriel drugged in your apartment and you in this abandoned barn. Whoever got you to the Crown and Thorn used Gabriel as bait, dumped him, and had you here for three days. They must have heard me coming so I didn't see anyone."

"Oh, Christ, was I speaking when you arrived? Did they ask any questions, did I say anything? Three days—oh my God, they could know everything in three days." I didn't even know what "they" shouldn't be told. However, I knew there was information that I wasn't supposed to share, such private information that I knew I carried in my head but couldn't access, like a password-protected computer file.

"Damn, why does my throat hurt so much?" I was ranting in a ragged whisper and thought of Clint Eastwood, wringing my hands. Oliver was watching me and moved closer, wrapping his gigantic arm around me. He handed me another bottle of water, room temperature, I noticed. The cold would have hurt more. "Thank you."

"Sophia, don't worry, love. I'm sorry I didn't get here sooner. I lost track of you when you left the office Wednesday. You took the wrong keys. Your throat hurts because you were screaming."

The keys had a tracking device, yes I knew. But how could I have taken the wrong keys? They were in my purse when I came to the office, and I was manic about keeping a conscious tab on them. Someone must have switched the keys to divert Oliver.

"Wait, what did you mean 'screaming'? Screaming what? What did you hear, Oliver?"

I turned toward Oliver, moving from his big bear embrace, facing him in the back seat of the car, calculating at lightning speed how fast the car was moving, where we were, and how I could get out of the car and away from him.

"Calm down, Sophia. I am not the enemy here. All I heard as I entered was you screaming that you were drowning, drowning in the pearls, can't breathe, can't breathe. That is all I heard."

I remembered the vision I had, but it was pleasant, this rocking on the waves of pearls. I couldn't recall Gabriel's face, but I wanted to see him. As if I had said it aloud, Oliver said, "He's already at your flat, resting. We'll be there shortly."

"Why my flat? I don't want him there. He's dangerous. He

touched me, and I blacked out." I was straining what voice I had left.

"Touched you?" asked Oliver. "Sophia, what happened exactly when he touched you? What do you remember? Go slowly, love." Oliver was very interested in hearing the details.

"I left work and was walking home through St. James Park." I paused for a sip of water. "There was a man on a bench, the same man who gave me the instructions to meet Gabriel before. So I went back to the same pub and found him there. He was completely put off by my showing up like that, but I thought it was his invitation, his same messenger sent to fetch me." More water. I could already swallow a little better. "Actually, 'put off' is way too mild. Gabriel was panicked, truly afraid. Then he grabbed my wrist as if he was about to drag me out." Oliver looked relieved and nodded his head as if he had expected this. "Pain, excruciating, and then I blacked out. Shit, Oliver, I don't understand this. What are you doing here?"

"I don't understand myself, Sophia. My work is to keep you safe."

When we arrived at my flat, Oliver turned new keys into a new lock. Gabriel was sitting on the couch, toweling off his hair, apparently just out of a shower. He stood and faced us as we entered while continuing to rub at his scrappy, unruly hair. I could see the bags under his eyes, his brow creased with fatigue. He looked worn out in his khaki pants and wrinkled polo shirt, the most casual I'd ever seen him. He was older than I had first guessed. He took a step toward me while I unconsciously stepped back, in sync with his movement, as if I'd known his move before he did.

I was standing next to the little entry table, the one that normally held my purse and keys in a little decorative dish. I touched the wall to steady myself.

"Stay where you are, Gabriel," Oliver warned and then

turned to me. "Sophia, please try to get your heart rate back under control."

I hadn't realized that I was on high alert again, the adrenalin a white water current through my veins. I was so agitated I could hear the blood rushing in my ears like an open faucet. My pupils were dilated and I scanned the flat in a millisecond before lifting my gaze to Oliver. Big, sweet Oliver, standing nearby but not touching, was looking down at me.

"Sophia, can you hear me?" he asked.

I nodded my head.

"Get him out of here, Oliver," I whispered. "I can't be in the same room with him right now."

Ten minutes ago I thought I wanted to see him; but now faced with him, I was violent in my need to see him go.

"Sorry but that's not an option. His flat has been ransacked, and this is the safest house we have for him at the moment."

I stood up on my tiptoes and noticed my shoes were missing. I motioned for Oliver to bend down so I could speak in his ear.

"Danger—danger—danger," I whispered with the Australian accent of the crocodile guy. Clint Eastwood goes down under. I must have sounded a little manic at the moment, but it was the only thing that came to mind.

"Steve was killed by the animals he loved, you know, Oliver?" I was whispering in Oliver's ear, but my eyes never left Gabriel's face.

"No danger," he replied. "Sophia, start counting your breaths, sweetie." He started to say my name slowly, in three separate syllables.

So

phi

a

I heard the name over and over "So – phi – a" and saw the image of the three separate syllables. My breathing started to slow, my pupils returning to normal. Gabriel, meanwhile, didn't move an inch. He was observing me with menacing clarity. He was making mental notes, I could feel it...what I was wearing, my greasy hair pasted to my head, make-up that had been smudged and worn off, wine cellar dirt on my clothing. I put out my hand like a traffic cop stopping a tractor-trailer barreling down on me. My hand blocked the view of Gabriel's face.

"Tell him to stop it, Oliver." I muttered, "I can't bear it right now. Tell him to look away."

Gabriel moved a fraction of a centimeter in my peripheral vision, and I grabbed something from the little table so quickly he didn't see it as it flew like a missile and hit him smack in his nose. He fell to his knees, trying to staunch the bleeding. I had barely moved, not even changing my foot position while launching the Murano paperweight. My heart rate hadn't changed during that little incident, I noticed. Only then did it strike me as odd that I knew what my heart rate was at all. Even more curious, Oliver also somehow knew. I filed that information away for a later time.

"Let's get you into the shower, Sophia." I felt the slightest pressure—Oliver's hand at my back. We walked to the left down the little hallway with Oliver putting himself between me and Gabriel, who remained stunned on the floor, holding the towel that was wet from his hair, now over his nose. The red blood exploded into the white hand towel like a rose petal opening in time-lapse photos. He was so silent it was startling. It must have been painful enough to moan or at least curse, but he was as quiet as a church mouse.

Oliver spared him a short comment on the way. "I told you not to move."

I stepped over the threshold of the bathroom, and the big man closed the door behind me. I was alone in the bathroom and had the chance to look at my face in the mirror, not a pretty sight. The shower was wonderful, washing away three days of dirt. As I began running my hands through my hair, I felt it was heavy with...sand. Sand???? Sandbox sand was pooling at the bottom of the shower stall. The dirt I could understand because there was dirt in the wine cellar and maybe the barn. But sand, sand?!!! I started to feel dizzy and slumping against the wall, I sank to the shower floor. Oliver must have heard the thump as I collapsed. He pulled aside the curtain as I whispered, "No, no, no, Oliver, Oliver, no, no, no. Get me out of my head...please put me to sleep, something, I am going mad," I pleaded and begged in a ragged whisper. He turned off the water and modestly wrapped me in a big bath towel. He was carrying me again.

"Please, please, Oliver, I beg of you. Give me something to sleep a dreamless sleep, please," my jaw trembling, knowing it was the only way to escape my own mind. He dropped to one knee and eased me onto my bed, left, and then returned with a pill and some water. I swallowed eagerly, the back of my throat still raw and burning.

I slept.

The body, like the mind, will have what it wants, despite any other desire. My eyes opened, and turning to the nightstand, I saw the glow—5:00 a.m. I didn't know how many hours I had slept, but I felt awake, well-rested. Oliver sat up. He was there, awake, in a chair near the window.

"Ah, good morning, Sophia," he said. "Slept well?"

"How long?" I asked.

"Since about 1:00 a.m., the day before yesterday. You're so tiny and the pill was a little too much for you."

"Holy shit, what did you give me?" I asked with a grin.

"What you needed. You have a visitor." I looked at him quizzically, and he told me Gabriel was gone.

"Looks like I could use a shower, finish the one I started the other day, and wow, I am starving!" I stepped out of the bed and noticed someone had put a big nightshirt on me, one of my own from the closet. I stretched and smiled.

"Excellent, I'll put on some breakfast and you go pop into the shower."

"I feel wonderful!" I chirped, surprised at the overall sense of well-being that flooded me, like sunlight through an open window.

I showered, washed my hair twice, conditioned, brushed my teeth, flossed, shaved everywhere, lathered in Yardley lavender body soap, cleaned my ears, applied eye cream, face cream, body butter, and dressed in a pair of faded jeans and oversized Yankee sweatshirt. I felt like I'd been hiking and camping for a week and then had returned to the refreshing comfort of home.

I smelled toast and eggs, cucumber and tomatoes, and English sausage in a skillet as I entered the little kitchen. As soon as I saw Marlow, I understood where that peaceful sense of well-being came from. My eyes lit up as he stood to greet me.

"Good morning, Sophia. You look well," he said. Marlow stretched out his hand, and it felt so warm, beach warm. I felt good all over. He pulled me into his embrace and wrapped his arms loosely around me. I felt safe—and warm—as if I had been cold for a very long time and his body heat was warming my core.

I released him, hungry as I was; and looking up into his face with a beaming smile, I said, "How nice to see you, sir."

"Sir? Sophia, please, I am a guest in your home. If you call me anything but Marlow, I'll feel as though I'm unwelcome."

"Sorry but I'm a little out of my element here, as well as out of my suit. This is an odd change for me, seeing a client in my home," I answered.

"You must surely know by now that I am more than your client, Sophia." He smiled a little crooked smile. It didn't look like the Caribbean sunrise that I had come to know in New York. It looked, well, different. I didn't understand his meaning, but I didn't feel a threat either. Sitting with him at the little kitchen table, I took in the feast Oliver had made. With a wave of his hand over the food, Marlow indicated that I should begin, and that morning he didn't need to ask twice. I filled my plate with some scrambled eggs, tomatoes, and cheese and topped it all off with a healthy dose of salt, pepper, and Tabasco. I was absolutely ravenous and dug in with a vengeance. I chugged the orange juice in front of me and helped myself to seconds. Boy, this was the best meal ever!

Marlow looked on, and his smile grew ever wider. He was happy for my appetite and commented, "I am so pleased you have such a healthy appetite today, Sophia. It seems the stress of the past few days has passed, yes?"

"You are so right, Marlow." I gestured toward him with my fork without thinking. "I feel better today than I have for months. It's odd, but I can't seem to recall the last time I felt this light—this well. I've been under the weather for weeks." I was beaming at him, all the sluggish weight of the recent weeks had vanished as if I'd been recharged somehow. I watched Oliver leave the room and wondered about the life he led when he wasn't babysitting me. Marlow suddenly leaned forward on his elbows, his lovely hazel eyes boring into me. He began a whispered chant—my name—and I re...mem... ber...ed him. Doing this. Before. While I slept. A memory of a dream...

So

phi

a

So

phi

a

It sounded like flutes on his lips and I felt...at ease. I smiled a drunken smile at him as he rose to leave. I was sorry to see him go, but Oliver took his place quickly.

"Sophia, would you like to take a walk around the park? It's a lovely day—chilly but sunny." He looked like an excited kid awaiting the recess bell.

"Oliver, what day is it?"

"Sunday—what do you say? I could use a little stretch in the legs myself, being here for the past two days."

"Sure, sounds like a great idea. I'll grab a sweater and be right out." We walked through the park. It was one of those beautiful autumn days offered up by the weather gods, a respite from dank gray clouds. Glorious—the trees of St. James still shedding their earthy colored leaves against the quiet stark blue sky. There were others in the park moving about, moms and dads pushing strollers or swings, and little Sophia with big burly Oliver walking side by side at a nice clip, I might add. Seemed we both had some pent-up energy to let loose.

A SHADOW IN THE VILLAGE

For ordinary men, it is a burning, fiery furnace...
only Bedouins and Gods find the desert fun.
~ Lawrence of Arabia

*A*chmed agreed with Lawrence of Arabia and was eagerly anticipating his return to the fertile valley of his Atlas mountain village, among the free people, his Maghreb. He continued to think about his nighttime travels and the woman, now knowing that they were connected.

As the long drive would soon be over, Hassan sought out the young Sufi and spoke earnestly, in hushed tones.

"Achmed, as you found the woman, you must keep her," Hassan told him one day.

"What is meant by keeping her?" Achmed asked, trusting Hassan to give him sound advice.

"It means you must provide for her with Allah's help. She may simply need a safe place for a time or she may remain for life. She was sent to you or for you, and you must take care of her. She'll be in our village now and should be made welcome."

Achmed accepted what he was told although the stranger was odd to him. She was so quiet, much more than other women he knew, certainly more than the girls he had grown up with who always seemed to be chatting. But she was similar to them in a most elemental way, accepting this new life, observing and adapting herself to the world around her. She didn't ask questions, didn't burden anyone with her presence at all. She acted with authority but was respectful. The tribe rode all day, every day; and in the evenings after eating, she would wander the desert, nearby but distant enough so that her wish to be alone was understood. Achmed was an early riser and could rarely remain awake until she returned in the late evenings to their tent. With each sunrise, the young man had the opportunity to observe the woman while she slept soundly nearby. He liked to watch her breathing, her lips slightly parted in rest, and to wonder about her life before. His imagination took him in many different directions as he tried to envision her story. Her face and lips were full with water and food now, and he found it pleasant to look at her, especially while she slept. She did not try to touch him again and gracefully moved into the rhythm of their journey as if she had always been with them.

As the caravan neared their Atlas village, they came upon one of the village boys on the lookout for them. They had been away longer than usual, although no one could say with certainty how late this arrival was. This was a land without clock or calendar, a place with no time. Surely the answer to relativity could be found here. The boy, no more than ten years old, excitedly greeted them, looking for sweets from his father who was returning with the men. Instead, he got an eyeful of the new addition to the caravan—the woman riding the spirited Arabian mare. He got his sweetie and raced back to the village to bring the news. When the line of camels trailed in, there was far more celebration and excitement than usual. The woman created a stir in the village, everyone curious to see her. That evening after a feast of fresh oranges, dates, and tagine, the entire village waited to hear the story of how this woman came to be found. Each of the men returned to his home and privately told his version of the tale, while Achmed and Hassan brought the woman to their home.

Achmed was relieved to be back in the fertile land of his village after the endless days and nights of desert landscape. As they entered the courtyard, he was reminded of all that he loved of his Atlas home. The red clay home with Majorelle blue door greeted his eyes like an old friend. The scents all around him, the courtyard bursting with pregnant citrus, fig, and pomegranate trees—he took a deep breath and closed his eyes. Jasmine and rose entered on the breath of his heart. His mother embraced him, the familiar perfume of henna and argan oil on her hair. The aromas flowed around him like a swirling vortex of scarves, earthy and fresh, drawn from nut and leaf. It was Achmed's first homecoming, and he was embraced with the love of his people washing over him. He felt the flame of a song on his lips, bubbling up from his most contented core.

Skoura, his beloved home, was a most peaceful place, everyone living according to his talent, moving during the days and seasons with the timeless rhythm of the land. Achmed saw it all as if for the first time, with the eyes of a child. The Atlas Mountains along the northern tip of the Sahara were fertile with wheat and fruit trees, sheep, and lamb. The villagers lived off the land and lived well and comfortably. Achmed wondered what the stranger saw upon entering the village. Did she see the beautiful faces of the dark-skinned children, plump with good food and love, smiling in greeting to her, a shy one standing a bit behind his friends, peeking around the corner of a shoulder to catch a glimpse of the visitor? What Achmed saw could not always be put into words, try as he might. His life was complete in these moments—measured by the love he gave and received.

Hours later when Achmed and his family were quietly sharing the evening meal, Alia, Achmed's mother, asked, "Madame, what shall we call you?"

The woman replied in the Berber dialect, "What shall you call me? What shall you call me?" she repeated slowly as if she were tasting the new words on her tongue.

Alia and the guest in her home looked closely at each other while Achmed and Hassan quietly sipped their mint tea. Hassan rose to go sit in the courtyard, and Achmed followed. The men heard the murmured voices of the women, the low melody of discussion, punctuated with gentle laughter, which went on for quite a while. After a time, Achmed rose to go indoors; but Hassan gently touched his arm, suggesting that he should remain outside. Finally, when all was quiet, the men rose to go inside.

Alia was waiting for them. "We will call her 'Amalu' as she has chosen. Amalu, a shadow, and like a shadow she will be," declared Alia. And so it was—and it was understood that she was to be a shadow in the village, unseen by outside eyes, protected in the village as one of their own.

Amalu's jalabia was replaced with a dress from Alia until she could weave her own. During the first weeks, Amalu spent her days with Alia. She observed and learned as Achmed's mother invited her to help with daily chores. She settled on the goats, and they upon her, moving each dawn from village enclosures to the lush fields where they had grazed since memory. Amalu soon became a shepherdess at Alia's suggestion. She was a natural, communicating with them with slight movements of her body.

From the moment Amalu laid eyes on Alia's full and gentle face, she felt a deep and abiding affection for the woman. Alia was a small yet sturdy woman, with soft brown oval eyes, a plump and wrinkled face, and a headscarf to cover her graying hair.

One day, the women gathered in a large group in the courtyard of Alia and Hassan's home. It was time to make seksu. Six women arrived in the early hours of the day, each with a large tin and cushions, seeking out the shady places on the ground. They came as they were, barefoot and prepared for a long day of communal work. The colors of their headscarves and clothes were as varied as their personalities.

Achmed returned with the goats after a morning of grazing to find the women laughing, full-throated belly laughs. They were not laboring, but loving their preparations. The making of couscous was a village event, the most talented hands coming together every so often to make a stock for each household. It is said that the seksu was only as good as the love with which it is made. Achmed knew this truth in his core.

Achmed enjoyed watching this labor of love—the artistry of their hands moving over the semolina, sprinkling oil and water, reaching into the tin and lifting the mixture, rolling again. The movement of those loving arms and bodies rising and falling over their grain gave him great pleasure. Achmed had tried many times to put this dance to song. Their devotion was as beautiful a melody as the winds moving through the wheat fields from which the seksu came.

The detail of each woman's technique was a lesson in her personality. Some of the women rolled in their hands, others against the tin. The rise and fall of the semolina in her hands or on her tin told a story of who taught her this art. One was known to be strong-willed and stubborn, another gentle and forgiving. Each would work her grain accordingly. Achmed was hypnotized by the cadence of each woman's movements, watching her technique and learning about her character.

Their undulating bodies moved like a dance over their grain, arms embracing the seksu, grain falling and rising between fingers and hands. Strong hands applied the gentlest pressure to create this fluffy and light dish beloved by all. There were spells of quiet sprinkled with chatter and laughter as the women applied their devotion to their craft and each other.

Amalu was sitting and cutting vegetables on this day. She watched and then sought out a small plate in the kitchen. She sat next to Alia and watched her for a time. Alia smiled, then with wet fingers, sprinkled some semolina into the young woman's tin plate. Not hiding his interest, Achmed sat nearby with his tea, wondering what would be revealed.

Amalu had applied herself to learning all their customs and traditions; and in a few short months, she had mastered most of the household chores. Achmed had looked on, seeing his mother's daily work as if for the first time. As with all the tasks that Amalu mastered, she watched Alia and tried, watched again, and tried again. But here with the seksu, her movements were uncertain, disjointed. She moved the grain, sprinkled some water, but her delicate fingers could not find a comfortable rhythm. Her brow was creased in concentration. She stopped and watched again. In a short time, Achmed saw that Amalu could not work the grain; she could move her body to most work, but this was not one.

Her delicate little hands were not up to this task. The women who made seksu had thick hands. Achmed watched as Amalu tried again and again until she and Alia finally burst out laughing. Amalu gave over her grain to Alia and said, "I think it best if I chop vegetables."

They laughed together, the sisterhood of women. They reassured her that making seksu was not for everyone. They already knew when they saw her dainty little hands that she might not feel the grain. So, finally, here was something that Amalu could not do.

Achmed watched the making of couscous in Alia's hands like a ballet. He had been seeing his mother sit before a tin of semolina his whole life, rolling and fluffing. But this was a new devotion he saw in Alia's hands. He watched her roll the semolina, add some water and salt, her fingers moving with gentle pressure, rolling the beads, tossing, catching. He saw her hands lift and fluff the couscous, over and over, like Allah's hands, guiding ocean waves, moving the tides according to his will. Alia's movements were the winds above those endless waters.

The pulse of this land Achmed knew. It was a gentle breeze, the motion of hands in a tin pan rolling out couscous, the movement of a herd of sheep in the rocky landscape of the Atlas mountains—this pulse was a constant of his life, the mooring of his poet's soul. The contractions of a woman giving birth struck the rhythm, the raising of children, the walk of elders. Achmed heard the heartbeat of his beloved home from the moment he rose in the morning until sleep claimed him at night. He never grew weary of these perfect moments and movements.

It was not a conscious thought among most of the villagers, but from childhood, Achmed was the village poet. He spoke aloud the blessings of their beautiful landscape, ached to put into words the beauty of the birthplace Allah had given them. Achmed was a man truly rich, full with a grand appreciation for his lot in life.

Every gesture, every movement of a leaf on a tree brought him great pleasure. The small kindnesses of the villagers, the way a young child would steady an old man's hand to help him on the road. Even as a young one, Achmed was well-loved and respected in the village.

When he was only eight years old, the boy saw a woman helping an old man on the road. He came close and asked them to bend down to hear him. It was such a strange request; they could have heard him from where he was, but he wanted to whisper. He was a bit dramatic. They played along and crouched down on their knees. It was then that he told them he had a great secret to share. And he said, "It is the little things that we do for each other that are the grand gestures of our time here together."

The villagers would hear this over and over from that time forward. It became a source of pride, sometimes jokes.

"Ah, here is Achmed with another story about a grand gesture."

They teased him, and he took it in good humor. But the villagers were all interested in his words. He was able to captivate them with his excellent skill at describing their common, daily labors. They adored his poetry without exception. Achmed worked hard to find the right words to describe the sublime beauty he observed; and when he spoke, the villagers saw their tasks as holy acts, each an honor to their beloved mountain home. They were not observant or religious in the traditional sense, but they began to see a sacred devotion in their everyday work.

The villagers called him the little Sufi after some years of his poetry. The Berber Sufi, or mystic, had a special role in their ancient memory, that of the musical chanter, a role well-suited to the young poet. During the fever after his circumcision, the elders were not surprised when he spoke of visions. Nor were they surprised that this was the boy who had grown to manhood and was chosen by the stranger in the desert.

One morning Achmed found Amalu waiting outdoors in the courtyard as he stepped out the blue door. It was time to take his goats out to the mountain pastures for the day. She rose as he moved toward the enclosures.

"What do you need?" he asked.

"I would like to join you with the herd for today," she replied. Achmed noticed that Amalu carried a sack (with food presumably, that she had prepared for the day). So, she had made a plan for this with Alia. Words of objection rose in Achmed's throat but went unspoken, as, beyond her, Hassan appeared and nodded his head. Set free, the goats moved along the familiar path leading away from the village. Amalu followed Achmed and watched all that he did that day, saying very little. When Achmed looked her way, he saw that she was lost in her own quiet thoughts.

The next two weeks passed the same, the woman appearing when Achmed was ready to leave in the early morning hours, returning with him for the evening meal. After several weeks of this, she picked up a good sturdy stick and began moving the goats as she had seen Achmed do. She rarely needed to use the stick. Amalu walked among the goats and they moved according to her wish.

Achmed liked his time alone in his mountain foothills, and in the first days, he felt Amalu was little more than an intruder. As the days grew shorter, though, Achmed began to enjoy her quiet company, until now he looked for her in the mornings. This became their new rhythm, and they moved well together.

One day in the early fall, Amalu was moving the herd along when she suddenly collapsed on a hillside. Achmed ran to her and tried to rouse her. "Amalu, Amalu, wake up. What's wrong?" She was lying there with eyes wide open, but not speaking. Her entire body was in spasm, arms and legs thrashing and jerking this way and that, her dress hiking up, almost to her slim waist. She gave no sign that she could hear his voice. Achmed gathered her up in his arms and cradled her against his chest. It took many minutes to quiet her movements, to bring her breath to his. Eyes wide, she remained unaware and unresponsive. Achmed tasted fear on his tongue as he rose from the ground with her. He had two thoughts—speed and care.

For three days Amalu suffered, from a wide-eyed coma to fits of shaking. Alia did not leave her side. It was on the second day that they talked of taking her to the city—to a western doctor. The village healer, Halima, was the fourth among them, and Hassan was speaking of the journey. A small sound emerged from Amalu's lips as she struggled to speak. "No, no, please. Let me stay. It will...pass." She began to retch violently. Achmed sat on the edge of the deep blankets, watching the cool cloth in his mother's hand. Amalu reached for him, and Achmed felt her fingers on his arm. She began to settle at the contact and was soon dozing again and breathing calmly. Halima and Alia took note that Achmed's presence was helpful. They whispered, talking about the djnoun, spirits known to possess people from time to time.

Achmed stayed by her side throughout the three days, coming and going with his need, his mother and the other women of the village trying their best to calm her during his absence, and Hassan taking over his shepherd duties. During the long hours of the evening, Achmed stroked her hand and she was soothed. The thrashing and fighting stopped. When he rose to leave, the shaking began again. Halima advised him to stay and stroke her skin; it seemed he had the healer's touch with this woman and at least could keep the worst of the pain from her. Exhausted, Achmed finally fell asleep, his hand on her wrist. He dreamed that night of sand dunes, dunes that crested and fell like waves on the water. He was afraid but when he woke he saw Amalu was smiling in her sleep. He caught his mother's weary smile. He was safe. She was safe. He slept.

Finally, on the third day, Amalu turned back the blankets and rose. She was weak and quiet. Rumors began in the village that she was a seer, that she had gone into a trance and had now awakened and would share her visions with the people. But no such thing ever happened. In fact, the following morning she was waiting for Achmed in the morning with the goats as if the intervening three days had never happened. She was still weak and let Achmed shepherd the goats up and along the hillside. At midday, he brewed tea over the open flame, and she gratefully accepted it. As Achmed handed the woman her tea, their hands touched.

The warmth that passed between them was instant and strong. Amalu caught his eye and smiled. Achmed was shy and uncertain with her; she seemed changed from her ordeal, more vulnerable.

In the days that followed, they spoke very little. They moved with the noisy demands of the herd, noticing a passing cloud, or a marker in the landscape guiding them in direction and distance from the village. They returned the goats to their enclosures each evening and parted company after a meal with Alia and Hassan. Then one night in the courtyard drinking tea, Amalu asked him to come to her room. He followed her quietly.

Standing at the threshold, she explained, "I haven't been able to sleep well. Halima tells me I was calm when you held my hand. I would ask you for this kindness for one night. I am weary with memory and vision and would welcome a peaceful night's sleep." The young man did not answer, remembering her vicious attack the night he found her in the desert.

"Please, Achmed," Amalu whispered, "I mean you no harm, but it seems you are the only one who can help me. Let's try now, sitting here on the floor first, to see how it goes if we touch fingers." He liked the sound of his name on her tongue.

Achmed was more than a little impatient, with his fear and curiosity warring over this petite creature. She was so sweet and vulnerable—just in the asking. Yes—he let his heart choose.

They sat on the floor among the cushions and faced each other. Amalu raised one hand, bent at the elbow, palm facing out and Achmed did the same. Coffee brown eyes were greeted by hazel as they moved their hands closer, each mirroring the other until their fingertips touched. For Amalu, it was the most calming moment of her day. Achmed watched as she breathed a great sigh of relief, shedding a great weight. Amalu let out a little sigh and he felt it, too, found it very exciting, watching her so. He kept his eyes on her face as she closed her eyes. The warmth from their fingers grew as Amalu laced her fingers deep into his and began to lean back into the cushions. Achmed reached forward, carefully keeping his hand in hers until she was lying down on her back and he was on his side. He could feel the pulse in his palm. After some time, Achmed heard the rhythmic breathing of Amalu's deep sleep. He felt good—like this healing was beneficial for both of them. He felt that all was right with his world for the first time since she came to him. He was content with her coming to him that night in the desert, relaxed that they were fulfilling their destiny. They slept and Amalu was true to her word. She did not ask again, although Achmed would have welcomed it.

The seasons continued to ebb and flow, one folding into the next as everyone settled into his place in time. Amalu was part of the village now, competent with the goats, and Achmed returned to his writing.

But Amalu was interrupting his thoughts. She began to drift into his mind more and more often. Achmed's poetry about his beloved mountain home was often interrupted by her image—over there—a silhouette emerging on the ridge of his landscape.

He began reading the poetry of the lovers, Layla and Qays, with new eyes. For her part, Amalu began teaching Achmed English. He was quick with the language, eager to please his new teacher. This shadow of a woman was a mystery; and he wondered, in small moments, who she was, and what she had left behind.

GABRIEL'S LESSONS

I went back to work Monday as usual, and no one questioned or commented on my absence. I was feeling well, physically and mentally. I had even increased my training routine, adding weight, running time, and an evening session of yoga. Gabriel went about his business, and I went about mine, and all seemed well in Sophialand.

We were out one night at Gallagher's (it had become our local haunt) when I asked Gabriel if any of the associates ever worked together on files. I was feeling comfortably at home and asked if he could spare some time on the Moreaux estate business interests. Adele had owned several interests in domestic and offshore businesses, and I wanted to understand better how they operated and, in particular, how they were taxed in the estate. England has an inheritance tax (which was long overdue in this estate) and I was researching whether the offshore businesses would be included in the taxable estate.

"Have you asked your senior partner to bring me into the matter?" Gabriel rolled his drink glass, cognac tonight, between his palms.

"No," I replied.

"Well, I don't know if this is appropriate then. I would

prefer that you speak to your supervising solicitor on this before you disclose any details," he responded as he brought the glass to his lips.

"Gabriel," I said, "there is no supervising attorney on this matter. The files were brought directly from the estate's executor." I sipped my beer, felt the foam touch my lips. "No one has seen or touched these files except him...from what I understand...ever. At this point, I heard he is rather senile and has full-time nannies caring for him at the Moreaux country estate."

"Sorry?" Gabriel replied, "I'm not sure I understand you. That cannot be possible. You report to no one? Why you're only a couple of years my junior. There must be some mistake or you are taunting me, Sophia. Seriously, I'm not enjoying this little game of yours."

I was surprised at the sharpness of his response. We had been very cordial to each other since our ordeal, never mentioning it in or out of the office. It was definitely there, just below the surface, like some distant childhood memory. I wasn't even clear at times whether it was a memory or a dream. *Here we go again*, I thought. Gabriel and his British tongue, cutting through a discussion like a paper-thin sharp paring knife. He couldn't believe that I had no supervisor. He was an arrogant little shit, and I suddenly wanted to smack him. I had taken a significant personal and professional risk in asking for help, help that I found painfully difficult to solicit. I never asked for assistance and I never expected it, thereby avoiding the twin agony of vulnerability and disappointment. Well, I had asked Gabriel for help and gotten slapped down in the most degrading way. I wouldn't make that mistake again.

"Sorry, Gabriel, I made a mistake in asking you," was all I could say. I drank the rest of my pint.

He continued sipping and muttering, shaking his head from side to side. I caught a bit of his commentary, "Really, no one?" under his breath as if I couldn't hear him.

I commented just as quietly, leaning over the table a bit. "Correct, asshole, not a one."

He wanted to continue the conversation as I reached for my wool tweed. He and the other attorneys were the closest people I had to friends in England, and he had reminded me in the sharpest way that we were no more than colleagues. There was no room for friendship in my workplace or any place at this point in my life. I left.

The next morning I arrived and found Gabriel waiting for me in my office. He stood as I entered.

"Sophia, about our discussion yesterday," he began.

"Never mind, Gabriel. I told you I made a mistake. I've got a lot of work to do today, so let's move on or part company or whatever it is that your people say instead of 'fuck off,' shall we?"

I was barking at him, surprising myself. He, of course, maintained that ramrod straight posture, learned at the hands of a well-heeled headmaster and the best nannies money could buy. I hung my jacket and worked my way around him to sit at my desk. He sat, as well, apparently not getting the message.

"I will not apologize for being the rude American, Gabriel. I have work to do here." I looked down and thumbed the combination on my briefcase.

"Sophia, I was simply trying to explain the firm policy."

"Oh, pleaaaase!" Head up and head on, "I work in the New York headquarters of this international firm, SIR, not some Mississippi trailer park, or north of Manchester, for that matter. I understand that you're a bit limited by your need to be an elitist asshole and couldn't comprehend what I said yesterday. Allow me to rephrase, 'Don't let the door hit you in the ass on the way out.' "

Again, the flare of anger, white and hot in my chest. Little images were snapping and popping at me, like grabbing the lovely Murano paperweight and launching it at his...no, not his face. His arrogant face was difficult to imagine with that heavy glass projectile smashing into it. I couldn't keep my temper in check with this putz, which only inflamed me more.

He walked (not marched) out of my office, no doubt thinking I was some loose New York cannon ready to shoot off my big mouth at the drop of a hat. Truth is, despite Albert's excellent training, I was impulsive by nature. I had spent too many years trying to grab words out of the air in front of my face until I mastered the art of thinking before speaking. This was the first slip in many years where I really did shoot off my mouth, big time, which only made me all the more frustrated. Uggghhh, this was going to be annoying if Gabriel wouldn't let it drop.

I spent the rest of the day researching offshore businesses and UK inheritance taxes. I figured I'd do it again the hard way, the same way I had researched the Family Moreaux. That turned out to be the story of a long line of European wealth, intermarriage among the elite, a child out of wedlock here and there, sometimes with an acknowledgment of paternity, more often not. There were French and British and Spanish bloodlines mixed up until sometime in the early 1990s. There was a vacation to the Caribbean islands that led to an extended stay in Jamaica. I decided to go to the estate at the next available chance and see what I could find.

By the end of the day, Gabriel had returned and told me, as he stood over my desk, that he'd been instructed to 'school me in offshore businesses.' Apparently, someone had heard our conversation. Gabriel suggested we meet after work, as he was busy on other matters. Our first meeting was in the firm library about 7:00 that night where he stood at the smart board and sketched out the structure of a domestic British corporation.

I am a quick student and was pleased to have someone with Gabriel's experience teach me. After two hours of taking notes, I asked him if he had ever taught formally, and he replied that he lectured regularly to the British bar on corporate law. Well, that explained his excellent skill and clear mental outline. He didn't need notes or references. I was excited about the opportunity and took full advantage of the private tutoring. He was likewise impressed with my pointed questions and gave me an assignment for the next week—I was to outline all the business entities (eleven in all) of the estate. We would then work together to determine how they were structured, review the corporate books and tax returns, and determine who the partners and shareholders of each entity were. With that information, we could analyze how each entity would be taxed in the Moreaux estate.

The next week, same time and place, I returned with my homework completed. I gave Gabriel a copy of the memo I had prepared outlining the business interests as he had asked. We spent the evening reviewing the memo together. It reminded me of my law school study group, and again I found myself grateful for the excellent help.

Our next three lessons were in corporate tax. It was painstaking and boring as hell. As good a student as I was, I wanted to jump out the window a few times. When Gabriel caught me daydreaming, he scolded me as a good teacher should. We laughed, enjoying the intellectual exercise. There was no ego involved, no one performing or stepping on anyone's toes, no competition.

One evening we decided to grab a quick bite to eat before beginning our lesson as neither of us had time to eat before our meeting. "There is a little bistro a few blocks away that serves salads and soups, if that sounds good to you, Sophia," Gabriel suggested.

"Sure, fine, Gabriel," I replied and we began to walk into the London evening. Despite my wool scarf and gloves, the autumn air was biting. I tried to make some small talk, as Gabriel was his usual clipped and formal self, which was starting to get old (and a little boring) for me.

"So, Gabriel, are you originally from London?" I kept my voice light.

"No," he replied, "Here we are. We stepped into the café and felt the warmth. We were seated at a table and ordered drinks, unsweetened iced tea for me, and Perrier for him.

I decided to try again despite his clipped answer to my earlier question. "So did you come from the countryside, Gabriel?" I pried again.

"In a manner of speaking," he replied.

This was going to be difficult, like a Shakespearian inquisition, I thought, and chuckled at my mental characterization, imagining lots of ruffled men with curly white wigs interrogating Gabriel.

"Something humorous that you'd like to share, Sophia?"

"Yes, you. Can't you loosen that starched shirt for a few minutes, for Pete's sake, Gabriel? We have to spend some time together, whether you like it or not."

"What gave you the impression that I didn't like it? I enjoy teaching and I especially enjoy teaching you. You're a quick study and a conscientious student." There he was—talking like an aging law professor.

"Are you really that obtuse or are you trying to goad me?"

He suddenly looked genuinely perplexed, a wrinkle forming in his forehead and then he did, unconsciously, loosen his tie. "Huh?" he said, so uncharacteristically dumbfounded that I burst out laughing.

Within a nanosecond I was giggling, peels of giggles that every so often would overtake me. I hid behind a cloth napkin, but it didn't help. He was so freakin' funny, sitting there looking goofy, that I couldn't hold back. *That's it*, I thought, *I'm not going to let him spoil my fun anymore. Nope. If we had to spend time together, at least I could have a little fun.*

His wrinkled brow grew deeper and he was scowling now, trying to cover his confusion with that formal British scolding look. "Well, are you having fun at my expense?" he asked.

"Gobs of fun, Gabriel. Here I thought you wouldn't be entertaining, but you don't have to say a word and I find you hilarious!"

When the giggles finally stopped, he was suppressing a smile.

"Try as you might, you know laughing is contagious. It might help to loosen that pole up your arse," I said quietly. The other diners had been staring during my episode but now all properly returned to their meals. Our soup and salads arrived and we both dug in. The laughing episode sparked my appetite and I enjoyed the food. We finished dinner with two teas, and he arched an eyebrow when I ordered Britain's national drink.

"Do you really have such a stereotypical view of all Americans?" I snapped. "What are you expecting, that I'll ask for hamburgers and ice cream next?"

"You know, Sophia, you're right. It seems we have a lot to learn about each other."

"Let's get back to work. I have an early start tomorrow".

That was the ebb and flow of our work together for some weeks. We were finally getting to know each other—and dare I say, appreciate the differences. He wasn't the elitist I thought —more of a professional acting out the role of solicitor. We Americans are just less formal. And he began to appreciate my rough Yankee edges. We got along well enough for two very different people but clung to our roles, avoiding any real connection.

A few weeks later I was on my way out for a day trip, a first visit to the Moreaux country estate. As I was getting into the car, a new driver introduced himself, then moved to the other side of the town car and opened the back door. Odd. There was no one else going. I turned to look, and Gabriel suddenly appeared and slid in beside me. Dammit—my aim was to visit the estate and get a "feel" for the family. It was one thing to understand holdings, investments, and history from a book, but quite another to be in the place where this family had lived (for centuries in one form or another). I didn't want company, especially not his. I was looking forward to the drive into the country and being by myself, without undercover surveillance. I didn't want to be on guard, especially with Gabriel in tow.

"Gabriel, what are you doing?" I asked.

"I thought I'd join you for your little field trip," he replied in an uncharacteristic informal Yankee speech. He was trying to endear himself to me so that I would accept his intrusion into my day.

"And who suggested to you that you join me on my 'field trip' today?" I asked again.

"Sophia, no one suggested it. My workload is light for a change, a big matter having settled unexpectedly early, and I have a little free time. Why the interrogation?"

"Honestly, Gabriel, I never told you I was going out today."

He looked appropriately chagrined. But he would not be deflected and stuck to a story he had obviously rehearsed.

"Don't you remember you mentioned this while we were out pricing antiques last week?"

I felt I should take his lead, not sure who was listening; and I didn't want to give anyone reason to doubt my confidence in Gabriel.

"I must be distracted to have forgotten. I've packed a bite to eat and truly welcome the company," I finally suggested to end this little chat. The rest of the ride, a bit more than two hours, passed quietly and peacefully as I enjoyed the view and England's warming countryside.

It was my first time at the country estate, and I was looking forward to seeing it. I'd done some brief tours, Oxford and Stratford, to see some of the historic highlights and hoped that the Moreaux estate might be worthy of Jane Austin.

We turned off the main highway onto a little two-lane

country road. After about twenty minutes, we turned into a drive marked by two pillars with a very intricate family crest carved into the stone. It reminded me of the necklace Marlow wore in New York at our first meeting. I hadn't seen it since, not anywhere, even on Marlow. I asked the driver to stop and stepped out to inspect it more closely. It was a beautifully detailed, very feminine filigree design.

I touched the crest briefly and closed my eyes. There was a flash of a door knocker, a paperweight in a library, a ring on a delicate child's hand. Gabriel's voice was next to me then, droning on about the history of the mansion. We returned to the car and continued the drive onto the estate grounds. It was a picture book, English garden grand entrance, to the stone palace. It was beautifully maintained and, in fact, there were gardeners at work in the freshly turned beds along the drive.

"Bulbs, no doubt. Crocus, daffodil," Gabriel was like a local guide, pointing out tree varieties and architectural details, filling me in on the historical significance of the location, naming the builder.

The car stopped before the grand carved stone entrance. The driver came around to open the door, and a butler greeted us. He was wearing a formal jacket and yes, white gloves. I was secretly thrilled—the romantic in me in full bloom.

"Good afternoon, Mademoiselle, Sir. Welcome to the Moreaux estate. I am James and pleased to welcome you. I trust your drive was uneventful." This was so English and so formal I wasn't sure how to respond.

"Nice to meet you, James," I said as I extended my hand in greeting. He didn't accept my hand but waved us on through. As we entered through the wood doors, I glanced up and saw the door knocker. To the right of the grand foyer was a library. It was a little chilly, and a fire had been set. We were offered tea and sandwiches and had a very civilized bite to eat. It was far better than my bagged snack, I might add.

Clearing the silver tea service, James asked if we wanted a guided visit or if we would prefer to explore on our own. We opted for the latter. It was a little strange the way I was given carte blanche of the grounds and the buildings, but I assumed it was the firm's doing. The rooms of the mansion were endless. I wondered how many people had actually lived here at any one time. Many rooms (more rather than less) were furnished. Everything was clean, fresh flowers everywhere, well maintained in every detail. There was obviously a full-time staff. I hadn't yet begun to account for the income and expenses of the estate. The accountants were preparing a formal accounting. The staff income alone must have been outrageous to maintain the buildings and grounds. There were enough bedrooms to accommodate a wedding party (which did, in fact, happen on occasion Gabriel informed me). The bathrooms were magnificent and abundant. The formal dining room was a catering hall. The kitchen was surprisingly functional and unexceptional. There were separate quarters for a total house staff of thirty and detached quarters for outside staff (including stable-hands, gardeners, and drivers) for forty-five. The excess was a little over the top.

We roamed the house at our leisure, and I didn't try to tune in at first. Gabriel was like an encyclopedia. He obviously loved history and art and architecture and was excited to have a captive audience. I was hoping for a few minutes of quiet. Places are like people, with memories. Like a body develops muscle memory, places become imbued with their own memories—imprinted with wisps of people and events that passed through. I could feel that this was a site rich in memories. We were passing through the kitchen, and I noticed a stairway off the butler's pantry, a room easily the size of my London flat. I started toward the steps, my natural curiosity calling to my inner voyeur. Gabriel resisted, telling me we had seen enough. He was uncomfortable venturing into the secret places.

"Fine," I said, "stay here. I like the hidden places, little nooks and crannies, what I used to call 'homey-homes' as a child. The smell and feel of a musty basement is the inner spirit of a place. You can have a rest if you're not interested."

Of course, Gabriel took that as a challenge and followed on my heels. The light was on and the basement served as storage and as a root cellar, stocked with all manner of canned fruits, serving dishes, and such. The foundation was stone, and several tree trunks stood as support beams. There was one largest beam, about two feet in diameter, a bit twisted and worn smooth by many hands. Gabriel was droning on about the architecture. I leaned against the foundation with my hands laced behind my back and closed my eyes.

"Gabriel, listen."

He continued to talk, his voice chirping in the background.

"Shhhh," I whispered.

He lowered his voice but continued his tour through English country home history.

"Please, Gabriel, please, please, please be quiet for a minute."

He did. He finally shut his yap, and I let out the tense breath I had been holding. I leaned into the foundation and closed my eyes. Now the pain in the ass was fidgeting. Gabriel's constant movement was so irritating, not to mention totally out of character for him—Mr. Pole Up the Arse who always kept up the façade of the self-possessed professional. Being here was uncomfortable for him for some reason. I heard him moving about, shuffling, pacing, and sighing, until he finally found a place to sit, on the stairs. I heard the creaking of the stairs while I began some deep yoga breathing. My rhythm struck quickly, in about three good breaths. Gabriel's tension was palpable; I could feel the tension in his muscles radiating throughout the cellar like a shock wave. In contrast, I began to relax into the wall, unlacing my fingers and splaying my hands out at my sides. The stone was cold, dusty, damp. It felt good, this space of the earth, below all the pomp and formal expectations above. I continued to breathe and relax each muscle, each exhale a letting go—first of my face, then shoulders, arms, and torso, pelvis, legs, and feet. I kicked off my shoes and stood there in my navy skirt suit and white-buttoned blouse, little pearl earrings and necklace. I was a grown-up seeking a child's bearings in this unexpected place.

There was a tunnel through the wood support column like a fox hole near the base of a tree trunk, and into it, I went. Through the wormhole, I flew steadily until my feet were again on the ground in the cellar. Two girls were playing hide and seek, giggling and skipping around in their beautiful dresses and petticoats, while outside the sound of rain pelted the house. This was a good place to play indoors on a stormy day. I heard a voice and recognized it as the nanny, scolding them.

"Don't get your dresses dirty before Papa arrives! Girls, he'll be here shortly. Come and tidy up before Papa comes."

As quickly as I was drawn in, I was shoved away, forced back, back to here and now. I opened my eyes and Gabriel was standing next to me, whispering in my ear.

"Sophia, where are you?" His lips were brushing my earlobe, his hand moving to my hair, his breath hot against my sensitive skin. He was leaning over me, his forearm resting against the wall. I felt trapped and excited by the moist heat of his breath on me.

"Sophia", he whispered, "you are intoxicating when you let your guard down...leaning here against the wall with your little naked feet dancing on the cobblestone, daring me to join you in this secret little world of yours."

Holy shit! His words were so unexpected and...and hot! He stopped talking. His mouth wasn't moving as he brushed his lips back and forth over my ear and neck.

I was trying to concentrate on what I had seen while

Gabriel dipped his head and nuzzled my neck. My breathing caught, then sped up—I couldn't focus with him all up in my head. I turned to look at him. He wasn't speaking, but I could feel his mood. His thoughts were a jumbled wave of emotion, rolling through his body. His entire body was undulating with the movement of his head. His eyes were glazed, like a sleepy boy or a drunk. 'God protects children and drunks.' That old cliché snaked into my head, as Gabriel looked like a child or a drunk in his intoxication.

"Gabriel—are you okay?"

Hmm, how did I get here? I was just on the stairs, wasn't I? I heard him distinctly, but he wasn't speaking; his lips didn't move. He didn't seem to mind so much as he smiled a crooked smile, his eyes connecting with mine.

Ah, okay, now I understood his tension and unusual chatter all day. I looked at his lips as his tongue traced their edges. *I'd like to do that,* I thought, to my surprise—no, amazement. Holy shit—when did that happen? Instead, I ducked under his arm as he began to tip and dip his lips toward mine. I picked up my shoes and walked up the stairs he had just vacated.

As the distance between us increased, Gabriel's expression cleared, and he seemed to wake from his slumber. I stopped short on the staircase. Gabriel, like Albert, had spoken to me without voice...he had fallen under a spell and it reminded me of Sally's little nap all those years ago on Long Island...the man on the steps behind me had taken a Sally nap, and this time it was not the weather that had shifted.

Gabriel followed me slowly up the stairs. He was tentative, the first time I had experienced that quality from him. Gabriel usually moved at a very intentional clip, the staccato steps easily recognizable and confident. As he followed me up the stairs, I heard him start and stop at irregular intervals, unsure of himself.

The drive back to London was quiet, both of us deep in

our own thoughts. Gabriel took a phone call while I tried to watch his lips moving without his noticing. But of course, he was quick to see me staring at those lips—those full, pouty lips, so soft and inviting. I wanted to lean over and bite him, feeling a little drunk myself. His look was thoughtful, not snarky or smirky, as surprised by his attraction to me as I was. I was equally interested in how he had ended up leaning over me without my hearing a single step. How was it I heard no movement at all?

I watched the countryside become small towns, then outskirts, then London. The day trip came to a melancholy close. We continued our work together on the Moreaux estate as if our visit to the country house had not taken place.

UNBEARABLE

$\mathcal{T}$hen one night as I was leaving Gabriel, gave me the two-cheek European kiss goodbye. On the second cheek, I made a purring noise in the back of my throat— "hmmm." The brush of his lips on my cheek was so fine. He stepped back and smiled his goodnight smile. I went home and meditated on that during my evening yoga. Hmmm, again, that was nice. Was this lust I was feeling? It was exciting...exciting was new to me. He began to invade my thoughts often during the day; I would listen for his step on the marble floor, imagine him sitting in his office down the hallway.

Our lessons on British Corporate Tax and Estate Law continued, as did our outings for property values, coffee, or a quick bite to eat. Then one Friday, Gabriel told me I had been such a dedicated student, he had planned a special field trip for the following day. I woke Saturday morning in quite a state, having slept poorly. It was a challenge to know what to wear. It was the first time I'd be with him out of my office clothes. I chose to be my most comfortable, an old pair of my favorite faded jeans and a warm cream sweater for the autumn mornings, now deep into the cold. I wrapped myself in a wool scarf and hat. I walked to the British Museum, and we met at the main entrance an hour before opening. He had a friend who ran the private tours that could let us begin earlier than the usual opening time. Gabriel was chatting with his friend when I arrived, and I paused for a moment to observe them both from a distance.

It struck me suddenly, how ordinary Gabriel looked and what a contrast that was to my growing interest in him. He turned to me in his khakis and collared shirt beneath his partially opened coat, and I swallowed for a minute, thinking I should have passed on the jeans. But in a moment of unexpected confidence, I thought to myself, *No, this is really how I want to be with him, my true self on the outside and inside, no more roles, no more 'being at the top of my game.'* I was not at work and wanted the freedom for once to be with him and be comfortable.

I strode toward Gabriel with that confidence, and his friend glanced at me and past me, no thought that I was Gabriel's colleague who they were waiting for. I walked purposefully toward Gabriel, and his friend didn't miss a beat when he said, "Good morning, Sophia. Meet John Walker."

"How do you do, John?" I put out my hand. John was as tall as Gabriel and also rather ordinary looking. That such a boring face could deliver the jolt I received at the touch of his hand was a startling reminder to...'pay attention,' as Albert would so often say. A chill crept up my spine to the hair prickling at the back of my neck. This man's grip was limp and cold, his fingers delivering an icy injection into my nervous system, the serum of menace seeping under my skin. He knew not to make full contact but dangled his fingertips, clammy and gray. That minimal contact was enough to halt the breath on my tongue.

He and Gabriel pierced me through with a knowing glance. The cool morning sun dimmed, and the scenery around us faded into the cloudy mist. Marlow was nearby. I could feel it and tried to search the area for him, but John and Gabriel both trapped me in their gaze. John's entire attention was focused on me, and I could feel his wiry fingers creeping around in my head. I let go of his fingers as quickly as possible; and the scene returned to normal, although the confidence I was feeling a moment before all but disappeared.

"Pleasure, Sophia. A new collection has been installed that I'd like to show you before the Museum opens to the public," John said. I was mute and now released from paralysis, I looked around to see if I could find Marlow. The street was quiet for 8:00 a.m. on a Saturday, and there were few other people about. John lightly touched my elbow to show me into the building.

Gabriel's friend escorted us past the security guards, and we moved up the main staircase to the museum. The British Museum could only compare to The Met; and I was an excited tourist now, listening to our personal guide's most professional docent explanations. After more than an hour, I noticed there was no offhand small talk between friends. It took me long to notice, so focused on the museum's offerings as I was. John stayed with us for a full two hours and then excused himself shortly before 10:00. At that point, we were both hungry; and Gabriel suggested we have a bite to eat at the Museum Cafe. We ordered tea and a chocolate croissant for me.

"How do you know John, Gabriel?" I asked.

"Shortly before you arrived in London, I was introduced to him in the office by one of the partners. I'm sure you've noticed the art collection in the office. One of the partners has an interest in art, and John is his personal buyer."

"So you don't know him personally?" I asked.

"Sophia, our office introductions are never personal, no," he replied while breaking off a piece of my croissant. "Have at it," I playfully waved at the dish, putting an end to that inquiry. We continued through the museum for another two hours, and

Gabriel continued to be a patient and knowledgeable teacher, especially excited about Art History. I mostly knew what I liked, but his enthusiasm was contagious; and I was soon caught up in his narrative, which was as good, or better, than John's. I let my emotions loose during that visit, loving a piece or hating it...it didn't matter, Gabriel taught me. What mattered was the feeling the piece elicited. It was a pleasant morning, and Gabriel finally started appreciating my humor. It was so sweet watching him laugh out loud when I commented on some British marm. It was fun when I would say something shocking, curse unexpectedly, and see him react with good humor. Later, with near-perfect timing, Gabriel suggested we take our leave. I was on overload by then and welcomed his suggestion as we left the Museum, heading toward St. James Park and my flat. By all accounts, it was the best time we had spent together yet.

The sun had warmed the brisk autumn air, and I welcomed the reprieve from winter's impending doom that fall had been offering in recent days. It was a comfortable walk, and Gabriel was pleasantly quiet. We sat at a stone bench near the lake in the park. I tipped my head back and closed my eyes, warm sun on my face and the cool air filling my lungs. I could hear the racket of geese and pelicans, the water fountain spray, a bicycle moving past, the patter of a runner, a child squealing on a nearby swing. I all but forgot that I was there with Gabriel, my mind occupied with the sounds around me and my inner chatter quiet for a spell.

I was awakened from my reverie with Gabriel's soothing voice, close. I was in no hurry to open my eyes but turned my head toward him. Still resting it on the back of the bench.

"Sophia, it's nice to see you so relaxed." I slowly opened my eyes. He was facing toward me, one leg bent and his arm resting on the back of the bench. His knee was almost touching my thigh, and his hand was a fraction away from my hair spilling over the back. He was right. I was really content.

"It's been a very pleasant day, Gabriel. Thank you for this. I don't have many friends in London, and this was a lovely way to spend some time here." I sat up and dropped my chin, rolled my neck, and came back round to him. "I love this park —it's been a real treat to be living so nearby while I'm in a strange city," I added.

"What do you think you'll do when your work here is done?" Gabriel asked. Was he making small talk? Oh, oh, those lips again.

"Well, we work for the same firm. You know as well as I do that they'll decide." I rubbed my hands along my jeans. "I have no preference really."

"Don't you have any personal plans of your own?"

"Not at the moment. Hey, what about you, Gabriel?" I settled back into the sun-warmed zone. Did he like hearing his name on my tongue the way I liked hearing mine on his? "How long have you been working for the firm?"

"Seven years now, right out of university they recruited me. It's been good and, like you, I don't have any immediate plans at the moment."

"Gabriel, I'm curious, how were you recruited? Did you find the firm or did someone approach you?"

"You know, it's nice to hear you say my name like that."

"Huh, like what?"

"Like you don't want to smash my face."

And we both started to laugh. So he did like to hear his name on my lips.

"Well, you have a biting tongue sometimes, Gabriel; and it brings out the worst in me," I said with a smile. "I imagine it's that British boarding school thing, that elitist history that I'm not very patient with. In any event, you confirmed your feelings towards the Yankees at our very first meeting. I think you do it on purpose sometimes, trying to get a rise out of me like it's a sporting event."

"There is quite a bit that you've assumed about me, Sophia."

"Perhaps because you don't give an inch," I replied.

"You are quite an enigma, Sophia. You're brilliant or you wouldn't be working for the firm. But then, you've got that rough edge that doesn't fit here."

"See, there you go. Apparently, someone likes that edge; sometimes that's exactly what's needed. Seems there was no one here or anywhere in the multitude of satellite offices that the firm has who was wanted for the matter I'm working on. Why do you think they chose me, Gabriel? And why did you deflect my question about how you were recruited?" I asked with a sideways grin.

"That's what makes you such a great solicitor, Sophia. You don't lose your train of thought once you're on it," and there was the Gabriel smirk.

"Oh, you're so irritating, Gabriel. That's lawyering 101— and you're doing it again. Is your family here in London?"

"No, I'm an orphan, Sophia, which I think you already know, although you're being coy for some reason." He was getting serious now. And he kept saying my name, each time, it made my heart skip a beat.

"I think you know all of the associates have little or no family attachments, as I'm sure is also the case with you." He looked down at his left wrist, at the same elegant and understated watch he wore every day. "Right, I have a dinner appointment and I think it's time we part company." He stood. "Would you like me to walk me to your flat?"

"No thanks, I'm going to stay in the park for a bit more." I was relieved our day together was coming to a close. He had given me a lot to think about. I stood with him, reaching out my hand to say goodbye. Those pouty lips toyed with a smile as he took hold of my hand, tugging on it with the lightest pressure, inviting me to step closer. I wanted to go there, take that first step into the unknown. Yes, but my tendency toward privacy prevailed as I kept my arm extended and taught. He got the message and let go, reluctantly, I thought.

"Well, enjoy the rest of your weekend, Sophia. I'll see you on Monday." I watched his back as he strode away with his purposeful stride. Yes, a man with a purpose and great lips.

A leisurely walk south through the park gave me time to sort through Gabriel, the sinister John, and beautiful museum pieces until I was returned to my flat. I picked up a couple of pieces of mail absentmindedly, all the while thinking about my day with Gabriel. Entering my flat, I deposited my keys in the little dish on the entry table, kicked off my shoes, and stretched out on the couch. Thinking of Gabriel's lips, I nodded off, his company, the walk, and the sun on my face had left me a bit worn out.

I woke about 7:00 and was restless, some unidentified and disturbing images having crept into my daytime nap. I phoned James to see if he and Philip were free and my good luck—they were. We met for dinner at the Horse and Hound. I ruminated with them for a bit on the Horse and Hound, the Rose and Thorn—what's with the names of the pubs?

Harry loved to follow office gossip and was the go-to guy when there was any scandal about, from mild scuffles among staff to rumored death and divorce of big-name clients. Tonight was no different. After a few pints of Harp and Guinness, "Black and Whites" they called them, he started on his favorite pastime, 'innocently making small talk.' But I knew better. Harry's talk was never small and never innocent. He was transparent enough for me to be wary. Philip, on the other hand, was reserved and not in the least bit interested in gossip or small talk. He passively sat gazing about the pub while Harry began his paparazzi assault.

"Sophia, it seems you've piqued our Gabriel's interest. Maybe you can loosen the pole up his corporate arse while you've got his attention," said Harry. I was expecting something along these lines at some point and was glad for the diversion. Truth was, Gabriel was on my mind way too often right now, and too intensely.

"Why Harry, whatever do you mean?" I replied with mock confusion. Apparently, Harry was too buzzed to notice the sarcasm.

"Well, we've been working with him for several years and have never seen him loosen his tie, so to speak. In a matter of months, you get private tutoring from him, one of the best young corporate solicitors in London, and a personal museum visit—ta-da!"

I was enjoying Harry's curiosity and irritation and started to poke fun at him. In a deadpan serious face, I said, "Aw, all right, Harry. I've been dying to talk to someone about this. I really need to get this off my chest. But you must swear on all that you hold sacred in the world, not to breathe a word."

"Me mother's grave..." True to form, Harry leaned forward with his elbows on the table in the little booth we shared. Like the long-time couple that they were, Philip absentmindedly moved Harry's beer mug aside before he knocked it over in his excitement to get closer to me. I good-naturedly registered that Harry never actually knew his mother.

"Seriously, I don't know what to do. When we first met, he was put off by my crass Yankee humor. Well, apparently, that was all for show. He likes the rough Yankees. He's been stalking me, asking me to 'talk dirty.' He sneaks up on me, just to get a rise out of me, and then gets excited when I'm angry. I could swear he'd like me to beat the shit out of him. Or maybe he wants to spank me. I don't know. I'm really at a loss. It sounds ridiculous, him using these words with that irritating accent. It should be ironic but it sounds wrong on him. Anyway, I finally agreed to dinner and he asked me if I'd like to tie him up at his place at the end of the evening. I'm really out of my element here." I grimace and stop my recitation.

Harry was dumbfounded, his mouth hung open. He

reached across the table and began to pat my hand, trying to comfort me in my distress. He never saw his partner's broad wink in my direction, didn't notice my struggle for decorum. I couldn't take it anymore and burst into giggles, roaring unstoppable giggles, clutching-my-belly-in-pain giggles.

Harry was pissed as all hell, snatched back his hand, and slammed his fist on the table. "Bitch!" He stalked off to the bar to order another beer.

"Really, Sophia, that wasn't funny," Philip quietly commented. "Harry will be in a state for a week over this. You shouldn't toy with those less sober than you. It's bad form."

But Harry's face in the bar mirror was so distorted with frustration, nose crinkled up and eyebrows furrowed, mouth in a bulldog grimace, that I couldn't stop laughing. He looked like a cartoon, one of those old wrinkled men made from stocking material. I finally calmed down enough to comment. "Really, Philip, it was hysterical. Harry's face was priceless, slathering over the scandal. His temper tantrum alone was worth the laugh."

Harry returned with his beer, attempting to hide his scowling face.

"Sorry to disappoint, boys, but I have in no way wiggled that pole up his arse in the slightest. In fact, I haven't seen his arse and...I have no desire to do so. Philip's backside is much nicer, in any event. Sure you're not interested in switching teams for the night, ay, Phil?"

"Sophia, you're absolutely scandalous. And you're right. Your New York humor is charming in the extreme," he bit back. "But Gabriel does have lovely lips, don't you think?" Philip added as an afterthought.

I blushed. Holy shit, I can't believe I blushed. I've been ambushed by Philip's feigned indifference. Here I thought I was doing a damn fine job of deflecting Harry, but these boys were no rookies. They were a tag team—and Harry smiled, suddenly not as drunk as I thought. Philip's smile matched

Harry's as they acknowledged each other with a nod and clinking glasses. *These guys are pros...two against one isn't fair*, I thought, stomping my mental foot.

"Ah, so you've noticed those full pouty lips, too, have you?" asked Harry, now fully recovered from his intoxication. "You're right about the arse, however, not as firm a bottom as Philip."

I tried to recover and hide my mistake, but even I knew it was too late. "Oh, he has what we call in my land of the crass Yankee 'the perfect apple butt.' I think it's time for me to push off, boys. I'll see you at work on Monday."

Harry and Philip stood as I got ready to leave, and as an afterthought, I asked, "How did you know about the museum?"

Harry replied without answering, "Sophia, don't fret. Seriously, my dear, your secret is safe with us. No one else cares or has even noticed." Phillip was nodding—smiling and nodding.

"Goodnight, fellas. As always, it was fun spending the evening with you. Yep, really fun."

Monday arrived and with it a growing excitement about seeing Gabriel. The slight pressure he imposed on my hand at the park on Saturday left an imprint in my thoughts all weekend. First thing in the morning Gabriel popped his head into my office—seriously, I was just putting my briefcase down.

"Good morning, Sophia. I'd like to wrap up our tax lessons this morning if you have time. I, ah, won't be available for the rest of the week."

"Good morning. Yes, Gabriel, why don't we meet in the library in fifteen minutes. I have a few items to dictate to Katherine first."

"Good, see you in fifteen."

I arrive in the library and you are already at the whiteboard, writing out your lesson plan for the day. I am preoccupied with your comment about wrapping up, realizing that this is our last lesson together. You begin your lesson and the morning drags, as I try to fabricate an excuse to continue our private time together. I draw a blank and you jar me away from my daydreaming.

"Sophia, it looks like you've got the concentration span of a tsetse fly today. Let's take a break for lunch. There's a new place I'd like to take you to."

"Sure, Gabriel, sounds good to me. I'll go grab my purse."

You follow me to my office. I lift my purse from the back of my chair and as I turn back toward the door, I see you've collected my jacket from the coat stand and are holding it out for me. This is such an unexpected and gentlemanly gesture. I reach an arm into a sleeve. You bring it up to my shoulder as I reach into the other sleeve. You hike the jacket up, and I feel your knuckles brush the back of my neck as you straighten the collar. That touch sends a radiating warmth from my neck down to my fingertips.

This lunch you suggest will stay with me for quite a long time. My heart is racing as we enter the restaurant, a dark and cave-like place, with crisscrossed concave ceilings, tiled in the azure and mustard tones I love. Of course, you found a cave in the middle of the business district, knowing today you would be wrapping up your instruction, our work together coming to an end. You sit down across from me in a booth and I'm a bit disappointed. But then, I do like the idea of looking at you, observing and examining the movements of your mouth and hands.

Our waiter, an older Italian gentleman, takes our drink orders, his voice accented with the language of Eros. You start talking about some new exhibit you'd like to take in, about the tax filings that I would soon resolve, office gossip, whatever. But I am thinking about something else entirely, lost in my thoughts all the time now. These thoughts are a fevered breath, short and tense and aching. I am breathing so rapidly, my mouth is parched. I take a sip of wine or water, I lose track. I sip the wine and wonder if you are watching me. I take a bite off an asparagus tip, dripping with cream sauce, and wonder if you are watching. Is asparagus erotic? Am I seductive? Do I want to be seductive? Yes, I think I'd like to be seductive but instead, I'm awkward and self-conscious. You continue to talk while I watch your mouth move.

As you chatter idly on, I see your hands move through the air. You punctuate with those hands, those elegant, strong hands. They are bigger than I had noticed before. The need to feel those hands on me is a raw ache in my chest, and finally, I say, barely above a whisper, "This is unbearable."

I think you don't hear me because you continue to talk. I think about those hands and am long gone, in an old rare bookstore...the one we visited during our research together, checking the values of some of the Moreaux antiques. But it's a different place I see, where I am standing tucked away in a corner, the smell of old parchment washing over me. The sound of gently turning pages is like the rhythm of sand tides. The store is so warm, like a parlor with a fire crackling. I know this place but I can't remember...I hear the pages turning, smell the musty books, and feel the sand tides moving around me. I close my eyes, tip my head back, and swim in the warmth, the dune waves warming my core. I feel hands on my neck gently massaging the tight muscles, knowing it is you. I am not afraid as your hands move to my hair, down my neck. I turn my head slightly to kiss your fingertips, your palm...

All the while you are talking, your voice a gentle cadence of the King's English. I've grown to like your accent, no longer annoyed by its elitist history. You pause for a moment and your eyes glance at my lips as you say, "You're awfully quiet today."

All the while I'm thinking I'd rather not spoil the music of your voice with my "afflicted" New York English. Do you remember when you told me I was suffering from a heavy

New York accent, sounded like I was stricken with some illness? I grimace and take another sip of wine. You look a little confused.

I raise my hand, elbow resting on the table, wanting to touch yours. I lean forward toward you as if I'd like to measure our hands against each other. We rarely make physical contact, each of us recalling the painful episode in the wine cellar. You look at me, elbow resting on the table as if we're about to arm wrestle, leaning toward you. You lift an eyebrow and put your arm on the table, same as mine. Our hands are a fraction of an inch apart. We don't touch but feel the pulsing energy in the air charged between our fingertips. You notice my little fingers for the first time and comment. I have kept them so well hidden all these months. You ask me what happened, but I don't want to hear my own voice, so I shrug in response, and move my hands to my lap under the table.

Giovanni is standing nearby, and I try to imagine what it is that he sees. He's been doing this a long time, watching a man and a woman have lunch. You say something that makes me blush. I resist the urge to hide my face behind my hands like a schoolgirl, not wanting to interrupt the charge between us. You sit like a gentleman, leaning a little forward and I feel ridiculous. How could you possibly be interested in me? You ask why I don't eat, and I answer with another shrug of my shoulders. I can't eat. I can't sleep. My mind is seized on you and your hands and lips, and I can think of nothing else. All the while I feel Giovanni nearby, and somehow I'm comforted by his presence. You are talking again and I am watching your mouth move.

I lick my lips.

You pause.

Giovanni smiles his seasoned smile.

"Gabriel," I whisper again, "this is unbearable."

You respond with a grave and terrible warning

"We must bear it."

I start to become angry, an anger that starts and ends with the yearning in my belly. Why can't I have my adventure? I ask myself. The answer is hidden deep, but I know you are right. Regardless, I let my mind charge ahead along the hormone trail of lust. I'm thinking of the warehouse, you pushing me up against the wall surrounded by gigantic erotic scenes—my mind escapes me in a fantastic scene that never happened, that I know will never happen. The food comes, but I am not so interested in eating as I am in watching your mouth move.

My thoughts move from your hands in the bookstore to your lips. I am thinking I'd like to trace your lips with my fingers. I'd like to dip my fingers in the wine and trace your lips. I'd like to dip my tongue in the wine and trace your lips. My fingertips are tingling, even the missing ones, I notice offhandedly, those phantom pains having subsided a long time ago. I twine my fingers together under the table in a white-knuckle grip, barely able to help myself from reaching out. I'm quite shocked at my own reckless thoughts, paralyzed with fear, adrenalin racing through my veins. Can you smell the adrenalin? Do you feel the searing pain of restraint?

I feel a chill and am acutely aware of my body. I'd like you to notice that I am chilled, my nipples hard with the heat between us and the cold in the restaurant, but then I think I shouldn't want that so I quickly put on my suit jacket while you look at me curiously.

Is this lust? I ask myself. You couldn't possibly feel this degree of lust. There is a pause in the conversation, and you squint at my lips again. You look at me, tracing a path with your eyes from my lips to my eyes. I continue this inner battle under your watchful gaze, weak with a force that saps my will. Can you know the turmoil I feel as I sit mutely, gasping in short breaths, waiting for you to move or stay?

You get up and come sit next to me, turning toward me so

that your knee is touching my thigh. You turn your face towards me and move one of your arms to the space between us on the seat, leaning closer. I feel every movement of your body. I hear your breathing and heartbeat pick up, see you move your other arm to rest on the table, effectively trapping me. You move your lips toward me, then tip your head so that your mouth is at my ear. You touch my hair so lightly, moving it away from my ear, and then say,

finally,

decisively

"Sophia, I want to take you."

Holy shit—the words are so erotic and startling. I am a shocked mute, trapped by your limbs and the booth. Suddenly, for the first time in my entire life, for the first time...

I.

Feel.

Beautiful.

I feel desirable and the pleasure of that feeling is acute and filling, a warm liqueur spreading through my limbs.

Yes, you want to take me. I understand what that means now, and I'd sure like to be taken, I think. It's good that I'm sitting because I am so weak in the knees I wouldn't be able to stand. But I'm more afraid than excited, sensing you have thought about the details in greater depth than I have. I have thought about your hands in my hair, your lips on mine, you touching my arms, my neck, but no more. I understand now that there would be more and I'm afraid.

You brush your lips against my earlobe, down my neck, your hand in my hair now, gently running it through your fingers. I am paralyzed, my heart sprinting as you barely touch my skin. Too soon, you move back to the other side of the table. Somehow we return to our meal and finish this lunch as if that moment never passed between us.

Ahhh, to be French. We know what we want. Why not lie down and get on with it? Little snapshot images nip at me as we prepare to leave. We are in the old estate home, taking inventory, me with my clipboard and you with yours. We are in the musty cellar, and you are schooling me in the architecture. It's warm and a little sweat beads up at my neck, but I keep my jacket on and you keep a polite distance. We are in the warehouse surrounded by all manner of priceless art and worthless junk, you again schooling me in the traditional European fare of culture and history, art and architecture. I would sure like to be schooled in something else entirely...and I let my mind wander.

Giovanni appears with the check after espresso and double chocolate dessert that we share. You stab your fork in the dessert and then I do the same. *We are forking the chocolate,* I think to myself hysterically. I can't wrap my head around this overwhelming lust—fear and excitement, the twin demons of my obsession.

I cannot stop the ebb and flow of the demons. In truth, I don't want to stop the adrenaline rushing through my veins. This obsession with your lips will obliterate me in its fire. This. Is. Passion. Then I stop thinking—I think of no one and nothing, consumed as I am with your lips and wishing they were on me.

I don't know how we get there, but soon we're out in the glaring sun on the sidewalk. We don't shake hands as you take your leave of me, on your way to an appointment, you say. And I am left on the sidewalk, bereft and confused, for a moment unsure of the time and where I need to be. I turn on my heels, angry with you, angry with me, and march back to the office. I know anger and use it to distract me and immerse myself in the work I have to do.

It turns out to be an incredibly unproductive afternoon. I try to separate the various expenses at the country house, payroll, personnel, but I can't concentrate. I dictate a memo to my assistant, and it comes back a confusing garbled stream of consciousness mess. Katherine leaves early, and I finally pack up and lock my office door at 7:00. I arrive back in my flat after passing through the park, unaware of anything around me.

I am back in my office the next day, the next week, and as you promised, you are unavailable for the rest of the week, having scheduled time out of the office. I am in my office for many weeks after, standing at the window, daydreaming again. I go to the door and close it, turning out the light. I lean back in my chair and close my eyes, reliving our lunch, unable to recall the conversation at all...while you are down the hallway, at a meeting, off at an appointment, living your life doing things I don't know about. And me, I am possessed with a longing that grows with time.

We bump into each other on occasion while I continue my work on the Moreaux estate. And you, you obnoxious prick, you continue to do what you do in your perfectly creased shirts and suits. I am tempted to follow you home to see where you live, but I don't. Instead, I try to busy myself, to get you out of my thoughts, but they entice me at all hours of the day and night. I am drawn to them over and over. Those thoughts of you are so much fun that I relive them like a child, watching a favorite television show over and over.

I am angry all the time now, frustrated with an unfamiliar ache deep in my torso. I start kickboxing to work out the anger, but it doesn't help. I've given up my yoga practice—I tell myself for a little while—unable to take a deep breath. I am possessed by a djinn, an evil spirit—a new word I discovered while researching the Moreaux family tree. I revisit our lunch daily and begin to doubt what you said or what I recall.

I alternate with being furious with you and admiring your restraint, thinking you either a coward or honorable for your inaction. Neither of those thoughts is a comfort to my growing desire and frustration. I think it will wane, but instead, it grows monstrously large in my mind. I am consumed with a wanting that keeps me company by day and haunts me most acutely at night.

I am at kickboxing one evening with my trainer, Jorge. He is built like a South American tank. I am going through our routine and my mind starts to wander. The moves are rote by this time, and Jorge is holding the mitts while I strike with alternating kicks and punches. My mind wanders back to our lunch, I see you tipping your lips to my ear and I hear:

"I want to take you."

"I want to take you."

"I want to take you."

I suddenly feel someone's arms wrapped around me, pinning my arms at my sides. It took two trainers to subdue me in that fugue state.

I am furiously violent. Jorge is on the floor, knocked out cold by my blows. I really want that to be you on the floor, as you have abandoned me in my need. I have never needed like this. I have never needed human contact more than now, and you have abandoned me to it. A rage has grown in me, a rage that stems from a seed planted long before we met. I am in an ambulance, strapped to a stretcher. I awake for a moment in the hospital, still strapped down, until I finally welcome the respite of drug-induced sleep.

Albert was sitting and waiting when I woke up on the couch in my flat. His voice was the first that I registered before opening my eyes, but there was someone else there. Marlow was with us, as well, and they were speaking quietly, while I heard all that they said. I was strangely reassured by Albert's comment to Marlow.

"Marlow, it won't be long now before she wakes. It's difficult to manage her while hormones are rushing madly through her body."

I sat up, and they took notice. I wanted to speak, but my tongue was thick in my mouth. I opened my mouth, but the tongue was in the way. Albert fetched a glass of water with a straw. I took a refreshing sip and again struggled to speak.

"Where is Gabriel?" was the first thing I asked. I sounded drunk, the words tripping over each other.

They exchanged a knowing glance. "Why would you expect him here, Sophia?" Marlow asked.

"I don't expect him, but I know you've sent him away."

Albert moved his head a bit too fast, giving away his surprise at my knowledge. "Why would you think that, Sophia?" Albert now asked.

It was as if they'd scripted these questions, the two of them. They were so confident they could control me, it was almost comical. They didn't understand that I'd already diluted the drugs in my veins. They didn't know that I could. In fact, I only discovered it now, while the seething temper hovered below the surface. I felt its heat burning up the drugs in my bloodstream. Marlow moved from one of the chairs to the couch next to me. He looked troubled, his brow furrowed. He was about to reach out to touch my hand.

I warned him, "I'm not so sure you want to do that just now, Marlow. It's going to be rather ugly." But he did. What he felt was my rage. He picked me up into his arms, and I did not resist. He was embracing me now, his arms wrapped around me. He was trying to draw the raw fury out of me into himself, but I held on in a death grip. I wanted to hold it and contain it for some reason. Meanwhile, Marlow was shaking in pain. I knew I was hurting him as he spun out of control in the tornado of this wrath within me. It was filled with disconnected debris of memory and emotion. I could not make any sense of it, but he apparently understood. And all he wanted to do was remove this agonizing anger from within me. I heard Marlow's quiet prayer.

"Sweet mother, is there no redemption, no forgiveness for me?" I didn't understand what he meant and I didn't much care. But I noticed Marlow's smell—it was ocean fresh and desert-dry all at the same time. His comfort was the seaweed of the shore while he scratched the blackboard of my fear. My thoughts moved quickly from Marlow's scent to you, Gabriel.

I am preoccupied with you, Gabriel; and your face is everywhere in the vortex of my rage. You have denied me, denied me, and I want to beat you until you give me what I want. Marlow slowly drew the image of your face from me. Then he showed me your face as it really was. You are sitting in a flat I don't recognize, but I know it as your own. You are on a couch with your head in your hands, shaking your head from side to side. You step out onto a balcony and gaze into the distance overlooking the city. You can see Big Ben from your apartment. Leaning on the railing, you are again shaking your head as if to rid it of cobwebs. You turn to enter the flat and I see your face as if I am in the flat looking out at you. You stop short for a moment, sensing a presence. Your face is a mix of fear and longing—but mostly fear. I want to reach out and touch your face, your confused and sad and frightened face. Your vulnerability touches me, and I want to comfort you.

Marlow pulled us away from there and we were now back in my flat, he was holding my upper arms and looking directly into my eyes. Marlow had shown me that you do indeed want to take me; your feelings for me are not some figment of my imagination. All these weeks I've been tormented by you, even beginning to think I had made it all up.

You are afraid of me.

After what I'd done to poor Jorge, I understood. It never occurred to me that your fear was greater than your lust or greater than my fear. I am weak with remorse for having been angry at you. Turns out you are neither a coward nor honorable. You've been warned, and you have abandoned me at great personal cost.

I turned my attention to Marlow, and I understood now that he was to blame for keeping you from me. He quickly let go of my arms, having held me for too long. He was drenched in sweat from the effort and recoiled from the pain he experienced when he touched me. He was unable to bear a moment longer.

"It's time for you both to go," I said clearly to Marlow and Albert.

They hesitated as I got up from the couch on steady feet and headed to the kitchen to make myself a cup of tea. I'm sure they were surprised at how quickly I'd recovered from the sedatives, but they made no remark. And neither of them prepared to leave.

"It's time for the both of you to go. Now," I repeated from the kitchen, a little more forcefully. I stood at the stove watching for the water to boil. The irony was not lost on me, that I was waiting for water to boil, waiting for the molecules to get so heated that they split the attraction binding the hydrogen, converting the liquid into a gas. My hydrogen molecules were starting to simmer, soon to bubble, and I was curious to see what happened when the attraction between them was broken.

It was a moment, an eternity.

The kettle whistled, hissing. They remained quietly sitting in my parlor, unwelcome intruders. I returned and sat at my desk, opened my laptop, and began surfing the internet. More minutes passed.

I turned in the swivel chair and faced them both.

"It is time for you to go now," I said again as I stood and headed toward the door. I held the door open; but again, neither man made a move to leave.

I headed toward Marlow first and gazed down at him sitting on the couch as I gently placed a hand on his shoulder. He felt the voltage of a taser as it traveled down his arm, a small taste of what I wanted to do to him. I removed my hand quickly before his muscles locked up.

Albert knew what I had done. He was not wearing a face

for the moment. I felt no judgment from him as he stood and collected his blazer from the back of a chair and said sincerely, "I hope we'll see each other again, Sophia."

I looked at him curiously, disinterested in the extreme, knowing with a calm certainty that we would surely never see each other again. Marlow stumbled to his feet and followed on Albert's heels.

CORRIDORS OF MEMORY

I took some time off, a couple of days, and spent many hours exercising. I ran, returned to Jorge, and apologized. I swam, I ran, I swam and ran and kickboxed for three long days until I got bored. I tried not to think and instead focused on the feeling of my strong body. This I could master—my body and my physical strength. This was the one thing that I could control in this life that seemed to be running away from me.

I especially tried not to think about Gabriel, but his face haunted me in the most unexpected places. I returned to the office and continued work on the estate. I saw his tortured face around every corner in this space. Then I saw his face for real several times. We smiled and nodded and went our separate ways, as I tried to suppress my obsession with him. His face was a floating ember in my eye, marring my line of sight. I immersed myself in work in an attempt to dislodge Gabriel from my life.

I researched the Moreaux family history. The exotic story satisfying—the family tree beginning with a French name meaning 'little dark' which related to the dark-skinned easterners or moors. It was likely that an ancestor had relations with the darker-skinned, which made me think of Marlow. Adele was truly a matriarch and master of all she surveyed. She took on the mantle of the family shipping business from her father as the only child. Imports from Jamaica included sugar, rum, and Bauxite ore. Adele was born in 1939 and died at 64. She had been married to William Edwards but uncharacteristically kept her family name. Both Adele and William were from blue blood British families, with no children. William had died at a very young age, only 50 years old. His death certificate indicated the cause of death was unknown. Adele was an only child, as was her husband, perhaps the result of all that inbreeding, I thought uncharitably.

I had reviewed enough birth and death certificates and researched enough online to conclude that I needed to return to the estate. The secrecy surrounding the decedent created unnecessary mountains of work for me, work that a good investigator or skip tracer could more adeptly handle. In any event, at the very least, I needed a break from my increasing obsession with Gabriel. I texted Oliver, unexpectedly wanting him to accompany me. True to form, the security chief asked no questions and arrived at my flat at 7:00 a.m. sharp the next morning.

As I stepped into the car, I reached over the seat to hand him a personal apple cake I'd made the night before.

"Sophia, what a pleasant surprise. Were you already at the bakery this morning?" I was pleased to hear his deep bass voice.

"No, Oliver. I'm a lawyer who can bake!"

"Where to today, Mademoiselle?" I had mixed feelings when he addressed me that way—with the formality of a chauffeur. On occasion, it felt right but I preferred him as a big brother.

"The country house, but I have a feeling you already knew that."

Oliver smiled his content closed-mouth smile, and I caught a glimpse of his sparkling eyes in the rearview mirror.

We were met at the estate by the surprised James and Alice. While Oliver had a cup of tea in the kitchen, I began ambling around. I found myself in the attic prodding through some old chests filled with clothes, china, photo albums, letters, and what looked like a hundred years of ancient leather-bound accounting ledgers. I was searching a bit voyeuristically, I admit, enjoying the free access into a complete stranger's most personal possessions. Sitting on the floor in my jeans for hours of careful prying in the dusty, hot attic was therapeutic. I lost track of time pouring over the Moreaux, Ltd. books and records. Alice stopped in every so often toting iced tea and the cutest little cucumber and chutney sandwiches.

Among the old trunks, I noticed one with a locked drawer running the full length along its bottom. I went in search of James and Alice and asked where I could find the key. Alice handed me more than a hundred keys on several chains. Oliver returned to the attic with me and about halfway through the keys, I turned a lock and we both heard the whisper-click that opened the trunk.

"Ah, sweet success, I leave you to it, Sophia. I have a gin game calling my name, and the old couple enjoys the company." Oliver's steps echoed on the stairs.

I recalled Albert showing me a similar drawer, the place where he kept "important papers" when I was quite young. Looking in this particular trunk triggered that memory, and I knew how to push a bit on the front bottom panel to release the spring lock. The drawer opened. Inside were journals and diaries, prayer-book size, all with Adele's name on the front leaf—Adele Moreaux. A while later, after sifting through the most tiresome rantings of adolescent drama, I stood and stretched. Arms up, stretching to the ceiling, bending to touch the floor, and several yoga stretches to take the kinks out. Was this the best that my search would produce—teenage drivel? The attic was warm, and I was getting a bit cross-eyed and tired. I took the sheet that Alice had brought up and set it out on the floor. I laid down on my back, the sun sifting in through the porthole windows, and watched the dust motes float about in the rays. I slipped into a deep sleep pretty quickly. When I awoke, there was no more sun and I was in almost complete darkness, the kind that fills every corner in the country.

Alice must have returned at some point and, not wanting to disturb me, turned on a small lamp. I was thankful, knowing it would have been near impossible to navigate through the full attic in the blind. I opened my eyes and turned on my side, trying to capture the memory of some sleeping image that troubled me. From the floor, I noticed the legs of dining chairs, a rocking horse, claw feet of a large dining table, and, among others, an old mahogany credenza. The base was peculiar. I got up to inspect, turned it on its side, and found another hidden drawer. Seems the trunks were decoys—I hit the jackpot and found one journal of Adele's travels to Jamaica.

Sitting in the quiet of that attic until the early morning hours, I met the adult Adele on a trip to Jamaica. Adele had kept journals from her early childhood until she was about 55 years old. Then they abruptly stopped. She traveled often, meeting shippers for the family business and developing personal relationships. Most of her trips were short business junkets, as logged in her journals. These were no more than terse entries—who she met, where they stayed, meetings, negotiations, and agreements.

This one was different.

1978

I am sitting outside a small shack on an aluminum chair, if you can call it that. I am watching him from here as he walks along the shore, pacing restlessly in the moonlight. He doesn't sleep well I know, struggling with his demons of discovery—sometimes that unveiling is exciting, a first kiss and newfound confidence in a young and virile body. At other times, it is unsettling, seeing that one might be truly careless with others' sentiments. I can feel the dread of some burden heavy on his heart.

Here is someone truly, objectively frightening. Not a body would guess what terrible thoughts flowed beneath the surface—but I, I could hear them. He is tall, with rippling muscles toned in the sugar cane fields and skin so smooth and earthy from the strong Jamaican sun, this beautiful young man. Fine silk fabric wrapped about the body— Ahhh, I could watch him for hours in his silent wanderings. I cannot get my fill of watching this godly work of art. But he corrects me and says it is a savage and unholy joke that he is so beautiful and still so damaged.

I cannot see any damage, blinded as I am by the curve of his mouth, his full lips, the thick waves of his black hair streaked prematurely with gray. His hands are strong and large but gentle. I am overcome with despair at his beauty. I have neither pride nor dignity while he holds me in his embrace. I am lost, lost at sea in a torrent of lust. I want to see that he is also kind, but in truth, I know he is not. I don't care. I want to see a small token of thoughtful grace, but I know he will come to me only to plant his seed when the mood moves him. And the mood moves him often. He is the Incubus who comes to me in the daylight. Sex is all about power I've heard. And I am powerless as he wields total control over me.

We first met some nights ago as I was wrapping up a meeting in the lobby of the Myrtle Bank Hotel in Kingston. My guest, one of the owners of a sugar plantation, and I were closing a deal with a nightcap when I saw him. A young man in his early twenties, I guessed, entered the lobby. He was wearing white linen pants and a loose linen shirt, barefoot. As I watched him open the door, he turned toward me. The room grew quiet; I saw my companion's mouth moving but couldn't hear a word, while he walked across the lobby in slow motion. Then he was gone behind the wall, and I was left with the fleeting image of his naked feet.

I turned back to my companion, and we said goodnight. I remained in the lobby for some time, hoping he would return. In the end, I went to my room and dozed on the balcony, waking now and then, gazing out at the beautiful Caribbean bay on this temperate evening. The ocean breeze was light as a feather ruffling my hair. Soon I was sleeping on the chaise and dreaming of a dark man (or was it a boy) while the tide moved rhythmically on the nearby shore. Awake again... He is there on the balcony in a chair next to the chaise, his face lit by the moonlight, his eyes deep pools of dusky ash that recede at the touch of my glance. He is resting his elbows on his knees, extends a hand toward me, touches my hair, moving the stray strands from my eyes. I feel drunk on his beauty, his fingers gently tracing my eyebrows, his palm cupping my cheek. He parts his lips a bit and wets them with his tongue; and I am seized with a languid, drunken desire. I see him coming closer, his eyes now black as pitch and not so friendly. But he closes his eyes, and I do not resist his gentle kiss. The tip of his tongue traces my mouth; and I am lost on the sea, the tide moving in and out.

We are in a one-room seaside shack. I don't know how we arrived here. I don't know how many days now since I left the hotel, missed more than one flight, I think. I am an addicted devotee, attached to my vows of lust in a most sluggish way. This is no cocaine addiction; I am drugged with the stuff of dulled senses, a veil before my eyes. I can barely speak from weakness and fatigue. But every few hours it seems, when he comes to me, he fills me with the drink of lust and I am awakened, allowing him license with my body, the demon spellbinder of my nights.

It seems after weeks of this work that he is done. He had something to do and it is finished. We don't really speak, but I understand he is done with me and that now he will return me to my own life. He helps me to check in because I need the help, quietly saying to the concierge something about finding me on the beach. I am so confused as the concierge escorts me to a room. Soon a doctor arrives to check on me, and I continue to be puzzled. He's gone and I start to awaken from this fugue. I take a shower with a nurse's help and am wrapped in a bathrobe afterward. As I brush my hair, the bathrobe falls open and I see that I have gained weight. My stomach is huge. I quickly tie myself in the robe and meet the doctor in the sitting room of the suite.

He is older, quick, and efficient, and without preamble asks me, "How far along are you, Mrs. Moreaux?" And I stare at him, dumbstruck.

"I, I don't know what you mean…"

He nods to the nurse who says "hysteria" quietly. But I'm not hysterical. I feel as if I'm waking from a long, long ago sleep. My hands rest on my belly, and I feel the skin is stretched and tight.

Returning to the bathroom, I open my robe and it's true. I'm pregnant; I see it when I look down and so definitely in the mirror's reflection. As if on cue, I feel a sharp pain in my back, and a small river of water washes down my legs. My water breaks and labor begins.

Furious pain roars, waits, and roars again. For two days I labored to deliver a child I was told my whole life I could not conceive. But as the labor continued, I became more and more alert, awakened to the fact that I had gone missing with him for nine months. Somehow, and without memory, I had written to England that I was enjoying an extended stay. William didn't even consider a visit—there was no need for alarm. He had my letter and I had for years run my own company and my own life.

After the birth, I heard the nurses whispering quickly and began to feel new pains. I heard the doctor's instructions, "Put her out."

But I didn't want to go back to sleep. I had been sleeping for nine months; and as the pain roared again, a beautiful black-faced nurse came close to my face and said, "It's the afterbirth, Madame, but there is a lot of blood. We'll help you to rest." Then she trapped me with her pitch-black eyes and inserted a needle into my IV. She wasn't there when I awoke with an unspecified panic gripping my chest.

For nine months I was with him on the beach in that shack. But time had folded in on itself. I didn't even know his name. We didn't speak much, the silence between us being all he would allow. I wondered if he had drugged me, but I knew that wasn't true. I knew in my heart what it was. I was a woman of practical expectations in the world, understood formalities and rules. I did my business well, fulfilled my roles at home and in the family empire, and never dabbled in matters of the spirit. I had accepted that I was barren with the stiff upper lip that is part of the British national character.

But this trespasser in my ordered world was something of another nature entirely. He was gentle and kind with me, but there was malice in his bewitchment. He was nineteen years old when he seduced me with his sinister intent. I was helpless to resist him and gave birth to a girl in 1979 whose name He chose, a name that came to me from a distant whisper on my mind

— Layla.

I look up from the journal as the name patters along the corridors of memory.

1979

I have returned to England with my adopted daughter. She is darker in the face than me, her hair is thick and black like his. I despise her. I hand her to a nanny when we arrive, like luggage to a porter. She does not cry for me, and I register that I am overcome with an urge to do her harm. I cannot understand how she managed to find her way into my womb, and I would like to cut her out.

But Layla is a pleasant child, the staff adores her as she grows into a toddler, and I keep my distance. I hear them muttering that I am not the maternal type. Well, the maternal type is available for a price, and they take care of her. Occasionally, I find myself wandering through our back gardens and think I catch a glimpse of Him, but it is my imagination running wild. At these times, I feel the need to punish Layla for her part in this mystery. I take the child to the shed, so much like the shack, the staff thinking I am walking in the gardens with her.

I stood up from where I had been reading the journal and went to a porthole. I felt nauseous. Looking out from the window, I saw shadows moving among the trees in the deep night, in the gardens...in the gardens. My knees felt weak.

I went down two flights of stairs and headed to the kitchen for something to settle my stomach. Opening the refrigerator, I found ginger ale. As I was closing the door, I saw a woman's shadow move outside the kitchen window. Dizzy, the bottle slipped from my hand...I reached for a chair at the table...too far as I slipped down to the floor. Trying to stay conscious...a small table lamp light came on. I saw Oliver heading toward me, shirtless, in pajama pants.

"Oliver?"

He didn't speak but scooped me up and gently placed me on a chair. He poured a drink and handed it to me. I couldn't stay awake. He put something under my nose and I smelled ammonia. Ouch, it was strong but the smelling salts aroused me.

I was more awake now as Oliver handed me the glass. "Here you go, love. Sip that."

I drank as I was told and then took his suggestion to retire for the night. I could get a couple of hours of sleep before dawn. I headed to the bedroom prepared for me, with Oliver on my heels.

"I'm fine, Oliver, probably just a little dehydrated." He ignored me and escorted me to my room, waiting in the doorway while I prepared for bed. Not until I was tucked in did he finally take his leave. He didn't close the door. It was only when I was safely under the covers that I wondered about Oliver. He was so respectful of my privacy, didn't ask any questions, and appeared when he was needed. I liked him, deep in my core, really liked him. He was so...reliable...reassuring. I drifted off to sleep with the soothing thoughts of Oliver nearby.

I awakened to a comfortable morning sun spraying into my room. It was a grand room with an old four-poster bed. There was another bed nearby, untouched. I showered, dressed, and headed down for breakfast. English breakfast rocks—cream tea and crumpets laid out in the dining room! I had a hearty appetite and ate alone.

Alice was nearby if I needed anything but did not interrupt my quiet breakfast with the newspaper laid out before me. I returned to the attic, a morbid curiosity sparking my enthusiasm to continue reading.

1982

One night I am at the shed and she's whimpering inside, and I see Him. I run to Him, but He evades me—behind a tree, past the stone walls, out into the street, down the lane. He continues to slip out of sight, and I run like a wild woman through the hallways of our home and the streets of Nettlebed. I am cornered near St. Bartholomew Church near High Street, taken to hospital with hysteria, drugged for real this time. I return to William and he is patient with me, but I resent his every kindness, intent on only two matters—finding him and killing her.

It is the same, night after night, drenched in sweat when I awake from a dream I cannot recall. Sleep is no longer restful, and I awake more fatigued each day. It is the same, day after day, as I lie resting on a hammock or a chair—my eyes are suddenly heavy and I drift into a dream state of confusion and lust.

September 1983

I don't know what day it is. It's raining and autumn chill is in the air. I've been on leave from work again, unable to focus. I hear Layla and her friend laughing, running through the house. The giggles drive through me like a freight train, and I call the nanny to quiet them. No sleep last night, visions of Him haunting me from every corner. I see Layla at breakfast, and she is chattering on about nothing. I look at her and want to cover her mouth, her face. From behind her, I see Him walking past the doorway to the kitchen and I jump from the table. But as always, when I enter the kitchen, He is not there. He is a shadow, I think sometimes, a ghostly apparition of my weakness. I am not afraid but overcome in my desire to drag Layla to the shed, to obliterate every reminder of Him that she is. The nanny takes her away, noticing my agitated state.

October 1983

He is with me all the time now, brushing the hair away from my face as I lie staring at the fireplace in the parlor. I glance toward Him and see those eyes, dark as night in the country, trying to threaten me. But I laugh hysterically...and nanny hides the girl in the basement.

When will they take her to school and finally leave me in peace so that I can lose myself in the soft contours of His lips?

He comes to me again, but His teeth are sharp and I think He's going to attack like a feral dog.

I saw Him again today, but He's getting more corporeal and the house less so. His features are not soft but angry. He scolds me silently —tells me a mother's love is like no other.

November 1985

The girl comes to me in the night and sits in a chair near my bed. She touches my hand while I'm catatonically staring toward the fire, where I see His face. Her touch is comforting somehow, but when I turn toward her, she looks like Him. Her eyes are dark and focused.

She's trying to force herself into my mind, I can feel it. And I know she is truly His daughter. But she is a child, and I think I can push her away. I try, but she resists and I hear her. "Be calm, mother. Do not fear. I can help you." But I strike out at her and watch with mild detachment as she and the chair fall over to the floor.

She gets off the floor and I feel her fury. I see her blossom to a distorted, clownish size, the fingers of her hands growing like ropes, reaching out for my neck.

1986

He came for real this time. At least I think so, but even now, I can't be certain. I was resting in the garden in the middle of the day, and I saw His image. We had an entire conversation. He asked about the child. I didn't want to speak of her, but He asked again and again, and I finally snapped at Him. I told Him I didn't like her. I told Him she was a wretched little imp, no worse, a festering pain, constant and sharp, a mental agony like the one of bringing her into this world. There is no respite for the mental torture of her presence, I tell Him. He was angry and asked me what I meant. "How could a mother not like her child?"

I asked if He had any children and he said no, only Layla. When He said her name, I cringed internally and He felt it. But I was not groggy now; I felt Him as he pushed and probed into my mind. I lashed back at Him, at the child who He so sorely wanted to know about. She was spoiling my first conversation with Him! I'll teach her to keep her place, I thought to myself with ice in my veins.

But He was in my head and I could hear Him shouting. "What do you mean? What will you do to my daughter?" He was a banshee yelling in my head, the screeching of His fear and anger hammering inside my skull. This is all her fault, every pain I suffer is her fault. He threatened me and I saw His awful eyes again, the ones that told me He was not kind. I began to retreat into nursery rhymes to get Him out of my head. "Jack Sprat could eat no fat. His wife..." but it was too late. He had stumbled upon my true intention—I would see the little beast buried sooner or later, throw roses gleefully upon her open grave.

1987

She is tied up in the shed again, and I am excited with the power I have over her, a power I didn't have over Him. William comes looking for me, calling out for Layla. I grab a shovel and hit him as he approaches—he falls to the ground and his head hits the cobblestone. My husband stops moving. He's dead, dead, dead and I don't care at all. I want to dance over his body and show Him that I have power. I have the power He took away from me.

Then He is there for real in the mist, and I charge Him with the shovel, but the shovel falls and it is Layla lying before me. She has escaped her binds. He is standing over her, protecting her, as she weeps over her papa's body. I try to step closer, but He moves between us and holds up His hand. From the hand, I see a wall emerge—it is a dense fog wall. I reach out to touch it, and it bends as my fingertips push into it, but I cannot penetrate the womb He has erected around her.

I begin to mutter under my breath, cursing Him, cursing her. He tries to reach into my mind, but He is busy protecting her and he cannot do both. I see a weakness and try to talk to him. I get louder,

"You—what is your name?" I shout at Him.

"What have you done to me? Four and twenty blackbirds baked in a pie. Ask me no questions and I'll tell you no lies".

He glances at me every so often, but mostly He is looking toward the little imp as she sobs over her papa. He tries to comfort her with a thought, but I drag Him back to me as I shout.

"Rock a bye baby...

On the treetop."

It works. He glances at me, and I begin to leap through the fog wall. He holds up a hand like a claw, and I feel it squeezing my chest. It squeezes my heart, and I feel the muscle spasm. I fall to my knees.

The wall has collapsed, but I cannot move. I look up as He towers over me, pulsing His hand in the air around my heart, grimacing in discomfort. There is no joy in what He does, in the power He has. He regrets doing it. But He will kill me. He will do it to protect her—of that, I have no doubt.

He releases the claw on my heart and moves His hand to erect the wall. As soon as the death grip is released, I begin to shout out nursery rhymes again. The staff start to trickle in from different places around the house, finally noticing we are missing. No one sees Him, but I cannot get past Him to crush her little neck.

Lights

Police

Ambulance

I am taken away again for hysteria. Will no one understand that He is haunting me? I spend a long, long time away, drugged to distraction. I return home and find that Layla has been moved to another's care, and I am relieved. I am acquitted of murder charges by reason of insanity.

1991

Many years have passed, and I have neither seen nor heard from Layla. She is somewhere off the continent, and I am longing to see Him.

I return to Jamaica, find the shack, and wait for Him. He comes as expected, but He is older now, His eyes are no longer earthy brown nor pitch but a beautiful hazel, Caribbean water color. More evidence of my damaged mind, I notice, knowing the color of eyes doesn't change.

I felt a chill up my spine but continued to read.

1991 (cont.)

He offers me tea, and I accept. He is still beautiful but in a more mature way now. There is no sense of malice lingering about Him, and He begins to speak, the first time I can recall hearing His voice.

"Layla is well, if you care to hear of it," He says.

I don't really care, that spawn of some dark and terrible sorcery that I cannot and will not name.

"Adele, I made a terrible mistake all those years ago. I was young and angry, and I shall pay the price for my sin for as long as I live. Please forgive me," but I do not want to reply. I want Him to explain. He continues.

"I was filled with anger and envy for a British father who raped my mother and left her to raise me on her own. I could recount the difficult childhood of poverty I suffered, but you cannot hear it. I know what you really want. You want to know what happened. You want to know if I caused you to lose your mind."

No, I think, I want to know how I can kill them both.

Suddenly, He stops speaking and His eyes become black, the way I see them in my dreams. He can hear my intent and He understands. He leans forward in the chair across the small table in that one-room shack. He moves his hands to the table as if He is about to reach for me; but I recoil, knowing if He touches me I will be lost again. I jerk back so quickly that the chair slips, and I find myself on the floor. He jumps to help me, but I begin to scream.

"No, no, no, don't touch me! I will be lost...Go away.." all the while thinking, "yes, yes, please stay. Please lay your hand on me so that I can escape this thing called my mind."

What do I want? What do I want? What do I want?!!!!! My mind is so completely damaged I cannot remember why I came here. I am homicidal. I am suicidal. I am filled with His malice and His seed. I am an empty vessel. I pray for death, His death, my death, but most of all Layla's.

He has done this to me.

He has done this to me.

He has done this to me.

He has filled me with violence that I cannot contain.

You, you, you, I scream in my mind—you have done this to me.

You have created a monster, a monster who lusts after murder, who wishes death on her daughter.

I hear Him weeping, His hands covering His face while He stands near the doorway. He understands everything and nothing. I am ruined and stay on the floor where He leaves me. I hear Him as He leaves, whispering in my mind, "what have I done? What have I done?"

A short time later an older Island woman comes to me, helps me to a cot, and covers me with a blanket. I hear a tea kettle whistle. I sleep then and awaken in the dead of night. She is still there, sitting on the same plastic chair facing the water where I sat those years ago. I sit up and feel weak. I stand and walk to the sink in the kitchen to splash some water on my face. I join her in her silent meditation. She is humming to herself, a Jamaican tradition I know to keep the evil spirits away. Is she keeping Him away or is she exorcising them from within me? What is within me, I wonder?

Sunrise brings a little warmth. She makes a meal of fruit and bread. I nibble and drink the tea she offers. This ritual continues for weeks, I think, but I can't be sure; time is once again folding in on itself in this parallel universe. She hums through the nights, and the Jamaican sunrises greet us daily. Then one morning she begins to speak.

"Adele, I'm going to tell you a story. His father, like you, was an importer and didn't think about leaving a broken pregnant girl behind. It is an old story of exploitation and indifference. Shortly before you arrived, his mother died of some infection that could have been cured with a few of your shillings."

"He was in deep grief which was soon replaced with rage against that cruelty. His mother's family comes from a long tradition of witchcraft, but it wasn't clear if he had the gift. He was always very much to himself, and his mother didn't have time to teach him. Perhaps he felt it, but like any skill, it must be taught and practiced to bear wholesome fruit.

"That rage tore a seam in the fabric of his spirit in an explosion *of raw power. When he saw you in the hotel, I don't believe he understood what was exposed inside of his burning self. He chose you as the target for his revenge. You might think that you were in the wrong place at the wrong time. We don't believe in such things. The world works its seamless magic, with or without our cooperation. He couldn't have known or understood the terrible sequence of events he would trigger, but he did know right from wrong. His fury was blinding and the grief so great he wanted to do harm—harm that has stayed with you, it seems. It is a scar that will be difficult to remove.*

"*That terrible power he used to seduce you left its mark. He saw it when you returned on this visit, and I've seen it these past weeks. I am his mother's sister, and I noticed the change in him after his mother died. I began to spend time with him and discovered the depth of his skill until he confessed his terrible sin to me one day. I went to the elders, and they allowed him to live with a promise from me to guide him.*

"*He long ago surpassed my skills and begs for forgiveness at his mother's grave every morning. His remorse is as great as his rage all those years ago. When the elders heard about Layla, they demanded that she be brought to the island, fearing that she may also be marked like you. But he has protected her, wanting to redeem himself by providing her with the best life he can. He has been successful in business and has a guardian with Layla who is teaching her the righteous path. Soon she will be brought to the island under his protection, but first, she must make a journey. That journey will be her test, to determine once and for all if she can choose rightly in the face of horror.*

"*The elders are afraid that Layla has also been damaged by you and that she will lust for violence. He is sorry for all he has done to you, but truth be told, he is not sorry for Layla. She's inherited skills that no one has ever seen on the islands. We pray that the guidance she receives will be enough in her time of trial.*"

I am listening and thinking that they have it all wrong. Layla is an evil little demon. They can't think she is worthy. She is the spawn of dark magic.

"No, Adele, Layla is no demon. It is you who have attracted the demon by his spell. You must be rid of the demon."

"Get out of my head!" I scream at her.

She hums a lot and tries to get into my head, but I block her with a stream of nonsense nursery rhymes I repeat over and over. In between. I hear a voice whisper, "Kill, kill, kill the spawn. That's your only exit to peace, your only redemption from this twisted nightmare."

After several more weeks of this talk, He appears and looks tired. He talks to her quietly for a time and then we are sitting together on the sand.

"It seems that the damage I have done is beyond forgiveness, but I beg you to forgive me. If you must hate, let it be me. If you must kill, let it be me. But please let Layla grow up, and let me protect her. She shouldn't suffer for my sin."

Suddenly, I feel a rage born of envy. He loves her and pities me which makes me want to see her dead even more. There are no boundaries to my vengeance. I envision her little body covered in blood, as it was when she was born—the blood of my envy, the blood of my passion, and I dance into the water. This is how I will punish them both.

He is grabbing my upper arms and shaking me. "Adele, Adele, stop it! Stop it!"

The woman is there, moving Him gently away and I hear Him weeping again. Not for me, no He does not weep for me. He's weeping for his precious Layla. And my envy grows—I covet His love of her.

He is gone again. I spend more weeks with her, His aunt. I am not interested in moving anywhere to carry out my vengeance, but I cannot stay still. I spend hours exhausting myself—pacing along the beautiful sea as He once did.

He returns, and I finally ask his name,

"Marlow," he says.

My lover's name is Marlow.

What.

The.

Fuck.

I dropped the journal and managed to get a paper cut. I put the finger to my lips and tasted blood...not the usual copper salty tasting flavor I was accustomed to. It was sharp, tinged with her bloodlust. Marlow...Marlow?

Marlow! What. The. Fuck?! The blood tasted like sulfur, bitter and vile. I have tasted this before. I returned to finish the entry.

He begs me to forgive Him and His youthful misguided sins. He promises that He will protect Layla until his last breath.

Marlow, I think, I don't give a damn about Layla and I don't give a damn about you. No one knows she's my child, and I dissolve the adoption with a few carefully placed British pounds. I left and never saw Him or Layla again.

I felt sick in that stuffy attic, the room seeming to tilt a bit as I got up from the floor. I made my way downstairs. Marlow, Marlow...why did he keep this from me? Did he think I wouldn't discover the truth? Did he want me to discover the truth? "But then why would he send me here?" I was surprised to hear my own voice as I asked the question aloud. He didn't actually send me here. I came to the country house on my own. But he sent me to England. Was he hoping I would find out his role in Adele's life? Did he want it kept secret? Perhaps the estate had already been searched and no one found the journals. My mind was working on overload and I needed some rest.

I spent another full day in the attic while Oliver and Alice checked in on me every so often. I closed the journal, phoned the office, and left a message that I'd be staying for another day as I retired to a second night of disturbed sleep. I knew that the Executor was residing at the estate, but didn't see or hear of him. I also knew that he was Adele's advisor and confidante of long standing.

The next morning at breakfast as Alice was placing my food in front of me, I took a breath and let it go, willing any ill feelings I might have away. Yes, that was better...I lightly touched her arm, felt her startle.

"Alice, I'd like to see William today."

"I'm not sure that's possible, Mademoiselle."

"It's important. Please do your best." I needed a distraction and walked out onto the grounds through magnificent French doors. After some minutes, I found myself in the back garden and was grateful for the clothing that found its way to my room last night. Push-ups, sit-ups, leg-stretches, and a small run. Lastly, a quiet place between tall hedges for yoga.

After a long, hot shower, I returned to the gardens, knowing now that Adele had an heir. That I could find this person through Marlow was, frankly, confusing. Why on earth wouldn't Marlow have told me sooner? And he knew where the heir was...what was this game he was playing? While strolling stone paths, the precision of this garden layout became apparent to me, as did the genius that had gone into making the estate grounds seem entirely natural. *What a beautiful art form, the traditional English garden is*, I thought. Organic illusions by design. Just ahead appeared to be a wide clearing—it was a clear lake, unseen until almost at its shore. It was quiet and very beautiful, and I was no longer alone.

There suddenly appeared at the water's edge an old man in a wheelchair, stationed by the lake. His skin was nearly porcelain; even from a distance, the blue of his veins was evident, a crisscrossing road map visible on the backs of his hands. He was wearing black slacks and a button-down shirt, had long gray hair almost reaching his shoulders. The hair was damp. If not a swim, which seemed highly unlikely, he had perhaps come from a recent shower. No one else was in sight, and I wondered if he had an absent attendant. *The Executor*, I thought. Perhaps Alice had helped me after all.

"Good morning."

The old man looked up at me and nodded.

"How do you do, sir? My name is Sophia." I put out my hand to shake, and he raised his left hand, his right one useless at its side. It was an awkward introduction.

"Yes, I know who you are," he replied. "You've been rummaging around here twice now. Have you found what you are looking for yet?" His voice was crystal clear, unlike his partially broken body. I sat on a low wall, which wound its way around this walkway bordering the lake. I noticed that he set a book aside and realized the wall was a convenient height for his chair, a side table of sorts.

"No, I haven't. Perhaps you could help me? Are you Mr. William Spencer?"

"No and yes," he replied to my questions.

"And why is it that you cannot help me? I'm researching the family tree and…"

"I know quite well what you are doing, and I cannot help you, Sophia."

"But you must know something, Mr. Spencer."

"What leads you to believe that, Sophia?"

Wow—I recognized his voice when he said my name. But it was wrong. The name was wrong.

"You know my name."

It was a question and a statement all at once.

"Yes."

I felt something growing inside me and I knew I could make him answer me.

"What is my name, Mr. Spencer?"

He didn't want to answer me and resisted the pressure I applied to his will. He remained silent.

I picked up a nearby chair and moved it directly in front of him. I sat. With a steady gaze, I looked at him. His eyes, like his voice, were a sky blue—clear and sharp. He tried to move but he only had one good arm and the brake was engaged. I was not sure I wanted to ask my question again. "I know the answer, I know the answer," I heard myself chanting. But I needed it said aloud, to break the spell, to release the dam of confusion. I leaned in a little and turned his chair slightly toward me. I wouldn't even need to touch him. He wanted to unburden himself. I leaned in closer, our knees touching as we met each other's eyes in an intimate invasion of his privacy.

I repeated, humming in a soft voice, "What am I called, Mr. Spencer?"

"You are called many things—depending on who is in the know."

"But what do you call me, Mr. Spencer?"

He delayed, his one good hand clenching the arm of his wheelchair. He couldn't look away as his body jerked in spasm.

I hesitated, knowing this would be the end of his resistance. I looked away and noticed a bird alight from a tree. It was a beautiful day, and I marked this moment, imprinting the image in my mind's eye—the earthy brown and rust feathers of the tiny finch, its perfectly round, black eyes. The finch spread her wings as she popped from the branch. The branch bounced a bit as she disappeared into the white-blue silver-gray lavender sky. The sky was so many colors today, not the usual blue but all the colors that mark this particular vision of the horizon. I followed the bird until it disappeared from sight. I held onto the images, reluctant to return my attention to Mr. Spencer. I looked instead back to the tree at the end of its autumn disrobing. The remaining leaves were mostly gray, the vibrant fall cascade having faded just recently. *It's appropriate*, I thought, *this season to my work here. I am in the final moments before the death of winter.*

I knew that everything would change in the next few seconds. The seed of my will blossomed, reminding me of Gabriel's blood detonating into my white hand towel. Like the reckless child that I was, I let go of the tree, the sky, the finch. I turned back to him and murmured, "What am I called, Mr. Spencer?"

"Layla. Your name is Layla," he replied softly. My world turned on its axis...a different time and place...I hear someone calling my name.

"Layla, Layla...come to the cellar. Let's play until your Papa arrives! Layla, quick, you hide and I'll seek...Layla, where are you?"

A woman's hands on my arm, squeezing too tightly, her nails biting into my wrist. I look up but cannot see her. She whispers, "Layla, this is your place" as she drags me to a shed. It's dark and there are garden tools in it. She whispers, "Layla...Layla...devil's spawn of the night and in the darkest night you shall remain."

Mr. Spencer was an evil man and I slid off the wall and ran from that place, trying to block the onslaught of memory as he called out my name, laughing maniacally, "Layla, Laaaayyylaaaaa."

I raced to the house at full tilt in search of Oliver, calling out for him. I smashed right into his huge chest in the parlor and he grabbed my upper arms to steady me. I screamed in pain and he quickly let go.

"Sophia, what's happened?"

"Take me home, Oliver, please," I heard myself pleading with him.

"Sophia, relax," he began.

"Stop it, Oliver!" I shrieked and he held his tongue.

In the car, he tried to talk to me but I was frantic with

worry and dread. I was at DEFCON 4 and couldn't hear anything he's saying but bits of sentences.

"We'll be home shortly...want to stop for a bite to eat? Do you want to speak to Marlow?"

"No!" I screamed, "not Marlow! I don't want to hear his name right now. Oliver, who are you calling?"

"Sophia, let's stop and take a walk."

"Drive, Oliver, and stop talking!" I shouted at him, my panic released in a torrent of rage.

He was on the phone while my head was spinning like circus plates but nothing made sense. I saw images and heard people talking, but it was all mixed up. I was hallucinating— no, I was remembering. Distorted images flashed at me, fireworks of memory bursting and cracking in my bulging eyes —landscapes and faces. I saw my home in Northport, Long Island, superimposed on an estate of epic proportions, watchtowers along the exterior walls gaping down at me. I'm with Albert, walking the dock on the Long Island Sound and he's teaching me. I'm sweating profusely and shivering at the same time.

Albert's face was suddenly with me here and I heard him, a true pedagogue. We learned everything together, philosophy and biology. He took me to the Cold Spring Harbor Laboratory to study with geneticists and to the bluff to exercise, running up and down the sand cliffs every morning through all seasons. He taught me self-defense and offensive observation. He taught by example the art of compassion and love, seeking places to help those in need—a soup kitchen, a rehab center, and a hospital burn unit. And there he was instructing me to command my mind, my memory so that I didn't know until this moment that it was he who had taught me these skills.

Albert and my life with him were clearly mapped out before me. I was in a state of blinding fury—betrayed.

Betrayed

Betrayed

Betrayed

Betrayed by everyone. Betrayed by no one. I am no one. I am everyone that I have been trained to be. I am not an orphan as I had been led to believe. I have been used and coached for some ugly purpose. The fury grew inside of me until I felt like I could murder. I knew I could murder. I had been taught to murder. I will maul them all—Albert, Marlow, Gabriel. They are all playing some treacherous part in this murderous plot they have heaped upon my damaged mind. I was overcome with a desire to do harm. I could feel the lust for their blood expanding inside of me. It was a virus that began in my chest and expanded outward, the blood flow of its poison ignited my entire being.

He has done this to me.

He has done this to me.

He has done this to me.

I heard Adele's words over and over in my mind. I wanted to dance in the blood of my enemies.

As surely as He infected her spirit with His malice, so has He infected the very cells of my body with His poisonously violent seed. What folly to think He could undo the damage to her and to me.

He has done this to me, and I feel Adele's bloodlust swarming through me. As surely as she wanted to sate her fury with my death, I want to do the same to Him.

He has done this to me.

Betrayed—betrayed, I think. How could I not have known? How did I end up inhabiting two minds? How—how—how? Images cracked and flashed at me from all angles. In my fury, I could not make any of them out clearly.

I was back at that gargantuan estate—no, no, this estate! This estate—I was here before! That was me playing in the cellar with, with, oh, it's right there, around the corner. I was torn between an overwhelming urge to know and not know.

Oh my God, what will this mean? I think, fear gripping my chest, a doctor massaging the new heart of a patient, bringing it to life. The dead heart slowly starts to throb, the blood of memories pulsing through arteries until there is no turning back. The valves to chambers begin to open and close with each pulse, the doors to memory suddenly flooded in the vilest surges of blood.

I was staring out the window as we drove back to London, Oliver still keeping up a running chatter. I had never seen him this anxious, this solid wall of a man. He was frantic with the overwhelming energy of my own splintered mind. He checked the rearview mirror often; I could see his eyes jump into it with frequent glances. I peered from the window at him every so often. I tried to focus on a tree or the road, like a ballerina finding her spot to subdue vertigo. Panic seized me and my mind couldn't focus. The landscape whipped past and I needed to stop moving. I asked Oliver to pull over and he had barely stopped when I flung open the door to vomit. I stepped outside the car and landed on my knees, heaving everything out of my stomach. I was sitting on the gravel roadside, shivering until Oliver wrapped me in a blanket, a living ragdoll whose black button eyes see nothing of this landscape. We were on the shoulder of a country lane, the view lost in the tangled knot of disjointed images. A repeating loop of snapshot images continues to burn behind my pupils.

I saw Albert cutting daisies from our garden on Long Island, the pillared turn-off to the Moreaux family estate, the view of Gardiner's Bay from Sally's house, my Manhattan office, the tax driver's evil eyes, and Marlow...

Marlow jumping into and out of each frame like a movie badly edited. In my wrath, I was laser-focused on Marlow's face. It began to transform, like a candle melting, losing shape, molding into something else. His head turned until I was looking through his melting eyes from behind, and I saw a group of men in a mountain cottage—cold. I clutched at the blanket, pulled it tighter, and saw the strangers step outside to build a fire. Now I recognized the acrid smell—the burning orange peels of cannabis. Warming up by the fire, they smoked ganga, while they talked about...me!

Who are they? Why is Marlow with them? What do they want with me? How can I see them? The avalanche of questions and confusion threatened to suffocate me as Marlow felt my presence and tried to force me out. No—no you don't —you, YOU brought me here. I am reminded of my fury and the peaceful image quickly morphed into images of me mauling him. I was clawing at his face with the fury of the she-bear and the curiosity of a bystander. I saw the slashes appear along his cheeks and the blood seeping out, running scarlet down his cheeks. I understood now what power and savagery I was capable of. I turned my back on his scarred and bleeding checkered face.

Oh, I understood Adele's hopeless desire for vengeance.

I threw off Oliver's blanket, got up, and began to walk, hoping the movement would settle my roiling stomach, but I couldn't hit a pace. I tried to breathe consciously, but I gasped and then found myself holding my breath. I began to run, then moved into a sprint, racing at breakneck speed across an open field. I was flying like a gazelle fleeing a tiger until I collapsed. The tiger was my mind and I could not escape her charge.

Oliver had kept this brutal pace a short distance behind me, but he lifted me with little effort, while I wheezed and gasped for breath. He carried me back to the town car and leaned me against it while he retrieved two folding chairs from the trunk. He sat and I joined him as he handed me a bottle of water. He was silent as the breeze in the field before us. I closed my eyes. The onslaught began again but this time, not moving, I was watching a movie, a hallucinating head case. We sat for a minute, a half-hour, I couldn't gauge the time.

I found myself thinking of Albert—the other Albert—only

recently revealed to my waking self...Albert shocking me with a Taser until I could convert its pain into a pleasant experience. Albert taking me to vacant warehouses at night, instructing me to memorize every detail until I could recall every crack in a windowpane. Albert bringing me to a meeting with ten people and making me find my way home in the dark. When I arrive, there is no comfort to greet me but a blitz of questions about the people who were there...what each wore, what the conversations were, the rooms of the house, the exits and threats.

Albert dropping me in the middle of New York City with little more than my wits and no money to find my way back home. As fatherly and kindly as the Albert of my eight-year-old memories, this Albert is a brutal drill sergeant. He never raises his voice or his hand to me, but there are many ways to bend a mind to a task, ways I do not want to revisit.

I heard Oliver breathing. I opened my eyes and realized that my breath had settled. I saw the field, a small farmhouse in the distance, some trees, a cloud. It was late in the afternoon, and this beautiful blue-sky day was a mournful contrast to my blackened mind and heart.

"That's it, Sophia, settle yourself," he said quietly.

"Who were you talking to—before, in the car?" I asked.

He didn't reply but turned his gaze to the green expanse before us.

"Oliver, I won't ask again," a simple, calm statement.

"Marlow," he replied.

We didn't make eye contact but both continued to look straight ahead.

"Is that who you report to? Do you work for the firm or him?" I snapped but worked to keep my head calm.

"I work for the firm and Marlow, Sophia."

"I'd like you to call him and tell him I'm fine. I don't want to see or speak to him now, Oliver."

"I can't do that, Sophia."

"You can and you will, Oliver," I replied, my courage fueled by rage, increasing by the second.

"Sophia..." he began.

"No. No, you don't...no 'Sophia.' " I interrupted him, looked him full in the face, and repeated, "Oliver, I said you will call Marlow and tell him all is well. It was a false alarm—that I had a little episode but am now fine."

Oliver's eyes were a little unfocused as he tried to look beyond me to a point over my shoulder. I was starting to swell with a feeling I could not name—not exactly anger but something that I knew would direct him. I knew instinctively that I could not plead or persuade. But I could command. It came to the surface, and I said again in a singsong hum, "Oliver, you will call Marlow and tell him I've had a rest and am fine." I found that I was repeating myself often today, practicing, tasting my new words. Albert did not teach this to me. But he knew of it.

I watched as he pulled his cell phone from his pocket and repeated my words verbatim to Marlow. I was calm and not at all surprised. We packed the chairs as the sun was setting and headed back to the estate. I wanted to return to the country house, and Oliver knew as much without my having to say so.

We arrived at the estate where James and Alice welcomed us as if expecting our return. Alice informed me that dinner would be at 7:30. I showered and I supposed that Oliver did the same. There were more clean clothes in my size laid out on the four-poster bed that Alice had thoughtfully provided, and I noted...even the right size panties and bra. I put on the clothes and sat down on a rocker near the window, brushing my damp hair.

Immediately, the hallucinations began again...bouncing a ball with Albert, no—I am playing in the cellar here in England with a young girl whose name I cannot recall, near my age. Albert speaking quietly on the phone late at night while I pretend to sleep; the family crest on Marlow's neck, on the wooden doors, downstairs. I am at Orient Point once more, then lying in the grass, reliving Sally's episode. Adele's oversized distorted face is here now, nose to nose with mine, spitting and spewing hateful words...but Adele, Adele I resist. I do not turn my eye to see her, for that would surely slay me. Instead, I focus my attention on all that has happened since then.

I stood and stared out the window, moved the curtains aside, leaned my cheek against the cool windowpane, and tried to breathe. I knew in an instant of searing and total horror that the torture shed was just there, down there where all that is left is a cement slab.

"Breathe, Sophia, breathe," I chanted to myself. I followed Albert's meditation and emptied my mind, found the void, and forced myself to move that terror into a place I could not reach. I headed down for dinner. Just below the surface, the panicked shadow of myself waited for a crack in the psyche to emerge. I suppressed her desire to devour me, ignoring the rage of "blackbirds baked in a pie," and held onto my sanity by the weakest thread of frayed cotton fiber.

I took the steps to the dining room slowly, uncertainly, wanting instead to submerge my entire being in a hot, hot bath, until it burned, my skin sloughing off the agony of this mind I could not escape. Could I sit at table now? No, I could not sit at table at this moment; turning back around, I measured my steps to the bedroom and locked the door, stripping down to a tank top and panties, the heat of the imagined bath scorching my skin. I went back to the windows, as I watched the moon climb and descend through the first night of my torment.

The giant paned windows projected the images of two lives for the long hours of this night. I clenched my hands around the heavy floor-to-ceiling Bordeaux draperies, twisting and pulling on them while I stared out the window through the endless hours, reliving the nightmare that was my life. I watched the black panes of the glass as I would a movie theater's screen, but the plot was in disjointed pieces. I saw myself in places I had never been, hallucinations without memory. I twisted and wrapped and tugged on the draperies. I continued to move slowly, the draperies winding around me like a snake coiling over my arms, my neck, my torso. The plaster gave way, the rods fell out and crashed onto the floor. I was weighed down heavily, heavenly, by the sensual fabric, until I was on the floor, buried under the weight of them. It was the wrappings that bound me together, keeping me anchored.

I was eternally grateful that the strangers downstairs left me in peace to wrestle with the demons of my mind alone. I remained on the floor, staring out the window at the setting moon, and was only vaguely aware of Oliver's footsteps entering the room. I was mummified in the draperies as he lifted me with the fabric and gently placed us in the bed, the draperies encasing me like the arms of a vicious lover. I liked the feel of the wrappings—keeping my body together—the tightness around me ensuring that I wouldn't break into the millions of little pieces that were the splinters of my brain.

Oliver sat in the rocker near the window, and I finally fell asleep to the rhythm of his conscious breathing.

Another day passed.

Oliver unwrapped my coiled fabrics and helped me to the toilet. I returned to see the piles of drapes on the floor. He removed the rods. I bent and grabbed hold of the edges, the edges of my sanity in the tightly woven fabric, and started the viewing and the wrapping again. The draperies were a heavy crimson velvet, the dense hairs comforting in the tight grasp of my fingers. Oliver watched as I stared out the window, my head moving from pane to pane, trying to organize the bits of brain matter splattered there. Disjointed images snapped and popped, exploding in the panes, some of them moving videos, others distorted snapshots of disconnected moments in time.

The twisting and wrapping continued until I collapsed under the weight again.

Alice brought tea and toast that I could not eat. Oliver coaxed some water into me. The hallucinations continued. I was not yet desensitized to the splintered memories. They accosted me over and over again. Oliver offered a pill, Alice offered food, but I declined both with a violent shaking of my head, mute and battered as I was. Oliver remained. I could see him with my eyes open and closed, while I was awake and while I slept. He was there all the time, even when he was somewhere else. I felt him with me, tethering me to some tangible pier, the dense mass of his being anchoring me to place, if not time.

Another day passed—three days—and I was again grateful that they left me in peace for the most part.

I needed to eat.

Ah, my first conscious, active thought. I have succumbed to my weakest nature, allowing a horror to seize me and control me as long as it cared to...as long as I allowed it. What an ugly commentary on my feeble state.

On the third day, she rose again—I was suddenly curious. On the third day, my mind started to ask questions. And the mind will have what the mind wants. I found the strength to shower again, and I finally joined the company of strangers for dinner.

IS IT JUSTICE THAT YOU REALLY WANT?

*D*inner was a household affair—me, Oliver, James, Alice, and Mr. Spencer were all seated. It felt like a choreographed scene from a drawing-room play that has been rehearsed for a very long time, perhaps all my life. We were at a table that was much too large for us. I was surprised to see Alice and James, the servant help who wouldn't even greet me with a handshake, joining us.

Of course, in my ignorance, I thought it was deferential that James wouldn't shake my hand. But it was fear—they were long ago warned not to touch me. It could incite pain or memory. But was there no pleasure to be had in my touch? Ever?

Albert touched me, I think. I was trying to remember our time together and if we ever touched—my fond memories of him lead me to believe he was a tender caretaker. But, did we touch? We walked, hiked, played games; we talked daily, but did we touch? Yes—the day I arrived, we made that lovely hand-over-hand promise. Was that the last day I was safe? This was a question I could not answer, strange as it was, considering all I do remember of Albert. Albert, Albert, my steadfast rock. I was now reliving our life together from a new lens.

Was I, was Sophia, ever loved? He named me I think, all those years ago, the day I sat on the swing in our yard. Why had Albert committed all those years of his life, perhaps sacrificing a family or friends of his own? Or maybe he was simply an employee committed to molding me into...some aberration for someone else's purposes. I am most betrayed by him. I picked up my steak knife from my table setting, ran my fingers along its edge, and put it back down. Albert filled my mind...he had given me tools to survive this awful reality. What did he think in all this? Where was he from? How did he come to be the one to train me? Does it even matter? It was most likely I'll never see him again. As he came into my child's life, he now disappeared like an apparition that I'll never be sure was really there. I was unfolding the napkin at my place setting, weaving it in and out of my fingers unconsciously. I noticed the table and its accouterments. The table was covered in a white linen tablecloth. Each setting had a delicately embroidered cream lace placemat. The napkins were held in place by pearl beaded circles, a spray at the tip embellished with the embroidered "M." Two clear small vases were filled with white roses and purple tulips to match the gentle lavender bouquet on the cream-colored china.

"Let us begin," Mr. Spencer said. He had seen my expression soften, my mind settling into the room, and directed his question at me.

"What would you like to be called?"

I was silent and didn't know the answer. I felt strong three days ago with Oliver. But now I was unsure of myself. I didn't know what I wanted to be called. Did I want to be named at all?

Mr. Spencer waited patiently. He was serene and measured in his waiting; there was no pressure for me to find an answer. I closed my eyes and contemplated his question without thinking. I found the void and also waited.

My mind drifted to the significance of a name. I recalled a lesson with Albert. I recalled the fucking lesson verbatim. A name defines the essence of a thing or a person. In ancient times, names had meaning. Both my names were derived from ancient tongues.

Layla, the name my father gave me, meant night in Hebrew and Arabic. I didn't know where this knowledge came from, but I was sure to find out sooner or later. In painfully ironic contrast, Sophia was the Greek word for wisdom...Sufi, the eastern mystic, came from the same root.

At the moment I feel dark as night, betrayal assaulting
*   me,*
invading every pore,
every fiber,
of who and how I am.

It was an unholy joke that my new name was imbued with ideas of righteousness and insight. The name plan was so transparent and demeaning I almost wanted to choose Layla as a lesson to them all. In their treachery, they may have recreated exactly the monster they hoped to avoid; a creature of the night torture shed, I have been cursed with profane wisdom.

The lies battered the inside of my skull until I felt the monster again. My eyes flashed open thinking about Albert and his fucking lessons about names and ancient tongues— teaching me pertinent roots, fucking prefixes, and fucking suffixes of Greek and Hebrew and Latin.

I closed my eyes again and sought the empty space. My

mind interrupted the attempt to choose a name for itself...still twisting in upon itself, unable to capture any stillness in the maelstrom. Minutes passed. I opened my eyes and saw Mr. Spencer, Oliver, Alice, and James all in quiet contemplation. They were waiting, each in his own thoughts, perhaps thinking this was the moment I would choose a name for myself and all it represented. I was not ready, not ready, not ready, the dark anger of betrayal keeping me from insight.

Mr. Spencer interrupted the silence. "May I suggest Sophia for the moment?" he asked.

I nodded my head, grateful for his kindness. Perhaps he was not so wicked...was I really hearing his laugh in the garden? Alice left the table and then returned to ladle a light vegetable broth. We ate quietly. I consumed very little, testing my stomach, making a mental note that I must maintain my strength. It wouldn't do for me to be sick. So I trucked through the meal, forcing myself to eat more than I really wanted to.

No one tried to make small talk. It was not a table for small talk this evening. It was a welcome respite as we enjoyed an unhurried dinner. After eating, I got up and walked out the doors onto the great terrace overlooking the gardens in the back of the house. Oliver quietly accompanied me into the dark. The smell of rotting leaves, musky and mushroomy, entered on an inhalation, seeping into my limbs. I breathed deeply of the soothing lozenge to my weary mind.

"How are you feeling?" Oliver asked me. He paused, avoiding the use of a name.

"Confused and tired," I replied.

"What can I do for you?" he asked.

"Just keep me company, Oliver. I like having you nearby. I'm usually fine by myself, but for now, you are a very welcome companion."

Oliver did just that. He didn't pepper me with questions or idle talk, as we strolled the gardens. He didn't ask about the side of the house I avoided, never questioned why I was retracing steps. We returned to the house and met Alice and James in the parlor. This was a very comfortable, inviting space. In the country house, there were rooms for every occasion and more than one for entertaining. This one was filled with oversized couches and chairs, thick with cushions, reminding me of a mountain lodge. The walls were covered in mahogany wood, and a stone hearth dominated half a wall. Area rugs were scattered about in all the natural earth tones of a country home.

Alice set out tea and sweet cakes. I asked for a cognac. James sat at the piano and started fiddling with a little tune. Mr. Spencer read a book. This could be a rendition of a still life 1700's classical parlor scene if only Alice and I were wearing dresses and the gentlemen sporting curly wigs. I tried to imagine burly Oliver in a wig and chuckled to myself.

I sat with my cognac and Oliver started a fire. It was all so very civilized, I observed with a menacing detachment. I reflected on the details of this English country house in its elegance, and I considered the damaged fiend within. It was the irony of public disembowelment before cream tea and crumpets. It was the southern belle in her hoop skirt presiding over the whipping of her slave girl. I was anxious about the wrath simmering below the surface of myself; part of me wanted to contain it, while another wondered what I could do with it. This newly-discovered power was seductive to me, most especially now, at this time when I felt so vulnerable.

I sipped on the cognac and felt it warming my core. It began in my chest and radiated outward all the way to my fingertips and toes. The fire and the drink began to remove the chill I had been feeling for days, although I hadn't noticed until this moment that I've been cold.

James continued to play a melody I recognized. He was slow and tentative at first, tapping out a haunting rendition of Beethoven's "Moonlight Sonata." I finished my cognac and

Alice refilled it. I kicked off my shoes and curled my feet up on the sofa. Everyone visibly relaxed, sensing I was calmer.

Oh, right, they are afraid of me. Oh shit, they are afraid of me. Oh well, they are afraid of me. Well, I'm fucking afraid of me too, so we can swim in our fear together.

The cadences of James' playing were tinkling in the background. The tempo increased with the piece, and I was enjoying the moonlight dance over the keys. Oliver poked the fire. Alice sipped tea and Mr. Spencer joined me with a cognac of his own. No one offered him help as he moved from his wheelchair to the couch. His spasmodic movements were a painful contrast to the music that James so expertly played. The Executor settled in next to me with his book and Alice set his snifter within reach. She did so almost absent-mindedly, reminding me of Phillip moving James' beer out of reach. I let the music in as the cognac washed over me and through me. I didn't try to calm my mind. I didn't try to do anything. I heard the pages turning of Mr. Spencer's book.

I remember something I once read...

Fear is the mind-killer. Fear is the little-death that brings total obliteration. I will face my fear. I will permit it to pass over me and through me. And when it has gone past, I will turn the inner eye to see its path. Where the fear has gone, there will be nothing. Only I will remain.

Dune—it was from the book Dune. I read it twice, Senior year in high school and in a Sophomore elective in college. Huxley got it right. The fear slipped from my core somewhere between the whispers of turning pages accompanied by Beethoven.

I awakened lying on the couch on my side, my hands in prayer under my cheek, the embers of a dying fire gently illuminating the parlor. Oliver was sleeping on the floor in front of the hearth, an arm's length away from me. Someone, likely Alice, had covered us both with blankets. I could see the outline of Oliver's body by the light of the embers. He slept on his topless back with his head resting in his laced hands, the lower half of his body covered. He was the king in his dreams, his mocha torso a solid mass of muscle. He was a beautiful man, soft and strong. I wondered about him and his story, from childhood to our workplace. Tears spilled from my eyes in my sudden affection for him. I was grateful that he was here with me. I raised my elbow and propped my face against my hand. I wondered if he had any treachery in him. "No," I whispered. I was confident this man was not treacherous at all. He was a good protector and I rather felt like I needed a protector. I didn't want to need a protector but I was weak with a deep ache and filled with gratitude for him. My aching was as bewildering as my rage.

Oliver opened his eyes and turned his face toward me. He was aware of any change in the atmosphere around him, and I was again thankful that he was here. He smiled a crooked smile, raising his eyebrows to question my tears. I shrugged my shoulders and grimaced back at him. We remained that way for a few minutes. I could feel that he'd like to comfort me, but both of us know it's grief. There was no comfort for grief except time and the presence of a quiet companion.

Oliver was someone who could sit in a hospital waiting room or a funeral parlor with the patience of one who has experience with grief. I tried to guess at his age, but he wore it well. Then I realized that it didn't matter. Age did not bless us with wisdom or experience of grief. Circumstances and heart did. This I was sure about Oliver—his had been a life with its share of heartache. He had learned to expect nothing and everything.

He moved from the floor at the same time as I sat up on the couch. Joining me on the couch, he fearlessly wrapped his big arms around me and I felt safe against the warmth of his naked chest. The tears continued to spill over silently. We sat for the next hours until the sun slowly began to dissipate the darkness. Oliver dozed off but his loose arms continued to cradle me. I recalled the five stages of grief, another lesson from Albert. I struck out at his lesson and banished him from my thoughts. He was an interloper here in this intimate moment.

Oliver woke with the morning light that scattered throughout the parlor. Sunlight shimmered off a piece of brass near the fireplace, a frame of a painting, a pen on a writing table. The parlor was filled with morning's gold and bronze. I knew it was beautiful, the morning light that danced in this space, but I could not find pleasure in it. My spirit was sad, I realized, unloved and unwanted.

"Of course you are loved, Sophia."

Every

one

is

loved."

Oliver stated plainly, my thoughts invading his mind. And I knew it to be true. Oliver loves. He even loves me, I noted with a start. He smiled at that, nodded in agreement. I would like to choose love, I thought. Maybe one day, but not just now.

Now I wanted vengeance.

I was reminded that my thoughts could slip into other people's heads when I was not on guard. It was something that Layla knew. Something that Albert taught Sophia to hide. It occurred to me that Gabriel may have trapped me in the cellar on our recent visit by the waxing light of my own lustful thoughts.

Except for that one evening with the help of cognac and the three sleepless nights before, it was difficult for me to sleep during my time at the country house. I tossed and turned in the blankets, entangling myself until I escaped the straightjacket of my own doing. Oliver and I shared a large room with two four-poster queen beds at either end. In the dead of night, each night, I disentangled myself and wandered the halls of the obscenely grand chateau. My black-faced angel would find me and follow. Mostly, we ended up back in the parlor, Oliver stoking a new fire, both of us eventually finding our rest on the floor before the flames. Alice took to leaving blankets and pillows in the parlor after a couple of days.

We spent days wandering the four wings inside when it rained or through the gardens when it didn't. Mr. Spencer was an eager companion in the gardens. A devoted bird watcher, he took great pains to introduce me to the native English fauna.

The country house, deep in Oxfordshire, was rich with water and land fauna. Mr. Spencer likened the birds to individuals. His favorite had changed with time, he told me. It was now the great egret, graceful in the extreme, movement he lacked since his stroke. I learned about the birds—his lessons an intellectual distraction from the labors of my fractured mind.

Spencer was not the demented old Executor I had been led to believe he was. Occasionally, he lost his train of thought but not often. I later learned that his manic shrieking that first day was a reaction to my invasion of his weakened mind. During the second week, one day we were sitting outside after lunch.

"Sophia, do you remember me?"

I looked into the man's face, unable to recall him except as a most intangible hidden reminder of someone I must have once known, a shadow of a memory. The pause must have been answer enough.

"Adele's neighbor to the south was my employer. I shuttled her daughter here to visit with you often." He was crumpling a handkerchief in his hand while I tried to dredge up a memory. His mention of a friend excited me—there was a whisper of a memory somewhere, but I couldn't quite grab hold of it.

"Oh, Mr. Spencer, what was her name?"

"Renee."

The name did not trigger any memory, but there were chasms still unexplored in my new mind. I had been working to organize my memories, but it was an excruciating, painful, and slow process. The pain was physical as well as emotional —I suffered caustic headaches while awake and disturbing dreams in piecemeal sleep. Renee and wherever she fit in was a great void. I was sure she was the girl I saw in my mind that day in the root cellar with Gabriel, but there was nothing more. I sighed in frustration but felt no urgency at the moment to know more. I was more interested in Mr. Spencer.

"Hmmm, are there any photos of you in the house?"

"Perhaps. You can bring some of the boxes from the attic, and we'll look them over. Renee was your only friend outside of school. You were eager to see her, not interested in her driver as a little girl, I'm sure." He smiled while contemplating that past. It seemed to stir some pleasant memories.

"What did you do for Renee's family?"

"I was the caretaker of their estate."

"How did you end up here?"

"Well, it began innocently enough with Alice providing me with a bite to eat on our frequent visits. We got on well, you see, and eventually, we were married. After the old caretaker here passed on, I gladly filled the post."

"No offense, Mr. Spencer, but how did you, the caretaker, evolve into the Executor of a multimillion-dollar international estate?"

"Adele's husband and I were about the same age when I arrived here." He rolled his chair over to the French doors. "It was an unlikely friendship that developed between us. When I took the post, he was actively looking for someone to look after you and his estate. Adele had been struggling with her madness for several years by then. I took it upon myself to look after things. About two years after my arrival, he died." The old man shook his head. "A tragedy, that was. I still miss my dear friend. He was a good man."

I recalled his grisly death in Adele's writing and shivered at the thought of those who had lost him, myself included. But I didn't feel anything in my own memory. I was quite still, breathing steadily, but nothing stirred. My memory had been suppressed by me or hijacked by Adele's overwhelming emotional bloodlust. Mr. Spencer had turned to face me and was watching me carefully.

"Shortly after Adele's husband died, I was called to his solicitor's office and told that he had appointed me as Trustee for Adele and Executor of his estate. Neither of them had any family, you see. You do understand that all of this," he waved an arm, "is yours."

"Um, no. I hadn't thought about it."

"Well, there's no need to linger on it now either. When you're ready, Sophia, we can discuss the management of the properties."

I remained at the country house for some more days, maybe a week or more—unaware of the amount of time that was passing. I didn't call the firm, knowing that someone had taken care of it. It could be Oliver or James or Marlow, any one of them. I didn't really care. It was such an afterthought, that silly job of mine. That silly job that seemed so prestigious and important became a footnote in my world. In fact, it was a footnote in the world at large, as well.

I aimed to sort through memories in a new context. Fury had subsided, transformed into a rage until it was dulled into an undercurrent of steady anger. Oliver kept me company, and I tried to learn from him. I tried to learn to let go of the past and not worry about the future. But this present was so mixed up with new and old memories, teasing me or tasering me, depending on the day, from behind different curtains in my mind. Some days were agonizing, sweat dripping from my forehead as I tried to sketch out drawings of events on scratchpads. I desperately wanted to understand, having lived in two separate minds for so long. More importantly, I started to believe that it was urgent for me to unravel my own mind, urgent in the sense of my physical and mental safety.

I thought that I wanted to be like Oliver, living so completely present that sometimes I resented him. Then I remembered that it was likely the consequence of a life lived hard. And I was angry at my childish self, wanting to rise above such petty emotions. Oliver was a good man. I wanted to wish well for him, not envy his present living.

Betrayed was what I am left with—I swam in it—literally swam laps in the beautiful indoor swimming pool. I swam twice a day. I woke up one morning and headed to the pool dressed in a bathing suit, towel thrown over my shoulder. The water was autumn cold, but I was immune, another consequence of Albert's first-rate training. I began a measured stroke and it continued for hour after hour, the persistent repetitive motion, hand overhead, head tipped to the side, take a breath, face in the water, other arm out. Kicking my feet, back and forth, back and forth, trying to empty my mind. Trying to eradicate all thoughts. But I was so adept at this stroke, I didn't need to concentrate on the movements; they were accomplished without thought, like breathing.

It occurred to me that so much of what I could do physically was muscle memory—learned at Albert's hands. Those hands revisited me in all their twisted contradictions, becoming a tableau of tenderness and discipline. The image of his hands transformed in my mind, weaving a tangled web of love and pain.

I was swimming and remembering Albert, walking along the shores of the Long Island Sound in all weather, while I swam laps parallel with the gentle tide, hour after hour. I was returned to a physical action that was graceful and meaningless. Perhaps this moving through water was taught, the practice supervised from a distance, as a refuge, for when I was overloaded with emotion that could not be contained.

Albert made me swim when it was cold until the water began to feel warm to me. He helped me to change every physical discomfort into a comfort, changing my thoughts about exhaustion, pain, even an irritating itch, until...it became my new sensation. Like...a Taser that becomes the warm tides of sand dunes, moving along a great desert, like a tide on an ocean...until my mind was accustomed to converting pain into comfort.

I am betrayed.

Am I betrayed?

Oh, fucking Albert had taught me to question all my presumptions and thoughts. Or was I protected...from myself and others?

Was I the evil spawn of Marlow's cruelty? Could I change my nature? What was my nature? Was it molecular? Why had he brought me here? I didn't find many answers here, but I did adapt to the new sensations. I could now recall both lives without getting dizzy. I could put some of the memories in chronological order, parallel to each other. But it was backbreaking work, this effort to untie the knotted weave of my mind.

I often tried to read from the vast collection in the library but found it difficult to concentrate. I could have lost myself in a trashy romance, but there was no such reading material to be found. Instead, I read a familiar favorite, *To Kill a Mockingbird*. Now I questioned whether it was my favorite or Albert's.

Revisiting my old friend, the small-town attorney, Atticus Finch, I fell in love with him all over again. He was my muse in my chosen profession. Oh, how I longed to be a whole person like Atticus; I longed to be that self-assured character, unflappable in my convictions, true to my love for all humanity. I loved Atticus so much it brought tears to my eyes, even after all these years. I examined what it was about Atticus that so moved me to my core. I could not pinpoint any one particular feature of the character—there were so many. He was modest and kind. But he was a fierce advocate, one with a commitment to justice. He was unmoved by hatred, intimidation, fear. He marched steadily into a frightening night and emerged as a great role model not only for his children but for ordinary folk, rich and poor, black and white. He fought what he knew was a losing battle, but fought nonetheless. I wondered if Albert shelved this book in our home library to influence my career choice...or if he felt his work with me was a losing battle.

But the injustice that reigned in the end no longer squared with my desires for justice in the real world. *I want more justice*, I thought. It was after a full day of musing on justice that Mr. Spencer greeted me poolside. He wheeled in and waited as he had at our first meal together. Once I got out of the pool, I joined him at a table set with tea.

"Do you want justice, Sophia?"

I was no longer surprised by the invasion of my thoughts into other minds. I supposed I'd have to learn to moderate that particular skill. I nodded my head in answer to his question. I felt a lecture coming and for a second I was reminded of Albert and reacted poorly, frowning. Mr. Spencer lifted his eyebrows and waited, giving me a chance to curb my irritation. I took one ujjayi breath and was grateful that Albert had taught me this art. I forced a patient smile despite myself.

"Ah, there you are, Sophia," Mr. Spencer commented on my smile.

"We were discussing justice. Your training as a lawyer has likely corrupted your grasp of its essence. Are you a victim seeking retribution?"

"I don't like to think of myself as a victim, Mr. Spencer. But I am angry at having been wronged so thoroughly."

"Why do you think you've been wronged?"

"Are you sure this Socratic dialogue won't corrupt our discussion?" I countered with a smirk, enjoying the intellectual exercise.

"How have you been wronged?" he asked without engaging in my attempt to distract him.

"Well, for one I have been lied to."

"Who lied to you?"

"Where shall I begin? Albert for one, then..."

He interrupted my recitation. "How did Albert lie to you?"

"He made me believe I was someone I was not."

"Really? How could a person do that to someone else? How could that occur without a willing participant?"

"I was an eight-year-old child," I replied calmly.

"Sophia, were you ever an eight-year-old child?" He waited, then added, "what would you consider to be just for Albert?"

"He should be punished for what he inflicted on me."

"What did he inflict?"

"A Taser for one."

"What would be an appropriate punishment? Should he be Tasered to feel its burn himself? Would that type of punishment seem fair to you?"

I was distressed at the thought of my beloved Albert being Tasered, and I immediately and protectively defended him.

"Of course not! " I replied.

"But why not, Sophia? Why wouldn't you want Albert to feel the same pain he inflicted on you?"

"He had a purpose for his actions. The thought of him coming to harm is upsetting to me, even though I am furious with him right now."

"Oh, how much harder must it have been for Albert then, to use a Taser on someone whom he loved so dearly for a purpose she couldn't begin to understand."

"You know, Mr. Spencer, Albert and I have had the justice discussion on many occasions. We've touched on all its components, including moral justice and legal justice, fairness, and equity. I don't think there is much more we can discuss."

"But we're not discussing an abstraction, Sophia. We're talking about you and your injured mind and broken heart."

I turned away from his penetrating attention as tears filled my eyes. I was touched by his personal comment. It was easier to be short-tempered just now. It was all so preposterous, this idea of justice. I was just sad and wanted someone to pay for making me sad. I felt used and manipulated and wanted someone to take it back—take the splintered bits of myself—and 'unuse' me and 'unmanipulate' me. I was thinking like a spoiled child, only about me, me, me, and my pain. Of course, I knew there was no going back. I could not now unknow the horrors that had been revealed. I thought of Albert taking that awful step of Tasering me, like a parent smacking a child who runs in the street.

"If it's true that Albert really loved me, then his actions were a great expression of self-sacrifice." I turned my attention to the flowers in the greenhouse.

"Do you doubt Albert's love for you?"

"Yes—he was not much more than a personal trainer for my body and mind."

"Your anger muddles what you know to be true, Sophia."

"I'm sure it does, Mr. Spencer. Incidentally, the name no longer works, so it's not necessary to use it so often. I know my name—I know them all, even if you don't. If you'll excuse me, I think I'll go put on some dry clothes now."

It was mostly a pleasant break, my time at the country house. It was the clichéd stay in the country for the pitiful woman who suffers from hysteria. The hysteria was treated with the quiet contemplation of nature's rhythmic breath and a stiff drink or two in the evening—exactly what I needed. We ate together twice a day, mornings at the counter in the kitchen and evenings in the dining room. We were content for the most part, we five companions. It would have been nice to remain indefinitely in this suspended animation of time and place.

But I sensed it was time for me to return to London.

A ROOFTOP REUNION

I headed back to London, my thoughts wandering to Gabriel for the first time in weeks. Although his anxiety about my whereabouts had lately crept into my dreams, in my self-absorbed state of mind, I had not found a generous moment to call him. I thought it was cruel that I didn't call him. I knew I was cruel, like my mother before me, like my father before her.

I finally called now on my way back to London and asked him to meet me for tea. I could hear the relief in his voice when he picked up the phone.

"Sophia, so nice to hear from you."

"How about a cup of tea, Gabriel? I'll be in town in about an hour."

"That sounds splendid."

We settled on a small café far from the office. I was nervous, wondering if he would notice any changes in me. I didn't want to let on that I'd been...that I'd been...what had I been?

I had been unmade, reformed, for a time barely maintaining my sanity, poring over memories and organizing them in my mind and on paper, trying to create a coherent story that I could understand.

What had I been? I'd been ravaged from the inside out. I'd been ravaged from the outside in. I was far from stable, great gaps still yawning in my memories. There were many that I actively suppressed, having no desire to revisit the one who would kill me. I was still so fragile that a pinprick could shatter the delicate psyche, the bits of glass shredding me to pieces. I didn't want him to see this needy weakened shadow of myself. Nor did I want him to see the parts that frightened Alice and James. I started to have second thoughts about our tea as I was walking toward the café.

As soon as I saw Gabriel waiting outside on the sidewalk, I was reminded of my attraction to him and dismissed any misgivings about him seeing me. I picked up my pace to get to him sooner. It was an awkward greeting, both of us wanting more than a handshake and settling for even less, a nod and a hello. Gabriel opened the door for me and we were quickly seated. He was sitting across from me and my gaze was drawn to his lips as if there had been no interruption these past weeks since our last lunch together. It was as if our time together was separate from the rest of the world spinning madly on. I thought of Adele and her lust. I found pity in my heart for that worship of hers, my worship—on this rather ordinary Wednesday in this quiet London café. I could hear my heart thumping.

The hunger will drive me mad if I do not feed it soon. I can't even remember what I wanted to talk to Gabriel about. I was the heroin addict, completely and exhaustively focused on the relief that I think those lips will bring me if he would only give them to me...give them to me. Give them to me. Let me have my way with those soft, full lips. I wanted to wrap my lips around them and move with his. I knew I must talk to him about something important, but his nearness drove me to distraction. I could not stop the ebb and flow of my desire, the demons returning with the adrenalin sprinting through my body. I tried to think, but there was no cogent thought in my brain. I thought of no one and nothing, only his lips and wishing they were on me. Give them to me. Give them to me. Give them to me. Give them to me. I started to become angry. I was astonished by my appetite for him. Perhaps the trauma of the past weeks had stoked my appetite even more if that was possible. Was it sex I wanted or control over him, indulgence in unrestrained being, finally letting go of all...

I chewed my lips, wiggled in my seat. He saw my discomfort. He smiled and anger spiked, white and hot in my chest. Lust, fury—it seemed that all manner of excess was destined to be visited upon me these days.

"Sophia, it is really good to see you." He was not usually so effusive in his language and it made me smile a bit. "When you called, it did sound as if you were interested in a bit more than my lips."

I was startled awake and lifted my gaze to his eyes. Gabriel's pupils were dilated. "Gabriel," I softly hummed and sighed. His nostrils flared. Yes, he definitely liked his name on my tongue.

I

Feel

Powerful.

He was excited by my fixation on those pouty lips of his, and I simply didn't care. I was no longer embarrassed. I was an addict and had no pride left, only a hope and a prayer for my fix. He pressed me.

"What's on your mind, Sophia?"

I really, really liked the way this name sounded...I was a little more tuned in now and tried to concentrate on what had been happening the past weeks. He might be able to help. I tried to put on my lawyer face and found it uncomfortable in the extreme.

"Are you well, Sophia? I've been wondering where you've

been. No one at the firm would answer the most benign questions, and I was beginning to think I wouldn't see you again."

He paused, unsure of expressing his next thought. But I knew it already. I knew his intention. He didn't like the idea of not seeing me again. I was reminded of Marlow's rendition of his face. I remembered that he wanted me. I was weak with that ache in my limbs. Gabriel waited. It seemed everyone waited for me lately. I was getting impatient with myself, even as those around me were not. I focused my attention on what I wanted from him.

"I'm not sure how to begin here or if you can even help Gabriel. You once said I was too inexperienced for this game. What did you mean by it?"

"I think you know," he replied.

"Yes, but I'm interested in what you know, Gabriel." During the weeks at the country house, I was able to piece together a working theory about everyone's part in the deception of Sophia. I had even drawn out a sketch of the players in an effort to put my thoughts in order as if I were working on a complex estate plan. It seems Marlow tried to surround me with people intended to protect or help me in some way. I'm sure they were also meant to protect and help him, as well. Knowing him, he only shared bits of information with each—Oliver, Gabriel, Albert—just enough information for them to provide their services. I was sure Gabriel had some information that would help me piece the entire story together.

"Are you going to try to play me again, Sophia? It didn't work the first time," he said a bit shortly. He was getting tense and abrupt. His arrogance ignited my humor this time, and I smiled a crooked smile. This was a sharp departure from my reaction last time when I was intent on getting into his head. I reached out and carefully touched the top of his hand resting on the table. I felt the swell in my chest, and Gabriel was at first wary but then began to relax. His eyes slowly lost their focus as I bore down on him. It was the gentlest push, all I needed now that I knew my iron will.

"Gabriel, what do you know about my work here?"

I could feel his attempt to pull away his hand, pull away his mind. This was child's play to me now, and I was smug about it. It's funny that I couldn't manage this during our first private meeting. His guards were weak in the most elementary way. I asked again, and I could feel the jagged electrical current beginning to form between us. I directed it to him and he was soon wincing in pain.

I repeated myself a third time in a flat command. His mind was now struggling, fighting within itself until sweat broke out on his forehead. I observed his pain, taking mental notes like a lab technician. Oh, I could definitely make him give me those lips that I so desire, I realized. Yes, yes, yes, give me those lips. Wrap those lips around my mouth and consume me in their moist heat. He leaned closer to me, torn by the pain and desire I inflicted on him.

I finally felt his pain and let go. This was Albert's doing, this clinical observation coupled with compassion. I was irritated with Albert's instruction and the way it interfered with my wanting to extract information from Gabriel's brain or a kiss from his mouth. Oh, fucking Albert again—the great betrayer. More infuriating, Albert was also apparently the great redeemer of my damaged gene pool.

Gabriel came out of his stupor and jumped to his feet, knocking over his chair. I had mixed emotions, torn between feeling remorse for my transgression, like an errant schoolgirl, and the joy of conquest. This feeling was as exciting as my rediscovered intoxication with Gabriel's lips. He gathered himself, righting the chair and putting on his face and his jacket as he quietly left. He paused at the door and looked at me with puzzled fascination, a much different face than the one he had been wearing since we met. He now understood the warnings he received about me, and the door echoed as it closed. I was left behind, staring at my hands. They were resting palms up while I examined them like a Muslim supplicant wondering what Marlow had given me, what curses these hands could inflict.

When I returned to my flat, I sent Oliver home, thinking it was time I found my own comfort again. I thought my old routine might help regulate my sleep patterns, but after waking up twisted in the sheets and gasping for air, I went to the living room and sat in the rocker, a light cotton blanket covering me. I started to rock and drifted off to sleep. I found myself gliding over the London streets. I heard someone calling the name I now recognized as my own...

"Layla, Layla."

I recognized the voice. I started to move more quickly over London, but in that dream state, I couldn't propel myself fast enough. I was flying down alleys and over rooftops, searching around corners, but I kept hearing her voice from a different place. She called out quietly

"Stop moving, Layla."

So I did. I stopped my frantic search and sat on a rooftop. I sat with my legs crossed, bowed my head, and closed my eyes, waiting for the voice to come to me. I took a breath. I took another. I heard the voice behind me, around me, in me.

"Oh, Layla, it's so good to see you."

I recognized that voice. It was the comforting voice of a dear childhood friend. She sat in front of me and touched my hands resting on my knees. I opened my eyes and saw our hands touching. But our hands were little, little girls' hands. Adorable, soft, pudgy, two in two little girl hands. I felt so reassured and excited here with my friend.

I followed the hands with my eyes, to her wrists and arms, and looked into the face of a young girl. She was small. Her round eyes popped open at me. Her little speck of a nose flared above her pencil-thin lips pursed together. Then she was smiling at me—a full-faced smile and I knew her!

This was my friend, Renni, Mr. Spencer's Renee, who I knew as a child in England. Her smile grew wider as she saw I recognized her. Ah, now I understand that it was she who kept our memories hidden, not me...not even Albert. She took them from my mind and now returned our shared memories to me with the fullness of her affection for me. I was filled from the inside out with her unconditional love. Oh, Oliver was right—everyone is loved. We both remained like that for a time, enjoying the feel of such unadulterated openness.

Her face began to mature, an aging video until I saw her adult face and she saw mine. We were still holding hands and she tugged on mine so that I stood. She turned and faced out above London, waving with her hand toward the east. Her hand waved brushstrokes into the night sky as she opened a curtain. Where the curtain had been was now an image of a desert. I saw her there in a small Atlas mountain village. Without words or map, I recognized Morocco. She showed me the twists and turns of the village roads and we crossed paths with a man who took her hand. He smiled at me—he could see me! Incredible! He was a shepherd, leading us through the landscape. Renee adores him—this unexpected Sufi shepherd with the kind heart of a poet.

We were floating and enjoying the drifting landscape below when Renee became alarmed. She glanced behind us and told me to wake quickly. "Silence, Layla, silence. Stay quiet!" I didn't want to let her go, but she was urgent. "Danger, danger, danger," she whispered to me.

I slowly opened my eyes and saw a shadow move on the balcony. I reached for the little table next to the rocker and put my hand on a paperweight. Closing my eyes to slits, I allowed the intruder to pick the lock and silently open the glass sliding door. As he stepped over the threshold, my arm flew into action, and he was beamed with the Murano glass right between his eyes, falling over instantly.

I got up and stepped over to him, seeing the handgun with silencer in his grip. As I reached for the gun, I heard the front door handle turning and stepped into my kitchen to wait. Whoever was at the door had a key and entered quickly and quietly. I raised the gun and came face to face with Oliver and Gabriel, almost shooting them both.

My heart was hammering in my chest as Oliver gently removed the revolver from my grip. The gun was unfamiliar in my hand, and I gladly let Oliver take charge. Oliver flipped the safety and pocketed the gun. He handed me a new leather purse and an overnight carrier. Gabriel, meanwhile, checked the corpse and looked at me curiously. No one said a word. The two men watched me pack the bag—a brush, deodorant, jeans, tee-shirts, a black sweater, one skirt, panties, bras, shoes, and a small bottle of perfume. We left together. My keys remained on the entry table. Oliver and Gabriel had already discarded their phones, credit cards, and identifications.

I dropped mine into a rubbish bin outside the flat, my first act of defiance against the deception of Sophia.

ESCAPE TO SKOURA

Oliver, Gabriel, and I headed to Heathrow airport. Oliver gave the cabbie forty pounds. No one spoke. We arrived at the counter for Air Morocco and purchased first-class tickets with cash, new passports in our possession that Oliver secured. The next available flight departed for Casablanca in less than four hours. We waited in near silence at the terminal gate, passing on the first-class lounge. We took turns standing, patrolling the area on foot. When one of us sat, another stood. A symphony of silent communication played among the three of us, one that only we could see or hear. Our movements were fluid, natural, incredibly self-contained in our relaxed vigilance. We had all learned at the hands of the same masters. We were experts at this calmly guarded waiting—moving from a seat to a window, then to the bar.

We boarded the plane and continued our waiting for the three-hour and fifteen-minute flight. Casablanca...I tasted the name of the city and perused my memory for references taught by Albert. Casablanca, the white house, I recalled. And I wondered if my damaged spirit could be cleansed in the white house. Casablanca, the place of exotic gatherings of colonial Europeans. Casablanca, Humphrey Bogart's haunt in American pop-cultural memory.

There was a much greater history to this city—one of centuries-old trade routes and time-worn passages between North Africa and Europe. We descended in time with all that I could recall, and I saw the city from the air. It was mostly a modern cosmopolitan city with an ancient Medina. We arrived early in the afternoon, the heat of the sun baking the city, every window reflecting intense light. We were directed to a different wing of the terminal and boarded a small twin-engine plane for another short flight to the tiny airport of Ouarzazate. "Our—zuh—zat." Oliver found his voice with this unfamiliar word and repeated it a second time. We landed on the edge of the great Sahara desert, a river of saffron, orange, and mustard sand. Something in me stirred, awakened in this endless expanse of sand river.

We were met at the airport by a driver who greeted us, looking for an English couple and a large black companion. He took us to a local riad. "Ree-ahd," Oliver shared the word with us. "The riad," Oliver explained, was architecture unique to Morocco, a traditional house with an interior courtyard. We were given two rooms, one for Oliver and the other for Gabriel and me (now Edward and Abigail Walker), a married South Hampton couple visiting this conservative kingdom of North Africa.

Lying down across a comfortable double bed, I started to feel a little relief, knowing the three of us were far away in time and place, hidden for now. The door on the wall joined this room with Oliver's, and I was profoundly comforted by his nearness. Hmmm...then there was Gabriel, my Mr. Walker. Interesting. I was not distracted by his lips, overcome with fatigue as I was. I wrapped my arms around one of the silk-covered pillows. The room was welcoming, the bed soft, the pillow smelled like cinnamon. I drifted into an exhausted sleep in the cool house, sheltered from the afternoon sun.

I awakened alone and saw the antique clock on the desk softly ticking out the seconds. Four o'clock shadows lengthening, not quite dusk. The room contained the one bed and comfortable Moroccan cushions tucked in the corner with pillows surrounding the nook. The desk was near the garden window. There was another door to the interior garden courtyard. The doors of Morocco were a sight to behold, a long tradition of master artwork adorning each one. The azure blue door to the courtyard was slightly ajar, and I glimpsed Gabriel sitting at a table drinking tea.

I looked up at the canopy overhanging the bed. The restful sleep had honed my senses, and I was stunned by the lush colors of this small, unassuming room. Here was a sea of Morocco's richness, alive with a vibrant Majorelle blue. The color swirled and repeated itself in the arabesque tile design throughout our suite. Oh my, it was impossible to describe the swaddling comfort of being in this place, this, the 'peace that passes all understanding.' There was a breeze blowing from the wood-slatted windows, and I could smell the jasmine flowers from the courtyard. I washed up and stepped into the fertile gardens that were awash with the care only a loving gardener could provide. Gabriel had left the table.

I knew we were on the edge of the Sahara, and I was delighted with this oasis of abundance. I sat on a wall surrounding a fountain and waited. It was quiet here after the traffic of London and New York and the roar of airplane engines. It was so quiet that the silence created a buzz in my ears. It sounded like the murmur of the desert out there...just beyond the walls of this place.

I closed my eyes and inhaled—a small breath, short and incomplete. I exhaled. I inhaled again, this time a little more satisfying, filling my lungs with the taste of jasmine, rose, and the nearby desert. I exhaled, a long unburdening release of breath. Several minutes passed until my breath found a natural rhythm. It was the tempo of this tranquil refuge. I was relaxed and opened my eyes to see Gabriel sitting nearby at the table again. He motioned me to join him. An old Moroccan woman, head covered, brought us mint tea and cookies. Her face was crinkled and warm and she smiled at us.

We sipped our tea and nibbled on delicious fig cookies. *I would like to stay here*, I think, but Gabriel broke the silence that we had kept for the past twenty-four hours.

"How are you feeling, Sophia?"

I was not sure about the name anymore. I didn't know if I liked it on his tongue the way I used to. Perhaps in this new place, my old name would be more suitable. He was observing me carefully, warily. I wondered if he was afraid.

Of

Me.

The thought made me sick. I wanted to be someone else—anyone but me at this moment. I didn't want to be scary. I didn't want Gabriel to fear me. But fear was what I smelled on him. And I wanted to curl up into a ball and hide under a bed. I wanted to run to a forest and hide in the trees. I hated that he was afraid of me, but I knew he was right to be afraid of me. I wanted to hide it. I wanted to take back all of the awful thoughts and become someone new.

I didn't want to be cruel and scary. He was right to be afraid. I was a monster capable of murder without remorse. I murdered yesterday, and I felt nothing today.

Marlow has done this to me.

All of these thoughts passed through my peaceful mind in a nanosecond.

"Good, Gabriel, how are you?"

"Well, it's been an eventful twenty-four hours. Do you need anything? Are you hungry? Would you like to bathe, walk, see the village of Ouarzazate nearby?"

"A bath sounds great and then a walk in the village. What about you, Gabriel? What would you like to do? Did you rest?"

"Yes, I woke up about a half-hour before you and went for a little walk with Oliver."

"Okay—I'll meet you back here when I'm done with the bath."

The conversation was a bit stiff and as if we were strangers. *Well, I guess we are strangers,* I thought. *We really know so little about each other. I'm excited to get to know him under these circumstances, unburdened by observers. There are no firm representatives, no Albert or Marlow, or any other authority interfering with our conversations or desires.*

My fear of doing harm had shut down the hormone trail of lust for the time being. I've heard that fear and lust were common bedfellows. But I was feeling neither. Like this oasis, I was calm, moving with the naturally forming space around me.

I returned to our room and noticed the disturbed blankets and cushions in the corner nook. I was mildly interested in the fact that Gabriel must have rested there as I entered the bath. I found some rose petals and dropped them into the water. The bathroom filled with the rose scent as I sank into the warmth. After a relaxing half-hour, I washed my hair with argan shampoo and was comforted by the intoxicating natural smells. What a peaceful respite from my usual routine. I couldn't remember ever being so out of tune with time or a schedule, except maybe in Sally's house. Those were timeless summer jaunts.

I remained still in mind and spirit, as I combed absent-mindedly through my hair. I put on a lightweight blouse and jeans. It was late November in the desert oasis, a lot warmer than the London we left behind. I retraced my steps to Gabriel in the courtyard and smiled to see Oliver. They both stood to greet me and Oliver looked surprised.

"Sophia, you look rested. How are you feeling?" he asked.

"Good—surprisingly good. How about you, Oliver? Did you get any rest?"

"Yes—quite well, in fact. This place is an oasis for body and mind if you get my meaning. You look excellent, like the girl I picked up at Heathrow."

Gabriel was still standing, observing me, wondering about my state of mind.

"I'm really fine, Gabriel. I feel relaxed. As Oliver said, this place is truly a sanctuary for mind and spirit."

None of us spoke of the intruder as we unconsciously moved through the courtyard into the riad and out the front door. It was as if our reason for fleeing London no longer mattered. This place insisted on each body being present in the moment.

Gabriel, ever the tour guide and fount of information, gave us a bit of this city's history. It had been the location for many films, most notably *Lawrence of Arabia*. We were in the center of Ouarzazate, nicknamed "the door to the desert" and populated by the Berbers. The name, Gabriel explained, comes from a Berber word that meant "without noise" or "without confusion."

I was walking through the streets of Ouarzazate, my mind still, without noise or confusion. I was filled with a pleasure of spirit that was totally unfamiliar—an inner contentment that I could only hope would stay with me. It was so alien and exquisite, this aching gladness of my heart.

As we strolled, I felt lighter with each step, my sandals leaving no imprint of a passage here...no beginning and no end in this prism. Gabriel and Oliver took turns glancing at me. We found a little outdoor café and sat down for dinner. The menu was governed by the day and the cook's wishes—a fantastic tagine of lamb, with prunes and onions, surrounded by a variety of picking salads, as I call them—eggplant with garlic and parsley, carrots with cumin and lemon, chickpeas, garden vegetables. It was a rainbow of color, a banquet of abundance. This place was pregnant with a richness of colors, aromas, and flavors. I couldn't find a happier moment to be if I tried.

As if on cue, Gabriel and Oliver said at the same time, "Sophia, you seem different."

"Well, I feel different here. I feel as different as a body could after a lifetime of confusion and restlessness, hidden chambers within my own mind, and manipulations from afar. I feel like someone else has been living in my body...and I have been returned to it." I forked a radish, popped it into my mouth, and enjoyed the sharpness and crunch. "I feel light as a feather—unburdened somehow—and thank you very much. I. Will. Gladly. Take. It."

"It's so refreshing to see you this...this happy, I should say," added Gabriel. He was smiling, a genuine pleasure beaming from his face. I could see that he was glad for my peace of mind as his smile climbed his face from his lips to his eyes. My burning desire for him had calmed with the rest of my usual tension. His smile did not ignite my libido but warmed me with his generous delight in my serenity.

We enjoyed our dinner and returned to stroll the streets afterward. This caramel-colored city was a salve for the three of us. We returned to the riad and I now noticed that there were only six guest rooms. The main living area was comfortably decorated with many floor cushions, sprinkled with beautiful lighting from the shuk, the nearby market, throughout. There were shelves lined with English, French, and Arabic titles.

We sat in the salon and I picked among the books until I found, unbelievably, *Mockingbird* again. My state of mind revived my old love for this classic. Unlike my stay at the country house, it was not Atticus and his decency but Scout who kindled my interest at this moment. She was awakened from the dreamy slumber of childhood, as was I. Her attachment to Atticus reassured me, and I could imagine that her adulthood would be imbued with her father's love for humanity. Had Albert given me this gift, I hoped and wondered.

I always feared that I had fallen far short of the bar Atticus set for our wee little American hearts and minds. And I considered myself American although I now knew I was born in Jamaica to an English mother and a father who I will not name here. I drifted into thinking that the American was indeed noble and honorable, in the most naïve and lovable fashion. Atticus was not naïve, but he was so American in that decent tradition of hoping for better, even in the face of such wretched injustice. I loved that he understood his world but still hoped. Was Scout loved enough, even after the terrible conclusion? Have I been loved enough...to, to hope?

Wow—I was so drawn to Scout and Atticus on the edge of the great Sahara desert. What an unlikely pairing of place and time—the small town in the deep South of American history to the North African fringes of the enormous Sahara. But somehow it all seemed to fit perfectly as if the two worlds were always meant to meet this way.

Scout and Atticus reminded me that everything was finally falling into place. I was exactly where I should be, with the people who should be with me, no matter where we have been or the trail we might follow ahead of us.

After a while, I got sleepy. "Gentlemen, I thank you for a lovely afternoon and a sumptuous meal, and now," I stood and returned my book to its place, "I'm heading to bed."

Oliver rose with me and followed us to our rooms. Gabriel remained where he was. I didn't want any excess of emotion to engulf me, and I think he understood. We were in front of our rooms, and I hesitated for a second. Oliver invited me into his room and showed me the adjoining door. I felt better. He opened this door and went ahead of me into my room.

"Where would you like me to sleep, Sophia?" he asked politely, his usual thoughtful self.

"Your room would be fine, Oliver. Let's just leave the door open, okay?"

I fell asleep quickly and didn't hear Gabriel when he arrived.

The next morning I woke up late and found that I had slept well again, for the second time in weeks. Gabriel had gone for breakfast, I supposed. His pillows in the corner nook were well mixed up. I was sleeping more than usual, a wonderful dreamless sleep that energized me in a new way.

I dressed and joined Oliver and Gabriel in the kitchen where our hosts had laid out breakfast. I rarely saw the man and woman that tended to this home. They were so unobtrusive but attentive to detail in providing for their guests, and we were the only guests at this unlikely time of year. Fresh figs were my favorite breakfast detail, along with a beautiful selection of homemade jams and pita.

"Sophia, what is our destination?" Gabriel asked, touching his lips with the linen napkin.

"Huh? " I replied.

Gabriel laughed, reminding us of his expression during our lunch when I burst into peals of laughter.

"Is that 'American' for you don't know?"

"Was it 'British' for you didn't know?"

We laughed together. It was contagious and Oliver joined us.

"Well, I'm not sure how we got here." I finally added.

"Sophia, you told us in your flat that we were heading to Morocco. On the plane, you asked the flight attendant about the flight here to Ouarzazate."

"What? What are you talking about? I don't remember any of that." How did this happen—that I could tell them but not know where our destination came from. Then I remembered quietly. It was not startling or jarring, this memory. Renni, no Renee, moved into and out of my consciousness like a ghost, whispering 'Morocco' on the way to Heathrow, then 'Ouarzazate' upon our arrival in Casablanca. She showed me the village as she did in our dream. I closed my eyes and thought of her. The name came to me as a hum on the desert wind. I opened my eyes.

Renee knew how to appear in my thoughts on demand and then hide herself. *This is a great skill that I'd like to learn*, I thought, as I could now answer the men.

"Skoura—we're going to a village named Skoura."

We sought out our hosts and asked where we could find a car. We would be driving ourselves into the desert. A jeep was hired and dropped off at the riad by mid-afternoon.

We were off the grid, having discarded phones, keys with tracking devices, and credit cards with tracers. We'd only used cash since we left my flat in London. We have new names and passports. We won't be using navigation, and the jeep was old enough that it had no tracking abilities. Nonetheless, Oliver inspected the jeep thoroughly, once and again, until he was satisfied.

It was late afternoon by the time we collected our things and began the drive to Skoura on the outer edges of the great Sahara wilderness. Maps in hand, we set out deeper into the desert. The excitement of this adventure tickled me deep in my belly.

THE COMPANY GATHERS

*A*chmed was alone grazing the goats under an overcast sky. The nearby trees quivered in the gentle morning breeze. He rested beneath a tree, thinking of Amalu. He had left her behind today. "Good morning, Achmed. Go ahead without me today, love," were her parting words. As he drifted off to sleep, he smiled, remembering those words on her lips.

He wrapped his mouth around those lips as he kissed her goodbye. And she welcomed the invasion of his tongue, smiling a contented smile. There were days when Amalu stayed with Alia, helping around the home. At other times, she joined the men in town for tea. Some days she would accompany the women gathering wheat. She moved from place to place, in harmony with where she could best help, and she was welcomed everywhere as a member of the tribe.

Achmed stood nearby his goats and turned his inner eye toward her. They had practiced their nighttime and daylight travels together until they were nearly one, calling on each other in thought as easily as they greeted each other on sight. It had become a habit, like reaching for a nearby lover's hand. But today Achmed couldn't connect with Amalu. Sometimes she would shut him out, and he would likewise do the same.

Everyone needs his private moments. As was his way, he didn't dwell on it.

Returning to the village after a morning in the fields, he found Amalu still among the blankets in bed. This was not like her. In the years since she arrived, she had only been sick the one time when the camel took her fingers.

"Amalu, what is it? What is wrong?" He dropped to the floor, his face even with hers. Amalu opened her eyes and there were dark circles forming under them, creeping into her beautiful cheekbones. Her forehead was wrinkled in concentration, and her lips were set in a thin line.

"Tired, Achmed. I am so tired. He has been trying to get into my head for days now. He wants to know where she is, but she doesn't want him to know. She thinks he is a danger to her. I am bringing her here where she will be safe."

Achmed knew who 'he' was. It was the man who visited with them in their dreams, the one with the grey eyes. Sometimes they called him 'Grey Eyes.'

"Amalu, who are you bringing here?"

"My, my friend. Her name is Layla."

"Layla, that's an Arabic name. Is she from here?"

"No."

"When will she arrive?"

"Soon, Achmed. She has two companions with her. We must find a place outside of the village to hide them. It is important that no one sees...I am too weak to make plans. They need a place to rest."

Achmed went to Alia, a little too distressed about Amalu's state to think clearly.

"We're going to have three guests arriving soon, Mama. We need a place beyond the village for them to stay."

"The tent you use with the goats will work nicely."

Sometimes when the grazing was sparse, Achmed would travel farther into the mountains with the herd. He and Hassan had pitched a tent there many years ago for overnight stays. Alia remembered what her son had forgotten.

Achmed returned to Amalu with tea and bread. She was sitting up and grateful for the tea. He watched her tear the bread, dip it into the honey, and sip the tea while he told her the plan and saw her relax as he took charge of the details. Night would be upon them in a couple of hours, and they needed to move quickly. Touching her arm, Achmed reassured her that he would see to everything. She finished her tea and the last of the pita, bestowing a grateful smile on her beloved Achmed.

Sophia's eyes rolled back in her head as Amalu stretched out a thought to her, directing them to take a different road. Gabriel was sitting in the back seat with her while Oliver drove. He was alarmed when her head dropped back, and he saw the whites of her eyes but willed himself to silence.

"Go left before reaching the village. There is a small stand with honey for sale just before the turn, usually with an old man sitting nearby," she said.

Gabriel watched as Sophia woke up, not recalling the interlude. They moved on through the desert until, just as spoken, there was an old man sitting near a stand, really no more than a few crates, with the jars of honey lined up. She pointed the rest of the way along a one-lane road, deep into the mountains. The road was narrow, with deep ravines on one side or another as they traveled. This was really one lane, not much wider than a horse path or a dog trot near the house in Oxfordshire. When they happened upon an old truck coming from the other direction, each car had to inch over to allow room, with a little more than a hair's breadth between the car and the ravine below. Oliver was a skilled driver, and they were safe in his very capable hands.

"Right...on...we...go...," he said, small beads of perspiration beading on his forehead.

Another passing donkey with rider smiled and waved.

After a long time of twisting, winding roads, they descended into a valley where the land leveled out. Fully dark now, Sophia asked Oliver to stop driving. They left the jeep together, the two men following Sophia into the darkness of the woods. She led the way through dense trees into a clearing where they found the Bedouin tent.

Amalu and Achmed were already there, having set out on foot with a pack mule from the village earlier in the day. The tent had been swept out, food and bedding brought from home. The guests would be comfortable.

Amalu heard them coming and stepped out as the three shapes reached the clearing. She had regained her strength, Grey Eyes having abandoned her a few hours earlier. Perhaps the invader was resting or searching elsewhere for Layla. Achmed followed her out of the tent but waited near the flap while she cautiously approached the three visitors. Oliver and Gabriel, likewise, stayed near the overhanging branches of trees that sheltered this small clearing. The men watched from a distance as the two women greeted each other in the moonlight.

They shared a similar petite frame. But where Sophia was rounder in the face and hips, Amalu was waiflike. They walked cautiously forward, stopping with a short distance—maybe three meters—between them.

Amalu and Sophia kept eye contact, each waiting for the other. Amalu took a small step left. Sophia followed, almost in time with her. Sophia stepped right and Amalu followed. Four times they followed the other's movements until they began to move in sync, two cats circling each other. There was a rhythm to their movements, an intimate knowledge of each other. Minutes passed as the dance was finely tuned. These movements reminded Gabriel of the time when Sophia returned to her flat in London, how she knew his action before he made it. It seemed the two women had moved to this waltz before.

They skipped in time to each other's movements, barely touching the ground with the balls of their feet. A bent knee, a bow, and a curtsey slowed the tempo, as they watched each other. These two little fencers poked for weaknesses in the other's defenses, charging lightly toward a hint of an action. One observed the tiny motion of a foot and feinted along with her partner. Instead of blades, they matched wits on a different playing field altogether, one completely unseen. Time was a circle here—one in which the mountains and the wood sprites whispered forward and backward.

Oliver and Achmed kept their distance, eyeing each other across the clearing. The two women continued their ballet, drawing closer in small increments. The nighttime sounds were still, every creature nearby paused...waiting. They skipped closer and closer, circling, each trying to feint. The excitement in the air grew. A quick dart by Amalu was just as quickly followed by Sophia. The tempo began to increase and the dance became less cautious, more exuberant. Each enjoyed the challenge and being met, feint for feint, by an equal partner.

Finally, within reach of each other, they stopped and shared a deep, heartfelt smile. They took the last, small step forward and leaned into an embrace, the conclusion to their beautiful ballet, finally enfolding each other in the comfort of friendship. Amalu wrapped her arms around Sophia's shoulders, encircling her. Sophia snaked her arms around Amalu's back and brought her in closer. Each let out a shared breath and hummed a contented recognition. Amalu leaned into Sophia's hair and took a deep breath, inhaling its earthy scent that held a day's travel in the Sahara. Sophia squeezed tighter.

Their silent reunion replayed itself in slow motion for the watching men. They moved their arms around each other, patting or squeezing, tears spilling freely from their joyful eyes. The moonlight played around them and through them as if they were illuminated and illuminating. Achmed was reminded of his first encounter with Amalu, the moon a laser of light through their bodies. When they separated, still holding hands, the moment stretched backward and forward in time—infinite and ephemeral. The bond between these two spanned millennia and could only be described in the most inadequate way.

Amalu whispered, "Oh, Layla, it is so good to see you. I have been looking for you for a very long time."

"I am glad you found me," Sophia replied with an ear-to-ear grin.

Gabriel and Achmed were both beaming, feeling the pleasure of this joyful reunion.

"Renee, meet…"

"I am known as Amalu here, Layla," Renee replied.

"Well, I am known as Sophia, Renee. Which do you prefer? I think I'd prefer Sophia. I'm afraid my name might call him and others to us."

"I can keep him out, Sophia," Renee said. "It's exhausting work, but so far, so good. He's been searching for you intensely these past days. Maybe we can do that work together. Yes, we can talk about it more tomorrow. But if you feel better using Sophia, so be it. Sophia and Amalu it will be for now."

"Oliver and Gabriel." The men had moved closer and spoke on top of one another.

"Sophia, meet Achmed."

"Oh, the poet." Sophia smiled as she took his hand in both of hers. Ah, his was such an uncontaminated spirit. She knew at the moment they made contact that she could trust him with all. And Achmed felt as if he had found another sister, one who could 'speak' like him and his beloved Amalu, over time and space.

After the introductions, the five moved to the tent. They shared a simple and excellent meal of lamb, cheese, sweetbread, oranges, and dates. The evening passed in quiet companionship. Sophia and Amalu did not reminisce—they caught up on all that had happened since they last saw each other some fifteen years earlier. Achmed had the chance to practice his improving English, mostly with Oliver. They spoke about the village, Achmed's family, and the land around them. Gabriel studied the map and wandered out of the tent several times. He alone seemed restless among them.

Sophia and Amalu maintained contact, thighs touching or a hand on an arm at all times. They gave each other strength. Amalu was reenergized, Achmed noted with relief. The burden of keeping out 'Grey Eyes' for the day seemed to have lifted.

As they reached for a dish, Amalu and Sophia held up their hands for everyone to see their damaged fingers. It was a comically interesting coincidence that they had both lost the same bits on opposite hands. The mystery of their friendship, in parallel realities, was fascinating. For this evening, the women were clearly joyful to see each other. When, finally, their eyes were heavy with sleep, Amalu and Sophia slept together, a peaceful and deep slumber.

The next day the five companions began their morning outside in the crisp air over a fire with mint tea. Amalu had made fresh pita before they woke. Achmed prepared the tea as they sat on small stone boulders around the fire.

Gabriel cleared his throat. "Amalu, you brought Sophia here. To what end?"

"Interesting that you should be the one to ask that question, Gabriel. You have some very important information that you've been withholding from Sophia since she arrived in London."

Gabriel's grip on his glass tightened just a bit.

"Amalu," Sophia continued, looking directly at Gabriel, "I am aware that Gabriel has not told me everything...yet. I'm sure he has had his reasons for doing so. I could compel him to tell me, but I would prefer he willingly shares whatever it is.

We need to trust each other if we are to work together. We need to understand the threats we face and what is to come. Now, it seems, is the time of choosing."

"Sophia," Gabriel replied, "I think we all know that the only one threatened is you. But the threat, it seems, is from more than one place." He turned a hostile eye toward Amalu. "Speaking of threats, what do you know about the Jamaican?" he hissed at her.

"I would not do that if I were you," Achmed's words were quiet but quite deadly. The men turned and measured each other.

"Achmed," Amalu rejoined, "Gabriel is seeking answers, same as we are. I don't think he means any harm. He wants to protect Sophia. He is confused and not sure whom to trust. I will tell you what I know of the Jamaican. Let's not use his name, although we all know it here. Achmed and I call him Grey Eyes. Let's begin by sharing what we each know of him. Then maybe we can determine if he is an enemy or an ally."

"I met him in my dreams when I was a young man. The first time we met, the water of the ocean burned my feet. He called me to him again and again and helped me learn to travel in my dreams," Achmed offered.

"I also met him in my dreams as a young girl, but he did not take much interest in me until I was attacked by the Obeah's messengers and left for dead in the desert. He tries to talk to me, but I am able to keep him away. It is very tiresome work," Amalu answered.

"Amalu, can you teach me to do that? I need to get him out of me. You, you are able to hide like a breeze among the reeds. Who taught you to do that?" Sophia asked. "I really need to learn how to do that," Sophia added, muttering to herself.

Everyone around the fire sensed Sophia's desperation and each turned his total attention to her.

"Sophia, you cannot do what you seek to do. You cannot

unmake yourself out of different material. Surely, you know that."

"But Amalu, you don't understand. He's evil. He has infected us, my very being."

"But I do understand, Sophia, more than I want to just now."

"Sophia," Achmed said with a frown. "What do you mean he has infected 'us.' Who else?"

"Did I say us? No, I meant me. It's me who has been poisoned. It is a curse of my very being, his invasion of me." Sophia was on her feet, pacing, waving her hands as she talked manically.

"Sophia, what has he done to you?" Gabriel asked as he stood and touched her shoulder, trying to calm her. She had been so content in Ouarzazate these last days that this change was all the more troubling to him.

Oliver stopped the train of Sophia's despair with a softly worded question,

"Amalu, who or what is the Obeah?" Sophia and Gabriel sat as Amalu responded.

"The Obeah are occult practitioners of the West Indies, like Grey Eyes. Some are older and stronger than him, but he is very clever. Often when I have seen him, I can sense others nearby. When they get too close, he cuts contact, hiding us from their prying eyes. There is also a multitude of other beings that surround the Obeah. Achmed and I have seen or sensed them too many times. They are lost spirits, souls that cannot connect to here or elsewhere. The Obeah use them to do certain tasks for them. I don't know if the Obeah keeps them against their will, but they are a frightening lot of damaged spirits. We call them The Host.

The Obeah can manipulate The Host like children. They are unsophisticated and trusting in their own way. But do not be fooled by them—they are a malicious mob, driven by envy for what they cannot have, neither the corporeal world nor the spirit world. They were searching for me, I assume, at the command of the Obeah. I don't think Grey Eyes knew. As I said, he took little interest in me until afterward. I was working in England, and the Obeah had been haunting my nights for some months. I learned about the Obeah many years ago. My mother had told me that I was adopted from Jamaica, and I learned all I could about the culture. I came across some obscure research about the Obeah, and it seemed to fit the nightmares I had been having for many years.

I planned a holiday to Morocco in hope of escaping the nightly torments. Three of the Obeah men found me in Fez, kidnapped and interrogated me for a week or so. They beat me pretty badly. I was so desperate that I tried to reach out to Grey Eyes, but I was physically and mentally battered.

I don't believe the Obeah men and Grey Eyes are working together. Grey Eyes does not seem malicious to me. The Obeah men use those other spirits for their errands, like looking for you and me, Sophia. One night while my captors rested and The Host was away, I was able to influence my guard.

When they awoke and found me gone, they were furious. They tracked me down a third time and left me in the desert to die. They don't like to murder, so they left me to the elements. Achmed found me, and I've been here with him since that time." Amalu finished with a quiet nod of her head.

"Amalu, you do not understand him. He is indeed violent. If you had read what I have, you might understand better." Sophia added.

"My heart tells me differently, Sophia," Amalu replied. She turned to Gabriel.

"When did you meet him, Gabriel?"

I was the one waiting for a change as Gabriel began his story. The men met in the office, same as we had—Marlow asked for him by name, just as he had asked for me in New York. It was, in fact, within months of the time that Marlow and I met. As he had with me, Marlow took several years to get to know Gabriel, until they had a strong professional relationship. Shortly before I arrived in London, Marlow had met with him to advise him that I would be arriving to work on an important matter of "keen personal interest" to him. He asked Gabriel to make an effort to welcome me and to "keep an eye on me."

As Gabriel reached the end of his story, he added, "There is one thing he told me that I've been reluctant to share. I think it was meant to protect you, Sophia; I was meant to protect you. I'm confident, in fact, that he surrounded you with people meant to protect you. I think it's time, though, high time that you understand the cause of danger, at least insofar as I understand it."

Amalu nodded to Gabriel, encouraging him to continue.

"He visited me recently to tell me about the assassin. He was sent, they were sent, by Adele. She hired someone before her death, and Marlow had been unable to make direct contact with the killer. The assassin is intent on finishing the job for which he's been handsomely paid. There have been other attempts. If we could locate the contact, we might be able to neutralize this threat, but...there is a second threat that concerns him more."

I heard Gabriel's voice coming through as if we were under water. I didn't react and he repeated himself. "It was Adele. Adele hired the assassin that came to your flat, Sophia."

I had no reaction. He may as well be saying that the garbage pail is really a rubbish bin. I could feel everyone waiting for me, to gauge my reaction. But I was surprisingly still. My mother hired someone to kill me before she died. Her dying wish was to have me murdered.

I understood her violent desire for vengeance. Marlow did that to her, as surely as he did it to me. I almost killed Jorge in my violent desire for Gabriel. I wanted to murder Marlow. I wanted to harm Albert. I killed an intruder without hesitation and never felt the slightest moment of remorse or regret for his life.

Marlow did that to her. It was irrelevant whether it was his intention. He inseminated her with a violence that I now understood. It was a violence that I sometimes enjoyed in the power it grants me. It made perfect sense that she wanted me dead. Marlow did that to me.

Amalu interrupted my train of thought. "Sophia, please try not to use his name, at least until we've decided if it's safe for him to know we are together."

"Oh, okay," I replied idly as I got up.

"Where are you going?" Gabriel asked.

"Just for a little walk, Gabriel. I'm fine, really. I just need to stretch my legs a little." I stood and dusted off my jeans; and as an afterthought, I turned to him with a question. "Gabriel, who was it that kidnapped me for those three days?"

"That is a mystery. It definitely wasn't the assassin. His job is to kill, not interrogate."

Amalu interjected, "It could only have been an agent of the Obeah. Maybe they weren't sure of your identity and were trying to confirm who you are. It's a testament to your guardian and your formidable skills that you were able to resist that kind of torture."

"I don't remember much, not really; I am sure you can understand—that event is one of the gaps in my brain that I do not want to revisit. Ever."

I took a long walk through the trees and returned to the tent before noon. I don't really recall where I went, what I saw, or what I did, and was startled to see Oliver returning to the tent with me. Not once did I realize he had been with me all those hours. I recognized the distracted blindness and wondered if Oliver was aware that I did not see him. While I was gone, the others continued the conversation without me, and now filled me in.

Oliver and Gabriel were confident they would find the assassin. They had some ideas that Marlow may be able to help. They will either convince the assassin to give up on his hunt by paying him more or terminate him. I was informed that there had been other attempts on my life. Marlow told Oliver that the assassin was likely to seek me out himself and stop sending his employees. It had been several years and he had lost a few expertly trained men in trying to fulfill this contract.

So that particular threat was to be neutralized somehow. The other threat was more disturbing and unclear. And for that, we would definitely need to consult with Marlow. I looked from Oliver to Gabriel, then to Amalu. Reality was swirling like a twister again, with Marlow's face at its violent center—the face that I now loathed. As I had called on Gabriel to choose, I knew now, we all knew, there was a time of great choosing bearing down on us. Amalu and Achmed must return to their village so as not to draw attention to their unexplained absence. They both sensed that their "guests" would like to rest. We bid each other a quick goodbye as they returned to Skoura while Oliver, Gabriel, and I remained in the mountain clearing.

My traveling companions were world-weary and cherished the comfort of these mountains. Weeks passed as we settled into a routine. Oliver was a very capable outdoorsman. Gabriel and I were both enthusiastic students as he taught us how to hunt with snares and collect the abundant fruits, almonds, and dates. Amalu and Achmed visited weekly with other supplies and news.

While sitting over tea one evening, Achmed and Amalu arrived and sent Gabriel and me farther into the mountains. They had been found by The Host who was poking around the villagers' dreams, creating quite a stir of nightmares. It would not be long before they would be hot on my trail.

"But what's the point of continuing to run, Amalu?

Sooner or later, we must face the enemy." I asked as we were leaving.

"There's no time for questioning right now, Sophia. We are working on reinforcements, but it will take time. There are ceremonies that must be performed, customs to follow, children to send away for safe-keeping. The elders have not called on their ancestors in many generations, and they need more time. We are not ready for the battle ahead."

Oliver volunteered to remain behind, to tend the tent as if we were all still there. "Sophia, you will be safe with Gabriel; and my presence here might confuse them, buy you some more time," Oliver offered. I reached up to hug him and he lifted me off my feet in a bone-crushing bear hug.

"Everything will be as it should be, Sophia," were his parting words whispered confidently in my ear.

We left on foot with bedrolls and supplies strapped to a donkey that Achmed and Amalu provided us. It took eleven days of intense hiking through the winding mountain passes until we arrived at our destination. We each had some bruising and scratches but nothing serious. Every so often, during those daily marches of twenty kilometers or more, Amalu would reach out to me and guide us ever on. Up steep mountains and down ravines we trekked, day after day, but always higher and higher into the reaches of the Atlas. My breathing was labored, as was Gabriel's, as we adjusted to the thinning air. Now and again, we would hear an approaching donkey with a lone Berber. We sought cover as best we could, quieted our donkey with handfuls of grain. If these strangers knew we were nearby, they respected our desire for privacy.

Our new refuge was a mountain dwelling overlooking a small lake along a river. The clay house was tiny but functional —one bedroom and a living area. There was an old tub in a small alcove off the bedroom and an outhouse uphill, hidden in a small grove of trees. The tub was a real luxury that I thought I might take advantage of at some point, a fair trade for the outhouse.

I took a moment to survey the accumulated contents of the house. There were two low stools, a small table, an abundant supply of blankets, pillows, and cushions. There was a narrow hearth for cooking and some rudimentary utensils and plates. It was perfect for our needs, and it was quite hidden in a thicket of brush. This was intended as a winter shelter, no doubt—complete with coal and wood, some preserved foods, already prepared for the winter. The house belonged to someone in the village; the people of Skoura shared with their needs and knew Achmed would replenish the stores when he could.

I took a moment to admire the spectacular view. The house was nestled in a shallow valley, protected on all sides by snow-capped mountains. We were, for all intents and purposes, living in the sky.

Gabriel and I got to work settling in. We looked around together and took a mental inventory of tools and supplies. In addition to the outhouse, there was a second, smaller outbuilding with a good supply of hand tools, an ax, a shovel, and room enough to keep our donkey quiet and comfortable at night. There was a great supply of fishing gear, which would come to good use at the lake. If it was to be a long stay, the two of us could be comfortable.

With a straw broom and some rags we discovered, we cleaned. Gabriel brought water from the hand pump that ran dry at first but then primed clean and clear. We could definitely survive the winter here, provided we could spend our days adding to the supplies. I made a fire, beat the carpets, shook out blankets and pillows until we had a comfortably tidy space to lay our heads. It was, as Gabriel remarked, "quite a luxury after being outdoors for the past fortnight, to be indoors with a fire burning." We slept in the main room, ignoring the bedroom, preferring instead the warmth of the fire.

We woke with the sunrise and began to fish and gather in earnest. The lake was abundant, and I brought in fish after fish with the worms and killies I collected with a net. I had twenty fish that first day, which we salted and hung in the outbuilding for drying. There was no electricity so we would have to cure everything we caught. There was plenty of salt, but we only had a few short weeks before autumn would be far behind us. Morning frost was the telltale sign of a quickly approaching winter.

Gabriel and I lived together during this time like good roommates. I think we were both afraid to let down our guard and allow our emotions (and hormones) to take over us. We fished and gathered and explored the mountains surrounding us. I learned how to live with the land and was at peace, for the most part. I maintained my daily exercise rituals—yoga and meditation, running, hiking. We swam in the frigid water in our underwear. I gave Gabriel lessons in these physical pursuits while he began teaching me French. There was no reading material to distract us, just the daily search for food, which was abundant in these fertile mountains. We didn't know how long we would be in the mountains, and it didn't weigh on us in the beginning. After some weeks of this, however, I started to get restless, wondering why it was taking so long to eliminate the threats. More than anything else, I wanted to help. I understood that if I were to reveal myself, we could draw "them" all out, hopefully to the same place, and put an end to this running and hunting game. I tried to reach out to Amalu, but she blocked me instantly with a grave warning of fear. She was afraid. I thought we had a good chance to defeat the hunters, but I didn't yet understand their nature.

The assassin's nature was clear to understand. He was paid for a job. I thought it might help if I could draw him out.

He would be easy to neutralize on a physical level. Kill or be killed. So I tried to find him. Before going to sleep, I meditated on the idea of finding him. If he was looking for me, perhaps we could 'connect.' I had been getting better at keeping my thoughts out of others' heads, but I didn't know if I had the ability to actively seek someone out. I thought there would be no harm in trying.

So I began to concentrate on feeling for a person who wanted to kill me. I tried during the day but was met with Gabriel's shock and anger. He was furious the first time it happened. I was sitting at the lake, concentrating. The mountains were reflected in the mirror of the lake as I began an ujjayi rhythm. I turned my thoughts to 'who wants to kill me?' While breathing, I chanted that simple phrase. I didn't consider Gabriel. Suddenly he was there, out of breath, having run from nearby.

"Sophia, what in bloody hell are you doing?"

I opened my eyes and looked up at him towering over me with his hands on his hips.

"Oh, sorry. I just can't sit around here much longer collecting nuts while everyone I love is out there trying to protect me. I thought I might find out some information that could help."

"Ohhh, sorry. Is that all you can say?" he hissed between gritted teeth.

I stood to face him, confused by this sarcastic bark of his.

"Have you lost your mind? Do you understand what a paid killer is, you fool? Are you really that ungrateful for all those who have put themselves at risk for you? Are you still so naïve?!"

I had never heard Gabriel raise his voice, and it took all his British self-control not to shout at me. This was so unlike him; I scrambled to my feet and reached for his hand, trying to reassure him. But he jerked his hand back, not wanting me to understand what had already passed between us in that second. I did, I knew in that contact—he was afraid for me. He didn't want to lose me. Immediately, I was filled with tenderness and remorse for being so thoughtless.

"I'm so sorry, Gabriel. I didn't mean to worry you. It won't happen again." It also occurred to me that he had heard my thoughts so easily. I needed to practice more if I were to keep them concealed.

We continued our daily lives, which were becoming boring. So we devised a schedule of exercise, lessons, storytelling, fishing, and gathering. To augment the salt in the cabin, we scoured the hills for local spices, finding thyme and sage. Along with the wild onions, we could make a tasty meal. I taught Gabriel what I knew of trusts and estates. He taught me what he knew of corporate and business law.

Nights were difficult on many levels. While at rest, I was vulnerable to the prying tentacles of strangers and kin. I tried often to connect with Amalu in the evenings, but she was intent on keeping me out of her thoughts. Achmed did his part, as well. Marlow and others were frantically searching for me.

The dark was filled with a jumbled mess of flashbacks from my early years, alternating with flashbacks of Albert, and now new raiders were trying to penetrate a gray wall of water that Amalu and Achmed worked at keeping around me. Occasionally, I would wake in a cold sweat, gasping for air, feeling like I was suffocating. Gabriel was always awake before me, sitting up, watching me. He never tried to wake me or interrupt those night terrors, and for that I was grateful. As uncomfortable as they were, these flashes of memory were necessary for me to sort through the confusing mess of my damaged mind. And it was indeed damaged.

Gabriel and I ignored the bedroom, both of us more comfortable (and warmer) in the larger room that I had organized into both a sleeping area and sitting area.

After a few weeks, the first snow fell. It was beautiful and terrifying. The snow struck an icicle of fear into my heart that was unfamiliar. I stood at the window all day and watched Gabriel from time to time out in the snow, splitting wood or fishing. I didn't want to leave the cabin. I was paralyzed by the idea of the snow falling on me. It was so irrational. I didn't understand it. I spent many winters in Northport with Albert in the snow. I didn't understand this unexpected fear. There was no escaping my mind in this isolated place—no pill or Marlow, no Albert or Oliver to soothe my growing panic.

I dressed in the sheepskins that Amalu had packed and decided to leave the cabin—I opened the door and stood there, as if a hand was pressed against my chest, like a wall where the door had been. Gabriel was returning with the day's catch. He stopped to watch me in the doorway, not understanding my internal panic. He tipped his head to the side, listening in to gauge my mood. His face moved from an expression of curiosity to surprise. This was the first time he had seen any evidence of fear in me. He was trying to penetrate my mind, glaring at me from a few yards away. I tried to take a step toward him, lifting my foot, not caring that he was trying to get into my head. I thought about moving the foot over the threshold as it hung in the air. But the thought would not move my foot as I withdrew it back, then returned to the window. Gabriel entered the cabin a few minutes later. He was completely respectful of my internal struggles and never pried me with questions, even under such odd circumstances. I practiced yoga and calisthenics in the cabin, anxious to release some of my tension.

I awoke from a nightmare screaming. Throwing off the blankets, I sprang to my feet and crouched low on my heels, ready to do battle. Gabriel was sitting on one of the stools, his face in his hands. His shoulders shook as he sobbed. I went to him and knelt on the floor before him. I was about to touch his knee when he slapped my hand away.

"Don't, Sophia. Don't touch me. I don't want you in my head."

"Gabriel, what is it?"

"Oh, I had no idea, Sophia...no idea. Do you remember your nightmare?"

"No, Gabriel, do you?"

"Yes, but if you cannot remember, it's best to wait until you're ready. It's not a good idea for you to pluck it from my mind. It's just so fucking unbelievable. It's so unbearable."

"Gabriel, please tell me what it was."

"No, Sophia, I've promised to protect you—your mind as well as your body. When it's time, you'll have to come to those memories on your own."

I trusted his answer. "I'm so sorry that I can't keep this from you while I'm sleeping, Gabriel. I have no way to block my dreams from slipping into your head." I had spent these months training my mind, using all of the skills that Albert had taught me in trying to master my thoughts. Occasionally, Gabriel would tell me if a thought had accidentally trotted into his brain; but while I slept, there was no containing the thoughts nor dreams, certainly not my nightmares. His mind was invaded and, unlike me, he remembered.

While we continued to linger, every so often I was able to feel for Amalu. I sensed that The Host was wearing on her defenses. I could feel it occasionally piercing the wall of water she and Achmed had erected. Its tentacles crept toward us like a living shadow on the land. Amalu was losing the battle. It would soon be on its way toward Oliver, then to Gabriel and me. It was a swarm of wicked creatures that I felt, crawling slowly but gaining momentum. I was confident it would be stampeding toward us on a foul wind very soon.

THE WORSHIP

I worship at the altar
of your body,
your flesh the shawl of my devotion.

your hands in my hair
are a prayer
for relief
reckoning,
beckoning.
I, atoning
for the sins of a day
each day.
I say god, it is holy?

I kneel at the temple
of your heart,
your breath a measured cadence,
a pulse in my ear.
It is the rhythm of
the sea
the cobalt blue sea.

Your voice chants
in exalted praise.
It is the gospel of Eros,
the symphony, my beloved.
I say god, it is divine?

I prostrate myself at the inner sanctum of your soul

inhaling the incense
saturating the shrine
invading every pore,
every fiber
of who and how I am.

I worship at the altar
of your body
and it is good.
I say god, it is holy.

THE WINTER OF LAYLA'S MIND

inter crept into the mountains as Gabriel and I hung on in a suspended state of being, literally living with no expectation and every expectation. It was unnerving at first, having no plan or schedule, no direction. Slowly, it became more comfortable, waking with morning light, attending to our immediate needs—water, food, fire. Providing food and water took up several hours of the day. We were creative at passing the time. We made a backgammon set and a chessboard. I taught Gabriel backgammon, and he taught me chess.

I worked at sorting through my memories, which was a very unpleasant task. Often I couldn't determine if the things I 'remembered' were Adele's journal entries, my true memories, or the nightmarish state of my confusion. Little by little, however, I recalled Adele and her sadistic nature. She took perverse pleasure in the little torments of my tiny world —a vicious pinch on the underarm if I happened to brush up against her, a yank of a loose strand of hair. Sometimes I could 'hear' her searching me out in the massive country house. Fortunately, there were many places I could hide; and the staff was often available to buffer the torment. Seeking out the order of those early years was like picking at a scab, over and over again, watching it bleed anew.

Most of the real trauma crept into my sleep and was sneaking up on me with greater frequency. Those visions were slowly becoming more vivid and alarming. My waking mind was not eager to explore those memories; but for some reason, my sleeping mind sought them out with greater intensity. In the end, the mind always has what the mind wants. Little by little, those daily pains, eight years of that other person's life, leaked into my daytime. I became more and more withdrawn, disinterested in our mental games or board games. I could stare out at the lake for hours, not realizing how much time had passed. Day after day, I became more consumed with my own mindlessness. I would find the void and look at the lake, weary with the mental exercises, frightened to the core of what they would eventually reveal.

Time passed.

Then one night, for a second time, I woke up screaming.

And I remembered.

I remembered it all.

The memories of those little torments were a protective barrier for the real terror. Adele had tried to kill me more than once. And I remembered each time in graphic detail. Worst of all, I 'heard' her planning and could not escape her reach. As I revisited each memory, each torturous revelation that she wanted me dead, my mind began to shut down. It was too much for the child Layla. And despite Albert's considerable effort, it was too much for the adult Sophia. I entered a state of suspended animation, unwilling even now to recount the grisly details. In psychiatric parlance, I was 'locked in.' When I tried to speak, I was unable to form my lips around words, like a stroke patient.

The traumas played themselves over and over in my mind, a slow-motion video, obsessing, turning in on itself, Adele's face in freakish disproportion, towering over me, dragging me by my hair to the shed, over and over, night after night, in the dark, the cold. I was as silent as a church mouse, hearing her wish me dead. Until the final hateful moment as she stood over the only papa I ever knew, dancing in his blood, while I sat mutely by waiting my turn.

I saw her snuff the life out of that man whom I loved. He held my hand tenderly when he was home. As evil as Adele was, he was sweet. Her journals did not do justice to the excitement she felt when she took that life. She was jubilant with her power, relieved of her pent-up desire to kill, the release of all that tension. The satisfaction was all too fleeting —the killing whetted her appetite for the release the act provided. She wanted to do it again and again and again. All of this I could feel flowing from her, a tidal wave of malevolence washing over the tiny mind of an eight-year-old child. There was no coherent thought, just the overwhelming tsunami of her feelings.

It was a vacuum of humanity—a black hole of the galaxy that welcomed me into its embrace. It was a place with no light or life in which she trapped me as she sought me out. Her desire for death would never be sated until I and all I represented—her break with reality—was gone from the world. I was the source of her unbridled loathing.

I did not move from the clay floor for the time I was locked in. I drank what Gabriel gave me, went to the toilet when he dragged me. It was agony for him to lift me, the shock of my being knocking him unconscious every time he tried.

I struck out at him in this drunken stupor when he came near. I surely hurt him several times, a feral cat, striking at the imagined horror. Unable to exercise the smallest control, poor Gabriel could hear the obsession, live through the graphic video, over and over, until my madness began to invade his waking mind.

Suddenly, Amalu was with me, reaching out. I saw her in

the garden of her childhood. It was a lovely place, verdant and peaceful. I saw her calling me from the path of an English garden. She was her little girl self again, as was I. I began a slow walk to her. As I moved, the dawn moved toward her with me, until we touched hands. I looked down at her little girl's hands, turning them over, interlacing our fingers, until I felt the warmth seep into my arms, moving up my wrists, to my elbow, shoulders, clavicle, neck. Oh, I took a breath, a deep breath after the drowning. My heart began to pulse, the oxygen rushing to my brain, clearing the congestion there.

Amalu was the breath of life, breathed into my nostrils. With that breath, she dispersed the evil memories into the wind. I looked into her little girl's face as she softly whispered, her breath smelling of buttercups, "Layla, it's time to wake up, sweetheart. You must wake up now, love. Please wake up."

And I opened my eyes. I saw the red clay ceiling with bits of straw from the floor in our mountain refuge. The details were so vivid, in high definition, I saw color and texture for the first time after a lifetime in the black hole. I moved to my side, then put a hand to the floor to raise myself up. Gabriel was again on the stool, his arms wrapped around himself as he withstood the nightmare of my damaged child's mind. I continued to hear Amalu. With her calming voice in my heart and mind, I withdrew from the nightmare. Gabriel's entire body let out the breath he had been holding. He looked up and was embracing me within moments, knowing finally I wouldn't hurt him.

"You must make a life of your own," I heard him whisper. "You must find a way to move on, to forgive, to understand—whatever it is that your mind can hold onto to have a life of your own." It was impossible to comprehend these words of his, to understand that a mother could be jealous of a child...that my mother could be jealous and murder her child. The words kept hammering at my skull until I thought it would burst. The words grew monstrously large in my mind's ear until I could hear little else. But still, I couldn't grasp them, couldn't quite wrap my mind around them...no, not my mind...my heart, my shattered heart would not hear. I railed at the truth of his words. I rose from the floor, my blouse clinging to my flesh, soaked through by the sweat of my proverbial brow. Tears were screaming to let loose, great balloons welling up and up from the core of my broken heart.

My chest was aching and I wondered at the physical pain I felt, as if every fiber, every muscle, and cell of my being had been fighting this knowledge all my life. Now, in this one horribly infinite moment, the knowledge was invading my body like a parasitic illness finally set loose upon a host. It was so tangible, this body ache; I thought it would surely kill me. All those years in the frigid waters of the Long Island Sound, the taser's kiss, could not compare to the entire body ache I felt. I walked to the fireplace and gazed into the flames sprouting up. I thought of the oxygen, the spark, the wood, all the components in the physical universe that came together to produce the fire. I thought of the sheer mass of it all, the elegant workings of the fire, how it could save a life or consume it. It could consume me and the life I had claimed as my own all these years. I hoped for it to consume me as the knowledge crept up my flesh from my toes, traveling in spiraling chaos through the years. I stepped on the knowledge for all those years, squashing that flame underfoot. But it returned when I moved and in the place where my foot had been, a smoldering ember of that knowledge gasped for oxygen to feed on itself. The heat from the fire did not warm me as I stood trembling, holding on to the wall, lest I fall or move into the fire and let it do its work.

Gabriel continued, "Your truth will never be hers. Perhaps your truth will redeem her in some grand gothic tragedy you have chosen for yourself. Perhaps she is not worthy of redemption. This speculation really matters very little. Either it was an accident that you were born to her or you chose her or it was some divine act or some unholy joke. None of it matters in the life you will make for yourself. Her nature is the nature of things as we know them."

I moved from the back wall, my nails scraping at the clay, toward the window, each step an act of supreme will, my legs scorched with the heat of the knowledge flame. It moved, millimeter-by-millimeter, creeping up my legs like an evil shadow. There was no way to douse the flame. I had been fed from the Tree of Knowledge of Good and Evil, and I could not stop the agony that continued to march through my limbs, an Army of the Almighty Intellect, forcing me to gaze out onto the lake and take notice of the ice, naked trees, a squirrel. I wanted to spring from the window into that lake, break through the ice to cool the heat burning me alive. My hands were pressed against the windowpane and then Gabriel was there, wrapping them in gauze, blood dripping down the length of my arm. I thought blithely, blood, water, all the same to me now—blood of the lake, water of my veins.

"This is my blood which I have given for you."

Where had I heard that? Is this how I could redeem her, reach into her soul, and heal her? The bright red rivulets of blood were soaking into my blue blouse, and I wondered if the blue and red would make purple. My soul was bleeding out the wounds, like leeches bleeding out disease. The fire had reached my neck. I couldn't breathe or speak or cry—or cry out. I was paralyzed with the knowledge that soon the fire would end the agony, and I welcomed it.

I heard Gabriel humming in the distance of a seaman's fog as I thought to myself, *Thou shalt not covet thy neighbor's wife...thou shalt not covet thy neighbor...thou shalt not covet...thou shalt not covet!* I wanted to scream, but I was mute, my lips sealed shut in disbelief.

"Thou shalt not covet thy child" was really the crux of it all. My mother coveted all that she saw in the world. "My mother covets," I repeated to myself. She is consumed with an envy, an envy that wishes ill on others. No, no, no I grasp—she does not covet all she sees in the world. She only covets Marlow's love for me. She only wishes ill on me. No, wait, she's dead now. She can't harm me anymore. But she has harmed me. The damage is done and cannot be undone. No wonder my mind is such a fucked up mess. How will I ever get out of my own mind?

Gabriel continued to hum, a lullaby of eerie childhood memories while I continued this manic conversation in my mind.

Who is rich? He who is happy with his portion in the world. Who is rich? Who is rich? Who is rich? WHO IS RICH? WHO IS RICH? WHO IS RICH WHO IS RICH WHO IS RICH RICH RICH RICH???!!!!?

Rich in spirit and love was all I ever really wanted.

I was on the floor when I awoke. Gabriel had wrapped his arms and legs around me, protecting me as I struggled to escape his powerful arms, his muscles flexing tightly every time I moved, my chest heaving with the exertion. The world about us faded away as twilight entered. Hours had passed, and only the outlines of the room were visible. The fire had gone out, but Gabriel would not relight it for fear of letting me go. He was still humming, but now I could hear the words.

He was pleading, begging the gods of his world, the stars, whatever. "Please, Sophia, please come back. I can't bear another moment of your horror. Please, please, please, Sophia, please let it go from your mind," he whispered over and over again. The heat of knowledge had faded, and I was suddenly chilled to the bone from sweat and blood and exhaustion. My voice croaked out, "My mother envied me, Gabriel. She did not, could not, love me."

It was the most precious moment of my life with her. I had eaten the apple, and it would not kill me. I ached for something that would never be. I ached to reach into her heart and heal her, to reach into my own heart and heal myself...

Gabriel, my unholy messenger.

Releasing my legs, Gabriel sat up, facing me, his hands still gripping my upper arms. "I'd like to wash up, I think," I said. Gabriel let go and got to his feet as I stood. I was dizzy and tipped into his arms.

"Give me a few minutes. I'll heat some water and sit with you," Gabriel replied.

"That's not necessary, Gabriel. I'll be okay by myself —promise."

I sank into the warm tub that Gabriel had filled, cleaned, and redressed the gaping cuts on my hands and arms, put on a tee-shirt and sweatpants. I toweled off my hair and did a quick brush through. When I came out of the bedroom, Gabriel had already started a fire and had prepared a light snack of pita, dates, olives, and some dried meat and tea. I sat and nibbled and drank while he quietly watched me.

"Gabriel, we need to leave soon. Amalu reached out to me and woke me up. How long...was I?"

I thought he would say forty days. The forty days from conception, the forty years in the desert. It felt like forty lifetimes, but in truth, it was a mere forty hours. Forty hours of unrelenting torment for both him and me.

He was observing my every move. "Forty hours," he whispered. He looked as if he hadn't slept or eaten.

"Let's go and sit by the fire," I suggested.

"I'm going to wash up also," he replied. While he was in the bedroom, I picked at the food and thought about what he had suffered these past days. I felt sickened by the food and shame.

I was ashamed of my weakness and my memories that were spilled like a vomitus mass of chunky spoiled milk all over the floor. The stench of sour milk and sulfur filled my nostrils, burning my sinuses. I was overwhelmed with my impotence to manage this fucked up mind.

I was sick of myself and so mortified that those private

traumas were now out there. I felt as if I were standing naked in front of an auditorium. Shame is the little killer. Unlike fear, which I could manage, shame is the little death that brings total obliteration. I will not face my shame. I cannot let it pass over me and through me. Where the shame resides, there will be a bounty of self-loathing. I will not remain.

I grabbed a couple of blankets and spread them on the floor among the cushions. I sat with my arms wrapped around my knees, facing the fire.

Gabriel returned and I hid my face in my hands as I whispered, "I'm so sorry. I'm so, so sorry, Gabriel. I never meant for you to bear witness to that ugliness."

He gently moved my hands from my face, held my chin, and made me meet his eyes. He had been crying. His vulnerability was so palpable that I didn't know if there was any redemption for my sins of suffering.

"No, Sophia, I am sorry for your suffering and your shame. You have no reason to be ashamed." He moved to sit behind me, his back leaning against some cushions, his legs on either side of mine. I felt his arms snaking toward me, touching my wrists, turning over the hands wrapped in gauze. He moved his hands slowly up my forearms, to my upper arms, then to my neck. I let out a breath and leaned into him. He spread his legs and pulled me closer to him. Both hands on my neck, massaging. I continued to stare into the fire while he moved up and down, from my neck to my wrists. I let out a sound.

"Hmmm—that feels nice."

"Yes, it does," he replied. He brought his hands around to my ribcage and kneaded the tense muscles. I was giving myself over to the sensation of his hands on me.

"Lift your arms, Sophia" he commanded.

I complied. Surprisingly, I was content to give him control of this time we have together. I was grateful he was so direct in his instructions. I didn't want to think. I wanted. I wanted. I wanted him...to take me. He removed my shirt and continued to knead my back, my ribcage, reaching around to my breasts.

I let out a sigh, feeling disjointed, excited. He kissed my neck, nuzzling me. I turned to look at him. His pupils were dilated as he cupped my cheek and leaned toward me. I was staring at his lips and realized I would soon feel them on me. He turned my face toward him as he licked his lips.

"Do you want me to kiss you?"

I nodded my head, unable to speak, I was breathing so fast.

"Do you want to feel my lips on you?"

I nodded again.

"Say it, Sophia. Tell me what you want."

He hesitated, his lips a fraction away from mine. All I could think was that I wanted to feel the doughy texture of those lips wrapped around mine. Instead of answering, I reached my mouth toward his. He pulled back a fraction.

"Sophia, you must tell me. I need to hear it. Not feel the overwhelming command of your mind. Nor do I want to be the man who takes a woman in a moment of weakness."

Oh, he is honorable in every important way.

"Please," I replied.

I leaned toward him while he moved back again. He knew what I wanted.

"Say my name, Sophia."

I could barely think while Gabriel kept me at bay.

"Gabriel," I said, his name a prayer on my tongue. I looked into his eyes. They were moist with emotion. I moved my hand and touched his face. Oh my god, I didn't know how I longed to touch him. I turned and faced him, full-on, topless, shameless. Sitting on my knees, I reached out to touch his face. I moved my fingers gently along his eyebrows, down below his eyes, to his cheeks. Finally, I reached his lips, the lips I've been lusting after for so long now. I did the things I thought about during our lunch. I traced his lips with my fingers. I reached for the tea and dipped my index finger in it. I wet his lips. His chest was heaving, his excitement and restraint warring with each other. I stared at his lips as I moistened them with the tea. I leaned forward at the same time as he did. I licked my lips.

He touched my lips with his, barely making contact, a butterfly kiss. The butterfly kiss moved languidly, our tongues tentative. We each felt the gentle touch, our lips molding and moving in time to a slow blues dance. We were battered and bruised, both of us, cautiously touching the other. His hands framed my face. I grasped his shoulders, moved down his upper arms, cupped his elbows in my palms. He continued to caress me, the most delicate devotion to the one he loves.

He loves me. He doesn't want to take me—he wants to worship me. And I, I am thankful for him, in a totally new experience for me. I am filled with gratitude for an undeserved devotion to my damaged self.

In my unguarded state, he commented on my inner dialogue. "No, Sophia, you are wrong. You are deserving. You are a unique element on the planet, an exquisite reflection of all that can be cruel and yet is still kind in this world."

He sees me.

And loves me just the same, in all my broken reality. The butterfly kiss picked up in tempo. The blues were rocking through our bodies, as we were engulfed in each other's mouths. Our limbs were the tentacles of the beat, as we were entangled in the dance of an ageless rhythm.

And I say god, it is holy.

Gabriel, my holy messenger. He brought me glad tidings after our forty days in the desert of my mind. He has reached into the treasury of souls and withdrawn Layla, born anew in the comfort of his loving embrace.

I woke at 5:00 a.m. and Gabriel was still sleeping. I stepped outside to stretch my legs and walked for a half-hour, thinking about our night together. It did not fall short of my fantasy. Gabriel was a kind and generous lover. He freed me from all that came before and all that might come afterward.

Then I considered the assassin. Although I had heard the news so many weeks earlier, it took all this time for my heart to hear the truth. I understood Adele's action, her desire for vengeance, and I thought I had accepted her and her damaged mind. But the dream awoke in me a paralyzing disbelief, a trauma to the heart of a child yearning for the love of a mother.

As I walked that morning, I said it aloud until I became immune to it. "The assassin was sent by my mother." Even after death, she would not rest until I joined her. That information, although not surprising, had set my mind into a tailspin. In addition to Adele's assassin, the clan in Jamaica had been searching for me in recent years. Their intent was not as clear. It couldn't be determined if they wanted to kidnap or kill me. It was only prudent to get those answers before making contact.

As I emerged from the woods and started down the hill toward the house, I saw two shadows through the window. Two men were beating Gabriel, his hands tied behind his back, on his knees on the floor. They were beating him with belts and fists. I had been so absorbed in my own thoughts, I hadn't felt any danger coming. Fury overtook me. I ran toward the house with my arms outstretched, my hands claws as I reached out to the invaders.

In those damaged hands, I held death.

Still running with my arms in front of me, I closed my hands over their hearts, and I choked the life out of those two little fist-sized muscles with a quick contraction of my hands. They turned to see me, fell to their knees, and dropped their weapons as I continued to barrel down upon them. My wrath knocked them over dead with the last pulse of my closed fists. I squeezed the life out of their puny hearts with pleasure.

Albert's training, a good dose of adrenaline, and muscle

memory took charge of my inflamed body as I raced into the house, jumping over the bodies, to untie Gabriel. As an afterthought, I remembered that Albert never taught me the use of any weapons. Now I understand why.

I am the only weapon I need.

Gabriel was unconscious, blood running from a gaping wound in his head. I moved with the calm precision of a paramedic, tearing my sleeve, applying pressure to the head wound, checking the rest of his body. His torso was bruised, a rib or two broken. I made a mental note on internal injuries.

For the moment, I had stopped the bleeding. I grabbed a stool to elevate his feet, I ran outside to the lake and wrapped some ice in a cloth, and applied it to his head. That was the best I could provide as first aid under the circumstance.

A more urgent threat was on its way. There were others coming, many others. They came on the wind, an army of apparitions. The sky clouded over, the wind whipped up, leaves and branches swirling about outside as I tended to Gabriel's wounds. It was the same menacing spirit that invaded my pleasant day all those years ago with my friend, Sally, the same that had crept around the day Gabriel and I met John at the museum. But this was a storm cloud of hundreds, thousands, of ghostly faces, coming to collect me. Ah, this was The Host that Amalu had spoken of.

It became clear that they were coming to collect me, not kill me.

I would not be collected. And they would not come close to my Gabriel.

I stepped outside and could see the storm cloud as it rose over the mountains. The cloud was composed of many faces, moving like an undulating body with many heads. It was Ursula with appendages of distorted faces. Young and old faces, gray and white, some dense with ash, others transparent human, monstrous parts. It was moving within itself as it glided over the mountain range. The faces were ghoulish, with bulbous features, the clouds moving in on themselves, limbs intertwining, hair trailing like fine jellyfish tentacles from the sky. It was a visual cacophony of fiends, devils, imps, monsters from our nightmares, made more terrifying because they were distortions of our human selves, not really monsters—clownish deformed and disfigured faces that were once people—men, women, children.

i
shall
not
fear

"I shall not choose fear," I mouthed meekly from my lips, a silent devotion to an inner strength I did not feel. The icicle of the abyss threatened to impale me through and snuff out any courage I had. My bowel was weak as water trickled down my leg. When I had invited the killer, I truly could not have imagined what thing I had called upon. This was the mass of our darkest nightmare, the place where the soul has been bled out. They sensed me as I crushed the life out of those hearts—it was a siren call, a beacon to light their way. I remembered the claw, its deadly strength, as I repeated to myself, more confidently this time,

I.
Shall.
Not.
Fear.

I closed my eyes and took, unbelievably, one cleansing breath.

Then another.

Albert was with me.

"Find the void, Sophia. Calm yourself. Breathe."

Anger bloomed in my chest upon hearing Albert call my name.

"Layla, I am called Layla, Albert. And with the night I will strike terror into the hearts of those who come to harm the ones I love." The wrath of my heart expanded into my chest, radiating out to my limbs. It made me strong—powerful—invincible. I remembered the claw again, and the memory dispatched the fear into oblivion.

I felt them trying to press in on me.

I continued to breathe—one breath, two, ten.

I found the void and opened my eyes, singularly focused.

My voice carried on the wind that surrounded me, a whisper amplified into the abyss between myself and the storm cloud. "Who comes for Laya?" I whispered.

"It is the we who are I," I heard. The cloud grew closer and larger. Its arrogance fueled my anger until it was a barely contained fury.

One, two, ten,

I breathed again.

"What are you called?" I demanded.

The specter hesitated, the many faces not sure of the direction of my voice. That was interesting.

I could move my voice. I searched my memory for all of Albert's lessons, knowing he must have taught me the skills I needed so desperately at the moment. Several seconds passed and I threw my 'voice' north, into the High Atlas mountains.

To my astonishment, the storm cloud moved north, away from me. I 'called' them from another place, and the cloud flew further north until it was gone.

I returned to the house to check on Gabriel. He was conscious but disoriented, trying to remove the ice pack that I had tied to his head. I was on high alert at that point, aware of any changes in the atmosphere. People were coming. I moved Gabriel's hand from the ice and whispered for him to stay quiet as he moaned. I stepped outside and hid in the copse of trees uphill to get a better view of who was coming.

Over the ridge came Amalu, Oliver, and Achmed...followed by:

Marlow.

OF ORANGE WATER AND DEATH MARCHES

*T*hey were racing up the hill, following the moving shadows as the cloud headed north. I stayed in the trees for a minute more as they approached and then stepped out so they could see me.

I started down the hill toward them. Within a few steps, my knees gave out. On my knees, I watched them approach. Oliver was first to reach me, and he picked me up in one swift move. We all moved into the clay house where Gabriel was lying on the blankets, the collar of his shirt between his teeth as he gritted against the pain in silence.

Oliver set me down on the floor and poured a glass of water. I could still feel the hoard of fiends moving further north, following my false lead.

Marlow pulled up a stool to sit near me. Achmed and Amalu turned their attention to Gabriel.

"Sophia, what happened here?"

I described, as best I could, the forty hours in the darkness of my mind, then Amalu waking me, the assassins beating Gabriel, the storm cloud. He was frustrated with my words and laid a hand on me to get a clearer reading. He was astonished.

"Sophia, have you 'heard' from Albert?"

"Sort of—I think we should make a plan to move. Can we move Gabriel?"

"We have some time, perhaps a couple of days. It will continue a mindless march toward your voice."

My eyes were getting heavy. I could barely keep them open as he continued to speak. I tumbled into a post-adrenalin slumber, unaware of the activity around me, and woke in the late afternoon to the sounds of quiet voices.

I was in the bedroom for the first time, covered in blankets and drenched in sweat. I sat up, feeling dizzy and weak. I put my feet to the floor and was overcome with a feverish shaking. Marlow was at the bedside there, beside me, with sweet orange water.

"Drink this—it will help with the trembling. It's low blood sugar and fatigue." He supported my back.

I did as he said, without hesitation.

I waited a few minutes until the shaking stopped and then stood, with Marlow's hand on my elbow. I felt as weak as a kitten as I headed to the toilet at the back side of the house. Marlow supported me to the outdoor convenience and waited for me. I leaned into him as we made our way back inside.

I was too weak to bathe, even though there was warm water in the tub. I settled on changing into dry clothes while Marlow modestly turned his back. But he remained as I changed my clothes, mostly sitting on the bed. I was panting with exhaustion by the time I finished. He gave me some more orange water.

"Why am I so weak, Marlow?" My voice was little more than a hoarse whisper.

"Well, you ran a mental marathon today with your activities. And you have had no conditioning. Your anger alone was enough to deplete you."

"Oh shit, where are the bodies?"

"Don't worry, Sophia, taken care of."

"Gabriel—oh, how is Gabriel?"

"He took quite a beating physically, but his mental injuries seem to be worse."

"What do you mean?" I asked, my brow creasing and my lips pursed. I struggled to keep control of my emotions, of the feel of Gabriel's lips, his fingerprints still warm on my skin.

"Why don't you come inside and see him yourself."

I got up and then hesitated.

"Don't be afraid, Sophia. You can handle this." But Marlow was right. I was afraid to see what damage my twisted memories and the beating had wreaked on poor Gabriel.

I stepped into the main room to see him leaning against some pillows, his torso wrapped with blanket strips to bind his ribs. He was staring out the window, his doughy lips stretched thin in his concentrated effort. His eyes were dull cataract blue, the intelligent sparkle gone. I walked toward him, and as I reached out to move a bit of hair from his eyes, he swatted my hand. He didn't look at me, just swiped at the annoying mosquito that had interrupted his work.

I moved behind him where he couldn't see me and put a hand on his shoulder. I didn't want to probe his mind in this state but I felt I must. I was sorry I did when I heard his inner dialogue.

"Cottleson, cottleson, pie—ask me no questions and I'll tell you no lies," over and over went the wretched rhyme. It was one of Adele's favorites. He was trying to bury or purge the torments of my youth, so disturbing and graphic they had been.

I turned to Marlow who was standing nearby.

"I don't understand. Why is this so difficult for him, Marlow? He was abused himself. And he was fine last night," I said with a blush.

"His childhood was a tea party compared to yours,

Sophia. You simply don't know any different. When he was trapped in your memories, it was as if he were reliving them with you. He's traumatized and responding as a young child would, perhaps as he actually did. Sometimes it comes on as a delayed reaction, like your reaction to Adele's death march on your life. The beating he took this morning seems to have been the last straw to push him over the edge. He needs some time to regroup. Unfortunately, we don't have time, and will have to move him in this state."

Marlow hesitated, opened his mouth, and then closed it. He rocked from one foot to the other. He put his hands together, interlacing the fingers, then dropped them to his side.

"What, Marlow? Is there more?"

He moved toward a window and looked out on the lake. I followed and stood beside him, our hands almost touching. For a change, I was the one waiting.

"What is it, Marlow? Keeping me in the dark won't help at this point."

He leaned his hands against the window panes on either side of the window and lowered his head.

"I am so sorry, Sophia. I had no idea. In the first years after Adele left for England, I had no interest in what was happening, so consumed as I was with my own newfound skills. I was taken in by the elders, my aunt in particular, and concentrated on learning how to manage my mind. When I finally sought you out, you were so silent, I thought you had not inherited any of the clan's skills, my skills."

"Adele's mind was bent on me, and I heard the first whispers of her animus toward you when you were only five years old. You were so good at hiding your heart and mind and body that I assumed...I, I didn't try hard enough to reach you. I thought Adele was calling me, but it was borrowed from you, the calling. I didn't understand the true danger to you until the night I held her back. I started to make plans as soon as I could, but it was complicated. It was only after the murder that I sought help more urgently."

Tears were spilling down his face as he spoke in an urgent whisper, unable to look at me. We both continued to look out on the lake. This was the blood of his veins. I am the blood of his veins. Take this cup and drink of it, the cup of the new and everlasting covenant.

"Sophia, I am so sorry. I wish there were some way to turn back time and undo the untold damage I have done. I didn't know. I didn't know. I am so sorry."

Some things just cannot be undone. He nodded and stepped outside. I wasn't inclined to comfort him, but Albert's words came to me on the mountain breeze. Forgiveness is for the injured, not the sinner.

Just now, I had no time to consider Marlow and our confusing relationship. There was work to be done, and I would be better for it if I could turn my attention to the task at hand. Amalu, Achmed, and Oliver were scattered about the tiny house. I turned my attention to them.

"Okay, is there a plan to move Gabriel?"

Amalu came to me and held my hand. "Yes, we will begin the trek back to the village tomorrow morning. Achmed and Oliver have put together a stretcher. It's going to be a difficult trail, but we need to get to the village as quickly as possible."

"Marlow said we have a few days, then what? They are hunting, and they intend to collect me. At some point, I have to make a stand. I don't know how seeing as the small effort I made today knocked me out for hours."

"Marlow can help you, Sophia, and so can we. Together we can make a stand, but not here. It must be in the village where we have more support," offered Achmed.

"Tomorrow cannot come soon enough for me. What can I do to help?"

"Rest, Sophia. We will need you to draw on that store of

energy you possess. Rest and eat and get strong," added Oliver.

"I'd like to get some air."

Oliver fetched my coat and boots and his, as well. He would stay with me as he knew I wished. We walked in the gathering dark and saw Marlow at the lake. He joined us in silent companionship as he and Oliver fetched gear and fished for our next meals. They had brought supplies with them and a pack mule, but we would need more. The trek down would take longer this time, as Gabriel would be on a litter, and there was new snow. I sat and watched, dozing every now and then, feeling an unfamiliar mental and physical fatigue.

We returned to the house with a dozen fish to be dried over the fire. Achmed, Amalu, and Oliver spent the evening packing our stores and tending to Gabriel. I could barely look at him. I love him, I have loved him and shredded his psyche, all in the space of some hours. What if he never came back to me? Amalu glanced up, and I realized I must quiet my thoughts, especially these very private ones.

After eating, we sat together in the warmth of the cabin, sipping at tea, each of us waiting for morning. Gabriel was dozing after Amalu put some herbs into his tea.

Oliver was the only one who could get near Gabriel. He approached as one would to a frightened animal. He moved into Gabriel's line of sight and waited until he was accustomed to seeing him. Then he moved closer, head bent, like a submissive, until Gabriel looked at him. Oliver would then offer what he had in his hand. It was a glass of water, pita, nuts, at different times. Gabriel would examine what he held and then finally take what was offered. Each time it took twenty minutes or more. It was a silent, patient effort. Oliver never spoke, while Gabriel mumbled quietly every now and again. In this way, Oliver got enough calories into Gabriel to sustain him through the night. I wasn't sure how we would get him on a stretcher. He was mute and unresponsive when anyone tried to speak to him. I stayed out of his head, trying to focus my attention on what lay ahead. Once Gabriel was sleeping deeply, I turned my attention to Marlow.

"Marlow, what can you tell us about the cloud? Where is it from? How can it be controlled? What is it?" Achmed, Amalu, and Oliver listened closely. They also would be facing that demonic cloud.

"It is a weapon wielded by the elders in the islands. They are lost spirits or damaged ones that have been unable to pass into the next world. The Obeah uses some of them for different purposes. This one was sent to find you."

"Can it do physical harm?"

"Probably. But the real danger is the psychological harm, which is much worse. It works by infecting the mind, like a parasite. If it is given entry, it will turn a genius into an imbecile, then use it for its own purpose, or deliver it to the elders for their purposes."

"Why are the elders hunting me?"

Marlow bent his head. It took a few minutes for him to answer. I was impatient.

"Marlow, I am still weak from my earlier efforts and don't want to expend needed energy on making demands. Just get on with it already."

"For breeding," he replied.

It was Amalu who got to her feet on my behalf.

"Like livestock—savages. I always knew they were savages." She was spitting the words out, pacing.

"No Amalu, I am the savage. Sophia's abilities are the direct result of my savagery. The elders have their reasons. I don't always agree with them, but they have their reasons to protect the clan, the Obeah, their way of life."

"I was right to spend all my time learning to keep them out and hiding from them. They are barbarians," Amalu added under her breath while she continued to pace the small space.

Marlow was suddenly keenly interested in Amalu's comment. He peered at her in intense concentration. He was taking the measure of her abilities and her anger.

She returned his gaze and raised one dainty little hand. She extended her pointer to him and slowly raised it until, in sync with her movements, Marlow rose to his feet as if he were dangling from strings and Amalu was the puppeteer. He was gasping for air with his efforts to resist. She let her hand fall gently back to her side and waited for him to catch his breath.

"Marlow, that little demonstration is the result of a life lived well...one without your violence; one with openness and honesty at its core. My parents were loving and kind, fearless and open-minded about the Obeah, my heritage. When they noticed that I could 'hear' things, they didn't dismiss it as a child's imagination but helped me to explore it with love and support.

It took me years to discover the ugly truth of the Obeah breeding plan. Like Sophia, I was adopted from Jamaica by a rich English couple. They were happy to buy a newborn baby girl who no one knew about or even acknowledged. It was the only dishonest act in a life otherwise lived morally. Unlike Sophia's childhood, mine was blessed with love. I always knew I was adopted, and my parents took me to my birthplace many times. It was there that they let me explore these gifts. I met a spiritual guide who helped to keep me hidden from the Obeah. Although she shared their gifts, she did not agree with their master plan—or master race. She helped me to find my biological father, and then she helped me to hide from him and his twisted notions of right and wrong."

Marlow was visibly shaken. He started toward Amalu, seemed to think better of it, and retreated. "What is your birth date?"

"You know it, Marlow, as you know that you have put both of your daughters in grave danger. And you still defend them?" Marlow was sitting on a stool, while Amalu was bent over, almost nose to nose with him.

"Wait...what? Renee??? I don't think I understand."

I could hear Marlow making a noise—something between weeping and trying to swallow tears, and then Amalu was beside me lacing her fingers into mine. She smiled and nodded, and it all made sense.

Marlow tried to stand but instead sank to the floor with fatigue. I enjoyed his discomfort for once, not being the one to control information.

"How, when? I don't understand," he said.

"Of course you don't understand, Marlow. You are the greatest danger of all, connecting us to them. In all your vain efforts to protect Sophia, you have brought them down on us, time and time again."

"After Adele gave birth to Sophia, there was continuing labor until the doctor realized another baby was on the way. They put her under and the doctor, with the help of one of the nurses, took me. It was common practice in those years."

"Amalu," I interjected, "I read about the birth in one of Adele's journals, and it fits now. But how did we end up being childhood friends? What are the odds?"

"The odds," said Marlow, "are quite good in favor of you being drawn together. It's one of the reasons that the elders seek out certain gene pools. With more of us working together with them, they and we have greater power. And we draw like kinds to ourselves, like roots of a tree drawing water from the ground. Think about it—you and Gabriel, Renee and Achmed."

He was sitting back on the stool again and shaking his head from side to side, reeling from the news that he had two daughters, not one. I again found myself enjoying his distress.

"We have a long journey ahead of us," Achmed suggested. "Let's all try to get some sleep."

"How will we get Gabriel on the stretcher tomorrow? How will we keep him calm, quiet?" I asked.

"I brought some sedatives, Sophia. We didn't know what we would find when we fled the village and came here," answered Amalu.

"Oh my, what happened in your village?" I looked from Achmed to Amalu.

Oliver spoke up and said, "Achmed is right. We will have time to catch up on the return hike. Let's get some sleep."

Marlow and Oliver took the bedroom while the rest of us took to the floor in the main room. I laid awake for hours, as did everyone but Oliver. He slept with one eye open so to speak, but he surely slept. The faces in the clouds haunted me every time I closed my eyes. It was a fearsome image; one that had been scorched into the gray matter of my brain.

Morning came and with it a speedy departure of our party of six. We left the little clay house in the mountain thicket and began the trek back to Skoura. Oliver got Gabriel sedated. The pack mule dragged the sturdy stretcher behind. After them came the smaller donkey laden with the food-stuffs we would need in the coming days. Gabriel's stretcher was strong and comfortable, with skis at the end to glide over earth and snow. Oliver and Achmed had done a good job.

Morning frost bit at us as we began to walk. We started out quietly, everyone wiping sleep from his eyes. As the sun rose over the snow-covered hills, we broke a sweat. Gabriel stirred every so often, and we would stop, check him, move on. We marched like a well-trained platoon, only stopping to eat and rest. Marlow led the pack and set a quick pace. He was strong and had the stamina of those of us half his age. Behind Marlow, I walked with Amalu while Achmed led the pack mule, and Oliver took up the rear with the donkey. I felt confident with my fellow travelers, even after a disturbing night's sleep.

After the first day, we had made good progress; and although I knew the direction, we were taking a different path. We set up camp and ate cold rations, Marlow insisting that a fire would not be a good idea. We went to sleep in a tightly knit circle, everyone close enough to touch, and I made up for the previous night.

The next day passed the same. That night, Achmed led us to a cave for shelter. There we made a fire and let the heat seep back into our bones. During the night, Amalu gently touched my arm to wake me and motioned for me to follow her outside. A short distance from the entrance to the cave, she took my two hands in her own.

"Sophia, do you remember the game?"

I didn't until that very moment when she shared it with me. Yes, yes, we would hold hands and one of us would form an intention. Sometimes it was a silly childhood desire, like snow falling in summer.

Snow falling in summer, I remembered.

That's why I couldn't step out of the cabin that first snowfall. We were playing one day in the gardens and we made snow fall in summer. Adele came upon us. I didn't hear her coming because I was too engrossed in my play with Renee. Adele screamed and chased Renee to her waiting car. I know now that it was Mr. Spencer who protected Renee from Adele's rage. I was not as lucky.

She took me to the basement. I could hear a plan forming in her mind. She had thoughts of one type of torture or another, discarded some, kept others, and settled on a most hideous violation.

She stripped me and then tied me with fishing line she found in a cupboard. She tied my arms above my head onto a hook in the ceiling and whipped me with a wire hanger until my lower back and backside bled. Then she left me alone in the dark for the night, where I whimpered as quietly as I could, peed myself, and waited for morning. I knew she would release me before the staff awoke. But it was a night of terror, as Adele paced the kitchen floor, thinking of other cruel ways to torment me. Her imagined torments were often worse than the torture itself. She considered filling the basement cupboard with rats or cockroaches, a thought she grew attached to for quite some time but decided in the end that she didn't want the infestation that would result.

It was the first snow that Renee and I had made.

It was the last snow.

As we held hands now and this nightmare came back to me, Renee sobbed and held me while I tried to comfort her.

"Renee, it's an old wound. It just feels new. I will let it go. You will let it go. Forgiveness is for me. And for you. Come, we can do better things with our talents." I smiled at her.

"Okay, okay, Layla. Let's try to see where it is."

"But won't it know I'm coming?"

"No, not if you come from behind; there's a blind spot...Here, I'll teach you with Marlow as the subject. He is sleeping, like Oliver, with one eye open. When you search for him, search for the back of his head, see his image as if you are standing behind him. Do not seek out his attention. Don't think his name." We were sitting at the mouth of the cave, facing each other, still holding hands. Renee told me to close my eyes, and as we did, she floated above, tugging me along.

I heard her wish to find him. But she was vague, not using his name mentally. We had some advantages. We knew where he was in the cave. He was asleep, and he wasn't seeking either of us. But the exercise was helpful. I was able to see Marlow from just a few feet away, hovering over him, but out of his line of 'sight' so to speak.

Renee led me back outside. "Let's try something a little more difficult. How about someone in England?" suggested Renee.

"I have an idea. Philip and James are my co-workers. The distance seems so vast. Marlow is nearby."

"Distance is meaningless in this endeavor. Okay, think of Philip, and let's try to find him."

We held hands, and I pictured Philip's face. Renee received the image, and I started to move over the landscape toward Europe. It felt like a long time was passing. Renee told me to just concentrate on Philip, not on the physical way to reach him. I tried and suddenly we were over London. I located his neighborhood, just south of Hampstead Heath. We entered his building and were standing in the bedroom, observing Philip and James in bed together, the night deep upon them, same as it was on us. This was a terrible invasion of privacy, and I felt awkward. Lying on his side, Philip felt for James, reaching out for him. James languidly rolled into his lover's arms. Renee and I were charmed by their intimacy.

Philip opened his eyes and looked directly at me. James felt him startle awake,

"What is it, love?"

"Sophia woke me."

"Just a dream—go back to sleep."

Renee brought us back.

"He saw me."

"Not quite, but he sensed you. The Obeah will truly see you, so you must come from behind."

"Renee, I'm tired. Let's practice again tomorrow. I'd like to seek out Albert, but I don't know where he is."

"You don't need to know where he is, but that will take some practice. We will continue tomorrow."

"Renee, how did you learn to do this?

"I told you, Sophia, my parents were very open-minded. It was a combination of their openness to the extraordinary and my mentor's help."

We returned to the cave to find Marlow awake, waiting for us. "This is a dangerous game you are playing, you two."

"Don't talk to me about dangerous games, Marlow," Renee retorted. I felt a little protective of Marlow, but Renee was very angry with him. She knew much more about the Obeah than I did, and I also wanted to learn more about it from her. We tucked into our bedrolls for the remaining hours of the deep dark.

The third day dawned with Gabriel in an agitated state. Oliver tried his usual approach, but Gabriel struck at him every time he got near. I tried Oliver's tactic and squatted nearby until Gabriel noticed me in his line of sight. He looked at me and made eye contact for the first time in three days. I didn't need to touch him to understand the cause of his anger. He was seething mad at me and broke his silence.

"You are poisonous, Sophia, or Layla, or whoever or whatever you are. You have poisoned my mind against itself." He tried to get up to attack me. His efforts were pitiful, which frustrated him more. He reached for something, anything near him that he could throw at me. He found a rock, but I easily moved aside as he cast it at me—a futile attempt. There was no answer to his accusation. He was right in the worst way. I had indeed poisoned him, as surely as if I had fed him arsenic. The cure for arsenic would be much easier to administer. Treating his bitterness toward me was a far different endeavor. His eyes sparkled menacingly like the Indian cab driver, and I felt an irrational danger from him.

I moved outside the cave. At least he was no longer mute. If Gabriel had to be angry to come out of his nightmare, so be it. I had already lost him and was aware of the bruising ache in my chest. Achmed came outside to interrupt my private thoughts.

"Do you know our story of Layla and Qays?" he asked. He bent his long legs and sat on his heels.

I didn't reply, annoyed by his presence beside me.

"Layla and Qays fell in love when they were young; but when they got older, Layla's father didn't approve of Qays."

Achmed glanced up and found my eyes. "He was given a new name, 'Majnun,' which means 'one possessed.' He was so consumed in his love for her that he could think of nothing else. When Layla married someone else of her father's choosing, Majnun went mad, talking to himself and wandering the desert."

"If I remember correctly, it didn't end well for either of them," I replied. "Majnun lived out the rest of his days in madness until his dead body was discovered at the tomb of his beloved, who also died of a broken heart. Sounds a lot like our Romeo and Juliet. What's your point, Achmed?" I snapped at him. His eyes sparkled and I was antagonized by his sympathy for me.

"So you do know the story." Achmed stood and touched his beard. "There is hope for you and Gabriel, the two of you together, for there is no one to come between you. Zayd, who tended the lovers' graves, had a dream and woke to leave us with a beautiful lesson. He told us, 'Commit yourself to love's sanctuary and at once find freedom from your ego. Fly in love like an arrow towards its target. Love loosens the knots of being, love is liberation from the vortex of egotism. In love, every cup of sorrow which bites into the soul gives it new life. Many a draft bitter as poison has become, in love, delicious...However agonizing the experience, if it is for love, it is well.' "

I watched Achmed as he recited from memory. He lifted his head a bit and looked up into the morning sky with a small turn of the corners of his mouth. He was at peace with the world around him. He was at peace within. I envied his confidence, the way he saw time in terms of the infinite moment.

"Thank you, Achmed. I will try to hold onto the bitter draft that will become delicious in time," I replied charitably. But in truth, I was pretty hopeless that Gabriel could tolerate a life with me in it. As we were alone, I thought to ask Renee's poet how our returning to the village would help.

"The Blue People will arise and help us, Layla." It was the first time anyone had used my given name, and he commented on my inner thought.

"Layla is a beautiful name. Its common meaning is night, but it is also the angel who comes at night. Do not regret such a name. It is said that when a soul is named, there is a mystical inspiration, and the name defines its essence. Embrace the name—it will be the source of strength that you shall soon need."

Achmed spoke like a person who had lived many lives, or many lived through him. I observed his face as he spoke. It was illuminated from within, a sheen of light imbued his skin. Although darkened from the sun, he was not yet leathered by it, holding onto the plumpness of youth. His eyebrows were thick, his smile genuine and large, almond eyes radiated a kind lightness above his full cheeks. Even his resting face was peaceful, a slight lift of the corners of his mouth reminding me of a Buddha child about to burst into laughter. His head was wrapped in the indigo turban that brought me great comfort. Whenever I noticed the soft cotton fabric infused with the Majorelle blue, I felt swaddled, comforted on the crest of my inner heart.

He turned to me in recognition of my silent observations, smiled, and continued.

"The Blue People are my ancestors—the name comes from the indigo turbans we wear. We have Sufis, mystics of our own, who will raise the Blue People from the dead to fight off the evil host of the underworld. They are led by the mothers, The Blue People. Dahlia will come in great need— and I believe this is a great need. The Blue People also call themselves the Amazigh, the Free People. They will not be ruled, although many have tried to do so. This is something you share with them, Layla. You cannot be ruled, even if you were to so desire it." I smiled at his keen perception of my true self.

"They, we, are the masters of the Sahara although we do not impose dominion. We are the free people—free because we understand our place in the world. We are free to accept the power and vastness of the desert. But the desert and her people will come to our aid when we need them.

Our great Queen Dahlia was a tall, dark woman with long black hair and large dark eyes. She was also called Kahina, a witch, most likely because she was intelligent or wise or had the gift of prophecy, or all of these. She was among the free people who would not be ruled. A chief terrorized her tribe until she finally consented to marry him." He shrugged, and a smile played about his eyes.

"And then she slew him on their wedding night with a nail through his skull. She would not be possessed. No, Dahlia, our beloved heroine, was the only one who could bring all the tribes together in a fantastic stand against the invaders of her day. All called her their leader of Africa—Berbers, nomads, and Romans. From her womb, the great Blue People have emerged."

Achmed turned to me, and he was formidable as he cut through me with his dark eyes. "Do not fear, Layla. We will defeat them with a brutal blow. They will be crushed. Many have tried to conquer us, and all have failed." At this last statement, Achmed drew himself up—he seemed to grow in height and breadth. The morning air around him pulsed with a dark light, the blue part of the flame.

Amalu was suddenly at his side. She reached for his hand. As they touched, I saw him shrink into himself. He was himself again, looking after his beloved, protecting her from the strange and wondrous power that filled his chest as he called upon his ancestors.

Achmed's presence was so well hidden in the cloak of his poet's gentle embrace. His true spirit was awesome and gargantuan, and I knew in a moment of clarity how his ancestors would greet him—with song and praise and awe. He pressed his forehead against Amalu's and glanced my way once before he drew her inside the cave.

Oliver eventually got Gabriel to drink, and then he and Marlow moved him to the stretcher. We continued to move through the snow and as we headed further south and down the High Atlas, the snow became lighter. We camped again that night in the open. Marlow set up a watch.

"They've discovered the false lead and are tracking you again, Sophia." I was awakened several times during the night by Marlow, then Achmed, Renee, and Oliver. They each took a watch and woke me as needed when they felt any invasion of my sleeping mind.

None of us were very well rested when we woke on the fourth day to an overcast sky. I thought it was a bad omen as we began a steep descent over the rock faces. Achmed was urgently pressing us on. Twice he went to Marlow and discussed the road that lay ahead. The second time they spoke, their exchange was heated, and they decided to put it to a vote. Marlow wanted to take a less visible route, stealth being his preference, a path that would take us longer to reach the village. Achmed thought that speed was the priority and the support of the villagers.

"It is not our bodies that they will see, but our spirits. It is safer if we move quickly."

"I disagree. There are lesser spirits who might see us and send word."

"What does that mean, Marlow?" I asked.

"They can use animals, like birds, as messengers."

"How many more days by each way?" asked Oliver.

"Two by my count if we go the faster route, three or more by Marlow's," replied Achmed.

"Achmed, why will we be safer in the village?" I asked.

Amalu replied, "The village has its own mystics, the Blue

Men and Women; and we will need the strength of their numbers. They will do everything to protect their kin and those they care for. They are already preparing for our arrival."

We sat quietly for a few minutes.

Oliver was the first to speak. "I prefer Achmed's choice."

"I agree," I replied.

"It is done," said Marlow. "Let's make haste."

We rallied and began a faster pace through the rough terrain, traveling well into the night. It was past midnight when we made camp, and we were up within four or five hours. We had not set a watch as everyone needed sleep.

They were getting closer; we all felt it. Maybe Marlow was right, a slow and cautious descent would have been better. We exerted ourselves, the pack mule and donkey also sensing a wolf-like danger as we moved quickly and with sure feet over the rocks and brambles. We ate on the move as the sky grew darker and darker, blocking out the midday sun. The landscape began to level out, and breathing became easier as we fled with a renewed sense of urgency.

Without warning, a wind came upon us. *Here it is*, I thought. *Sally's nap had come again.* Oliver kept looking up and over his shoulder in the rear. The sky was volcanic ash. The knowledge came upon us all at once, that we wouldn't make the village in time. Gabriel remained awake throughout the day despite the sedatives, his sharp eyes drawn to the sky, but mute, in a deeper trance than usual.

Marlow gathered us, with Gabriel, the mule, and the gray donkey, too, in the center of our circle. "We have to try a diversion. We are still a day away," he whispered and instructed us to hold hands. There we stood under a grove of trees, Oliver, Renee, Marlow, Achmed, and me, all of us surrounding Gabriel. It began to rain, a black soot rain, the pellets beating down on us like hail. Gabriel was turning his head this way and that, then spasmodically jerking his whole body and wincing at the pain of his broken ribs.

"Just follow my lead as best you can."

The only sound above Marlow's whispered words was the wind whistling a haunting tune. I knew the melody. As I tipped my head to hone in on the tune, Marlow shouted,

"No, Sophia, don't follow the melody!"

And then I was gone.

How much could a body take, I wondered, as I was carried on the wind into a void of epic proportion.

BATTLE OF THE BLUE PEOPLE

*A*malu, Oliver, Achmed, and Marlow watched as Sophia's hands slipped from their grasp, with the oily rain covering her limbs. She fell forward in slow motion as if the wind were cushioning her fall. They each tried to grab hold of a dangling limb as she was raised up in the vortex of debris flying about them. Rocks, branches, mud—they were caught in a tornado of flying debris as they watched her disappear into the abyss in the sky.

The wind died and they were left one person less, filled with despair—gutted by her loss.

Gabriel smiled and said, "Let them take her. She will finally be where she belongs—with the perverse witches of the southern seas."

Marlow turned on him and it took Oliver, Achmed, and Amalu together to restrain him from choking the life out of poor, wretched Gabriel.

"How wicked are the ways of Obeah, infecting the weak mind and turning it against the one it loves most," said Oliver. He lifted Gabriel back onto the stretcher and gave him some drugged water. Then five people and two pack animals, one dragging a litter, ran as fast as their legs could carry them through the night.

When morning came, not a body would know. No sun met them on this day—no blue water-colored sky, no lacy wisps of cloud—this day the sky remained volcanic ash. Their sprinting through the night was rewarded as they had made good time. The elders, both men and women, were waiting just outside the village walls when the travelers arrived, and all were dressed in indigo jalabias. The children of Skoura had been sent to another village to the East, far from the approaching storm, some three days prior.

There also stood Albert—covered in an indigo jalabia and turban. He was a magnificent image, draped in that haunting color, brought to his full height, come to help his beloved Sophia. He was akin to Lawrence of Arabia—grand in the English tradition of composed determination, tanned in the burning sands of the great Sahara. His inner beauty shone through in the movement of those long-fingered hands as he waved them into his embrace. His face fell, an excruciating pang of despair written upon the creases of his brow when he realized his Sophia was not with them...

His Sophia

Renee's Sophia

Marlow and Oliver and Gabriel's Sophia—gone now

Each face a reflection of Albert's grief, he did what he knew best to do.

"Come now, my friends," said Albert. "It's not time to worry just yet. We have work to do."

The village was draped and painted in blue—Majorelle indigo blue. Every doorway had been covered with it since Achmed and Amalu left; great swaths of fabric had been dyed and hung across the fronts of homes and as drapes in windows. Every man and woman in the village was covered head to toe in that exquisite color, wrapped in the blue that evaded the best poet's words. The party of five was overcome in this womb of cerulean and sapphire, azure and cobalt...blue.

Several women quickly and calmly took charge of Gabriel and moved him directly to Alia's home. There they tended his body and his mind, humming Sufi tunes to infuse his spirit with a wholesome love of place and person.

Marlow, Albert, Amalu, Achmed, and Oliver met with the remaining elders in the center of the village, at the oldest and largest well. They drew water and each drank from a common skin.

"Water is life," each murmured a blessing before drinking.

They sat in a circle, broke bread, and smoked hashish.

A drumbeat started, low and regular, the heartbeat of this group. They began to move to the rhythm, coming together as one moving organism. The fiddler joined in, his one-stringed fiddle wailing a perfect single note that went on and on and on. Then a double clarinet joined in, harmonizing with the fiddle, releasing a firestorm of agonizing joy into the sky. This was an ancient music, drawn from the treasury of the Berber tribes. This was music that came from and returned to the earth. It reflected the land and its people, animals, and stones in a thousand reflections and refractions of dizzying harmony with the world around them. This was a music that drew from the earthen core of man and beast and spirit. This was music that praised mother earth.

The amydaz, or village poet, began his chant, Majnun chanting into the wild winds of the desert, calling on the beasts to return his Layla to him.

"Layla," he called with a keening clarity into the void, with the words of her beloved.

Every breeze that blows brings your scent to me;
  Every bird that sings calls out your name to me;
  Every dream that appears brings your face to me;

Every glance at your face has left its trace with me;
I am yours, I am yours, whether near or far;
Your grief is mine, all mine,
Wherever you are.

They all joined in the chant. They continued this tune and many others learned at their mothers' breasts to banish evil spirits. The tempo increased, and it continued for five minutes, ten minutes, an hour or two, or four. Time was unmeasured here. They were calling to the Layla of Majnun and the Layla of Gabriel. They sang to Allah, asking for His divine help. They called for the intercession of the Prophet, of the Messenger Gabriel. He was not only Gabriel the orphan of London. He was Gabriel the Messenger of the Holy One. They called on them all.

But mostly they called to the earth and sky. They drew the darkness down from the sky until it was concentrated in the center of the village. This continued for hour after hour. Amalu, Marlow, and Oliver were tiring. Albert was indefatigable. He needed neither food nor rest. He was awesome in his tirelessly calm, considered chanting.

Marlow touched Albert's arm. "Let's go to Alia's for some tea, Albert," he coaxed.

Albert followed Marlow to Alia's courtyard.

She brought tea. The two men sat cross-legged and gazed into the gray skies. The air was thick with an oily haze. They peered into it and saw the doughy texture of distorted features moving in and out of the clouds. They retired indoors where the disturbing skies could not penetrate. Gabriel was huddled in the corner on some blankets with two villagers nearby. Seeing Gabriel in this condition, Marlow was sorry for his outburst and asked forgiveness. Alia touched Marlow's hand—offering her strength. The two old friends begged the help of Dahlia as they walked back to the well where they took up again—the chanting with the villagers and their companions.

Achmed came to them every so often with food or water, a well-placed cushion. He was at the center of the communion. When the amydaz's voice weakened, Achmed continued. His voice was a godly instrument, as clear as the long note on the villager's violin.

The darkness of real night descended, and the communion was finally broken for a full meal. This work could not continue without tending to the earthly needs of its men and women. Amalu, Oliver, and Marlow did not eat but slept in place. Their fatigue was deeper than a night without rest. It was the invading doom of the void. They were connected to Layla and felt her despair from within the nothingness. It was a distant voice on the cusp of their fearful hearts.

Amalu fell asleep with tears streaking her face. The villagers calmly, assertively, continued their work well into the first night, keeping Amalu, Marlow, and Oliver within their protective embrace.

Amalu dreamed of Layla and saw her in the void. Her face was blotched with the ash of the volcanic mountain. Her eyes were empty coal-blackened sockets. She could not ask for help. She could not speak. She could not think or feel. She was within the vast oblivion. She was part of it. This was no treasury of souls; it was the chasm of a broken spirit, beyond redemption. There was no deliverance, no salvation for a being here, living or dead.

Amalu awakened and Achmed comforted her. "You have seen her. If you have seen her, we can find her. Do not despair."

"It is not her," Amalu sobbed. "She, she is gone. Her spirit has been bled out of her. There is no earthly or heavenly body in that abyss."

"Do not fear, my beloved. We will draw her forth with the

strength of the millennia. Our ancestors will come. They are, we are, the Amazigh, Free People, the Brave People of the desert and mountains. Our spirits will douse the flame, and the blackness will shatter in the light of a thousand suns." Achmed rose to his full height and self, reminding Renee of the deep well of his spirit.

"She is gone, Achmed. I cannot feel her anywhere."

"No, Renee, she is not gone. The doom above us prevents us from seeing within." It was the first time he had used her given name, and she heard his truth.

On the second night, the dark skies opened and spewed forth the bodies of the hellish host. They tormented the villagers; they infected the sheep and goats. The villagers were forced to slaughter their own livestock as the beings attacked. They took on forms drawn from the clouds to beat down the people of Skoura.

The villagers began a new chant, calling to their ancestors; and from a nearby mountain pass, a legion of Berber fighting men arose. They took on the form of the earth and trees. They were made of the substance of the mountains. The hellish host began to multiply, spewing forth from the sky and dropping like dough onto the earth. They didn't have the substance of the Berber warriors, less tangible, they rose from the dough and took on a monstrous shape.

The Berber warriors were called out of the branch and stone of the mountain, a giant wave of humanity, risen from the dead. These were the men who defeated the Romans, the Spaniards, the French, all who invaded their land and hoped to rule them. These were the free people who would not be ruled. They came robed in the azure blue of the gods, armed with the weapons of their times, swords, machetes, picks, and axes. At their head was Dahlia, their warrior queen. Her long black hair fanned about her head in the savage winds, her charcoal black eyes determined and deadly. Behind her, the legions of Berbers, loyal to her mystic power, followed with vengeance in them. In her hand, she held a single nail—the nail she used to kill the man she was forced to marry.

Queen Dahlia swept down from the mountains to charge the host of demons. They clashed and the blood of the dead flooded the dirt streets of Skoura. The people helped their ancestors as best they could as the fighting moved to the alleys —fiends and monsters and warriors hacking at each other. The battle raged for hours with no respite. Here there was no ebb and flow, only the firestorm of brutal carnage.

The demons were defeated that night—the fragments of spirit withdrew to the blackened skies only to return a second night and a third, each time weakening the defenses of the villagers—killing, maiming, and enjoying the flow of blood.

For three days and three nights, the village fought for Layla. At times, the winds descended upon them in a violent expulsion of vomitous bile. They stood and fought, men and women, warrior descendants of the Blue People.

After three days, they all needed rest. Gabriel began to awaken from his nightmare. He walked with help, a few steps each day. But he cowered beneath the violence of the void and returned to the safety of Alia's home.

On the fourth day, Oliver went to visit Gabriel. He was sitting in the courtyard of Alia's home. Oliver sat next to him. "Gabriel, I think we could use your help."

"How can I help? I am a fearful shell of a man, weak with the blackest shame and remorse. Oh, Oliver, take a close look at me." He was openly weeping.

He bent closer to the big man and whispered, "They will feel that weakness and exploit it. I'm not strong enough, Oliver. I'm a fucking bloody mess."

"Do you love her, Gabriel?"

He held his silence.

"Do you love her?"

"I don't know her. I can't know her. She is something I do

not understand, a woman with a split mind and a broken heart."

"Love does not think, Gabriel. It feels the truth of a kindred spirit. You are a thorny man, as well, with two very different lives you have lived."

"Love cannot cure the damage she has suffered." Gabriel's fists were clenched tight to keep his hands still.

"Perhaps not, but we are not looking for a cure. We are looking for Layla, to recover what is left of her."

"Oliver, I'm afraid. That thing, that place, that world they inhabit is only a breath away, living alongside us. It is the soulless place of the universe. It is the net that catches all the detritus of our worst evil. It is indescribable and horrific. It cannot be unseen, what I have seen at their hands."

"Yes Gabriel, it is. It is all that you describe. And that is where your beloved Layla resides."

THE VOID

I am listening to a melody. It is haunting and soothing. It feels so familiar. It rises and falls like a nursery rhyme, the simple rhythm of rosies and posies, the black plague lurking beneath. The plague is my friend, it seems. The specter of disembodied spirits is drawn to me, wanting to drink from the goblet of my spirit. They crowd around me, touching with a ghostly limb here, a tongue there, hoping for a taste. They cannot feel the corporeal body, which drives their desire more intensely. They crawl into my heart, the tentacles of their craving seeking to devour. They are not as much filled with malice as they are with a wanting that cannot be satisfied. They are infused with a yearning, an ache for the thing they cannot have.

Life.

I don't resist, interested as I am in the character of this thing and the way it reflects the sleeping fiend within me. I observe with Albert's clinical detachment and they turn their interest toward my vision of him. The faces begin to change shape and they mimic the contours of Albert's face. I find it fascinating, the way we communicate. But Albert's face is spiritless as if they have bled it dry of all that makes it living.

I am bothered by the way it makes him lifeless, but I continue to observe. I begin to see individual faces. They are caricatures, cartoon-like. They recoil at my characterization and try to strike fear into me. But they cannot harm me. I am the objective observer of their madness. I am not afraid as they part like the waters of the Red Sea before my inspection. Where the shadows part, there is a great tunnel of the blackest night through which I move, floating through a wormhole.

At the end of the tunnel, I find the Obeah, two men and six women, communing on the beach over a fire. They peer into the tunnel as I emerge. They are the truest evil here. They are practically rubbing their hands together in their greed for me, excited beyond control. They have finally captured the prize. They are gluttons with wanting, thrilled at the prospect of collecting me, like a collector of insect trophies, the prize lifeless and stretched, pinned under glass. These are no art collectors. They are collectors of gene pools, and they think they will overcome me with the force of their will.

I peer back at them, each in his turn. One old woman tries to prick my brain with her cataract eyes. I stretch out my hand and touch her temple with the tip of my middle finger. Her appetite for me is insatiable—she wants to see me writhing in childbirth. She is revolting and incites me to Adele's homicidal madness...I tap her once on the forehead and she is blinded.

She screams, her brown leather face contorting in pain. I sadistically enjoy her pain and whisper to her, "Be careful what you wish for." I smile a demonic smile at the simple task. I am filled with the swelling of my dark power, and I turn to her companions, my face lit with a blue light, a halo of dark shadow surrounding me.

"I am come again. Do you not recognize me? You shall love me in your desire...and despair. Come to collect me, you think? I shall collect your skulls for trinkets to wear about my neck."

My voice grows larger, filling their ears with pain. My face glows with the blue light of the darkest fire.

"Collect me? Breed me like some backyard broodmare? I don't think so." As I reach out to each of them, they recoil in fear. I can command any one of them at will. I am transfixed by my own dominance. I feel...I feel large, expansive, as if I could fill the world with this sinister and tempting power.

Albert's voice returns to me on the wind. "Forgiveness is for you, Layla. You can bring light to this terrible place. Or you can be consumed in it. You have always known this."

One of them smirks, an arrogant little smirk, belittling the words of my Albert. He intends to inflict harm. I swing my arm toward him, my hand the claw skewering his fleshy heart. He gasps, mouth open, and falls over dead.

I like the claw. I like the way it sings with electricity when I wield it. It is no longer my damaged hand, no, this is the claw of personal doom. *I can exercise it at will, with cause or without, upon you or you or you*, I think loudly enough for Them to hear me. The claw is so simple and effective and terrible.

"Be warned."

I return the way I came. I am back in the clouds above the village. My friends and the villagers have been working tirelessly to bring me back. They do not know what I have done. They think I am lost in the void. I turn to the storm cloud and push it back with two hands, my feet rooted in the sky. I am Hercules. I can leave it at will. But can I return to the village? Will they know me? Will they fear me even more? How can I live among them? The Obeah men and their words come through the melody that captured me with a sing-song persuasion. "You cannot live with them. They are not worthy of you. Come to us, Layla."

They toy with my struggle between vulnerability and limitless power. I strike out at them and they retreat. But I remain floating in the timeless limbo. I delay and dawdle, like a child. I am tempted to...to do nothing, as the wanting of me surrounds me. I will be worshipped by the living and the nonliving. I will be feared by all. Or I will return to my small life, lived out in a small way.

I hear Achmed the child say it again, "It is the little things we do that are the grand gestures of our time here." Really? It is the grand gestures of great power that define our time here, as well. It is quaint and naïve, not really enlightening at all. Wait, that's not my thought. It's one of the Obeah women, snuck up from behind through the wormhole, planting her poison in my heart.

I hear Achmed telling Gabriel about the burst of a thousand suns and I test it. Yes, I can shatter it like a delicate teacup. I linger amid this gloomy and terrible weight. My vision begins to fail—a curtain hanging in front of me. It is a supernatural apparition, one that I can control and direct to my own ends. Time has turned upside down. I have no way of knowing how long on earth my friends have worked. I don't want to care. I see Gabriel and despair. He is weak with worry for me and fear of me. I see Albert—but he is no longer the Albert of my memories. He is larger than life—beautiful in a wholly constant way. He is the mooring to which I may attach myself again...or not.

How can I be loved? Oliver was so sure of it. When I think of him, I feel him with me and I remember his words.

"Everyone is loved."

I rest and float in the tragic and oily embrace of that dreadful place. The spirits are longing to drink from me, but they are impotent, without enough breath to take a sip from the well of my heart.

Everyone is loved.

Gabriel cannot love such a dark and twisted heart.

I rest some more. I hear Albert whispering on the breath of my failing heart. The rhythm slows, a thumping surrender to the fatigue I feel.

"You will be whole and beautiful, Layla. You can raise the

peaceful embrace of night's angelic rest. You may enjoy the evening of your worthy heart. You may choose, you who I know to be forgiving and kind." Albert sings.

I close my eyes, but my retinas are seared with the images of all that I have seen.

What I have seen is finally laid bare before me—with the weight of the sadistic tormentors surrounding me.

What I have seen and heard and felt.

Adele, the mother who would murder me. Murderers for hire, manipulators near and far.

I have forgotten much of what was said.

But I recall what I felt in exquisite detail—the Host brings it to the fore, over and over again. It stimulates and excites— the pain of my youth. And I am overcome with fatigue, a weariness of the spirit that is close to death, ready to give It what It wants, has wanted, for all eternity.

Time passed—sometimes floating, others a driving wind— hours or days expired while I languished in that place, caught between hell and, well, a different kind of hell.

Back on the ground, Oliver helped Gabriel in longer walks each day. He maintained his silent companionship, waiting patiently for Gabriel to find his courage.

Several days went by, I thought. The villagers continued their work. Marlow was feeling the dread of imminent failure. He, Amalu, and Achmed all tried to penetrate the cloud. Albert continued to commune with me. He reminded me of our pleasant times together.

But they could not find Layla. They could not feel her and began to despair. I could not find Layla—I was emptied of the light. I felt the weight of the Bordeaux drapes, now blackened with soot and oil, slipping from me as I threw off all I knew of myself and allowed the millions of little bits of me to dislodge from myself. The bits began to disperse, like dustmotes into space.

Gabriel joined them one evening. With Oliver, they followed the chanting in Arabic. They did not understand the words, but they began to repeat them.

Layla saw Gabriel with Oliver. Oliver reminded her she is loved. "Here he is, Layla, with a fear gripping his heart. Here he is. He is braver than any of us. He loves you, Layla. You can be loved. You are loved."

I wanted to choose, but I am weaker now than I was at the beginning. It was the extended time of non-choosing that had sapped my strength and bludgeoned my will. The void closed in on me, sensing a finality in my existence; the Obeah men punched through the wormhole and were here with us. I was in the nothingness of no existence.

I have no weapon.

"No weapon," It repeated.

I have no strength.

"No strength."

I have tarried too long.

"Yessssss, yesssss, too long—but you will be loved here with us, Layla."

I can be loved here, as well.

"Yessss," the snake whispered. "We will worship you."

Its excitement was palpable. My mind knew it was the viper, but my spirit was so tired, so tired.

I was weak with a drunken surrender, ready to deliver myself into nothingness. It would be nice to let the bits disappear into the oblivion of the void. I could rest, rest, rest my broken heart and tortured mind. I could let go of thinking anymore about anyone, about me and my scrambled eggs of a brain. I could let go of caring for Oliver and Gabriel and everyone I have ever known. I would only hurt them if I let them in.

Gabriel tentatively reached for me and I felt him.

IT reached its long tentacle arms, with grotesquely curled and long fingernails, toward my Gabriel. IT wanted to scratch his brain. There was dirt under the nails, saffron bits of sooty ash. The nails reminded me of a different time, but I could not place it. I was missing the fingertips of those same nails. Something teased my mind, but I could not connect the thoughts.

"Sophia," he called my name from those beautiful lips.

"Layla," he called her, as well.

And he loves them both.

I will only hurt him.

"Yes, yes, Layla—he is too weak for the likes of you."

The arms were close to him, and I saw his eyes bulge from the scoring near his brain.

I awakened dreamily, my arms pushing at the soft cloud—with no purchase to resist. Gabriel grimaced. I rolled over and bent my knees, pushing with my hands against the cloud. It was so hard to stand with no resistance. But IT cannot keep his face hidden from me—our genetic material was interwoven now after our infinity here together.

He moaned with the nails that draw blood. I was upright on my knees, adrenalin filling me with renewed strength. I bent at the elbows with my hands flat against the sky. The hands were gargantuan, expanding into the void, growing with a light.

The hands were whole and perfect, undamaged, and casting radiant light into the specter of faces. They turned their heads, the light scorching them, blinding them.

I stood, my feet planted in the sky and my arms outstretched, and I thought of the shattering teacup.

The Obeah men turned their attention away from Gabriel, desperately united against me. The dead pressed their dark and gloomy despair onto me, a weight on my being.

I thought about the shattering teacup.

"Sophia, you don't need a weapon. You are the weapon," Albert reminded me.

I am the only weapon I need.

Behind me charged Dahlia, flying upon a beautiful steed, her host of Blue men and women at her flanks. Miles of blue fabric billowed in the wind. They flew like gazelles from the ground upon a pathway of white, white, sand. Hooves beat, feet thundered into the sky. I was surrounded by the cotton fabric of the most intimate cobalt blue at both my flanks, streaked with sapphire and cerulean and indigo. I was in the womb of the world, the beginning of all things. It was not the blood-red womb of a bursting sun or a woman but the earth's blue ocean and sky. Here at the beginning of all things I felt the earth and sky at my call.

The many-tentacled heads of the host and the Obeah men grimaced and screeched and wailed. Their loss was imminent. The Blue people struck at them, a wall of hands, feet rooted in the sky next to mine, and we pushed against the darkness as one.

The light of the shattering teacup splintered, splitting the darkness into a thousand refractions and reflections of crystal. The light exploded in an atomic blast, shattering the doom into a vacuum. In its place, there were millions, billions of little grain-sized illuminated pearls, iridescent, moving like a tide above the earth. It was Achmed's thousand suns. It was Oliver's certainty about love.

The Host was released in the explosion. There was a great release, relief, joy almost, in the spirits that were no longer trapped. They were gone—on to better or worse places but gone on. They were freed, and I heard the collective sign of liberation.

It was the ancestors of the millennia who came and guided me home, as I fell from the sky into Achmed's waiting arms, Gabriel by his side.

There were losses—many of the people were lost, among

them four of the village elders. It was a keen loss. Albert—
Albert was lost to me, and I despaired at the news. Oliver was
gone. Unbelievably, that great wall of a man, steadfast and
true, gave himself for Gabriel. All lost. All gone to leave me in
further sadness and regret.

I awakened with Renee's delicate little face smiling down
at me; I was in Alia's home where I had been unconscious for
days. Renee spoke, telling me that Gabriel did not visit.
Burials were had. This was a good resting place for Oliver.
Gabriel and Marlow left soon after Oliver was lowered to his
final rest, each to his own destination. I didn't see them go,
and I was glad of it. The children were returned home. I
could not speak of Albert.

I remained in the village for more than a year. I found the
rhythm of that place and joined its peaceful reprieve. No one
spoke of the battle. No one spoke of the man I had loved and
lost. I could not say his name aloud, lost to me as he was, as
surely as if he had died.

I returned to New York after a brief stop in London.
Someone else had settled the estate. I collected some personal
items, and the estate was distributed to its one true heir. It
brought me no joy but gave me the luxury of wandering some
more. I returned to the anonymous city where I didn't feel the
worry of those around me. And for six months more, I
wandered the city streets. They left me alone, and it was a
comfortable place to be.

THE LOVE MONSTER

A short time after I returned to New York, Marlow appeared and took me to lunch. We were in a private dining room at some Michelin restaurant whose name meant nothing to me. He looked different—kind and thoughtful, not how I remembered him after the harrowing days in the mountains and sky. We sat down and he reached across the table, inviting me to feel the touch of his hands. It felt good. His hands were warm and tender. Without letting go, he got up and moved to the chair beside me. It was a comfort, having him so near me. In my wanderings, I often wondered if this would be so and began to cry. Here, over a piece of bread broken between us, in this safe, beautiful place with Marlow, I could finally allow the feelings to wash over me and through me.

Marlow, Marlow, Marlow.

I sang in praise—a hymn or a lullaby.

Marlow could sit beside me, be silent and comfort me in my broken core. Marlow could know that silence would be the only cloak of respite at this moment, and he gave me the silence I demanded for the many weeks that followed.

Here with Marlow, I cried in desperate frustration for what

could never be. The tears fell onto my plate, as our nameless waiter brought sparkling water, closed the door, and left. We moved into a quiet companionship during those lunches and the many walks in Central Park that followed in the weeks afterward. Marlow appeared at my building, rode the elevator, and waited patiently while I got dressed, usually in jeans and a warm fuzzy sweatshirt. The world had turned to autumn again; New York's cement canyons were already getting cold. Marlow let me take the lead and often reminded me of Oliver, letting me be, but guarding my steps. I was directionless in the West 50's, stopped often at the FAO Schwarz windows, but always ended up in Central Park. We would walk for hours, in silence, sometimes until I collapsed and he would call his car to get me back home. Marlow knew enough to leave me to my silent musings and wanderings and kept me company like this for weeks on end.

One morning he arrived and snow was falling. I lay on the couch, staring up at the beige ceiling as I had all night. He brought clothes from the bedroom closet, but I made no effort to move. Rolling over on my side, I began to talk. I told him everything I could remember of the void, the Obeah, with all the detail I knew he wanted. He didn't interrupt with questions or nods. He let me talk well into the evening until I was done. It was done. I awoke the next day in my bed, unsure how I had arrived there. Marlow had stayed the night, was still there in a living room chair, and I had a peaceful sleep.

"Marlow," I whispered over his prepared tea and toast.

"I know, Sophia," he replied before I could thank him for staying. I glanced at him and saw his arrogant smile; and it annoyed me, that all-knowing smile of his.

"Marlow, should I thank you or curse you for your part in this? Did you see where this journey would lead us? Would you have done differently?" A surge of anger was bubbling up while he sat impassively at my kitchen table. He was taking my measure, testing my state of mind before he would take his leave. There was so much I knew about him without him uttering a word. It was painful and irritating to know so much about this stranger—my father. I could not reconcile my desire to love with the awful agony of my loss. I could not believe he made the best choice, knowing all those ulterior motives. I wanted to be rid of him and the confusion he created in my heart.

His name was no longer a psalm on my tongue.

"I can't bear the sight of you or your presence here in my world. Not anymore. Go away and don't come back. Go back to where you came from...wherever that may be. I want a life without you, as comforting as your presence might be to me." It hurt me to say these words to him, but I had to rid myself of him and all his calculated machinations. I could feel his concern at leaving me unattended. He was weighing his options.

"Stop that—there is no danger of me ever sharing our story with anyone, ever, in the universe, as I'm sure you well know. As for the options that you are weighing, you know full well I can send you where I want. Consider it my commitment of silence that I'm letting you choose."

He knew what I told him was true, of course. But this was the first he knew that I knew. His mind was jumping back in time to determine when I became aware of the depth and breadth of my influence over others. He stood and went to the window, looking out at bare tree-tops, while I answered his unspoken question.

"When I woke up after my attack on poor Jorge, that's when I first had an inkling. I began testing it shortly afterward and have been honing it ever since. Think about it, Marlow, when did you 'decide' to come to New York."

He turned on his heels as I drilled that seed into his skull. He was finally

Truly.

Afraid.

Of.

Me.

Well, I thought to myself, loud enough for him to hear, *everybody close to me is afraid of me. I didn't want to leave you out, seeing as you are the one who has made me something to fear.*

He took a step toward me where I was sitting at the counter. I held up my hand to stop his advance. He didn't want to leave me.

"Please leave," I said quietly.

He pleaded with his eyes to remain a little while longer. There was something about being with me that pleased him, although what I couldn't imagine. He took another step closer, a supreme act of will, as I was actively trying to stop him.

"Go away," I said louder this time. He continued his advance until he was within reach. He gently touched my arm on his way out. I didn't see him again for many years.

Finally bored with my wanderings and grieving, I returned to the work of trusts and estates law. People were always dying so work continued at a steady, grueling pace, which suited me just fine. After three years, on one unremarkable Tuesday, I was having lunch with a client. On our way out I noticed Marlow seated nearby with a younger gentleman. Funny, I hadn't heard of his arrival in New York, or that he had ever been in this restaurant. We had respected each other's privacy in recent years. At least if he was poking around in my head, he had become so adept at it that I never felt him.

I found myself saying goodbye to the client. As soon as he saw me coming toward him, he stood to greet me with a gentle kiss on each cheek. His smile came back in full force, reminding me of our first meeting in the conference room with Richard. The Caribbean sunrise had returned, and then I was genuinely glad to see him. I returned the smile tenfold.

Time had begun to heal his wounding of me.

I understood in a moment of soothing clarity—I love him. And he heard it.

He was so genuinely joyful, I 'repeated' it for him.

Yes, Marlow, I love you. I am the love monster.

I recalled our first meeting when his presence removed the shawl of my burdens. Here he had returned to remove the cloak of my grief. It was an unexpected and very welcome reunion.

"Sophia, it's so nice to see you. Meet my son, Jonah," he said.

His son.

My brother.

Would the wheels never stop their relentless churning of unwelcome information grinding into my brain? I pushed that negative thought quickly aside. Perhaps this was welcome news.

My brother.

"How do you do, Jonah? Have you been rescued from the mouth of the giant fish yet?" We both knew who the giant fish was, and I watched as he threw back his head in a deep belly laugh.

For his part, Jonah burst into spontaneous laughter, healthy, sincere, and contagious laughter. Ah, how refreshing the sound was.

"Oh, Sophia, we're going to get along just smashingly," he replied with a good dose of authentic joy. He wrapped his arms around me. He embraced me with a fearless and genuine hug. It felt wonderful.

Fearless and pure.

I whispered to him, "Yes, you have indeed been delivered from the giant fish."

I turned to my father. "Marlow, I'm glad you are here. Where are you staying?" I glanced at my watch and saw that I would be late for an appointment.

"I have to go back to the office, but we could meet after work tonight if you'd like."

"That would be great," Jonah replied.

Jonah, my brother. Jonah the prophet.

Does not follow in our father's footsteps.

Here was our father's chance to get it right. And he had indeed done so. I became weak in the knees as Jonah gently guided a chair to my collapsing legs. I smiled a crooked, drunken smile at my new brother, all my bitter thoughts swiftly diffusing into his beaming smile.

THE OCEAN SHALL BE MY MOTHER

I have raged against you all my life,
a churning tempest
on the waters of my aching heart.
and now, the fury of the gale spent,

I weep for you.

I weep an ocean of tears
in all my unrequited
hopeless
love for you

on the dunes of a white, white beach at winter
    midday
in the blinding sun.

the pulse of the tide soothes me
a gentle breeze, rich with the scent of seaweed
tousles my hair.
I am mute with the tender caress
and whispered lullaby of the shore.

and I wonder,
can the ocean be my mother?

after all these years,
I am still.

but still
searching for my mother.

I lie down, my cheek pressed to the warm sand,
a mantra swirling in my clever head.

let the ocean be my mother.
the ocean may be my mother.
the ocean shall be my mother.

the temperate sand
shall be the fire lit at mother's hearth.
the blanket of her soothing hush shall
    swaddle me.
her salt shall be mother's perfume.

with one ear to the ground,
the ocean tide enters my heart
on the breath of a lifetime hope

her rhythm mother's heartbeat

it shall be the sea,
the cobalt blue sea
and her eternal love

the ocean shall be my mother.

EPILOGUE

*I*n the end, all was not right with the world. I was no longer working as an attorney, having tired of the endless worship of all things powerful and cruel. Renee, Achmed, and I had built a sprawling ranch on the Atlantic where we found some peace. I spent my days walking, thinking of Gabriel, and tending our beautiful gardens, while Renee invited guests for her spectacular French and Moroccan meals. Alia had her own rooms and was the mother to all. Sally visited once or twice a year with her brood of children. It was a welcome distraction from my brooding life. Marlow and Jonah also visited on occasion, and Jonah was a great companion.

But all in all, I was lonely beyond repair. Beyond losing Albert and Oliver, I was wounded by Gabriel, a wound that would not heal. He could not see me. All he could see was the rotten work of my hands, poisoning his mind. Renee worked diligently trying to find a suitable partner for me. But no one interested me. Or I frightened them until, finally, I accepted that I was destined to be alone. I worked hard to hone my skills to keep out of other minds and keep them out of my own. The temptation to seek out Gabriel died a quiet death.

One day, I was sitting on a beach chair reading a book. I removed my sunglasses, dropped my book, and turned my face to the waning sun. I looked at the ocean, my refuge, and smiled. I was watching the beautiful play of ocean light on the crest of the waves, listening to the gentle cadence of the ocean tide. I found pleasure in the sound and sight and smell of the ocean.

Someone came into view and blocked out the sun.

I looked up from my beach chair and before I could see his face, he was on his knees, his head in my lap. His hands moved along my thighs to my arms resting there. I tentatively touched his head, then thoroughly ran my hands through his unruly hair. I wasn't sure if this was real or another dream. I had thought of his hair and the feel of his hands on me for so long now. It had been three years in Manhattan, and four more in a house above this beach. I still awakened regularly longing for his touch.

"Oh, you're really here," I whispered, afraid I would break the spell. "Are you really here?"

He sat up higher on his knees and wrapped his arms around me. I moved forward into his embrace.

"Gabriel, Gabriel, Gabriel," I hummed over and over while he chanted a silent devotion.

And it was good.

ABOUT THE AUTHOR

Audra Dehan is married for 35 years and has three children. When she is not writing, she keeps busy running a law practice concentrating in trusts and estates. This is her first novel